I0824991

THE SILVER FISH

THE SILVER FISH

CONNOR MARTIN

THE MYSTERIOUS PRESS
NEW YORK

THE SILVER FISH

Mysterious Press
An Imprint of Penzler Publishers
58 Warren Street
New York, N.Y. 10007

First edition

Interior design by Maria Fernandez

Library of Congress Control Number: 2025942799

ISBN: 978-1-61316-735-9
eBook: 978-1-61316-736-6

10 9 8 7 6 5 4 3 2 1

Printed in the United States of America
Distributed by Simon & Schuster

To Penny Ratcliffe

AUTHOR'S NOTE

This is a work of fiction and a product of the author's imagination. None of the characters are real people or are intended to resemble real people, living or dead. None of the events in the plot really occurred or are intended to resemble real events.

In most instances, phrases in languages other than English are written phonetically to reflect how they are commonly spoken. Spellings are chosen for clarity.

PROLOGUE

He wasn't supposed to be here.

An hour passed before they found the body. Billy Demirjian should have been long gone. Instead, he was across the road, watching through the railing on the second floor of the neighboring building.

Traffic buzzed by in both directions. Coach buses, tro-tros, mopeds beeping past hand-pulled carts. Billy crouched low, hidden in shadow, with a good view to the car where a Nigerian telecom executive named David Ibrahim lay dead in the front seat. The sky was hazy, reddened by the harmattan winds. Billy waited, motionless. The wind coated Ibrahim's car with a thin layer of dust the color and consistency of cinnamon.

Then people began to yell. A sudden crowd congregated around the car—men pushing to the front, scolding each other excitedly, banging on the hood and the windows with the flats of their hands. The door was wrenched open, the dead man pulled from the passenger seat. He was big. They could only get him halfway before he slipped from their grip and his torso flopped onto the pavement.

Billy felt empty. Shocked. It wasn't the killing: during his three tours of active duty, he had been personally responsible for removing four people from this life, that he knew of. It was the killing *like this*. Up close and intimate. With his hands. In the quiet of a parked car, twenty feet away from where ordinary people were walking down the street.

This had started three days ago, when his case officer had sent him a signal for the first time in months. Billy had been visiting the same café he was required to report to every morning for exactly this purpose. He'd taken a bite of his bread roll and was stirring powdered milk into his Nescafé when the vendor had said, behind his back, "Did you hear? A ship sunk in the harbor last night."

Billy had turned around slowly. "Run aground?" he asked.

"Capsized." The vendor's face was stenciled with a lifetime of poverty. He shook his head, convincingly rueful. "Bad weather."

By these codes, Billy knew which drop spot to check for his orders. When he did, he couldn't believe what he was seeing. David Ibrahim was a big deal in West Africa's telecom industry. He imported millions of dollars' worth of the equipment that made cell phone networks functional and kept the internet online in Ghana, Nigeria, and Senegal. And according to the paper Billy held in his hands, he was being run by Chinese intelligence. Targeting somebody like this was a major escalation.

But it wasn't Billy's job to question. He was the sharp end of the stick, and the protocol was clear.

Do it quick, do it clean, and be gone.

Last night, his case officer, a man who went by the name of Ford, had met with him to review the plan. Follow the target to his girlfriend's house, where he spends an hour every Tuesday and Thursday after work. Slip into his car while he's inside. Hide in the back seat. After an hour, the target will get back in the car and close the door. He's thinking about going home to his wife, he's rehearsing answers to her questions. He's freshly showered, as he always is at this hour.

"And then you do it," Ford had said. "Knock him out, no drama. In his pocket there will be two cell phones. They never leave his side. You secure them, and you bring them to me."

Quick, clean, gone.

After Ford left, Billy had stayed awake until dawn, turning the orders over in his hand. The manila envelope had contained two sheets of paper, with information on Ibrahim corroborated by a double agent, who was pretending to work for the Chinese while funneling information to the United States. There was something touching and insubstantial about this packet. He wondered whose soft hands had pressed down the stapler, in what hushed office. The small, precise motion—as conclusive, as violent as anything that Billy would do afterward.

The instant Ibrahim had shut the door to his car, Billy had hinged upward from the floor of the back seat where he'd been hiding and in the same motion grabbed Ibrahim's throat from behind and pulled it against the headrest. Ibrahim was a big man. But when you surprise someone there's nothing they can do. Their hands fly to their throat. They don't even realize yet what's happened—only that something is wrong with their body, very wrong, which they are desperately trying to fix. Soon enough the lack of oxygen causes them to pass out.

But that was when the plan had stopped working.

Ibrahim had continued to struggle, his large hands grabbing blindly at Billy's face, scratching, pulling, twisting. A finger dug into Billy's eye. Reaching across the steering wheel Ibrahim managed to pop open the glove compartment, and a long knife fell out of it onto the passenger seat. Billy could feel that this man was still strong, still dangerous. He was fighting for his life.

And then something happened inside Billy that had never happened before. A blank white space opened up. A sensation of falling.

Suddenly he was leaning over the front seat, and the knife was in his hand, and with a burst of energy he was stabbing Ibrahim through the neck and ribs again and again and again and again and again. He heard shouting—heard himself screaming the names of Ibrahim's wife and children and cursing them and promising that before today was over he was going to kill them all too.

Finally the man died.

In the abrupt silence, Billy's panting had filled the car. He had looked down at his dark T-shirt, slick with gristle. Startled, he threw himself to the floor of the back seat, away from the glare of the daylight that was now pouring through the car's windows on all sides. The silence rang like a bell. He felt watched, as though by an audience that refused to applaud. He felt, in a strange way, humiliated.

Be gone, the protocol said. Ditch your clothes and your weapon, *now.* Resume your cover identity and await your next order, as though nothing has happened.

Prepare to wait a long time.

But when the body was finally found an hour later, Billy was still there, crouching on the second floor of the deserted laundromat across the street, frozen, Ibrahim's bloody phones in his pocket.

Everything had happened just like the intelligence had indicated. Which meant they were now in business with an honest-to-god double. As he watched the growing commotion, watched as the world discovered what his hands had done, Billy thought about this Double. What would he think of the scene inside the car?

Of course Billy had never met the Double. Intelligence wasn't his job; if anything, he was the last to receive it. Only Ford saw the whole picture. It is the case officer who approaches somebody like Ibrahim. Say they learn that the target likes to play golf on Saturday mornings. They show up the next weekend with a terrible swing. Shank one shot after another, until the target takes pity and comes over to give him some pointers. Maybe the target and the case officer shake hands. The next Saturday, maybe they go for coffee afterwards and talk about their wives. The officer makes sure his golf swing doesn't improve too quickly.

It doesn't always end in violence. More often, the case officer will try to turn the target—bring him on the payroll. When that fails, somebody like Billy gets the call.

And when Billy fails?

Because that was what was bleeding all over the car seat: Billy's failure. Nobody had told him to murder David Ibrahim. He had lost control and disobeyed orders.

He was sure there would be blowback. Billy wasn't dumb, no matter what Ford and people like Ford thought of him. In the forty-eight hours that he had tailed David Ibrahim prior to killing him, he had observed plenty. At least once a day, Ibrahim had passed in and out of the offices of a Chinese-owned shipping company called Dongsha, near Madina Market in the city center. He had worked out at a public gym by the beach. Pull-ups, push-ups, sit-ups by the hundreds. And he had liked to dress stylishly, expensively—especially on the days he visited his girlfriend. On the afternoon he was killed, Ibrahim was wearing a pair of pressed chino trousers that stopped well short of his ankles, and a green satin coat with wide lapels, like a smoking jacket. On his feet were immaculate white Adidas trainers. As Billy watched the crowd haul him out of the car, his open throat flapping, a little boy, whom nobody knew, pulled off one of the trainers and ran away with it, evading outstretched hands.

ONE

DANI HAD BEEN REPORTING in Ghana for three weeks. She was not in danger of running out of money, but she was beginning to feel that she was running out of time. Today she had finally landed an interview that really mattered. If it was a failure, she was going to have to start asking herself hard questions.

"Have you been to West Africa before?" Kwesi Adjepong put his Nokia face down on the table.

"Yes," Dani said. "Many times."

"Do you hear the Twi?"

The wind off the ocean kept whipping her hair into her eyes. She tucked it behind her ear again. "A little. Wo ho te sen? Eh yeh."

"Ah!" Kwesi Adjepong's eyes spread wide, he flicked his fingers at the air. He said something in Twi she couldn't follow.

"Sorry," she shrugged.

"You will take some food?"

Danielle Moreau did not like the food in Ghana. For the last several days she'd had intermittent diarrhea. "How about a Smirnoff?"

Men were always pleased when she offered to drink with them. It usually got her out of eating.

Adjepong called to the skinny boy sitting a few tables away—the restaurant's waiter, and its only other occupant. He snapped his fingers impatiently, an expensive watch poking through his shirt cuff.

Dani looked away towards the sea. The waves thundered thickly, relentless, without any space between them. The silent boy set two Smirnoff Ices on their table. Adjepong took a roll of cedis from the pocket of his suit and pressed a few into his hand.

They clinked bottles. Kwesi Adjepong leaned back in his chair, at ease. In the distance, Dani watched a fishing boat make a run for it, rocking violently back and forth between the swells.

"So," she prompted him, picking up her pen. "Mr. Adjepong. The Chinese investors."

"Ah," he shook his head slowly. "Troublesome Chinese."

"When did they first approach you?"

"They approach me . . ." He frowned, furrowed his brow. "I do not recall."

"Was it July 2016?"

"I do not recall. What are you writing?"

"I'm writing that you do not recall."

"Hm," he grunted.

Parked in front of the restaurant was an immaculately polished government-issue Mercedes. The driver sat on its hood, looking at his phone. Dani was seated in the shade, sheltered from the sun, wearing her foreign correspondent's uniform: running shoes, khaki pants, a blue linen shirt rolled up at the sleeves.

It had been more than three years since she had reported like this—out in the field in a country she did not know. There was a time when her whole body would have hummed with the energy of this encounter. Sitting across from an interview subject like Kwesi Adjepong would have made her lean forward in her seat, waiting for him to underestimate her, watchful as a hawk. But today Kwesi Adjepong's winking disdain, his obvious lack of shame, did not make her feel eager and powerful and hungry to catch him out. It just made her feel small, and stupid.

"Can you confirm or deny for me that two investors from Dongsha Limited approached you in July of 2016? To be specific," she flicked through her notebook, "July 24, 2016? At the offices of the Energy Ministry in Accra?"

"I do not know." He parried her with easy smiles.

"You do not know, or you won't say?"

Silence. Silences are useful to an interviewer. Most people feel awkward and want to fill them. But Kwesi Adjepong was a pro. They waited, watching each other.

"If you want, you can be on background. That means—"

"I know what on background means, madam."

"Of course. I'm sorry."

Dani had landed in Accra three weeks ago, with her new sneakers, a plastic-wrapped brick of fresh Moleskine notebooks, a first aid kit she had purchased in a Boots on Oxford Street. She had been tipped off by a friend to look into Ghana's oil industry and the deep-pocketed Chinese investors who were circling it. There was a story here. She knew it, she could sense it, just out of her reach.

But time was running short. Not because of money. The arbitrary conditions of Dani's birth meant that she was wealthier not just than 99 percent of her fellow Americans but more prosperous, when adjusted for inflation, than almost anyone who had ever lived—and she preferred to live cheaply and hard. Time was running short because Dani's belief that she could still do this—could still be a reporter—was growing weaker every day. She could not sustain the illusion much longer without something to show for it.

And this was the first interview that really mattered. She was finally getting to speak to someone who had been at the meeting on July 24, 2016, where executives from Dongsha Limited had met with Ghanaian officials—one day before Dongsha formally bid for the rights to explore an oil parcel off the Ghanaian coast, parcel number 42, near the maritime border with Côte d'Ivoire. Dongsha had purchased the rights for $231 million. But no oil had ever been discovered in Parcel 42—even as nearby parcels managed by American and European oil companies had yielded reserves worth ten times what Dongsha had paid.

"Ah," Adejpong clicked his tongue impatiently. "What is the point of your questions, eh? The Chinese buggered off in the end, when their parcel turned out to be dry. Everybody knows that we have the lovely Texans, your countrymen." He tipped his Smirnoff Ice bottle at her. "And we have the lovely British. Why do you concern yourself with the Chinese? But I am not confirming, unh? Not confirming anything, you understand. I am just curious. Your story seems—not a story."

Dani picked up her drink, watching the hawkers who were working the beach, selling necklaces and plastic bags of filtered water. The beach was full of people selling things. There were acrobats, fire swallowers, a teenage boy holding two woebegone ponies by the bridle. Obruni were everywhere—Chinese, Lebanese, Germans in Speedos.

She was not new to West Africa. Right out of grad school she had spent two years in Senegal working for Reuters, covering the UN, the World Bank, the IMF. That was where she'd really become a reporter. She'd learned how to press, how to cajole, how to threaten. How to let out some slack in the rope your subjects didn't realize you had handed them.

But all that had been back then. When she was confident and fearless. And young.

"Mr. Adjepong." She turned her gaze back to him. "Please work with me here. This is your country. These are your people's resources. I am merely trying to make sure they are not misused."

"Would you like to know what I think? I think that you Americans are obsessed with the Chinese. You see their shadow everywhere. It is an unhealthy concern."

"Surely it is of concern to Ghanaians as well? Who is benefiting from their oil, who is not?"

"Let Ghanaians worry about what concerns Ghanaians. We do not need a lecture. If a Chinese company wants to spend 224 million dollars on a patch of empty seabed, that is their business."

Dani's pen paused in the air above her notebook.

"Sorry," she said. "How much did they pay?"

"As you very well know, they paid 224 million."

For a moment Dani did not trust herself. She flicked back a few pages to double-check. There it unequivocally was—the figure she had found on Dongsha's annual public financial statement for 2016, filed with the securities regulators in Hong Kong.

$231 million.

She tried to keep her tone steady, not to give herself away. "Where can I confirm that figure, please?"

Kwesi checked his watch, looking bored. "Really, must I do your job for you, madam? All Energy Ministry auctions are recorded in the public register. Parcel 42 was no different."

"Of course," Dani said. "But I am confused—maybe you can help me."

"Why are you confused?"

"Well," Dani said slowly, "because Dongsha's own financial statements report that Parcel 42 cost 231 million, not 224 million. I have a copy right here, if you would like to take a look. What happened to the missing seven million dollars?"

A flash of hatred passed over his face, so brief and terrible that its clarity emerged only when it was over: like lightning at night. As a journalist and a woman, she was alert to that moment when the politeness of men ran out and she became an object of scorn or rage. It could happen very quickly. "Now you listen," a senator had snarled, back when she had been doing a stint at Politico before she went to journalism school—she had followed up his compliment of her earrings by asking about his vote to approve a military aid package to Saudi Arabia. "You won't get far in life being a rude person."

Being a cunt, is what she knew the senator had wanted to say. You won't get far being a cunt.

"I deny your allegations," Kwesi Adjepong said now. "I deny the veracity of your supposed proof. What are you writing?"

"I'm writing that you deny it."

Adjepong grimaced. *Cunt*, he was thinking. Or some Twi equivalent. "Anyway, I am not the one who can help you."

"Who is?"

For several long moments Adjepong deliberated with himself. "Talk to Oscar Aidoo," he said finally. "He is the deputy energy minister, he is the big man on Chinese issues in the NPP." He reached across the table and ripped a page from her notebook, snatched the pen from her hand. "Oscar Aidoo, he is the man in charge."

"He lives in Accra?"

"He has a home here, but his family is from Takoradi, in the west. Big shots, big shots in the west. Check him on Google, on Baidu, you will see. This is his phone number. But you must not tell him I sent you. You must tell him—"

"On background."

"Quite." He handed her the piece of paper, frowning.

Dani looked down at the scribbled address. She was unsure whether this counted as a victory or a failure. Should she press Adjepong further? All her instincts were off.

"Now I think it is time for me to return to my office, enh? If you have no more questions."

"Thank you for meeting me." She offered her hand.

Ajdepong polished off his drink, ignoring her handshake. "Chinese, British," he muttered to himself. "Your Texans are far worse, you know. Warrior for what? Warrior for shit, I say."

"What do you mean?"

"So, you have never talked to me, you agree? You will talk to Oscar Aidoo, but for me, this conversation did not take place."

"Mr. Adjepong, I can only keep off the record what you tell me to keep off the record in advance. I cannot lie and say I never met you."

She waited for his reaction. Kwesi Adjepong pulled on his jacket, shooed away a female hawker viciously with a growl from the back of the throat. His eyes found Dani, who had also stood up, and was again holding out her hand for him to shake. This time he shook it, with an expression of distaste, not looking at her. He seemed regretful now. "The Chinese buggered off in the end," he repeated, looking out at the sea. Then he left her there, striding away through the pale-skinned obruni in his dark suit, whistling his driver to attention.

DANI WROTE DOWN A set of notes quickly, transcribing the interview, making sure she got everything he said. Her most important interview in three weeks, and she had captured a key new fact. Dongsha had paid $7 million more than the Ghanaian Energy Ministry had recorded, for an oil parcel that had turned out to be worthless. She had Kwesi Adjepong on the record confirming it, and now she had a new lead, even higher up the political chain: Oscar Aidoo.

Good enough for now. Good enough to keep going.

The sun had shifted and was blasting her with its ridiculous heat. She got up and moved her chair a few feet to the left, into the shade. She took down all of Kwesi Adjepong's quotes, added in notes about the make of his watch, the color of his shirt, how much he paid for the Smirnoffs. She was diligent about detail. She had no publication backing her now, no name like Reuters or *The Guardian* to wield as proof that she was not a joke. She was a freelance reporter for the first time in her career. An American, a woman, alone. She bent her head and wrote with furious concentration. When she was finished she wrote the date at the top of the page: October 29.

There was still plenty of daylight left. The old Dani would have gone straight to Oscar Aidoo's address, the scent of the story yanking her forward like a predator tracking its prey.

But today something held her back. For a while she wandered around the restaurants and shops. Wandering is part of a reporter's job too, especially when you're in the early stages of a story, when you're trying to get your arms around a place you're not from. Dani remembered the rules, even if her reflexes were stiff. She heard the voice of her old professor at Columbia, Alma Hortensia: *Wandering plus curiosity: soil and water.*

She paused in front of a series of large, faded posters on the wall, from Ghana's last general election in 2016. She took out her notebook again and started writing down the names of the previous candidates for Parliament.

"People hate this man," said someone behind her. A teenager, a Ghanaian. He was not holding anything to sell.

"What man?" Dani said.

The boy stepped around her, jabbed a finger at a poster showing Ghana's current President, the leader of the NPP, the New Patriotic Party. He'd taken office in 2017 and would be up for reelection in December 2020. The NPP was also the party that Kwesi Adjepong belonged to—as well as Oscar Aidoo, her new lead. "This man, people hate this man."

"Why?"

"Because, under this man," he moved his finger to a poster of the president's predecessor, "things were cheaper." The predecessor had been from the opposing party, the National Democratic Congress or NDC. "But the president overthrew this man. Now, under him, things become more expensive."

"I see." Dani was intrigued by his use of *overthrew*, when in fact Ghana was celebrated for its peaceful transfers of power. "My name is Dani. Eh te sen?"

"I am Wisdom." He ignored her attempted Twi. "You are welcome."

"Tell me, Wisdom. Do you hate the president?"

"Not hate, no, not hate." He stabbed his finger against the poster again. "But things were better under this man. Things were cheaper."

"Can you spell your last name for me?" She held up her notebook. "I'm a journalist. I am writing about politics in Ghana."

"I do not know." He seemed not to understand the request, or else he was uneasy.

"Why were things better under the NDC?"

"I do not know."

"If you could just spell your surname." She was practically shoving her notebook under his nose. Wisdom ignored it. With a shy smile, he tapped the poster again and walked away.

There was a time when Dani would have pursued him—would have flattered, flirted, bullied, whatever it took to get his full name, his picture, a better quote than just "Things were cheaper." But today she watched him go with something like relief.

DANI HOPPED A TRO-TRO back to the city and went straight to To God Be the Glory without bothering to drop her stuff off at the dorm where she was staying.

Back in cell service range, she saw she had another missed call from her mother. That was no surprise. But there was also one from her younger sister, which was.

To God Be the Glory was a restaurant she had stumbled upon in her first days here, popular with foreigners—a sprawling establishment on the corner of a busy intersection, with tables and seats that spilled out into the street. It served Guinness and local Ghana Star lager by the case, and harder stuff too if they liked the look of you.

Dani listened to a few seconds of her mother's voicemail before deleting it; she saved Izzy's for later, when she could listen properly. She ordered a gin, no ice. It stung the back of her throat, flushing the dust and the dirt that had accumulated there. Burned, then cooled. Like an anesthetic. Her stomach was bothering her again.

She closed her eyes for a moment, rested her palm on her forehead.

"All right, Dani?"

"Hi Bruno."

Bruno was an Australian she'd met a few nights ago. Former military. He was a contractor for a security services firm whose employees guarded the Ghanaian elite, and he drove around in a shiny white pickup truck. Friendly enough, in the way of men who could obviously kill you with their bare hands.

"Killer hot out huh?" Bruno said through a mouthful of food. He was eating a heaping portion of fufu, his huge body curled protectively around the bowl, like a wary dog. The smell of it turned her stomach. Fufu was a cassava dough that formed the base of a spicy stew of meat or fish, which you ate with your hands. The first time she had tried it, on her first night in Ghana, Dani had been put down for forty-eight hours with apocalyptic diarrhea. You haven't known true humiliation until you've shit yourself as a grown adult. The body quivers, the mind rebels—*hold it*—but when the connection fails, the collapse is total. The physical weakness does not impress you as much as the emotional one: failing at something you've known how to do since you were two years old. Hard to forgive the food responsible for that. So Dani had been subsisting on rice and plantains and McVities biscuits she bought at the European Mini-Mart. And the odd plate of fried rice at one of Accra's many Chinese restaurants.

"How's work?" she asked.

"Busy," Bruno grunted. "Bloody ECOWAS coming to town, city's chockers with ministers. Everyone needs their motorcade. Not for security, not really, I mean—this ain't Côte d'Ivoire. But you've got to have one if the next fellow does. Well, you know what Africans are like."

"Mmm," she said noncommittally. ECOWAS was the Economic Community of West African States, a grouping of regional countries that had free trade agreements with one another and whose leaders met to coordinate policy.

"Yeah," said Bruno wistfully, picking a tendon from his teeth. "It ain't like Côte d'Ivoire, for sure. Sometimes I do miss the action. I mean, the money's good in Ghana, don't get me wrong. But I haven't fired me weapon once since I got here."

"How old are you, Bruno?"

"Forty-three."

"Kids?"

"Two. You get the picture." He grinned, waved his massive left hand—a gesture of disrespect, if he'd done it to a Ghanaian—showing where a wedding band cinched his ring finger like a tourniquet. Even Bruno's fingers had muscles. "Money's good, right? Wife's happy. Kids happy. Therefore"—he licked his fingers—"Bruno's stuck. I'll be babysitting Togolese deputy ministers till I'm old and gray. Buy you a drink?"

Dani paused. She had to watch herself. The Smirnoff Ice and then the gin; that was enough for now. "How about a Coke?"

"Right you are."

Her first stint in West Africa, nearly eight years ago now, when she was a girl charging through Senegal, Dani had gotten drunk every night. She had eaten whatever she wanted, she had given her malaria pills away (until she got malaria). How careless she had been back then. This time around, by comparison she felt silly and frail—with her good sense, her reasonable caution, the bug spray and hand sanitizer and iodine tablets in her bag.

"One Coca-Cola," said Yaw, the owner of To God Be the Glory. He smiled and took hold of Dani's right hand, asking quietly, "You are all right, Danielle?" He was a tall, thin, older man, with the most marvelous soft palms. Dani was a little in love with him.

"I'm okay, Yaw. Thank you. How did your son do in his exams?"

"He passed."

"Mashallah!" Dani said. Yaw frowned. The phrase was a reflexive habit, picked up in Lebanon. "I mean that's wonderful, Yaw. Please give him my congratulations."

"Yes, he is a good boy. His mother and I will give him a party here, when he gets accepted to university in Britain or America."

Outside, the sun was setting, the air tinted red by the dust from the harmattan winds that blew sand down from the Sahara across the whole of West Africa from November to March. It was a little after 6:00 P.M., rush hour, and the streets were surging with tro-tros and taxis and trucks, racing down the wide boulevards before they inevitably slammed on the brakes.

Dani sipped her Coke, warm and sweet. She thought about the boy at the beach this afternoon—Wisdom. And Kwesi Adjepong with his hands in his pockets, looking out to sea. She was on the tail of a real story now. Seven million dollars of Chinese money had gone missing, and senior party leaders in the NPP knew what had happened to it. If she'd had an editor, they would have been thrilled. But something was wrong with how she was approaching these interactions. They could all see right through her. More than likely this new man, Oscar Aidoo, would give her the run-around and send her on her way, smiling indulgently.

Who was she kidding? To think she could still do this?

The night got hotter and windier. The music got louder. Ghanaian men danced with each other unabashedly. They were not gay—because you couldn't be gay in Ghana, you would be dragged out of your home and lynched in the street.

Dani had had enough of the syrupy Coke. She ordered another gin. Ruddy-faced Bruno clinked his glass against hers. "That's the spirit."

Drinking had been a problem, off and on, for most of her life. She had recently started again, after the year when she couldn't. She remembered that first sip of wine, back in London, in the barren flat where she had been crashing after she had left Ben, her husband. Ex-husband. Her first night alone, clutching a hot water bottle to her stomach. The first sip had gone down too easily.

Still, she told herself that now she would be cautious. Not just because of what she'd been through—but because she was thirty-two, a grown woman. And so far, in Ghana, she had managed to stay in control. You had to be careful in the developing world. You had to keep your wits about you. In Senegal, she had made friends with a British war reporter who was covering the Ivorian civil war next door. Laurie Balfour: beautiful, blonde, posh—an Oxford woman, distantly related to the House of Windsor. She had a huge scar down the side of her neck, a shrapnel wound that spilled across her collarbones, faded to a vaguely sexual pink. Dani had worshipped her. Laurie could drink absolutely anybody under the table, burly men, ex-SAS types like Bruno, it didn't matter. Laurie would rip shot after shot until they toppled off their chairs, then calmly continue her conversation. She had drifted in and out of Dani's life unpredictably, but had always seemed to turn up when Dani needed her the most—needed advice, needed a friend, needed a woman who would not judge her. But one day, when Dani had been living in Beirut, Laurie had turned up dead in Côte d'Ivoire, in the alleyway behind her hotel. She'd been robbed and raped and shot in the head.

Now there was a commotion in the street in front of the bar. An acrobat troupe began doing tricks. Dani had seen them before. A crowd gathered, forcing traffic to go around them. Clapping, cartwheels, somersaults. One of the troupe was a dwarf. He vaulted onto the shoulders of his partner to screams of encouragement from the audience. They came around for contributions.

Dani's mood had darkened suddenly. Her stomach hurt, and she knew it would hurt even more in the morning without the numbing effect of the booze. There was something *wrong* with her. She did not take care of herself properly; she lacked some essential feminine nurturing instinct. And there was something wrong with To God Be the Glory. The way the white people here would look at each other, like they shared a secret handshake. Too many Westerners, with that arrogant, lazy mindset she had spent a lifetime trying to escape.

"Oh please can you give me some tips, some small monies?"

Not a performer, this one. Just a child begging.

Dani studied his face. She reached into her bag and pulled out wads of cedis. It was all the cash she had—about fifty bucks' worth. More money than this child had ever seen, probably. She pressed it into the boy's little hands. "Take it, take it," she gushed. He moved on without a word. When Dani looked up, she saw Yaw watching her with a look of disapproval.

Goddamn it. She was drunk.

In a flash of panic, she pulled her bag towards her, checked to see if her notebook was still there. She comforted herself by running her finger over the page where Kwesi Adjepong had scribbled Oscar Aidoo's address. "The big man on Chinese issues." The man in charge, if Kwesi was to be believed.

Tomorrow she would find him. And she would find her story.

Dani put her phone to her ear and listened to the voicemail Isabelle had left her.

> *Dani, it's Izzy. How are you? How's Ghana? . . . Guess what? Josh proposed! I know, I know, I'm screaming, sorry, sorry . . . I mean, it wasn't a surprise, remember how I told you we've been talking about it? But this is real! Like actually real! Just this morning he did it. . . . It's so weird, I have a* fiancé. . . . *Anyway, call me when you get this. I hope you're feeling okay, Dani. I love you. I love you. Call me!*

She put her phone back in her bag.

It wasn't so bad, To God Be the Glory. To God *be* the glory, indeed. Late at night, when the music got loud, Yaw came out from behind the bar and drank Jack Daniels with his customers and clapped along with the drummers and the dancers. The hands of men found the waists of women. Bruno was dancing with a Ghanaian girl who wore a top that said PINK in sparkly sequins. Dani watched him take off his wedding ring and put it in his pocket.

THE POWER WENT OUT again at the dormitory that night. Dani startled awake sometime after midnight to the sound of her own voice moaning in pain. She was covered in sweat, her hair matted, the blankets itchy, her stomach cramping so badly she could barely stand up.

She went out into the hallway of the building, which was open to the city, and stood at the railing trying to breathe. Desperate for a breeze. But none came. Accra lay silent, the night air damp and heavy. In the trees, unidentifiable insects clicked and hissed.

She heard a door open behind her. Priscilla, the woman staying in the next room over, emerged wrapped in a towel.

"Oh," Priscilla said softly, surprised. "Hello Dani."

"Hello." God, her voice was like a bag of glass. She swallowed. "Hello Priscilla."

"Are you okay? You look, you know." She pointed at her mouth. "Sick."

"I'm," Dani grimaced. "Just . . . need some air."

"You will come and see me tomorrow? Your dress?"

Priscilla was a seamstress from Lagos, who traveled to Accra every few months to buy fabrics and make sales. The moment they met, she had sized Dani up and offered to make her a dress. Dani had been putting her off ever since.

"Tomorrow," Dani said. "Tomorrow—ah," she gasped. "Yes."

Priscilla shrugged and walked off towards the communal bathrooms, her shower shoes slapping the concrete. Dani stayed outside for another few minutes, fanning herself with one hand, the other on her belly, until the cramps passed. Then she went back to her room and drank half a liter of water. She put some baby powder in her armpits and lay down on top of the scratchy blankets beneath the motionless ceiling fan. She dozed uneasily for another couple of hours, until she woke in the smoky light of Accra's predawn to the nagging feeling of a task left undone, the sound of roosters crowing, and men's unhurried voices in the street below her window.

TWO

THE DOUBLE WAS NOT so heedless as to have expected that his life would be simplified by giving the name of David Ibrahim to the American intelligence officer. Still it surprised him how abruptly and irreversibly everything had gone wrong. He had not expected Ibrahim to be *killed.* Certainly not in such a violent way. From what he read in *Ghana Today*, the man had been slaughtered like a beast in a frenzy: throat slit, nearly decapitated, stab wounds all over his body.

Was he sorry that Ibrahim was dead? He supposed so. After all, he had known David Ibrahim. He had shaken the man's hand, eaten at his table—had even bounced Ibrahim's young daughter on his knee.

But the primary difficulty with his death was not emotional but logistical. Ibrahim had goings-on with half a dozen women, so the police might suspect a spurned lover. The Chinese, however, would immediately begin looking for a mole. The Double had to proceed on the assumption that his movements, his activities, everything he said and did were being scrutinized. A clock had begun ticking. He had made a decisive leap to the Americans, and he was now exposed: no longer able to retreat to the Chinese, nor yet secure in the Americans' good offices. He needed to close the deal with the Americans before the Chinese discovered his betrayal. The clock would not keep ticking forever.

THE DECISION TO GIVE up David Ibrahim was his own: the act of a grown man. But the decision to spy for China had been made for him long ago, when he was still a boy.

He vividly remembered the day it had begun. He was fourteen. He had been told to wait in the small room at the back of his family's house, a place where he was typically sent as punishment. This had confused him; he had racked his mind for what he could have done wrong. A thread had come loose from the soccer jersey he had been wearing—a Chelsea shirt, for Michael Essien, of course—and he had been fidgeting with it when the door had opened and the Chinese intelligence officer had entered. A man whose face, voice, whose very smell he would come to hate. The Chinese officer had laid his thin hands on top of the Double's. "Thank you for helping me."

That day began the second part of his life: his career as an intelligence asset.

Every few months the Chinese officer would make contact, and the Double would be required to make a report. Always the same perfunctory questions. What were the boys at school saying about the government in Accra? What mobile phone brands were his friends using? What social networks? The Chinese officer received his answers expressionlessly. And after a few years, working for China felt like just another chore, like doing his laundry.

Until one Sunday, when he was twenty-three, he had heard his name being called as he was leaving church. It was the second

Sunday of Lent. The Double was more interested in girls than religion, but he still went every week, at his mother's insistence. The congregation was streaming out into the parking lot, when the man who had been sitting in the pew behind him had fallen into step with him.

"Hello, brother." His accent was American, which made the Double stop short. The American had patted his stomach. "May I join you for some fufu?"

The Double knew that he was supposed to say no. But a part of him had always believed that this day would come. The truth was, he had been waiting for it for many years. He had known that destiny would not keep him trapped in Ghana, that America would come and save him. And now that the moment was here, he was somewhat startled at how excited he felt. How unfrightened. Everything had an air of inevitability.

"My name is Ford," the American said, once they had collected their fufu at the chop shop down the road from the church and taken their seats on the blue plastic stools. "Like the car."

"You are welcome," said the Double cautiously.

Ford did not waste time with pleasantries. "In the United States, we believe in God." He leaned in, the spicy smell of pepper stew on his breath. "Do you believe in God, my brother?"

"We have met in church," the Double said contemptuously. He would not let this man patronize him like the Chinese officer did. *I am an adult,* he wanted to say. *Come to your point.*

"America is not perfect. Far from it. It is a nation built on the backs of African slaves. I sometimes wonder if my own ancestors might have passed through the Door of No Return at Elmina, just up the coast from here. Impossible to know, because of how brutal the Americans were then. Savage people, monsters." Ford's voice rose, then fell away. "But America is a living body. It gets sick and gets better. In waves, of course, not in straight lines. But it does grow up. And it keeps its eyes on God. God lives in America. The Chinese, they have no God. The Chinese, they are," he lowered his voice and hissed, "atheists."

The Double was not impressed. He felt Ford perceive his hesitation and pivot his argument.

"We cannot pretend that America is blameless." Ford waved his arm to include both of them. "As Black men, we know America's sins. But those sins are public. They are visible. But the Chinese—what does anybody know about what they want, about who they are? You think their investment will be a good thing for Ghana? They care only about themselves." He waved his arm again. "America's sins are in the past. China's sins are in the future."

The Double hesitated, and the other man's eyebrows rose slightly. It was as if he could smell the Double's love for Ford's country. For America had been the place of the Double's dreams ever since he was a boy, since even before he had been forced to work for the Chinese. America was the place where the most fantastic inventions emerged from thin air and materialized in people's hands. A land of mystery and infinite riches—its movies, its music, its skyscrapers, Oprah Winfrey giving three hundred audience members free cars, Bill Clinton playing the saxophone in sunglasses. The place where people drove in convertibles with the top down, underneath palm trees, on clean, empty highways, the place where ordinary people lived ordinary lives filled with infinite and wondrous gifts, Coca-Cola, Microsoft, McDonald's, Whitney Houston, Michael Jackson: all of it had long ago ignited a fire for America in the Double's young heart, a sense of wonder and hope—and a gnawing sense of shame about his own country and his own people. America was where the future was born every day. It was almost too intense to permit himself to imagine, even for a moment, that he could actually be a part of it.

"It is dangerous, talking to you like this," the Double had said, returning his attention to Ford. "I should not be here."

"If you feel that way," Ford said, "we can part ways, and no hard feelings. This isn't about forcing you. That's not how we do things. But if you were interested, we would protect you. That is a firm promise. If you got into trouble, all you would have to do is signal us. And we would give you whatever you asked for."

The Double sat for a moment in the middle of two lives. He tried to work out the calculations in his head, the risk and reward, the geometry of the scenarios that might unfold, but adrenaline was flooding him and he couldn't think clearly. Inside himself he felt his histories and his futures already diverging. It was one of those moments where the voice speaks the truth before the mind has quite accepted it.

"I want to become an American citizen."

Ford betrayed no hint of triumph or even surprise. He scooped some fufu into his mouth as though he hadn't heard. The sauce ran down his chin; he wiped it away. Then he nodded once, sharply. "That can be arranged—if things go well."

SO THE THIRD PART of his life began.

At first the stakes had remained small, almost frivolous. His Chinese handler would meet with him as usual, and then the

Double would signal to Ford that he had a message to pass. They would meet in shops, at gas stations, on remote roadsides on the outskirts of Accra—never the same place twice. The Double would tell him everything the Chinese officer had asked about, and even though these were the same perfunctory topics the Chinese had been asking about since he was fourteen, Ford was always interested. Always diligent and focused. The Double was gratified to feel that Ford understood the risks he was taking and the sacrifices that living this way demanded. He valued the Double in a way the Chinese never had.

In his own life, the Double felt a sense of purpose he had never experienced before. He moved through the world like a commander of men. At his job, with his friends, talking to girls in the KFC on a Friday evening, he had displayed a new confidence whose authority was private to him but whose effects everyone noticed. He had a goal, and he was taking decisive action to achieve it. At night he dreamed of his new life in the United States.

But after about a year, the flow of events began to reverse. Ford began signaling *him* to meet, giving him proactive assignments to find certain pieces of information and return them. These assignments, over time, gave the Double a picture of what the Americans were focused on: cell phone networks, and the various hardware and software systems that allowed Ghanaians to communicate with each other and with the world. They wanted to know which companies were gaining market share in West Africa's telecom industry, and who funded them, and who supplied the component parts that went into their systems. They wanted to know who was winning the government's contracts to transition Ghana to 5G technology, which pinged signals between cell towers so much faster than 4G that it would make possible an entirely new set of technologies: the Internet of Things.

And they wanted to know what China wanted to know about all of this.

On his own time, the Double surreptitiously read all he could about these issues. And what he learned was that a great decoupling was underway. Ever since the US had welcomed China into the global economy in the 1980s, the two economies had been binding themselves closer together, a happy marriage of US money and intellectual property with China's vast cheap labor force. As a consequence, China had grown rich and powerful—modern megacities blooming atop muddy farmland, hundreds of millions of people emerging from a poverty as severe as that of the poorest Ghanaians into something approximating a middle-class American lifestyle. But since the late 2010s, these wheels that had been spinning for nearly forty years had begun to sputter and grind to a halt, and in some cases reverse direction. China was pulling apart from the US, led by its confident ruler Xi Jinping. And the US government, over howls of protest from its private sector, was pulling apart from China. A world-changing event was underway, and the Double was watching it ripple into the beaches and markets and chop shops of Accra.

THEN, THREE MONTHS AGO, Ford had come to him with a specific question.

"Do you know what a vampire tap is?"

The Double did, but he had played dumb. "I'm not sure."

"Vampire taps," Ford said, "are small pieces of plastic that you connect to internet routers. Fiber-optic cables carry the internet beneath the ground. But every so often the cables have to terminate in one of these routers. From there, a new set of wires carries the data on to its destination. But if you put a vampire tap *inside* the router," Ford made a pinching motion with his thumb and index finger, "You could pull information about all the data traffic crossing the wires, including encryption protocols. Then you could hack into whatever private networks that data later traveled to. You with me?"

The Double had known all of this. It was elementary stuff. But he'd nodded, frowning with concentration. "Yes. I think so."

"Now," continued Ford, "We believe the Chinese are using these taps to hack into the networks of American companies whose cables run through West Africa. So what I need to know is: who is bringing the vampire taps into the country?"

The answer was David Ibrahim. He was the primary importer in Accra of Chinese-made vampire taps. But the Double had hesitated. He had never before been asked to give up a fellow African by name.

"Let me remind you that we are giving you the most powerful gift the United States can supply: our protection," Ford had said. "I will not let anything happen to you, while you continue to help us."

The Double had looked away. He disdained the lack of subtlety in Ford's words, the crassness of the implication. But then he had looked at his hands. He had thought about holding an American passport in them. The blue cover and the gold seal. He had thought about flipping it open and seeing his own picture, his name, and the words UNITED STATES OF AMERICA.

"There is a certain man," the Double had said. "A Nigerian. His name is Ibrahim."

AND NOW DAVID IBRAHIM was dead.

The Double was not a violent man. In grade school, when the other boys would fight and scuffle and get their shoes dirty, he preferred to stand off to the side. But he had committed an act of violence now. Were it not for his choices, his decisions, the words he had spoken aloud, David Ibrahim might be alive today.

But he could not be sorry for what he had done. The circumstances that had put him in this position were the work of others. The decision to spy for China had been made for him, long before he'd had any say in the matter. He would admit no moral condemnation for his efforts to free himself from a prison in which others had placed him.

Besides, if the US and China really were pulling apart, such messes were bound to happen, not just in Ghana but all across the globe. When two giants fought, the ants at their feet were crushed. It was the mistake of people like Ibrahim to believe they could dodge being trampled by anticipating the footfalls—when the real key to survival was to ascend. The Double's only job now was to keep himself alive until he was firmly on the back of the particular giant that he thought would win.

So he did not feel sorry for the act of violence he had facilitated. Events beyond his control had forced him into a world where such an act was required. He had had no choice.

Still—what an act of violence it was. As he read the news in *Ghana Today* about the condition in which David Ibrahim's body had been discovered, the Double felt nauseated. The savagery of it must surely have been deliberate. The Americans never did anything without careful planning. And the message it sent was clear, to the Double at least: work with China and you will die, like the worst dog.

Ford could not have been the killer. Too mild mannered—and anyway, the Double could tell that Ford preferred to keep his hands clean. That was why they worked well together: both men knew that one's brain was one's deadliest weapon. So there must have been another American spy out there in Accra who had actually killed Ibrahim. The Chinese were no doubt hunting them too—just as they were hunting the mole who had given up Ibrahim for death.

The giants were fighting. The ants were scrambling. The clock was ticking.

THREE

DANI STRUGGLED AWAKE THROUGH her hangover haze, memories of To God Be the Glory flickering behind her throbbing eyelids. A dancing dwarf. Bruno's hand on that woman's waist: PINK. A shot of gin, and then another.

She ate a couple of Hobnob biscuits and mixed herself a Nescafé with the little water that remained in her bottle. Her head was killing her. Good. She was ashamed of herself.

But when she looked out the window and saw the bright Ghanaian sun, she felt herself go taut, like a sail in the wind.

The story!

Seven million dollars was unaccounted for—and she had the name and address of the man who knew where it went.

She swallowed her malaria pill with the last of her chalky coffee, slipped her passport in her bra, and tied her red bandana around the strap of her backpack. Then she set off in pursuit of Oscar Aidoo.

The address Kwesi Adjepong had given her was in an upscale neighborhood near the center of the city. Dani took the tro-tro to Makola Market, wedging herself into a seat beside an older woman and her granddaughter. The old woman looked her up and down. "Hello," she said gravely. "You are welcome."

"Thank you," Dani said. "Good morning."

The little girl stared up at Dani, silent.

The tro-tro flew and weaved around men leading goats on ropes, around motorbikes and taxicabs, around girls hawking sealed baggies of filtered water from buckets balanced on their heads. "Aaaaacewata!" they called. "Aaaaacewata!" At one point, they passed another tro-tro that had spilled on its side. The minivan's wheels slowly swiveled in the air, like an animal's legs. The driver was standing under a tree, waiting patiently while the city's backed-up traffic edged around his wreck, honking.

Oscar Aidoo's house was down a side street of abrupt tranquility. An unpaved rust-red dirt road, lined with complexes ringed by concrete walls embedded with broken glass along the top to deter intruders. It was a world away from the traffic and chaos a few blocks over. Inside the walls, glimpses of well-kept mansions painted in fresh orange and yellow, and gardens flowering with trees. Through one gate she saw a German shepherd watching her. At another, an armed guard sat beneath an umbrella.

When she got to his address, the gate was locked. Dani pressed the intercom call button and waited.

"Hello?" A woman's voice crackled on the speaker.

"Yes, hello," Dani said, raising her voice. "Good afternoon. My name is Danielle Moreau and I am a journalist. I'm looking for the Honorable Mr. Oscar Aidoo. Is this his home?"

A beat of silence. "Journalist?"

"Yes, my name is Danielle Moreau. I am a journalist. Is this the home of Mr. Oscar Aidoo?"

"One moment."

"I can show my credentials."

"One moment."

A harmattan gust made her sneeze. Dani untied the red bandana and blew her nose. "Bandanas are infinitely useful things," Laurie had told her once. They could be a tissue, a washcloth, a maxi pad, a tourniquet. You could tie them around your neck to protect yourself from sunstroke, or wedge them under your head if you were sleeping rough out in the field. The bandana never complained.

The gate opened with a rusty sigh. Dani stood looking at a heavyset woman in a maid's uniform, who stood with her arms crossed. "Who are you?" she said at once. "What are you doing here?"

"I'm Danielle Moreau," she repeated. "I'm a reporter working here in Ghana."

"British?" The maid's tone was like a meat cleaver. Each word a short, heavy blow.

"American."

"Adjoa!" A new voice rose up from behind them, from the house, which was still hidden behind the half-opened gate. "Bring her here, please."

Adjoa held Dani's gaze for another moment, then turned aside. Dani stepped into a neat, well-kept yard. On the veranda sat a pair of young men. One was handsome and tall, wearing an orange T-shirt that bulged with muscles. The other, sitting down, was slightly pudgy, wearing glasses. A deferential buffer separated the two of them from the employees, but neither could be Oscar Aidoo. Far too young.

The man in glasses greeted her. "Howdy," he said, in an American accent.

Dani was surprised. "Uh, hi. Good afternoon."

"Good afternoon," he repeated seriously, gently mocking her. He got to his feet. Short, almost her height. He was not smiling, but the shadow of a smile dogged his expression, as if it might break out any moment. "I'm James Aidoo. How do you do, Miss . . . ?"

"Danielle Moreau."

The promised smile appeared. "What a beautiful name. You French?"

"I—my mother is." Dani was flustered by this unexpected American directness. In a foreign country, when you meet a stranger, you calibrate your behavior by the local mores. Which, in Ghana, tended towards scrupulous politeness and an almost Victorian formality. "You must be Mr. Aidoo's son."

"Guilty as charged. And this," he clapped the tall man on the arm, "is my best friend, Kofi Oppong."

"Hello," said Kofi. "You are most welcome." His voice was deep and slow.

"It's lovely to meet you both," Dani said.

"You are a reporter?" said Kofi.

"Yes. I'm here because I have some questions for Mr. Oscar Aidoo. Is he in?"

"A reporter with who?" James asked.

"My bylines have appeared in Reuters and *The Guardian,*" Dani said. "And Politico, if you've heard of it."

"Oh ho," said Kofi. "Now you are in real trouble, James." He said something in Twi, his syllables flowing more rapidly in his native language. Then he switched back to English. "I shall take my leave, for you to ask your questions."

"There's no need—" Dani started to say.

"Nah," James cut her off, swatting the bigger man's arm again. "Kofi was heading out anyway. He's got a date." He winked up at his friend, who frowned. "But I'm sorry to tell you that Dad's not here."

"I hope we shall meet again," Kofi said, taking Dani's hand in his. "You are most welcome here in Ghana."

"Thank you," she said. She was disappointed that Oscar Aidoo was not here: the predator found the nest unguarded but empty. But in their own way, these two young men had caught her attention. A rich neighborhood, a maid, two friends joking around. Where was the handsome man going? And why did the pudgy one talk like he was from the Midwest?

The critical thing, as a reporter, is to be honest about your own prejudices. Best of all would be to not have them, but that is impossible. The trick is to recognize your prejudices right away when they do arise and then correct for their distortion. Fall back, let the scene come into focus afresh. Ask yourself: what is it you're noticing? What is it you're discounting? Why do certain details stick out for you? Resist the temptation towards drawing premature conclusions. Resist it resist it resist it.

"JUST KEEP PRESSING, DANI." That was what Laurie had told her, long ago. "Don't let them turn you away."

This was in Senegal. Dani had been twenty-six years old, working for Reuters. She was in real danger for the first time in her life. It had thrilled her.

Dakar was full of Lebanese businesses, a legacy of both countries having been colonized by the French. Lebanese owned all the gas stations, all the hotels, all the supermarkets. It was at a hookah bar one night that Laurie had introduced herself to Dani.

"I work for a wire service," she had said, extending her hand and exhaling a plume of sheesha smoke, as American rap music played in the background.

"I'm with Reuters," Dani replied, feeling like a badass.

"AFP for me."

Laurie was a real war reporter. She had been in Afghanistan and Gaza, and now she was in West Africa to cover unrest in Côte d'Ivoire. Tall and thin and blonde, with the long scar on her neck. They started talking about the story Dani was working on at the time, about a famous Senegalese musician who was suing a German DJ for copyright infringement.

"Keep pressing," Laurie had admonished her.

"I really think the story is done, Laurie." Dani's head was gently spinning from the tobacco. "I think it's ready."

"No, no, no. Keep at it. The more people you can speak with, the richer your reporting becomes."

"Just keep speaking to people? Indefinitely?"

"You just keep pressing. Don't let them turn you away. You've got to be fucking savage about it." Dani had giggled at this, at Laurie's BBC newsreader accent. "Every time you press and you feel some give under your hands, some weakness, you know you have them on the run."

"But *how* do you know when you're finished?"

"When you press and there's no more give. Then you know you've found a set of solid, true facts. Hard as rock."

In the silence after Kofi Oppong departed, Dani assessed the young man standing before her on the veranda. She was still single-minded in her determination to get to Oscar and to press him about the missing $7 million. But suddenly she was thinking that maybe it was lucky Oscar was not home. A frontal assault on a man like that was unlikely to work. In Dani's experience, you almost never got to the big man on the first try; he was always "too busy." You got some flunky instead. Better to try to sneak through a side door.

Like the big man's son.

"And do you . . . live here, in Ghana?" she said.

"You mean, why do I talk like this?" James grinned and patted his belly, one hand resting on the soft paunch. Everything about him was slightly round: face, cheeks, even his forearm, cinched with a Rolex that cut into his skin. "Went to school in the States. At UT Austin. I'm guessing you're American?"

"Guilty as charged."

"Right," he chuckled. He rocked on his heels, hands in his pockets. "Anyway, like I said, my father is not here. Sorry I can't help you."

"When will he be back?"

"No idea. He's in Takoradi. Family business."

"Could you tell me where I could find him?" Dani touched his arm. "It's important."

He raised an eyebrow. "No offense, Miss Moreau, but I don't know you."

"Of course."

Her flirting felt crass, somehow illegitimate. Young Dani would have had this kid eating out of her hand. But now she was just a random freelancer. His first question: *A reporter with who?* She wiped the sweat from her face with her red bandana.

"Can I offer you some water?" he said apologetically after a moment. "Some coffee?"

He was being generous. But she was not too proud to accept. "Coffee would be great."

She followed James into Oscar Aidoo's house. When the door shut behind her it was like she'd been vacuumed out of the midday heat into a vault of muffled darkness. Heavy lace curtains blocked all the windows. There were green velour couches along the walls, green velour chairs in the middle of the room—concentric rows of green velour, like a furniture showroom. In a corner, a huge television played mutely, tuned to CCTV, China's English-language news channel. Down a hallway, she saw the swish of a maid's uniform vanish through a door.

"Coffee, Adjoa darling," James drawled in the direction of the kitchen. He turned to Dani. "How do you take it?"

"Black's fine."

He shook his head. "I'll never understand Americans. As if sugar was poisonous. All the girls in Austin too."

"How old are you, James?" She consciously elongated her vowels to match his vaguely Southern drawl. "If you don't mind my asking."

For a moment he looked offended. "How old do you think I am?"

"I'd always rather ask than assume."

"So you are interviewing me now?"

"I'd be happy to interview you, if you consent." She pulled out her notebook. "Let's say we're on the record now, okay? If you want to go off record, you have to tell me."

"I feel like Tom Cruise."

"Let's start again. How old are you?"

"I'm twenty-five. How old are you?"

"Thirty-two. What did you study in Texas?"

"Electrical engineering. Don't you have a tape recorder or something?"

"To protect my sources I never record my interviews digitally. Just here." She patted the notebook. "And when a story is finished I lock them in a safe."

"Afraid you'll be hacked?" James nodded. "Smart."

"So. Austin? What was it like?"

"Austin was okay." James chewed his lip. "I enjoyed my studies, met some good people. But I was homesick. Now I'm very glad to be back in Ghana. And Texas was—you're not from Texas, are you?"

"New York."

"Whoa." His eyes widened slightly. "So cool."

Adjoa appeared with two coffees in small teacups painted with flowers. She gave Dani a dirty look as she set them down.

James took off his glasses—thick square frames—and cleaned them on his blue linen shirt. "So, Miss Moreau."

"Call me Dani, please."

"Dani. My turn to ask a question. Why do you want to talk to my father?"

"I'm writing a story and his name came up."

"A story about what?"

"Chinese investment in Ghana's oil resources."

James nodded and sipped his coffee.

"What, specifically?"

Through the side door. "Oil has been such a boon for Ghana's development. That's what my story is about—how the government has been using the country's natural resources to grow its economy. One of my sources told me that your father deserves much of the credit, and I wanted to ask him about it."

"Who gave you my father's name?" he asked.

"I can't divulge."

"Oh, come on. Tell me." His tone tried to be intimidating—but he was too short, too young for the effect.

Dani blinked back at him. "No, actually. I won't."

"You know what? I think I'd like to go off the record again. Please."

"All right." She closed her notebook.

James rubbed his chin, considering her. "So you grew up in New York? What is it like?"

She laughed without thinking. "What's *New York* like?"

"I mean." His eyes dropped. "I've never been. Just the airport."

"You should go. Maybe I can show you around."

"I bet that's what made you want to be a reporter, huh? Growing up there."

She felt a flicker of impatience. But even though she was here with a job to do, there was something about this kid she found disarming. He seemed shy of his own inquisitiveness—like he knew his questions were foolish but was unable to stop himself. With his baby-fat cheeks, slightly short of breath. *How old do you think I am?*

"In some ways, I suppose yes," Dani said, trying to be generous with him, as he'd been with her. "New York forces you—it puts right in your face the fact that nothing separates you from other people's lives. That there is no real reason I'm me and you're you. Just random luck, and a few inches of space on the subway. But any city's like that. Accra is like that too. Isn't it?"

He nodded somberly. "Accra is like that. Dad doesn't like it here—that's why he goes back to Takoradi every chance he gets. You know Takoradi?"

"Tadi's a great city."

He snorted. "'Tadi' sucks. I grew up there, I should know."

"Will he be back in Accra soon?"

"Dunno." His shadow of a smile returned, a twitch in his cheeks that tailed every word. "But hey, if you want to go and find him there, be my guest. I'd be happy to tell you where to look. I'm sure he would love to talk to you about his achievements." Did she detect the slightest note of bitterness in his voice? "But I think you should be careful," Aidoo continued, tipping back the rest of his coffee. "Out here in West Africa, the oil industry is full of rough sorts."

She frowned. "That's not a threat, I hope?"

"Not at all." He smiled broadly. "Just friendly advice."

Somewhere in the silence of the house, a grandfather clock clicked minutely.

IN DAKAR, DANI HAD felt more sure of herself than she ever had in her life. She had filed stories on foreign investment, on the misdeeds of the IMF and the UN. She had grown thin and tan. She'd caught malaria, and spent three weeks in the hospital. Laurie had come to visit her there, and brought her a fifth of Gordon's Gin to keep under her pillow.

And then Reuters had moved her to Lebanon. She had learned Arabic, studied for hours every day. *I do not like Cairo because of the traffic. The weather in Jordan is very hot.* She found the language beautiful. She loved how they greeted each other in the mornings. "Sabah ewahrd." *Morning of flowers.* "Sabah eyasmeen." *Morning of jasmine.*

But more than the language, she had loved the danger. Beirut was a buzzing city, tense with the potential for sudden violence. Dani was becoming addicted to it. Her assigned beat was politics. She covered the city's factions, learned how to use burner phones and fake email accounts to cover her sources' tracks. SIM cards were cheap; she went through them like candy. Laurie had told her never to record sensitive interviews—"It puts your sources in danger"—but instead to transcribe them by hand as soon as they concluded. Dani herself had been threatened, a trickle of anonymous WhatsApp messages: *Be careful* in Arabic. *Go home.* It had made her feel bold and powerful. She switched SIM cards and the messages ceased.

One day she had witnessed the aftermath of a bomb blast. It was pure luck: the explosion was around the corner from the café where she was working. She had been on the scene less than a minute after it had happened. Disembodied limbs scattered in the street, pulsing like hearts. Cracked glass, car alarms, and grown men holding their heads, weeping for their mothers. It had been her first byline to make the homepage:

CAR BOMB KILLS 12 IN BEIRUT AS
SUNNI-SHIA DISPUTE TURNS DEADLY

DANIELLE MOREAU / REUTERS

BEIRUT

Dani had felt herself picking up speed. She had felt superior to her mother, her sisters, to everyone she had ever known back in the US. She was braver than them, out here on the wild frontier of the world, where the stakes were real, where the floors were hard and dirty.

And then she had gotten the text from Dakar. Laurie Balfour was dead.

DANI HAD THE SENSE that the maid Adjoa was just out of sight, listening to every word she and James said.

"What do you do for a living?"

"I work for Ghana Telecom—Vodafone Ghana, I should say." James smiled. "We used to call it Ghana Telecom when I was a kid. Don't you do that too? Call things what they were called when you were little?"

"Do you like it?"

"It's not very challenging. But it pays well." He threw out his chest slightly. "And I'm proud to be part of the development of my country."

Dani kept her tone light, disinterested. "Is that how you know Kofi? Is he a friend from work?"

"Kofi? Nah, he and I have been friends since we were small boys. We grew up down the street from one another. His father is an MP, like mine."

"And how does your father feel about your job contributing to the development of Ghana? He must be proud of you."

James cocked his head. "You're so eager to meet my father for your story, which, forgive me, sounds like a bit of a puff piece." He leaned forward and lowered his voice, conspiratorial. "But have you seen his videos?"

Google him, Kwesi Adjepong had said. *Check him on Baidu.* What she should have been doing last night instead of getting sloppy at To God Be the Glory.

"No," Dani admitted. "I haven't."

"You will learn a lot about his worldview there."

"What should I expect?"

James seemed pleased she'd asked. "Look, my father has been enormously successful in the world he knows. In the world that you Westerners gave us," he added pointedly. "But as for me, it's not the world I want to go into. Oil is not what will make Ghana a great nation. I deal with data, bandwidth, download speeds. Mobile phones and Wi-Fi. Ghana doesn't need to tread the same path as the West. We can leapfrog you. We can go directly from premodern technology to the internet of everything. We don't need the clunky phase in the middle, where the West is currently stuck. That's where I see Ghana's future. In data. Not in oil wells and brute force."

"But your father doesn't agree?"

"My father has his beliefs. Everyone does. But a new generation is growing up. Like Kofi and me." He patted his belly again, as if for reassurance. "We do not share the same history as our fathers. We know we don't have to let the West make us feel ashamed. We are as good or better than anyone." He gave a small nod, like a student who had proved his thesis.

He was an interesting kid. But Dani was out of patience. She needed to get to the $7 million. She needed Oscar.

"Here's a proposition for you," she said, as if the idea had just occurred to her. "Why don't we go to Takoradi together? You can take me to your father, and when I write this 'puff piece,' as you say, you'll get some of the credit."

James leaned back and assessed her, his hands threaded behind his head. Dani knew it was a risk. She didn't know this person; he could take her anywhere. And even if he did bring her to Oscar Aidoo, Takoradi was a good six hours away. She'd be far from anyone she knew, reliant on somebody who owed her nothing. And most of all, it was sketchy craft, even potentially unethical. James Aidoo was the son of the source she was pursuing; he might, himself, become a source in time. She shouldn't be soliciting favors from him.

But he was the shortest way to Oscar. The story demanded it.

"I suppose that would be fine," James said. "You know, I actually do need to head down to the West anyway at the end of the week. I could save you the bus trip. Yes. I don't see why not."

"Here's my number. Dani ripped a scrap of paper from her notebook and wrote down her cell number. "Just call me when you want to go."

"How about on Friday?"

"Friday works." She shut her notebook neatly. "I look forward to our road trip."

James Aidoo laughed and shook his head. "American girls."

THEY NEVER CAUGHT WHOEVER had killed Laurie. Dani's friend had been drinking at a bar in Abidjan, the largest city in Côte d'Ivoire. She had left to return to her hotel. The next morning, she had been found in an alleyway, half naked, a bullet wound to the back of her skull.

But the imagined scenes burned into Dani's psyche, no less horrific because they were conjecture. Laurie being raped, a gun pressed to her head. Laurie pleading for her life. Laurie's brains caught in her blonde hair. The images and sounds burned into her memory. As real as the rows of cholera victims in body bags she had seen in a Senegalese village, rain pouring down on their white plastic. As real as the face of a dead woman after the car bombing in Beirut, hanging open, empty space behind it—like the frame of a building after a tornado.

In the months that followed Laurie's death, even as she had continued her work in Beirut, Dani had suddenly had enough of men with guns. Of men's angry voices, of men's leering laughter. Of the metallic taste of alcohol and the papery taste of cigarettes. She was tired of living in the world where Laurie had died—a world where people died every day, violently and for no reason.

So when *The Guardian* had offered her a position in London, covering a new beat—the informal economy in emerging markets—it had been too good a job to pass up. It had been the chance to be a desk reporter and to see what that was like. But more than that, it had been a chance to catch her breath. Dani wanted to shelter for a while in the developed world, in safety.

And there was another thing.

She wanted a child.

THAT WAS MORE THAN three years ago.

Today, after Dani left Oscar Aidoo's house, as she walked back through the bucolic streets to the main drag in front of Makola Market, she vibrated with the quiet energy of the hunter.

She was going to Takoradi, and she was going to confront Oscar Aidoo, escorted by his son. She was going to find that $7 million.

She was going to get her story.

The heat and the noise of Accra, after the dark isolation of the green velour living room, pushed on her from all sides. It was the middle of the day and the bursting traffic had slowed, as if the cars themselves were sluggish. She ducked into the market, looking for some gingerroot. The strong coffee had riled up her stomach again. She found some at a stall stacked with rows of cloves and cardamom.

Dani bought a bag of water from an aicewata girl and tore it open at the corner with her teeth and wandered slowly down the market rows, sucking on it and checking out the wares. Pig hooves, T-shirts, salted fish, jewelry. Racks and racks of dress shoes. The markets were where she stuck out the most as an obruni, a foreigner. People stared at her; occasionally catcalls followed her, men made a sucking sound with their teeth.

She was rediscovering that the rush of a story is unbeatable when you're inside it. Human sources are challenging, because you only ever get a little sliver of truth from them at a time—mixed in with masses of half-truths, untruths, fantasies and speculations. You have to go through bags and bags of shredded documents to find the one strip of paper with the one word on it you need. You have to fish out the slivers, you have to lay your slivers against one another and see if they cohere. And then you have to verify, corroborate. And for that you have to find more human sources.

She was freelance now; no publication, no editor to push her. No husband, no child. No employer, no reputation to protect.

Until yesterday it had made her feel vulnerable, but now that she was making progress, Dani experienced her isolation as a kind of superpower. It meant she was completely free.

She knew what Laurie would say about this trip with James. Stupid; risky; shoddy craft. But Dani didn't care. If there had been a faster way to get to Oscar Aidoo, she would have used it. As a journalist, you made it your business to go where others weren't, to see what they couldn't, and to report it back. You didn't do it because it was easy. You did it because the truth had its hooks in you.

You did it because if you didn't, who would?

FOUR

MORE THAN A WEEK had passed since he had botched the operation to steal David Ibrahim's phones. Billy had been braced for consequences—for his bosses to recall him to the States, to fire him, even to turn him over to the Ghanaians. But he had heard nothing. That was how they treated you. Huge expanses of time went by in silence. Then, just when you were sure they had given you up for dead, you got a call at 0100 that told you to report by 0130.

He was at the beach, having a beer at a chop shop after another day of fake work at his cover employer. Alone. Down the beach from where he sat, there was a tall building, a skyscraper that had been started but never finished. It had been constructed ten years ago, when Ghana had a mini–building boom after the discovery of the Jubilee Oil Field. Financed with Chinese money. But something must have gone wrong, and now it was just an empty husk, the harmattan winds whistling through the holes that had been cut for the windows.

When he was in the Army, Billy found that he had a talent for being in the shit, just like he'd had a talent for football. Don't think. That's the key. Thinking will just make you afraid. And honestly, in the chaos you're better off, because thoughts simply don't have the time to form. See the target downfield. Know where your guys are, know where their guys are. Head on a swivel but eyes focused. Know the play but be ready to audible. Keep your breath steady as best you can. Don't think. Just do. Trust your body and let it tell you what needs to happen next.

His hands twitched around the beer bottle, long since gone warm.

That was the one thing he had too much of in Ghana. Time to think.

WILLIAM JEFFERSON DEMIRJIAN WAS named by his father for the man who was President of the United States on the day he was born—January 22, 1993. Once he got older his dad said he even looked like Clinton. Billy's mother never expressed an opinion on it.

His parents had been the pioneers. They were the ones who had fled from Armenia during the first of the wars over Nagorno-Karabakh in 1992, when their town near the border with Azerbaijan was overrun. Billy was conceived at some point during the journey, and by the time his parents and his older sister landed in Rochester, New York, clutching their I-589 asylum visas, his father was alight with a love for the United States that would last for the rest of his life.

His son never felt the same wonder. English was Billy's first language; America was his only home. It was just the water he swam in. But he worked hard to match his dad's enthusiasm. Billy's whole childhood, they would spend every autumn weekend together in front of the TV watching football—college game day on Saturday, NFL on Sunday. Davit was learning the language, Billy was learning the rules. He paid desperate attention to the emotions behind his dad's reactions and tried to inject commentary to show he agreed. His dad would wince in disgust, and Billy would shout, "Should have been a flag on that play!" "The Jets' QB is scared to get hit." "USC's D-line is too good."

In the course of a single weekend, ads for the US Army would play what felt like thirty times. "The Army is for real men," Billy would say, not even needing to turn around to see his dad incline his chin in approval.

Over time, Billy really came to believe it. *Be all you can be.* It was a challenge, but it also sounded like a promise.

Billy was never great at school. He didn't see the point of questions that were designed to make you get the wrong answer.

"Try harder," his mother Mariam or his sister would say, sitting with him at the kitchen table.

"This is stupid," he would complain. "'If I make five pancakes in one mile, in a car going ten miles per hour, how long will it take me to make twenty pancakes?' Who cares?"

But he was good at sports. On the field there was no confusion. A straight line from cause to effect, from problem to solution. Billy joined a Pop Warner team, where his coach was the owner of a local Greek diner who took a shine to the Armenian family because they both hated the Turks. Coach Michaelides gave Billy a chance at quarterback, and Billy excelled. He pointed his body down the field and the ball obeyed him.

Then 9/11 happened. Billy had just started third grade. The week afterward, three boys from sixth grade told him to come with them one day in the playground after lunch. They led him to an unobserved corner and kicked the shit out of him, battering his ribs, his legs, his groin. "For the Twin Towers," one of them said.

Mariam was distraught that night, tending his bruises. Davit just looked at Billy. He didn't have to tell him what to do. A few days later, when the boys tried to lead him away at lunch again, Billy set his feet and punched the biggest one right in his mouth.

That solved the immediate problem. But Billy was still troubled. He did not understand why those boys blamed him for something that Arab terrorists had done. Objectively, he was white. He looked white, talked white. His name was William for Christ's sake. But now his family was learning something else about being American, which was that it wasn't a title you could claim but a club you had to be invited into. It didn't matter that Davit and Mariam Demirjian and their children loved this country, had been saved by it. It didn't matter that Billy was captain of the football team. They were still foreign. Foreign enough.

So Billy had joined the Army right out of high school. He had figured: put it all to rest in one go.

"You'd be a natural candidate for a paramilitary officer," the agency had told him at the conclusion of his third tour of duty, when he was at a loss for what to do with the rest his life.

He still remembered the polygraph exam. "Do you have an older sister, Anush?" the examiner said, laying a picture of her on the table.

"Yes."

"Good-looking girl. You ever had sexual thoughts about her?"

"Of course not."

The examiner looked skeptically at his monitor. "Never? You sure about that?"

Billy had clenched his teeth. "Yes."

"Happens to everyone, you know, there's no shame in it. You're twelve, thirteen. All these weird feelings. Hot summer day, Anush is wearing a dress you've never seen before. You have a reaction?"

"No."

"I remind you the consequences of not being truthful with me can include up to ten years' imprisonment. No weird feeling in your pants?"

Billy had wanted to get up from his chair and strangle him. Which was exactly what they were trying to make him do. He took a breath and reminded himself that the guy was just doing his job.

"How'd you feel on 9/11?"

"What? I was eight."

"I didn't ask how old you were. I asked how you felt."

It went on like that for hours. The questions swerved randomly, the examiner messed with him nonstop, pulling his emotions one way before yanking them in a completely new direction. Every few minutes he would remind Billy of the consequences of lying. And when it was over, he gave no sign that Billy had passed. He just frowned and said, "I think I've got all I need, soldier."

Two months later his clearance came through. The next day he was on a plane to Angola. He had no idea why the agency had picked Africa for him—he didn't exactly blend in. But here he was. His first posting was in Luanda, the capital. The scale of the corruption made Afghanistan look like nothing. The president there, dos Santos, had been running things for more than thirty years. During that period the country had discovered major oil reserves. Glass towers had risen along the coast, overlooking the deepwater port where the container ships rolled in and out. There were stores that sold Cartier watches, there were Ukrainian and Brazilian prostitutes in the hotel bars, and Rolls-Royce Phantoms sped down the streets, running over goats and chickens, and sometimes children.

Billy was learning a whole new trade. Learning how to recognize others like him—spooks. They were his enemies, but he felt a strange affinity for them. They spoke different dialects of the same language. The Portuguese were around, the former colonizers. So were a handful of Russians left over from the Cold War. The Japanese had built the Angolans a highway, and a good chunk of money flowed in from the Gulf states, Saudis and Qataris trying to outbid each other. But China was sweeping all of them away. Every single construction project had Chinese lettering on it. Every single flight was packed with Chinese faces. Hidden among this flood, the Chinese intelligence services were relentless. They flipped Africans at an aggressive rate, spending cash like it was nothing. Billy had never seen so much money. Even the Arabs couldn't compete.

But he was also learning his place. He was told what he needed to know, and not a word more. Nobody wanted his opinion on Angolan politics or Chinese tactics. They wanted him for his body. Billy wasn't asked to kill anybody—they had promised him that killing was rare in this job. Mostly he followed people. Watched where they went, and who they met with, and fed the information back to his case officer. Once he was ordered to grab a target off the street. A young man with East African features—Ethiopian, maybe. Billy had pinned the man's arms behind him, shoved his knee into his back, and thrown him into the trunk of a waiting SUV. The car was driven by others like him, fellow Americans he would never meet, who also got told what they needed to know and no more. They sped off and vanished.

And then, shortly after his twenty-sixth birthday, they sent him to Ghana. Another confusing placement. This country was not Angola. It was developing quickly. It had democratic elections, and a free press. Billy bought newspapers at the market every morning. If a Rolls-Royce hit a kid in Ghana, the driver went to jail.

In the week since it had happened Billy had not been able to get David Ibrahim out of his mind. It came back to him at unwanted moments—like last night, when the power had gone out and he couldn't sleep, lying there hot in the dark.

His knife scraping a rib bone. A chunk of flesh sticking to the window.

But it was the loss of control that disturbed Billy the most. For the forty-five seconds that he had spent attacking David Ibrahim in that car, he had no longer been sovereign in his own life. He could not say *why* he had done what he did. He only knew that he had been overpowered by something nameless and much stronger than he was. Something dominant. He glimpsed himself in mirrors and could not meet his own eyes.

WHEN HE GOT BACK from the beach it was dark. He opened his door and stopped.

On the floor, just inside the apartment, was an envelope.

It was addressed to his cover name, written in blue ink, in a shaky hand he didn't recognize. Inside was a message from Ford. A single sheet of paper with a date and time and a code word.

Lemon.

Billy drew in his breath.

He was going to meet the Double.

FIVE

THE HARMATTAN WINDS GOT worse. Accra was quiet; people stayed in their homes. James had said Friday, but the waiting felt like torture. What could Dani do to stop herself climbing the walls?

She could work.

And she could drink.

She bought a bottle of whiskey from the European Mini-Mart and sat on the floor of her room at the boardinghouse, organizing her research—she wrote out facts on index cards, moving them around like checker pieces.

Dani had first learned about Ghana and its rich oil deposits two months earlier, back in London, in the flat she had been renting after she had left her ex-husband, Ben. Long nights. Summer was ending and autumn was seeping into the city: low buildings, low sky, drifts of dead leaves that cracked beneath your feet like shells. Her whole body had hurt and she had been utterly alone.

When she had been pregnant, she had withdrawn from the world, physically but also intellectually. She had not wanted to know what was happening in Syria, she did not want to hear about the latest tantrums in the US Congress, the outrage of the day. She had avoided them all like toxins. She was responsible for a child. You quit drinking, you watched your mercury intake. Dani had figured you should monitor your cynicism just as seriously. And it had been surprisingly easy to stay ignorant. You simply changed the channel when the news came on. You read different magazines. Was this how other people lived?

And then suddenly she was no longer pregnant. There was nothing left to protect.

Taking pity, a friend had invited her to dinner one night—Marc Rutland, a reporter for *Der Spiegel.* He had been Ben's friend originally, but he was too good-natured for her to resent the association. Very German: icily competent, abjectly silly. Great at parties. His beat was the Bundesrepublik's foreign policy in the Merkel era, and he was spending a lot of time in Benin and Togo, where German charities were active.

"You need a new story, Dani," Marc had insisted, waving his fork. "You should go to Ghana."

Dani sighed. "I've done West Africa, Marc."

"Nonsense. You did Senegal, and that was five years ago, things have changed. The new Africa is being born before our eyes." He wiped mustard from his moustache with his napkin. "What about Ghana's oil? There's a story."

"Oil? No thanks."

"Listen, *listen.* So you have Ghana, politically stable, English-speaking, yes? The democratic leader in the region, relatively transparent government, and so on. And it has oil deposits similar to Venezuela's. The oil was discovered in the 2000s, order the champagne, Ghana will rule the world, et cetera. But now that it's really pumping, the questions begin. Which will Ghana become? Angola or Norway? And of course, who benefits? Exxon Mobil, Gazprom? The fucking private equity firms in New York, in London, die blödes Arschloch!" Marc's eyes had gleamed with excitement and fury. "These are the questions, Dani! They are there for your taking!"

Alone in her rented flat in the cold nights that followed, poring over the coverage of Ghana and its oil had felt like opening windows in a long-abandoned house. Dani was rooting for this country. The record was stacked with worrying precedents, but Ghana was putting up a fight. "We are not ignorant," the energy minister—Oscar Aidoo's boss—had said in an interview, when asked about the deal terms being sought by the major oil companies. "We are not fools. We know it is not fair." And it was too perfect, really, that the story was in West Africa, where Dani had come of age as a reporter, where she'd met Laurie—where she had felt like her real self, not whoever she had been pretending to be in London. She missed the stinging heat, the humidity that stayed low to the ground all day, that put its hands all over you and practically sucked the air from your lungs. Sitting in chilly London, it sounded like paradise.

BEFORE LONDON, BEFORE LAURIE, before Dakar—before any of it—there had been the feeling. Dani could not have said when she first felt it. Only that for as long as she'd known, since she was a little girl, she had been living in the shadow of a vast unfairness, and her own inescapable complicity in it. She had understood that somewhere out there, there was a thing called the truth, which was immutable, which could not be destroyed. But she had also understood that the truth, by itself, was inert. It waited out whole human lifetimes patiently. And the people in her life were not looking for it. Her family and friends weren't stupid. But their lives lacked urgency. They weren't sufficiently afraid of what they might be failing to see.

She had grown up in Manhattan. Her father was an investment banker, a vice president at Société Générale. For college, she went to Berkeley—as physically far from her family as she could get in the States. It was here that Dani's need to understand her own position acquired an edge—turned inward and became self-criticism. She burrowed into herself, obsessive, relentless. She knew that she could never sufficiently disavow the blood-soaked history that allowed her to exist at the pinnacle of every political and economic structure on earth. Worse, she didn't even have the courage of her convictions. Flying home for school vacations, she hated herself as she settled into the business class seat her father had paid for. When she spoke to classmates who were going into debt to get their degree, her face burned with shame. She had started eating less and going for long runs in the midday California sun. Her stomach had ached with hunger. Her hip bones began to show. It helped. When her body hurt, she felt a little less guilty.

And then an English professor had assigned Michael Herr's *Dispatches*, and Dani had become obsessed with war journalism. She read Bao Ninh's *The Sorrow of War*, and Martha Gellhorn and Marie Colvin's reporting in *The Sunday Times*. A new possibility had appeared: *This* was what would validate and excuse her presence in the world. The truth was out there, but it was hidden—split into shards and dispersed. And journalists were the people whose job was to collect the shards and reassemble them. She needed to do what they did. She needed to put her body on the line.

After graduation, she got a job in Washington, working for Politico. Twenty-two, a kid, eager and angry. She had felt a giddy rush the first time she saw the Speaker of the House in the flesh. At first, Dani had found a ferocious satisfaction in hating these politicians, in cataloging their hypocrisies. But gradually she realized that the problem was bigger than Washington. The truth was bigger than the latest administration, it was older than the United States, it was more diffuse than she had imagined. The shards were tiny and they were scattered all over the world.

After Politico she went to grad school at Columbia. This was her formal training in journalism, its mechanics and craft. She'd been back in New York, near her family. Their proximity made her itch, like pet dander. She was as restless as ever, but she directed her anxiety downward, to her books, her studies.

One of her professors was a Spanish woman named Alma Hortensia, who had become famous in the '80s for her coverage in *The New Yorker* of the death squads in El Salvador and Guatemala. Dani fell in love with her from their very first class together, when she had them read excerpts from the memoirs of Bernal Díaz del Castillo, the conquistador who had accompanied Cortés on his expedition to Mexico. Del Castillo had been present when the Spaniards first met the representatives of the Aztec emperor Moctezuma. He had recorded the moment that set in motion the decimation of Mexico's original civilizations and the bloody birth of modern Latin America.

"You must never take a subject's hatred personally," Alma had told them. "As a journalist, you are neither Aztec nor Cortés, but a third person, watching them shake hands. Even though you know what disaster awaits them both."

Dani was breathless with adoration.

"Journalism is relentless," Alma told her a few weeks later, when Dani had bought her coffee after class. She had said it like a warning. "The moral demands are exhausting, and they never let you off the hook for an instant."

"I know, professor." Dani had been desperate to prove just how much her own privilege weighed on her. "I was thinking about this the other day. I was crossing 116th Street, and there was a boy coming towards me, a teenager, a Hispanic boy. He was carrying this huge tray of coffees, you know, like a delivery. And he just . . . tripped. Tray went flying, coffee spilled everywhere. He was sobbing 'Puto, puto, puto,' with his head in his hands. This poor, skinny kid. Honestly, I started crying too."

"Hold on." Alma had set her mug down forcefully on the table. "You don't mean to tell me you didn't pay for the fucking cups?"

"No, I—" Dani had blushed. "It didn't occur to me."

In the long silence that followed, Alma's face had gradually hardened into a look of pure contempt. "That was a vacuous oversight on your part, I should say. Thank you for the coffee, Miss Moreau." She'd left without finishing hers.

And for almost the entire rest of her two years at Columbia, Dani could not get this woman to acknowledge her. Walking the streets of Morningside Heights she had found herself looking for the boy with the spilled coffees, staring into the faces of deliverymen rushing by. She berated herself, curled in her comfortable bed, unable to sleep. *Pay for the fucking cups!*

It haunted her to be found wanting by the woman whose career she most wanted to emulate. Alma had been tortured by government troops in El Salvador. She had watched rebel soldiers impale babies on bayonets. And now she lived alone on the Upper West

Side, and wore black clothing, and never cried. She understood the truth. It was ineffable, it couldn't be looked at directly, it couldn't be taught. It had to be experienced.

Couldn't she see that was all Dani wanted too? That Dani was willing? That she was ready?

Then, a month before graduation, Alma had finally spoken to her again. Dani had been crossing the quad in front of Columbia's massive steps—its imperialist homage—when she had appeared, absurd in all black in the heat of late spring.

"Miss Moreau. You are leaving us, then? Congratulations."

Dani had been wary, but eager too. "I'm leaving for Senegal. Reuters hired me. I'm going to report on oil and West African politics."

Alma had nodded tersely. "I wish you good luck," she said. "And safety."

"Thanks," Dani had replied uncertainly.

Alma had already begun walking away. "Remember," she had muttered over her shoulder, so softly Dani almost didn't hear: "They never let you off the hook."

AND NOW, THREE WEEKS after arriving in Ghana, here Dani was—trapped inside as the winds raged, sipping her whiskey and moving the index cards around, trying to make the facts cohere.

She pushed a card forward.

- Dongsha Limited's filing with the Hong Kong securities regulator showed the firm had paid $231 million for oil parcel number 42.

Another card beside that one:

- The Ghanaian government's official figures from the Energy Ministry showed that Parcel 42 had been auctioned off for a price of $224 million.

Another card:

- Her first interview in-country, with an employee at the Ghana National Petroleum Company—an excitable young man she had approached as he left the office one afternoon. She had him on record claiming to have been present at the meeting in the Energy Ministry building in July 2016, when the Chinese investors had approached Kwesi Adjepong.
-

Three cards below that one.

- Her interview with Kwesi Adjepong, who had started out by trying to deny that the meeting ever took place, and who had blundered into revealing the $7 million discrepancy and ended by referring her to Oscar Aidoo, "the point man on Chinese issues."
- James Aidoo, who hadn't said much on record, but who had pointed her to Oscar Aidoo's videos on social media.

A final card, mostly blank: *Takoradi—James Aidoo—Oscar Aidoo?*

Pushing the dorm's spotty Wi-Fi to the limit, she watched as many of Oscar Aidoo's speeches as she could. He had a significant social media presence, with tens of thousands of followers on Twitter and almost as many on Baidu, Twitter's Chinese equivalent. Aidoo was a natural politician, his booming voice now empathetic for Ghana's children, now full of contempt for Ghana's oppressors, now high-pitched making fun of his NDC opponents. "The time of the Anglo-Saxon imperialists is over," he breathed, looking straight into the camera. "We do not need their lessons, we do not need their money, we do not need their weapons. With friends from Asia, Arabia, Russia, Ghana is among equals. Africa is rising and we are leading the charge!"

Dani scrolled through the comments and the coverage in Ghana's newspapers: the *Daily Guide, Ghana Today.* "With the appointment of Oscar Aidoo as deputy energy minister, the NPP has sent a strong signal that Ghana's energy resources will be tapped for the benefit of Ghanaians and not foreign corporations."

She felt the picture becoming clearer. Aidoo was a populist who welcomed Chinese investment and heaped scorn on the West. It seemed incongruous that he had sent his son to be educated in an American university—but then again, even China's leaders did that. She could barely contain her impatience to get to him, to throw the missing $7 million in his face and see what the resulting chaos revealed.

NIGHT WAS FALLING AND the winds continued to howl. Restless and a little drunk, Dani crossed the hallway and knocked on Priscilla's door.

"Wotcher, Dani." Priscilla flashed the peace sign, sleepy-eyed.

"Sorry, did I wake you up?"

"A little nap. I have my," Priscilla gestured, "you know, my period."

"Want some ginger? Good for the stomach."

"Come in, come in," said Priscilla. "Eh, finally, we can make your dress."

"Priscilla, to be honest," Dani said, crossing the threshold, "I'm not really a dress person. They don't suit me."

"You are a woman, yes?" Priscilla clucked. "Then you should be beautiful. You should wash your face. And you should wear a dress."

Dani laughed. "Fair enough."

Every surface in Priscilla's room was piled with dresses, fabrics, bolts of cloth. "I like you in this," Priscilla said, holding up a bolt of aquamarine fabric. "No—better this. For your pale skin." Forest green chiffon with a pattern of jagged yellow lines, like the stripes of an unlikely tiger. She ran the back of her hand lightly along Dani's forearm, admiring the contrast. "Yes, this one for you. Stand up straight, please. Arms out—like this." She stretched the measuring tape under Dani's bust, around her waist.

"Priscilla," Dani said, "what are your thoughts on China?"

"China?" Behind her, Priscilla laughed. "I do not know any Chinese people. Breathe in."

"Aren't there any in Lagos?"

"Yes. But they do not mix with the Nigerians. They are, you know, isolated. In their camps. They do not live with us."

"You've never made a dress for a Chinese customer?"

Priscilla looked at her strangely. "Do Chinese men wear dresses?"

"I guess they would all be men, around here."

Priscilla bit down on one end of the tape, stretching it along Dani's shoulder blades. "My cousin, he is a tailor as well," she grunted. "I believe he has made suits for Chinese men in Ghana." She removed the tape measure from her mouth. "Big shots. He meets them at the Holiday Inn."

"The Holiday Inn? Next to the airport."

"Holiday Inn," she repeated. "You may lower your arms. We are finished."

"You didn't write down any of my measurements."

"I will remember."

Priscilla was young—early twenties, Dani guessed. She cleared a space on the bed of clothes for Dani to sit. Dani drew her legs underneath her and lay on her side, resting her head in her palm, listening as Priscilla worked a tuft of beige fabric, her sewing needles clicking softly. The wind rocked the window in its frame. It felt cozy in Priscilla's room. It was like being inside on a rainy day.

"Okay, different question. Has oil been a good thing for Nigeria?"

"Oil?" This time her response was unhesitating. "It has been a disaster. A disaster."

"Why?"

"There used to be civility. Now there is rapacity." Priscilla shook her head slowly. After a minute of silence she said, "My brother was killed for a jerrycan of condensate fuel. They attacked him in his truck."

Dani sat up. "Priscilla, I am so sorry."

"You are writing about the oil here in Ghana, yes? God save Ghana. Oil is a curse. A curse. A curse."

"Condensate fuel." Dani dearly wished she had brought her notebook and a pen. "Now what exactly is that?"

"Cheap gasoline. The oil workers, they sell it. It is illegal." Priscilla waved her hand. "Many young people make income this way."

"Do you mind if I run and grab my notes? I would love to record what you're saying. For my research."

She had said the wrong thing. Priscilla stood up impatiently, turning away and busying herself with a stack of fabrics. "I am sorry, Dani. Now I have to work."

Dani hesitated. She did not want to go back to her room, to the solitary whiskey bottle and the whistling of the wind. "Shall I leave you the rest of the ginger root? Your cramps?"

"Thank you." Priscilla flicked her eyes, a brief acknowledgment.

"Knock on my door if you need anything. Please?"

Priscilla's back was to her now. "Yes."

"And will you let me know, please, when I should come back? For the dress?"

"Yes. Soon. Soon."

THE NEXT DAY THE sandstorm finally cleared. A sudden silence fell over the city in the early afternoon. Dani went out to the balcony and stood for a moment, listening.

The sky blue and empty. The air cool and still. She felt it again: the excitement of the hunter. There was only one more night to kill until her trip to Takoradi, until her chance to spring tough questions on an unsuspecting Oscar Aidoo.

No way she could stay in her dorm room.

Dani walked to the tro-tro stand, past open canals on the roadside filled with a porridge of rubbish and piss and dust. Her phone began to buzz. *No Caller ID* said the screen, and Dani felt a small thrill. Maybe this was a source: Kwesi Adjepong, James Aidoo, or even James's muscular friend Kofi?

"So you just weren't going to call me back?"

"Izzy," Dani sighed, "I can't talk right now."

"Don't you dare hang up. It's been two months. You can give me five minutes." The voice was crystal clear despite the great distance it was traveling. Dani could picture her younger sister sitting in their parents' apartment on Park Avenue. The yellow wallpaper, the dish of butter sweating on the countertop. Izzy was the baby. Everyone's favorite. Dani was the middle child. Caitlyn, the oldest, was married to an architect and had two daughters of her own—Emma, eleven, and Claire, six.

"I'm sorry, Iz. You're right." Dani plugged her other ear with her finger so she could hear better over the street traffic din. She forced herself to say the things you were supposed to say. "Congratulations! The ring looks *huge*!"

"Wait until you see it."

"What's the rule? Two months' salary?"

"More like three."

"Poor Josh. I could have gotten him something cheaper if he'd asked. The diamonds probably came from around here."

"Where are you, exactly?"

"I'm in Accra, in Ghana." Dani squinted. "To be specific, at the tro-tro stand in the Legon neighborhood near the University of Ghana."

"Tro-tro?"

"They're these minibus things that drive all over. Sort of an unofficial public transit."

"How are you feeling?"

"I'm great!" Dani's voice was too loud, startling a couple of Ghanaian women standing near her. "In fact, I'm sorry Iz, but I'm actually on my way to meet—"

"I meant, how are you feeling about everything?"

"I'm fine, Iz. Really, I'm fine. Good as new. Feels like London never happened."

"I'm going to see you soon, right? You're going to come?"

"Come to what?"

"My engagement party."

Dani laughed, then instantly regretted it.

Now Isabelle's voice was angry. "Don't be a bitch, Dan. I'm the only one who sticks up for you around here."

"I'm sorry."

"You didn't hear any of us complaining when we had to get on a plane to London for your wedding, even though the red flags were already there. We showed up and we were *happy* for you. Because that's what families *do.*"

Her wedding. God, it seemed a million years ago, though it had been less than two. A summer night in the Cotswolds. The white tent rose tautly above the heads of the guests, who danced atop portable floorboards trucked in the previous day by Polish-speaking men who had pounded the pegs into the earth with sledgehammers. Outside the tent, just beyond the light from the dance floor, Dani had watched her nieces Emma and Claire playing, chasing each other in the long summer grass that grazed their ankles. Beautiful girls in crepe de chine dresses. High-pitched giggles floating out of the darkness.

"You're right. I know. I'm sorry, Izzy." Dani took a deep breath. She was sweating in the bright sunlight. "That was rude of me. I would love to come, okay? Will you email me the date and the details?"

"It's at Maman's place in Bedford."

"Email, *please,* otherwise I'll forget."

"Promise you'll be there?"

"Sure—yes." She cleared her throat. "I promise! Now, I'm sorry, but I really do have to get to work."

Dani hung up before her sister could say anything else. The keypad of her phone left a sticky indentation on her cheek.

Of course, she had no intention of going to her sister's engagement party. It was bad enough that she would have to fly home for the eventual wedding. She would have to face everyone's questions, their slightly indulgent smiles, their belief that Dani's journalism was a lark, an escapade, somehow cute. Her mother would say she was too skinny and criticize her hair. "What *are* you getting up to, Danielle?" And she would have to see her nieces. Caitlyn's babies. She was not sure that she could face that yet.

Problems for another day. Right now she had important things to do.

The Holiday Inn directly overlooked Kotoka International Airport. The neighborhood around it had that same sense of melancholy Dani recognized from airports in other cities: people are forever passing through.

She could just tell, even before she entered, that the hotel's interior was going to be aggressively air-conditioned. As she walked through the lobby, her sneakers squeaked on the marble floor, and Beethoven's "Ode to Joy" piped softly through unseen speakers. She was dirty and underdressed, but attracted barely a glance; she was a white woman.

The lobby was quiet. Two African men in dark suits were sitting side by side in plush chairs, texting on their phones, but she saw no one else, certainly no Asian faces. The AC froze the sweat in her armpits and on the nape of her neck.

Dani continued through to the pool deck in the back of the building. But here too, there was no sign of any Chinese big shots. At a table nearby, she saw a large, fleshy European sitting with another man over glasses of beer.

But wasn't that . . . ?

"*Marc*?" she said, incredulous.

The European turned and flashed a goofy smile. "Wo ho? Guten abend, my intrepid friend."

"What are you doing here?"

"Here at this pool, or here in this country? I am working, of course. Meet my friend." Marc indicated the thin, dark-eyed man sitting beside him. Lebanese, she guessed. "Dani, this is Carlos Rivera. Carlos, Dani Moreau."

"Pleasure to meet you." His accent was American.

She reassessed. Not thin so much as dense, compact. She had a feeling he'd be a head shorter than her when standing up. Yet he seemed sure of himself, somehow immovable. A diplomat? But too young, no suit, not nearly bombastic enough. A money man?

"Carlos is with UNHCR," Marc said.

Ah. A bleeding heart.

"He is American, like you are, Dani." Marc caressed her shoulder. "Like the rulers of all things."

"Marc, are you drunk?"

"A little," he admitted. "So! You came to Ghana, just as I advised. Are you learning much about the oil?"

"Not enough. Which is why I'm here. I was told there were some Chinese moneymen who hang around this hotel. Instead I find a German and an American." She jerked her thumb rudely at Carlos.

"Not very helpful," Marc agreed. His beer left a thin film of foam in his moustache. "But this is serendipity! You should drink with us instead!"

"I can't, Marc."

"What aspect of Ghana's oil are you reporting on?" Carlos's voice was soft. He did not raise it to match the ambient sounds of the bar. You had to lean in to hear him.

"It would take too long to explain. But I'm on the trail of a real story, a big one." She couldn't keep a note of self-satisfaction out of her voice.

"Come now, come now," Marc said. "We are going to watch a taping of *Stars of the Future.* You must come!"

"What is that?"

"It's an *American Idol* rip-off," said Carlos. He said it innocuously, but Dani was roused. It was as if the mere appearance of this other American made her defensive on Ghana's behalf. She would not stand for the condescension of this soft-spoken obruni. She would stake her reputation on the caliber of *Stars of the Future.*

"Couldn't be worse than the original," she snapped.

"It's wonderful to see you working again, Dani," Marc cut in. He *was* drunk. "I mean," he faltered as she turned a deadly stare towards him.

"I'd love to hear more about your work," Carlos said. In spite of herself Dani leaned in to hear him. His forearms looked strong, resting there on the table. "Sounds maybe relevant to some of the human rights work I'm trying to do here."

"I doubt it."

"Ah, come on, Dani—don't make us beg. Won't you have a seat?"

Dani deliberated. She had an early morning tomorrow with James Aidoo. But she felt an involuntary pang of grief picturing herself in her room in the boardinghouse an hour from now—when she would peel herself out of her sports bra and sit on her scratchy bed, alone, unable even to go next door for company with Priscilla, who had been markedly colder to her since their conversation last night.

"All right." She sat down at their table. "*One* drink."

An hour later, the three of them went in a taxi together to the national theater, where *Stars of the Future* was filmed.

It was indeed an *American Idol* rip-off, right down to the three judges—one mean and terse, one motherly and encouraging, one sexy and ditzy. The finalists were Bethany, a confident teenager from Kumasi who belted Whitney Houston; Justice, a muscular bald man from Tema, who brought the crowd to tears with the story of his sick mother; and Esther, a shy girl from Accra who Dani could see shaking from stage fright as the hometown crowd whooped and stamped their feet for her. "Your pitch was not so good," said the mean judge. The crowd roared its disapproval. Marc became a partisan for Justice and left his seat to join the cheering section.

Now she and Carlos were alone. The three gin and tonics she'd drunk at the Holiday Inn gave her limbs a warm, loose feeling. But underneath she felt sadness, remembering the surprise Marc could not keep off his face when he had first seen her.

Her arm brushed Carlos's. Somewhere in the mess of feelings crisscrossing her body, she registered excitement. It stuck out because it had been so long.

"I'm still thinking about your story," Carlos said. "Do you really think the Energy Ministry is in the pocket of Dongsha Limited?"

"I don't know," she sighed. It had been a good day, but she was tired. The right thing to do was to stop drinking and go home. Wake up well rested for Takoradi tomorrow.

Carlos watched her with questioning eyes. He was young, younger than she had realized at first glance. And he was an American. He was as burdened as she was—he could not escape it either. But he was a man. He didn't care.

She leaned across the chair. "Listen, dude, I'd like to get a drink with you some night. Just us."

He held her gaze for a moment. The whites of his eyes were very bright, perfectly still. Like the bubble of a level measure. "Okay. Yeah. I'd like that."

Just then, Marc came galumphing back to their seats, his shirt drenched in sweat, cheering, shit-faced. Justice had won.

SIX

THE NEXT MORNING JAMES Aidoo picked her up outside the boardinghouse in a white Toyota SUV, country music playing on the stereo.

"Kenny Chesney." A grin split his baby-fat cheeks. He pushed his square glasses up his sweaty nose. "Texas habits."

They had some trouble getting out of Accra—a truck had overturned in a roundabout, spilling sacks of rice across the motorway and stopping traffic in both directions. For nearly an hour they were stuck behind a school bus that had EXCEPT THE LORD written across the top of its rear window. It took Dani a long time to work out that they meant ACCEPT. Once they got past this bottleneck the trip was easy going. James gunned the engine of his Highlander to pass a tro-tro.

"My father knows you're coming," James said. "We googled you."

"And?"

"We like your stories from Senegal. And your stories from Beirut. You're the real deal, I guess."

"I'm flattered."

"Dad likes that you are skeptical of US and European talking points. Not a—what do you call it? A shiv?"

"A shill."

Dani was feeling jittery, and not just from the hangover. She reviewed the facts in her head and rehearsed how she was going to put them to Oscar Aidoo once she was sitting across from him. Neither Aztec nor Cortés. Seven million dollars that belonged to the Ghanaian people was missing. Where did it go?

A government minister, receiving her in his home, personally escorted by his son. The side door approach had worked—which meant that someone had failed to run the traps. That was what it was called when a person, usually a subject's PR team, dug into a reporter's history before an interview and tried to get a sense of what questions they would ask. If googling her was all Oscar Aidoo had done to run the traps, then he deserved what was coming to him. Maybe her "puff piece" pitch had really fooled him. Maybe he was betting that he could intimidate her. Or he was simply underestimating her and assumed he could brush her off with a bit of star power. She *was* just a freelancer, after all.

His mistake.

The sun was bright, the sky was clear. Dani was back in the driver's seat of her life. She was on her way to interview Oscar Aidoo, she was going to meet Carlos Rivera for drinks tomorrow evening—and goddamn it, she was going to go home with him. For a moment there, it had all nearly fallen apart. Her identity had been slipping from her, she had almost lost herself. But now she had it all back. She had her story. She had a job to do.

James's car zipped west along the N1 motorway. From time to time the ocean appeared on their left. Dani knew that the oil rigs lay just over the horizon, invisible, enormous.

"You know, I was talking to my friend the other night," she said. "Her name is Priscilla, she's Nigerian. She said oil has been a disaster for her country."

"Is she Igbo? Yoruba? What?"

"I don't know. I'll find out."

"It matters."

She offered James a biscuit. "Hobnob?"

"No, thank you."

The Kenny Chesney CD ended, and a Garth Brooks one started.

"You know they make good music in America too," said Dani.

James laughed loudly. "This was what I'd listen to on my road trips. At UT, my favorite part about college was leaving campus. I would take my rental car and drive into West Texas. The badlands." He waved his hand over an imaginary landscape. "I have never seen anything like this. Hundreds and hundreds of miles, not a *single* person. You do not see that in Ghana. It's far too crowded here."

"Even in the bush? There must be empty places deep in the jungle."

"'The bush?'" James rolled his eyes. "Dani, you will find people everywhere. On their cell phones, these days. That's what happens when a continent has been inhabited for two million years. But in the American West, you can really see what the world looked like before human beings. What it will look like again, after we are all gone. America invented the idea of the national park. Amazing foresight, really, for a country that otherwise just takes, takes, takes. So that is what I would do, when the other kids were at frat parties on Sixth Street, I would rent a car and go west."

"Where was your favorite place you saw?"

"Zion National Park," he said immediately. "Have you been?"

"Oh yes, when I was in college too, at Berkeley." For the first time Dani felt a twinge of guilt at the position she was putting James in with this interview. Despite the bombast and the servants and the cheesy jokes, he was a nice kid. The son of a famous politician; so little room for error. And yet he seemed to carry these burdens lightly—more lightly than she would have, if the roles were reversed. In another life, in different circumstances, they might have been friends.

"Sometimes still I find myself there in dreams," he said now. "Close your eyes. Come on! Can you picture it? The red rocks at sunset. Aspen trees in the wind, leaves shaking like coins."

It was almost enough to make Dani love her country, hearing a foreigner describe it like this. "Something small and furry?" she tried. "Diving into a pile of dead needles?"

"And me," James continued, "sitting outside my tent, in the hollows of a rock that has sat *just like that* for tens of millions of years, since long before hominids appeared—in Ghana or anywhere else."

After a moment Dani asked, "And you were alone on these trips?"

"There *was* a girl, for a while. Marina. She was from Mexico City, or De Efay as she was always calling it. El Distrito Federal. She was studying architecture at UT."

"Was she beautiful?"

"She was. She is. Married now, and back in DF. We got along because—well, because we were foreigners." He exhaled. "*That* is America too."

But they would never be friends, of course. Not after today.

The highway brought them through the northern precincts of Cape Coast city and then veered down to run right alongside the ocean. The spray from the thundering waves misted the windshield. They drove past the slave castle at Elmina, gleaming white in the distance. The Gulf of Guinea shimmered behind it.

James spoke again. His voice was flat. "You ask me, I think they should knock it down."

"Why's that?"

He glanced at her momentarily. "If it's not obvious to you, you won't understand."

"Try me."

"As a Ghanaian," he cleared his throat, "as an African. To have that—*fucking* thing sitting there. They should knock it down and send the bricks back to London."

After a minute of silence, Dani said, "What about the argument that you preserve it because of how awful it is? So it never happens again?"

James pulled on the gearshift and they raced around a sputtering minivan.

"I'm just playing devil's advocate," she felt compelled to add. "That's not my view."

"So you agree then? They should knock it down."

"It's not my place to decide. One way or the other."

An odd smile rose on James's face. "It doesn't matter," he said. "It's too much at the heart of our country's identity. Tourists love it. The politicians will never allow us to move on."

"Politicians like your father?"

"Dad thinks for himself. He can be tricky, even when people are on his side. You will see! But I can at least say that for him: he thinks for himself, he is not a slave. I can't say the same for the rest of the government, and not for the opposition either. NPP, NDC, it makes no difference, they're all just as bad."

"What about Kofi's father?"

James carried on like he hadn't heard her. "All these African politicians, they go to America, they go to the UN, they act the Big Man. Their children get into Harvard. But they must do what Washington says."

"Would it be all right with you if I wrote some of this down?"

James waved a hand, unconcerned. "Everyone knows what I'm saying is true."

"But isn't that exactly what the Chinese are doing?" Dani said. "And in some ways, aren't they even worse? More money, more demands for oil and natural resources. Less interest in Ghana's welfare."

"Are you interested in Ghana's welfare? Is that what this trip to Takoradi is about?"

"Why else would I be here?"

"Just like you were interested in Senegal's welfare? Lebanon's?"

"I know it might sound hard to believe, James. But some people genuinely do just want to help. Not all Americans are here to take oil from the ground."

"Oil is not interesting. It's like I told you the other day, it's not what the world is *taking* from Ghana that's important, it's what they are *bringing*. Telecom, internet, payments systems, mobile phones. Data, Dani!" He grinned. "The richest trove of all. Just by sitting there, you create an inexhaustible resource of incalculable value."

She was skeptical. "Just by sitting here?"

James reached across and plucked up one of Dani's Hobnob biscuits from the roll. "The makers of this car want to know how comfortable you are, and how your legs are positioned. Advertisers want to know what you are looking at while we drive. The makers of this radio want to know how often you reach for it. And then as soon as you stand up, you'll be creating infinitely more data with every action you take. How you look. Your DNA. It's all for sale."

"Sounds creepy."

"Facts about the world, Dani. That is the currency. Isn't it the same for journalists? And China is at the vanguard of this—*not* the United States. All of us Ghanaians, when we think about who is leading the technology of the future, we look to Chinese companies. Cheaper and easier than the Western versions. And with no lectures attached, no judgment." He grabbed another Hobnob. "All over the world, the Chinese have done this. They're in America too. They are even in Austin! You are trying to keep them out, but China's goods are too cheap, too easy to use. And they're patient. They believe being a dominant power in the world is their rightful destiny. They believe that they have been around long before America, and they will be around long after."

Dani's pen skidded across the page of her notebook with the motion of the car.

"And what do you believe, James?"

"Honestly?" Crumbs spilled into his lap. "I believe the Chinese are right. America is in trouble. The world has realized that your promises are false."

TAKORADI BEGAN TO APPEAR thirty minutes later. They rolled through crowded neighborhoods of one- and two-story cement buildings, punctuated here and there by taller, newer constructions. James was continuing to drive at highway speeds, beeping the horn madly, frightening off motorbikes, handcarts, market women.

Eventually the traffic thickened sufficiently to slow him down. He started bobbing his foot impatiently.

"Paragon," he said, pointing a stubby finger at a building. "That's a nightclub. We used to drink there as teenagers. Me and Kofi, and all our friends." He laughed. "Good to be young. Drinking and dancing all night, enh? Here." He changed the CD player, and the voice of Bob Marley filled the car. "That's better, yes?"

"Were your parents strict?"

"I was raised Catholic."

Dani thought this an odd answer. "Tell me more?"

James honked the horn. "I believed in God when I was a child, like everybody does. But at a certain age, I suddenly realized it was all horseshit. You know that Ghanaians are very superstitious. These shop names and everything, Praise the Lord this, Blood of Jesus that. It's one of the big weaknesses of this country. We should grow up. St. Paul says it in his letter to the Corinthians: *When I was a child, I thought as a child; but when I became a man, I put away childish things.*"

"How about Kofi, was he raised Catholic as well?"

"You ask a lot of questions about Kofi. Should we have invited him along as well?" There was a hint of jealousy in James's voice.

"Ah," he grinned. "Even Kofi, you know, he is very devout. He still goes to church every Sunday. Imagine!"

"Does it bother you?"

"It used to. Kofi and I had some incredible arguments over it. But he has realized he has no chance of persuading me. Superstition is fine, even going to church is fine, but you mustn't actually believe the horseshit. The smartest people are atheists. The Chinese are atheists."

"You believe in the Chinese?"

"I believe in Charles Darwin." There was a long pause in which the only sound was Bob Marley's voice. James jerked his chin at the radio. "And I believe in him."

THE FIRST THING SHE noticed was the size of the house.

It was a mansion on the top of a hill on the outskirts of Takoradi, twice as big as any of the other homes in view. White stucco, with a balcony all along the second floor beneath a roof of bright orange terra-cotta.

The second thing she noticed was the satellite dishes. They crowded the roof, a row of them angled in different directions, connected by bundles of wires thick as an arm, which ran down the side of the building before disappearing into the earth.

It had rained recently and James's Highlander fishtailed a little in the mud as they ascended the hill. Ten-foot-tall concrete walls surrounded the compound, studded with the ubiquitous jagged glass pieces along the top, for scooping out the palms and kneecaps of potential intruders. He swung into the driveway with the same peremptory speed with which he'd been driving all day—not caring who he knocked down. A sense of ownership. A casual disdain for the space his body moved through. It gave him a certain muscular quality, even with his sweaty round face and his belly flab.

Finally, James cut the engine, and in the sudden silence Dani realized how high above the city they were. All she could hear were birds. Impatiently he beckoned her through the front gate and up the steps through a large, muddy yard. He pushed open the mahogany front door. A maid, standing at an ironing board in the kitchen, looked up in surprise.

"Ah! Hello!" she said. "You are here?"

"Hi, Yaaba, hello, my dear." James gave her a hug. The maid wrapped him in her arms and covered him with kisses on both cheeks; he made a show of pushing her away but Dani could see the real pleasure in his eyes.

"Such a good boy." Yaaba seemed old enough to be his mother. Both she and James were half whispering. "You are here to visit your mommy? She will be so happy to see you."

"Yes, yes," said James. "But first I must speak to Daddy." James cleared his throat. "Daddy," he called, marching deeper into the house. "Daddy, where are you?"

Dani stayed put, unsure whether to follow. "Hello," she said quietly to Yaaba.

"You are welcome!" Yaaba kept her voice low, almost hoarse.

"My name is Dani." She cleared her throat, raised her voice. "Dani Moreau. I am a journalist."

"You are welcome, you are welcome." Yaaba clicked off the iron and stood with her hands clasped in front of her. "Would you like something to drink? Some water? Coffee? Tea?"

"I am fine, thank you." Dani looked around. Like the house in Accra, it was very cold, air conditioners in every window. Lace was draped over tables and countertops. The thick curtains were drawn shut against the sunlight, giving the rooms an underwater feel. On one wall was a display of pictures: Oscar Aidoo with various grandees. She recognized Ghana's current president, and some of its past ones. On the opposite wall hung a heavy gold crucifix.

There was something indefinably *off* about this house. James and Yaaba's whispers; the slightly chemical smell that hung in the air.

"Is Mrs. Aidoo here?" Dani said. "I would like to introduce myself."

Yaaba cocked her head, like it was a strange question.

"Dani!" Now James's voice came echoing down the hall. "Come here to Daddy's office please."

Dani walked forward, gripping her notebook. On the left, a room she recognized from Oscar Aidoo's videos on social media: a large Ghanaian flag backdrop, the black star and the stripes of red, yellow, and green covering the entire wall, with a director's chair and professional studio lighting.

A little farther along was another door, standing half ajar, revealing a darkened room with a large bed and the shadow of a person asleep. The chemical smell grew overpowering. It was a hospital bed.

She walked more quickly, to where she could see James standing in the bright light of the office at the end of the hall. "Daddy, here she is," James announced. In the sickly stillness his voice was wrong, too loud.

Dani stepped into the room, and Oscar Aidoo looked up. He was older than he appeared on camera, with stooped shoulders and gray hair framing a perfect circle of bald skin on the crown of his head. He was wearing a suit and tie, even in his own house, and thick, square spectacles, like his son's.

"This is Danielle Moreau," James continued. "She is the journalist from New York that we spoke about."

For a moment Oscar stared at her. Then he spoke sharply in Twi, his eyes fixed on Dani. His voice was raspy, far from the bellowing tenor she had heard online. An instrument out of tune.

James answered in English. "Yes, exactly right. She wants to ask you some questions about how Ghana's oil is helping the country develop. About how we do not need the West."

Neither Aztec nor Cortés. Dani extended her hand. "It's a pleasure to meet you, Deputy Minister Aidoo. You have a beautiful home."

Oscar Aidoo regarded her cautiously, ignoring her outstretched hand. "Indeed."

"As James mentioned, I am a reporter, and I'm hoping to ask you some questions."

"A journalist from where? What publication?"

She smiled. "Your son asked the same thing when I met him. I'm formerly of Reuters and *The Guardian*. Now independent."

"Independent."

"But, of course, my relationships with my former editors at those outlets remain strong. And I'm confident that with the right piece we could put something in front of them. I think *The Guardian*'s readership, in particular, would be interested in how much success you've had developing Ghana's natural resources for its people."

Oscar Aidoo merely nodded and scratched his chin. But she saw his chest rise slightly. She felt his calculations changing, his annoyance turning to curiosity.

"I'm mindful that you are a very busy man," she continued. "I appreciate your time."

"I'm going to go say hello to Mommy now," said James. "I'll leave you to it."

Oscar Aidoo smiled at her. It was his son's smile: sudden, warm, unguarded. It surprised her.

"What are your questions, my dear?" He leaned backwards in his chair. Dani had found, interviewing smart men, that the lazier their posture, the stronger their confidence. Good. She wanted him to feel at ease.

She opened her notebook. She was glad James had left the room for this part. "As James said, sir, I'm here in Ghana reporting on the development of the oil industry, especially the Jubilee Field off the coast that was discovered in 2007—"

"A great achievement of the nation," he interrupted. "Please, my dear." He motioned with his palm for her to sit. Dani thought back to her two hypotheses for how this interview might go: intimidate or underestimate? So far underestimate had the lead.

"Is it all right with you if I record our interview?"

"Will I have quote approval?"

"You know *The Guardian* would not agree to that, sir."

"Of course, of course." But his smile remained as he said it, as if he was winking at her. "Come then, young lady. What would you like to know about the oil fields?"

"Let's start at a basic level. How does Ghana get paid on the oil in its territory?"

Oscar Aidoo put his hands together like a steeple in front of his face. "Revenue from oil production accrues to the government of Ghana in three ways," he rasped. "One, the national oil company owns some of the fields outright. We can develop them ourselves or sell the development rights to friendly partners. Two, the Energy Ministry collects royalties on the production of oil in the fields we have already sold. And three, all oil revenues accrued within Ghana, whoever is earning them, are taxed by the government at 35 percent."

"And do you think the contract that the previous administration negotiated on selling development rights to foreign firms was a fair one?"

"No, I would hardly call it fair. What Jim Ofori did was unconscionable."

"Former Energy Minister Ofori?"

"I call him a prostitute. You can write that down. It's Jim Ofori who is the criminal." Oscar Aidoo shifted in his chair. She could see the energy building, a performer warming to his audience. Even better. Overconfident and riled up. That was when they said the thing they wished they hadn't.

"What did Ofori do?" she prompted.

"The finder's concessions, of course. Just because they found the oil, we give them everything, these foreigners, these Texans." He scowled. "Just because they found the oil first, they have the right to suck it dry before Ghana benefits? Ah? Where is the justice in that? Where is the equity? Jim Ofori spread his legs for the Americans, just like John Boateng and all the rest of the NDC sycophants."

She wrote it down. She was conscious of him watching her. "Just a moment ago," she continued, looking up from her notebook, "You said, 'It's Jim Ofori who's the criminal.' Do you accuse him of corruption?"

"I accuse him of being an imbecile. I accuse the NDC of mismanagement, which the current government under the leadership of the NPP is attempting to rectify."

"But terms like 'prostitute'—are you saying there was a quid pro quo involved?"

"I'll not slander the man. But he is a prostitute."

"Mr. Deputy Minister—"

"Please call me Oscar."

"Oscar, you say that America is bleeding Ghana dry. But what about China?"

"Ah." He brushed the question aside. "China is a minor player in the oil market here. The Americans and British dwarf them."

Dani cleared her throat and went for the kill.

"What would you say if I told you that I have records showing that a Chinese firm named Dongsha Limited paid 231 million dollars for the rights to Parcel 42 in 2016, as recorded by the authorities in Hong Kong where Dongsha is registered? And what would you say if I told you that your government's receipts list the sale price of that parcel as 224 million dollars—leaving seven million USD unaccounted for?"

There. She'd struck something.

"And further," she said, keeping her voice steady, watching Oscar Aidoo's anger build, "what would you say if I told you that I have evidence that in July of 2016 representatives of this same

Dongsha Limited met with Kwesi Adjepong, who now reports to you in the NPP government's Energy Ministry? What would you say to that, Oscar?"

He stood up abruptly, and for a moment Dani thought he might reach across the desk and hit her.

"James," he bellowed. His voice had leaped several registers, to the pitch of contempt she recognized from his videos on Twitter. "James!" he yelled again in English, before switching to a stream of furious Twi.

She twisted around in her seat to look behind her just as James came hurrying back into the room.

"Sit down," Oscar said in a simmering voice. "Next to your American friend."

James sat. His whole body had tensed, and he was not looking at Dani.

"Is this how you punish me?" Oscar said. "Is this your funny joke? Ah? Speak up, boy."

"I do not know what she has said to you," James said uncertainly. "I thought she had only a few small questions."

Oscar erupted in a burst of Twi, concluding with the English words "fucking shit." He pounded the desk so the room shook.

"It is a lie!" James yelled desperately, in English. "She is all full of lies!"

Oscar came around from behind the table and grabbed his son by the scruff of the collar. The sounds his palm made as it slapped James's face once, twice, three times were specific and individual—like tennis balls bouncing off a wall. One, two, three. It was over before Dani had time to process what was happening.

"Stop it!" she said, standing herself, looking around crazily for a weapon—a paperweight? —but Oscar had already finished and was returning to his side of the desk. James sat there speechless as the echo of the three slaps died away. Dani saw tears rise to his eyes.

"I categorically deny," said Oscar slowly, breathing heavily, "that I have dealt with the Chinese in any capacity as related to Ghana's oil resources," he said. "Your data is wrong. If you have proof that anything illicit was done, let us see it."

"I don't—" Dani was stunned. "This is how you answer a journalist's questions? With violence? This is what you want the readers of *The Guardian* to know?"

"Publish whatever you like. I will hold James responsible for it." Oscar pointed his finger at her—a vicious, slashing motion, so that she flinched as if he had slapped her too. "He is a young boy, who does not understand as much as he thinks he does. But I decline to sit here and listen to your slander."

"James had nothing to do—"

A ceramic figurine exploded against the wall behind James's head. "Out!" Oscar yelled. "Out of my house!" He picked up another statue, made of some heavier element, and heaved it at his son's head. It connected with a sickening soft thump.

"Go!" Dani yelled at James, pushing him in front of her. "Go, go."

The kid stumbled out of the door, one hand covering his face. He was bleeding where the second statue had cut him. Dani tried to take James's hand but he wrenched his arm away.

"Tell the readers of *The Guardian* we have no need of Western help!" His father's voice followed them down the hallway. Dani stayed close on James's heels, rushing past the open door where

James's mother lay motionless in her sickbed, unaware of the commotion.

"James," Dani said. "James, wait."

He ignored her, his hand still flung up in front of his eyes as they reached the end of the hall, where Yaaba stood at the ironing board, watching the scene with a horrified look. Oscar's voice continued to echo down the hall, a barrage of abusive Twi.

For an instant James paused in his fleeing and stood still before Yaaba. They embraced. "Kafra, kafra, kafra," he whispered, tears in his voice.

"You may quote me in your article, if you wish!" Oscar Aidoo's shout carried from a distance. He had switched back to English. "Use the quote about Ofori being a prostitute!"

THEY PULLED OUT OF the muddy driveway in silence, in the late light of the afternoon sun.

"Are you okay?" Dani said again.

With a savage jab at the radio James silenced Bob Marley. For a while they drove along in silence, zipping past diesel trucks and taxis, cushioned on the pitted roads by the Highlander's smooth four-wheel drive.

"I'm sorry," Dani said. When James still didn't reply, she decided to just be quiet. She ran her hand along the leather seat, her body humming with fear. The sudden violence had shocked her as much as it had appeared to shock James and Yaaba. Oscar had used only his hands—not a gun, not a bomb, not a knife. But it was the switch-flip of it, the explosive, irrational destructive energy of it, that was flooding her with adrenaline now, that made her want to turn around and check that she was not being pursued by Oscar, even as they were speeding away from him.

"James," she said at last. "What happened back there was not right. I don't care who your father is."

He turned his head to look at her. "Need to stop," he said, his voice unnaturally low. "We're low on petrol—gas." He grunted. "Does that ever happen to you? Brain reaches for different words depending on who I'm talking to. Am I pretending to be Texan, or pretending to be British?"

He was breathing heavily, his words halting. He drove slowly, letting others pass. Dani recognized, in hindsight, the reason for all that honking as he had sped through Takoradi's streets, all that yelling and bluster as he pushed his way through the house. James had been psyching himself up.

"So you tricked me," he said eventually. "You used me." He shook his head. "Honestly don't know what I expected. What a fool."

"I'm sorry," she said again, feeling useless. "I didn't expect he would be violent."

"Of course not." His voice was soft. "Only someone who has spent their whole life in safety would assume you could play games like that without the possibility of violence. You threatened my father's reputation, his freedom, maybe even his life. And you thought—what? That he would bow to your cleverness? Fold and confess? This isn't debating class at school. You know, you Western intellectuals come to Ghana and think you are uncovering a great secret. But you are no better than anyone else, trying to make their fortune off our suffering."

"James—"

"And *don't* tell me you are sorry again."

They fell into an uneasy silence. After a while James pulled the Highlander into a truck stop overlooking a dip in the highway. Distantly Dani could see the rooftops of Sekondi, which was Takoradi's older sister city. And beyond them, the Atlantic Ocean. The sky glowed smoky yellow above it. Dani waited for him to speak while the pump filled their tank.

"You know, I'm used to this," said James heavily. He was calmer now. "Back there, that was nothing. You should have seen when I was little."

"He's a beast."

James did not contradict her. He touched his face lightly where his father had slapped it. "Are you hungry?"

They took a pair of plastic seats on a triangle of gravel by the side of the truck stop. "I will get us something to drink," James said.

Watching his fleshy back move through the crowd, a feeling rose in Dani's chest that she had only ever felt once before. An enveloping aggression, a desire to surround, to enfold: unmistakably maternal.

How could she have done that to him? Used him like that? Here Dani had thought that she had found a new identity, or rather rediscovered an old one: the journalist, the hunter, the defender of the truth. But the shock she felt at what had just happened was evidence that maybe it just didn't fit anymore. She couldn't be a ruthless killer, even in pursuit of a story. She couldn't watch what had just happened to James without wanting to make it better.

The truck stop was bustling with hawkers selling bread, water bags, batteries. James returned bearing two Smirnoff Ices and a plate of goat kebabs. The kebabs were so spicy they made Dani's eyes water, but they were delicious. She washed them down with the cold, sugary alcohol.

"I don't know why Smirnoff Ice of all things has established itself in Ghana, but I can't say I'm complaining." Dani set down her drink, wiped the grease from her chin with the back of her hand, and looked out at the yellow sky above the ocean. She waited for him to say something.

"In Austin I tried to drink tequila sometimes, but I couldn't do it." James chewed his kebab. "But I do miss Mexican food."

"I'd like to hear more about Texas sometime. And Marina."

"Right." He laughed bitterly. "That can be your next article."

"I did not know your mother was sick. I'm so sorry, James," she couldn't resist adding again. "I'm sorry for everything."

He gathered up their empty plates, ignoring her. "We should be going, enh? Long drive back."

As they were pulling out of the truck stop, a policeman stepped in front of the hood of the car.

"Whoa, hello, hello." He waved his baton at them.

James rolled down the window. "Good evening," he said cautiously.

"You have a crack in your windshield. That is against regulations."

"Ah!" James cried, disgusted. "No, no, no, I don't have it."

"There." The policeman pointed. "It's very small."

"Show me."

The policeman glanced fleetingly at Dani. "I tell you it is there."

"It is not there," said James.

"Do you want trouble this evening?"

Grumbling, James shoved a few hundred cedis into the policeman's hand. The cop tipped his cap to Dani. "Good day to you."

They drove on eastward in silence, back towards Accra.

"It's because he saw me with an obruni," James said eventually.

"Why didn't you drop your father's name? Maybe he would've backed off."

Suddenly James seemed to find the whole thing funny. "If you have to ask," he laughed, "then you won't understand."

SEVEN

THE DOUBLE LAY ON his mattress, restless with anxiety, watching the minutes tick by on the clock in the corner of his computer screen: 8:42, 8:43. At 10:00 P.M. he would leave his home and make his way to the meeting place with Ford, whom he had signaled that he needed to meet. Urgently.

Next to the time was the date: NOV 8. Ten days had passed since David Ibrahim's death. It was time for the Double to execute his next move.

Most people never experienced the kind of clarity he now possessed. They went through life in a vague fog of uncertainty and doubt, sensing dimly that there was more to the world, but never able to take action to seize it. The Double had a purpose. To be a US citizen was to be among the holy, the elect. Their passports were sacred objects, and he would not rest until one was in his hand.

But the Double was not stupid. The Americans did not give anything away for free, and he knew that despite the risks he was taking, he had no real leverage over Ford. David Ibrahim was already forgotten: his business continued uninterrupted, and his wife and children had fled back to Lagos. What if the Americans' demands were never satisfied? What if, after

Ibrahim, Ford asked for another name, and then another and another? Even worse, what if Ford stopped asking the Double for anything at all? What if Ford himself were killed, or recalled back to the States? The Double had no way of proving what the two of them had shaken hands on.

And though the Double flattered himself, he was certain that he was not the only Ghanaian that China had co-opted. A well-known analogy said that intelligence collection was like stealing grains of sand. If the Russian way was to send a tactical team under cover of darkness to grab the sand in huge buckets, China would instead send a thousand ordinary families in broad daylight to collect it one grain at a time. The Double was just one sand-collector among many: a diligent ant, but an ant nonetheless. That was why his Chinese handler's questions had always been so perfunctory. And it was why it was highly likely that Ford had also approached other Ghanaians like him—thus diluting his leverage still further.

That fact was, if he permitted the Americans to let him dangle, he would die. Sooner or later the Chinese would trace the betrayal of David Ibrahim back to him, and the Americans would conclude that he was not worth their effort to protect.

That was why the Double was putting forward this new, aggressive scheme tonight. He needed to push the pace of this dance forward. He had to make himself indispensable. It was like a math problem—each step revealing the one that necessarily had to follow.

But now that the hour was here, the Double's nerves would not calm down. The sheet of red satin that he lay on felt itchy and damp. His pillow felt greasy and thin. The Double punched at it and repositioned his head, trying to get comfortable.

9:12. His eyes drifted to the row of hardbacks above his desk. *Heart of Darkness. Great Expectations. Invisible Man. The Fire Next Time. The Holy Bible.* Abruptly he stood up, took the Bible from its perch and flipped open to a random page. Zechariah chapter 7: *This is what the LORD Almighty said: Administer true justice; show mercy and compassion to one another.* He snapped it shut and ran a hand along his computer's surface—buzzing with warmth beneath his fingers.

A sudden sensation launched the Double to his feet and sent him running into the washroom next door, where he vomited into the sink. It was thin and watery—he had been too nervous to eat today. For a long moment he did not move. His head hung above the basin, throat stinging.

HE TOOK A TRO-TRO to the location of the meeting—an address clear across Accra, close to the Tema port. Sitting wedged between the tired, silent people, he felt sure they could hear his heart thumping in his chest.

"Mate, mate," he called to the driver's assistant. "Let me out here."

He continued on foot. The night air felt good on his skin. This was a part of the city where obruni never came: he passed chop shops where old men scooped steaming handfuls of fufu to their mouths and bars where everyone was drinking Star Beer, gathered around beat-up televisions that flickered gray and blue.

Everton was playing Liverpool tonight. Everyone wanted to watch Liverpool's young Ghanaian midfielder.

The Double's feet crunched in the dust. His hands were clammy in his pockets, but walking made him feel calmer. He heard a cry of dismay go up from the bars: Everton had scored. A shadow darted across the road in front of him. A cat, maybe, or a large rodent. He smelled cook-fire smoke and, faintly, underneath it, human shit.

It had been many years since the Double had been able to feel anything but shame about Ghana. Not necessarily because he loved America; he liked to believe he had no illusions about the country for which he was risking his life and the lives of everyone he loved. America was not paradise. But America *was* the world's only reliable guarantor of power and safety. To the Double's mind, too many Americans, especially young Americans, mistook the fact that no other nation dared bomb them to pieces while they slept for a fixed truth about the peacefulness of modern existence—rather than a tenuous result of the relentless vigilance of the human beings in their military and government. Men and women whose job, day and night, was to imagine and prevent all the horrible ways in which the world could and would bring violence to American families. That was why 9/11 had been such a trauma, a rip in the fabric: quickly papered over. The Double had heard young Americans say contemptuous things about "national security," as if it were only about diverting money from investing in health care and bridges, as if it were only bombing children in Afghanistan. But national security was the right to fall asleep without fear, and the right to sit in the sunshine on the first warm day of spring. National security was the right to vote. It was the right to think and say whatever you wanted, without fearing you would be thrown in jail for it. It was the right to make as much money as you pleased and spend it how you liked.

Americans might be hypocritical, but there was something real about the universal values that they lived by. Something ineffable and true. The Double wanted to be safe and powerful—yes, why not, who wouldn't? But more than that, he wanted a life where his destiny was unmolested by the needs of others. Fairness, equal opportunity, agency: *they* were what the Double really loved about America. The sacred right to be sovereign in one's own life. If such values had been allowed to be expressed in China, he would have gone to China. But they were not. In China the state was sovereign, and the Communist Party was the state. Your life was not your own. Your job, your family, where you lived, the very air you breathed were subject to the shifting internal dynamics of the Politburo. He could never consent to such an existence.

And he could not live in Ghana either, because in Ghana his opportunity was bound to his willingness to serve China. He could have been "free," he supposed, if he had rejected the arrangement that had compelled him to work for the Chinese since he was a fourteen-year-old boy. But it would really have meant trading one loss of freedom for another. He would be left completely destitute. All the privileges that flowed to him in Ghana depended on the people who had arranged this. If he rejected them he would be cut off, and he would be exposed to the violence of the global economy, as vulnerable as the poorest Ghanaian. He would literally be out on the street. And not the street in America, where at least theoretically there was the chance to pull oneself up. On the street in *Ghana*, where it would take generations to recover the basic dignities of modern life—with only rats and the smell of cook fires and human shit for company.

So here he was. Almost to freedom.

If he could keep his nerve.

THERE WAS ANOTHER MAN in the shadows behind Ford tonight. He stared at the Double, silent, arms folded. The Double was instantly unsettled.

"A friend," Ford explained. "He will be another resource for you. He'll watch your back."

"What do I call you?" the Double said.

Ford answered for the other man. "A friend."

The Double turned his head away. He didn't like the way the other American was staring at him. And whatever Ford said, it was obvious that the same sort of person who could protect him from harm was also capable of inflicting it. Watch your back, indeed.

"So," said Ford expectantly. "You wanted to meet."

The Double set his feet and stiffened his shoulders. Focus. "Yes," he said. "I have something extremely important to share with you."

"I'm all ears."

"You are interested in vampire taps, yes? This is what David Ibrahim imported—"

"Who's that?" Ford interrupted. His tone was expressionless.

"Well, yes, yes," the Double stammered. He started again. "Vampire taps—you are worried that China could put them in the server racks of Western telecom companies, inside landing stations for the internet cables. Yes? But this is about playing defense. There will always be another David—another person to bring in vampire taps. Defense never ends. If you really want to succeed, you should play offense as well. You should not only worry about China getting inside your Western networks—but about whether you can get inside China's."

"I'm listening," said Ford.

Standing behind him, the other American shifted his weight impatiently.

"But first," the Double said. "I would like to discuss my situation."

"Your situation."

"As you know," the Double raised his voice a little to be sure the other man heard, "as we agreed, my helping you is in exchange for American citizenship. So I would like to know when I should expect to have that. To have my passport."

"Of course you will have it," said Ford smoothly. "But these things take time."

"Time is not a luxury that all of us can afford. Not when incidents such as—not when the Chinese are now paying close attention to what is happening in Ghana." The Double tried to make his voice sound hard. "If you want me to keep helping you—if you want to get inside China's networks—then I must know *when*."

"Soon, my brother, soon."

"Do not call me 'brother' if you will not help me," said the Double, genuinely affronted. "You are turning your back on our agreement."

"Oh no." To his surprise, Ford smiled. "Everything that you asked for you will receive, when the time is right. We are in this with you." He gestured at the man behind him, who watched their conversation silently.

The Double stood his ground. "I need to know when. I need a date. So that I can begin to organize my affairs. Quietly, of course."

"But I cannot give you a date." Ford's tone was apologetic.

"In that case, it would not be smart for me to tell you what I know about the new network that China is building to route their embassy communications through Ghana. And it would not be smart to tell you that you have a month to get inside before they finish construction—at most. And that only I can tell you how to do it."

He sensed the energy of both men pulling towards him, an invisible current running through the room. The power had reversed direction. He held it now. It was an addictive feeling. America, that vast and mighty nation, was only these two men, in a foreign land, fumbling in the dark, listening to every word he said.

"What is it that you know?" said Ford.

"I have heard it personally from the lips of my Chinese handler." The Double could not keep a note of pride out of his voice. "The network for the embassy will be air-gapped," he continued, "so to have the best chance at getting inside, you will need to be quick and try to compromise it before they finish construction. You have a month, as I said. Afterwards it will become much harder."

The other American spoke up for the first time. "Give us the coordinates." His voice was thin, almost reedy. Not the harsh baritone the Double would have expected.

"Not without my passport. Just like you, I need to be safe, enh? I need to have assurances. Last time I gave you the name of the man importing China's vampire taps that threatened American networks. Now I am offering the keys to China's networks. These are valuable pieces of intelligence, we all agree. But I am not an NGO. Give me a date that the passport will be in my hands, and I will tell you what else you need to know."

The attention of the room settled on Ford. He stared at the Double, his expression impossible to read. After a long silence, Ford said. "You will have your passport one month from today, December 8. I will personally make sure of it." He extended his hand. "Deal?"

The Double looked down at the open palm, waiting for him to shake it. Was it enough? Could he survive until then?

"One week," he said.

"Three weeks," Ford countered instantly, his hand still outstretched. "Best I can do. There are processes involved. Approvals."

The Double considered. It was still a long way off. But it was a concrete date, at last: December 1. He had survived this long without being detected, he could make it a little longer. By Christmas he would be safe in his new life in the United States.

"Three weeks," he repeated.

They shook hands.

"Excellent." Ford smacked his lips. "So?"

"So." The Double cleared his throat. "There is a town called Bekwai. North of here, outside the city of Kumasi. The construction project is there, in the bush. I will give you the coordinates. It is to be the biggest landing station for Jushu Marine in Ghana—one of the biggest in West Africa. A routing point for all the Jushu Marine fiber-optic cables that run along the African coast. And it is more secure than the ones that have been built previously. Air-gapped, as I have said. That is why the Chinese will route their embassy communications through it."

"You're sure of this?"

"Oh yes. When you get inside the network, you will be able to see and hear everything the Chinese do, without them knowing." The Double leaned forward, looking into Ford's glittering eyes. "*Everything.*"

EIGHT

THE MORNING AFTER SHE got back from Takoradi, Dani woke up to the ping of a WhatsApp message on her phone. It was Carlos Rivera, checking whether they were still on for drinks.

She almost canceled. She couldn't get the image of Oscar Aidoo beating James out of her head. The interlude of silence after the three slaps. The furious twist of Oscar's face. And James, cowed beneath him, all his cheery bombast evaporated. A scared, bullied kid, with a sick mom, whom Dani had put in danger. She was not sure how she could live with herself after that—let alone how she could go on a date with some random dude.

Still, she dragged herself out, if for no other reason than as a distraction.

They met at To God Be the Glory. A good rule of thumb for a woman abroad—meet your date at a place where the staff know you.

But right away she was having a bad time. She couldn't remember why she had found him attractive. His eerie stillness, his wide white eyes. The too-strong grip as he shook her hand hello. His youth, his awkwardness, his naivete—everything she had found endearing now irritated her.

"So tell me your story," she half shouted. The bar was thronged with foreigners in town for the ECOWAS conference, and they were having a hard time hearing each other. "How'd you end up at the UNHCR?"

"Well, I got my master's in social science." And he still spoke softly. "I decided I had to apply what I was learning to help people in undeveloped countries." Carlos sipped his Ghana Star. He had a small, womanly mouth. "My family is from Mexico. I have a lot of firsthand experience of how the policies of the global North can hurt people in the global South. What's good for the American consumer is not good for everyone else. When I see suffering, it's just within me that I have to help." He shrugged. "It does burn me out, though." His elbow brushed hers, leaning on the bar.

Dani fingered the lip of her own beer bottle. "I know what you mean," she said. She had looked up what *kafra* meant, the word James had repeated to Yaaba on their way out of the house as Oscar's shouts pursued them down the hall: *I'm sorry.* She kept thinking about how James had paused, mid-flight, to comfort this elderly woman. Such control and poise for such a young kid, such presence of mind—even amid the chaos of his father's rage.

A shout rose behind them. "Good evening, Dani!"

"Damn it," Carlos sighed. The first sign of irritation she'd seen from him.

"And Mr. Rivera! Oh ho." Marc Rutland wagged his finger at them. "What's happening here? Dani, I want you to meet my friends," Marc nodded at the crowd of white men around him. "Let us have a roster. American, Dutch, Swedish, British, and I think Patrick is Irish—no, British also, I'm sorry!" He slapped the muscled shoulder of the man nearest him. “This is my friend I was telling you about. Danielle Moreau. She is writing an article on corruption in Ghana’s oil industry.”

“Journalist?” said one of the Brits. “Why don’t you fuck off, love.”

“I’m not on duty tonight,” said Dani mildly. “I won’t bother you.”

Carlos seemed uncomfortable around the men. “I’m just going to use the restroom,” he said, touching her hand briefly.

“You have this word, *opfer*?” said Marc to the Brit, watching Carlos walk away.

“‘Op-far’? What is that?”

“In German it means, technically, *victim*. But it means—ah, it’s complex. It means this kind of person who is a weakling, but also an asshole.”

“Like a pussy,” said the American. “A douchebag.” He jerked his head at Carlos across the room.

“Ja. This is opfer.”

“How do you all know each other?” Dani interrupted.

“We’re drillers, love. Exxon brings us in, thirty-day course on the rig, teach the locals. Then they fly us to the next place. Easy money. All we do is tell these Africans how to do what we’ve been doing our whole lives. Just got back to Tema port and tomorrow morning we fly out, crack of dawn.”

She felt bad thinking it, but they were more fun to talk to than Carlos. “All of you are oil workers?” she said, looking around the group.

“You can call us roughnecks darling, we ain’t offended,” said the other Brit—the one who had told her to fuck off. “We’re roughnecks.”

“Rich ones,” the Swede piped up.

"That's right, Henrik, rich fucking roughnecks, I tell you. You ever been on an Emirates flight? Three-course meal, four different vintages to choose from. I like a Bordeaux myself. Hot cappuccino, fucking *love* it. Specially after a month in this fucking African hellhole. Although," the Brit burped, "not as bad as Jeddah. Here at least there's booze."

Carlos was crossing the room back to them. He was holding two Ghana Stars. He smiled at Dani from a distance. She found herself focusing on his arms again, as she had back at the Holiday Inn. It wasn't Carlos's fault he was awkward. He probably knew how to fix cars. Probably used his hands as well as any of these other assholes. She smiled back.

"How's the pussy round these parts?" the American said loudly, timing the question to greet Carlos's return. "Ghanaian girls?"

"Nigerian are best," said Marc, nodding seriously, sipping his whiskey.

The Dutch guy spoke up. "For me, I like Chinese pussy. I got yellow fever."

"You have?" said Marc, alarmed.

"Different kind of yellow fever, mate."

All the men laughed.

"Let's get out of here," Dani whispered to Carlos.

SHE HADN'T BEEN WITH anyone since the baby.

She had met Ben, her ex-husband, by chance one evening in a bar in Carnaby Street, shortly after moving to London from Beirut to take up her job as a desk reporter. He had been wearing a double-breasted suit and had broad shoulders and the shadow of a beard across his jaw. He'd been a rower in Cambridge; now he was a real estate developer. Solidly upper-middle class: Middleton class. When he had introduced her to his parents as a reporter for *The Guardian,* she had seen his mother visibly wince.

"Do you think your parents view my job as a provocation?" she had asked him once.

They'd been lying in bed in Ben's flat in Mayfair, tangled in his sheets. Cut into the ceiling above their bed were two small skylights, like a second set of eyes.

"Definitely. Possibly a communist."

"A communist?"

"And worst of all, an American communist."

She'd slapped his shoulder. "Be serious."

"I am being!"

"My mother's French."

He'd pulled the sheets off her, exposing her breasts to the air. "Thank God for that."

Ben had been so charming those first months. But she had known from the start they did not share a point of view. Ben was not curious about the world. He had never needed to be: the world came to him, coddled him, overlooked his faults and smoothed them out. He was decent enough, she had thought, and ordinary enough. And he was rich. He'll do, you say of a certain kind of man. And Ben did.

Carlos was not like Ben at all. Now, as they sat on the couch at the next bar after To God Be the Glory—a quieter spot down a side street in East Legon—Dani watched him carefully. When he spoke about the things he'd done at the UN, the intensity of his sense of duty rose off him like heat. He was not a careless man, as

Ben had been. The alcohol had softened him, but he remained precise. The way he was moving his body, the words he chose. Like a sharpened pencil making perfectly formed check marks on the world.

"Where were you before West Africa?" she said, stirring her gin and tonic.

"Kabul. With WFP—World Food Programme."

"Really? What was it like?"

"Just . . . so much poverty. You wouldn't believe it. I wanted to stay, but they said they needed help in Angola, and I don't have seniority, so I didn't have a choice. Then they sent me here."

"You've been with the UN your whole career?"

"Oh yeah. I've got my problems with it, don't get me wrong. But at least they show up for people. Sometimes, the least you can do is all there is to do."

"God, it's true, isn't it?" There was a looseness rising in her limbs that she recognized. It wasn't just the alcohol. "That's all we're here for, right? To do the least we can. But sometimes I worry that being a journalist is just another kind of exploitation. I mean, why am *I* here?"

"Meaning what?"

"You're here to directly make people's lives better. But I'm here because there's a *story* in Ghana—I can feel it underneath my hands, and I know the techniques for how to find it and tell it."

"And what are those?"

She thought he was patronizing her, but she didn't care. "When you're starting a story in a new country, the most important thing is to talk to people. Ask all the questions. Even the obvious ones. Read everything written *about* the place, then all the writing *of* the place—not just the speeches of the great men but the newspapers, comics, gossip rags. Watch television. Find out what the people who live here want. What do they do for fun? What do they do when they're bored?"

"And you've done all that for Ghana, we can assume?"

Definitely patronizing. Definitely didn't care. "This guy Oscar's house, man, you should have seen it. There is an incredible story here. I can just feel it. He had the telecom infrastructure of a major news studio. How did he pay for it? Where did that seven million dollars go? Chinese investment is changing this country. Do people know who stands to benefit, who stands to get hurt, from sucking Ghana dry at the same time the internet is wiring Ghana to the gills? Economies are changing, politics are changing, laws are changing. And no one has put all the pieces together yet."

"It sounds like you know exactly what you're doing."

She tipped back the last of her gin. "I know my craft, at least. But that doesn't change my question. Is it moral, is it *right*? Or am I no better than anyone else who comes to Ghana to make money off it, and doesn't care who they hurt along the way?"

"I guess it depends on what you do with the story."

Dani shook her head. "Even if my story wins the Pulitzer, will I have made one Ghanaian person's life better? Will I have fed one mouth or saved one child?" In sudden desperation she gripped Carlos's arm. "Do I have any right to be here at all?"

His eyes were steady on hers. "Excuse me." He flagged the barman down—ever solicitous, his voice soft. "Can we have two Johnnie Walkers please?"

"What are we celebrating?" Dani asked. He didn't answer. She realized that her hand was still on his forearm. They were passing through the transit zone. Like an immigration hall, it was neither here nor there—but you could not stay.

A long time since she had kissed anyone. The whiskey grew warm on the table, forgotten.

But when they got back to the guesthouse, it was all wrong again. The power was out, like it always was. They rolled into each other, fell onto the bed, Dani laughing but Carlos with a kind of silent, desperate intensity. There was something faintly pathetic about the way he pushed against her, his erection pressing into her thigh through his pants. His tongue was too much, his moustache scratched and tickled.

Maybe she had just lost the knack.

She pressed on, determined to enjoy herself. Fuck it, she deserved this.

He was naked, she was naked, she was trying to guide him but he thought he knew better, the idiot, and she tried to enjoy it, to enjoy the feeling of his weight bearing down on top of her, a glimmer of something familiar, of a life she had once lived, and maybe she *was* enjoying it now, it was totally fine, it was good enough, it was—

And then suddenly the power was back: the lights, the fan, the sound of a television from the room down the hall.

In a startled moment, Carlos whipped his head around and gripped her arms so hard that she cried out.

"Ouch—what the fuck?"

He reared away from her, as if she'd hit him.

"Sorry," he said, dully.

"I—it's okay," Dani said. Her arms *hurt*. She knew he hadn't meant to do it, but still. "Let me turn the lights back off."

"Wait," he said.

"Oh come on." But something had changed. What little rhythm they had achieved was lost, the illusion shattered. She pulled him towards her again but felt nothing, no response. She ran her hand along his arms but they were lifeless.

"This was a mistake." Carlos had straightened up in the dark.

"A mistake."

He was pulling his shirt back on. "Yes. I'm sorry, I have to go."

"What do you mean?" Suddenly she was furious with all of it. The UN sob story, the shyness, the intellectual bullshit. "You're leaving?"

"Yes." He was cinching his belt, one hand already on the door handle.

"What kind of a pussy are you?" Dani exploded. "Fuck you!"

She was shouting so loudly that Priscilla next door could surely hear. She grabbed at the nearest thing she could find—a flashlight—and threw it. Her aim was worse than Oscar's. It broke against the wall next to Carlos's head. From across the room he was just a silhouette, framed by the open door. For a moment they looked at each other in silence. Then without a word he was gone.

THE DAYS THAT FOLLOWED were bleak. She was out of time, out of road, out of friends. She had used James Aidoo, an innocent kid who had only ever been generous to her, and she had put him in unacceptable danger. She had tried to drink and fuck her way out of a corner but that hadn't worked either. All the old tricks were tired, all the old clothes didn't fit. She had played at being a journalist again, a real one, like the one she had been when she was younger—but she had lost the steel to charge forward and damn the consequences.

She kept reliving James's look of betrayal when he had realized what was happening—what she had done to him. Alma and Laurie had taken their discipline to the very end, to the exclusion of all other possible lives. Dani could imitate their fanaticism, but she couldn't bring it over the line. It wasn't in her.

Maybe it had never been.

She thought about leaving Ghana, but where could she go? There was nothing for her in London. She had spent her whole life avoiding New York. Maybe South America? India? China itself?

And what—lose a whole month of solid reporting in Accra? She had a *real* story here. A Chinese investment firm had overpaid for a useless patch of sea floor, and $7 million of the Ghanaian public's money had vanished into somebody's pocket. Was she supposed to start over from scratch in some other country, where she would be just another interloper?

At night sleep came only when she had drained a sufficient amount of the whiskey she bought at the European Mini-Mart. She dreamed of Senegal, of Beirut. She dreamed of her wedding. A summer evening in the Cotswolds—the air dense with the smell of wildflowers. After dinner, as the dancing had gotten wilder, the laughter more drunken, her nieces had begun chasing each other through the long grass. Bored of the adults; Dani couldn't blame them. She had seen Emma emerge momentarily into the light outside the tent, laughing, her thin blonde hair done in a pink barrette; Dani had helped her comb it that morning. A streak of huckleberry pie smeared on the corner of her lips. That was the dessert they had chosen. Huckleberry pie, à la crème anglaise.

Dreams of shadows. Her nieces flitting over the spotlights that were wedged into the ground, illuminated for an instant. Huckleberry streaked across their baby-fat chins like jagged mouths. Like phantoms. Like ghouls.

In the end there was no alternative: she had to keep going.

It was another hot morning. Dani tied her red bandana around her neck and hopped a tro-tro heading east towards the port at Tema. Those roughnecks at the bar with Marc the other night had given her an idea.

She got lucky with a seat by the window—the breeze threw passing smells from the street up into her face and cooled the ridge of moisture along her hairline. In her bag she carried her notebook and her phone, some cash, and, tucked inside her sports bra, over her heart, her American passport. That was the safest place for it—if you didn't mind the way your boob sweat warped the corners, or the BO that sank into the ridges of the presidential seal. More than one immigration officer had wrinkled his nose and given her a hard stare when she handed it over. Dani didn't care. Passports were just paper and plastic, in the end. You could always get another one.

It was hard to find Chinese people to talk to in Ghana. It had been like that in Senegal too. Most of the Chinese who came to Africa were poorly educated laborers from rural China, sometimes all from the same village, shipped en masse by some conglomerate based in Shanghai or Guangzhou to build the huge infrastructure projects their government was financing. Lonely years toiling in the sun, far from home. They lived in camps with long tents, like army Quonset huts, with signs in Mandarin characters hung along the fencing.

But Tema was the largest international port not just in Accra but in all of Ghana—a vast complex where massive container ships unloaded their products from all over the world. If there was anywhere she would find a Chinese oil worker, Tema was it.

The port was not like the city center. Here there were few pedestrians, no sidewalk. Truck after truck trundled heavily past her. For more than an hour Dani walked alongside the road, choking on the dust the vehicles kicked up. She drank most of her water; her passport stuck to her chest. Gradually her excitement and determination began to wane. A faint taste of whiskey stuck at the very back of her throat. Her nose was beginning to run. Her body protesting.

Dani, Dani. *Enough.*

Then, at last, she reached a real neighborhood. She felt relief surrounded by the bustle of actual human beings. She sat on a tree stump and pulled her map from her notebook. As a woman, broadcasting helplessness like this was dangerous, but she didn't know what else to do. She was thoroughly lost. "Fuck's sake," she murmured, tracing with her finger. All the bottled-up impatience she had been keeping in check was suddenly urgent. She was tired, she was hungry, she was thirsty, she was horny.

Then she looked up—and through the crowd, she saw an Asian face.

Three of them, in fact. Dressed casually, in jeans and sneakers and T-shirts. One was wearing a red baseball cap with the logo of what she thought was an NBA team. They were young men, laughing and talking to each other, threading their way through the indifferent Ghanaians.

She followed them. The crowds were thickening, the streets had narrowed, there were no more 18-wheelers rattling past. This part of Accra felt anonymous and transitory. Scaffolding was everywhere. Several of the buildings had blue tarpaulins for roofs.

Up ahead, she watched the Asian men disappear through the doorway of a building of unpainted concrete, several stories high. A sign in front said China Hotel.

Dani went inside.

It took her eyes a few moments to adjust to the darkness. She was in a restaurant. The three men were the only customers, sitting around a table at the back. An Asian woman stood near them, hands curled into fists on her hips, head turned half away—a pose of not-quite-persuasive disinterest. The men were chatting and laughing. Then one of them made eye contact with Dani, and they all fell silent and turned to stare.

Dani walked right up to the table, wielding a chipper American attitude like a battering ram. "Hi there. May I sit with you?"

For several moments the whole group looked at her uncertainly. The waitress stepped lightly away, disappearing into the kitchen. The smell of cooking filled the room as the door swung behind her, and Dani saw an older man prodding a wok, cigarette wedged between his lips. The eggy, salty smell made her salivate.

"My name is Danielle Moreau. I am a journalist."

One of them shifted his chair a little, opening a space. Dani pulled a chair from an adjacent table and sat, smiling brightly at each of them in turn.

"What are your names?"

Nothing.

"Do you speak English?"

Two of them shook their heads vigorously. Then the one in the baseball cap said, "I speak English."

"What's your name?"

When he didn't answer, she pointed at herself. "I am Dani. You are . . . ?"

She felt certain he understood. But there was something hard behind his eyes: maybe suspicion, maybe contempt.

"What are you doing here in Ghana?" she asked.

He shrugged. "Work."

"What kind of work?"

The older man and the waitress emerged from the kitchen with three steaming plates piled high with fried rice. It smelled delicious.

"Boss," said baseball cap, nodding at them.

"Excuse me, sir," Dani said, half rising.

Without a word the older man beckoned her impatiently to follow him. He was wearing rubber sandals. Ash from his cigarette fell to the carpet and on the bare tops of his feet. The kitchen was lit by a single light bulb.

"What do you want?" he said, in perfect English.

"My name is Danielle Moreau, Mr. . . . ?"

"Wang."

"Mr. Wang. I'm a journalist. And I'm looking for Chinese people who work in the oil industry in Ghana. To talk to them about what their lives are like, and how they feel about being here."

"Okay." He was piling more rice from the wok onto a plate. He handed it to her. "Thirsty? My daughter will bring you some beer."

"No, that's all right—"

"Tsingtao." He grinned. His gums were swollen, his teeth stained a deep brown. "Real Chinese beer."

They sat all together in the restaurant's main room. Dani couldn't control herself and spent several minutes silently eating, pausing only to gasp down sips from the warm beer bottle the waitress had brought her. Her body closed around this nutrition with a desperate gratitude. A weakness she had barely noticed in her arms and legs was filled up and soothed. When was the last time she'd eaten a proper meal? The old man was watching her with a satisfied expression. He lit another cigarette.

"Now," he said. "Your questions."

"Do you mind if I . . .?" She pulled out her notebook. "Mr. Wang, where are you from?"

"Chengdu. Sichuan Province."

"And these men?"

"The same."

"How long have you been in Ghana, Mr. Wang?"

"Many year. Ten year."

The daughter had reappeared and was sitting at a little remove from the other men, all of them watching this exchange with interest. Dani felt suddenly self-conscious. "I'm here to ask you," she said, projecting her voice, trying to sound stern and official, "what you know about China's presence in the oil industry in West Africa."

Wang looked nonplussed. "China is strong, yes," he said. "China was strong always. You know Admiral Zheng He?"

"Zheng He," echoed the men at the table, picking out a name they recognized.

"Can you write it down for me, please?" She put the pencil in his hand. Wang nodded and drew out the Chinese characters in fluid, elegant strokes. A nib of cigarette ash fell onto the page, and he brushed it away. Dani guessed the admiral must be pretty famous, given the men's reaction. But she had never heard of him.

"Mr. Wang, can you tell me what brought you here, to Ghana? What do you do for work?"

"Import/export."

"What do you import and export?"

He shrugged. "Doesn't matter. Import from China, microwave, refrigerator, air con." He asked his daughter something in Mandarin. "Yes, air con. And export to China, cocoa, wood, palm oil. Doesn't matter. China buy everything."

"And these men?"

"These men work on construction. I build this hotel."

"Can I ask you to write your name here, underneath Admiral Zheng He?" She tapped her notebook. "And their names as well?"

Wang pulled the paper towards him again and wrote out a few characters. "Me." He tapped. "Daughter." He pointed.

"And these men?"

He blew air through his lips, a bored sound, and shook his head.

"Mr. Wang, I'm hoping to speak with some Chinese people who are involved in the oil industry here in Ghana. Do you import or export any oil? Petroleum?"

"No, no, no."

"Do you know where I can find Chinese people who do? Who export petroleum from Ghana?"

Wang folded his arms across his chest and leaned away from the table, peering into the empty dining room like there was something important there. The workers had ceased following their conversation and were busily eating, but the daughter was rapt.

"You go to Holiday Inn, in Accra?" the daughter suggested quietly. "Many Chinese there."

For the first time in hours Dani became aware of the pressure of her US passport wedged above her heart. After a while its weight felt soggy and vaguely repulsive, like gauze in your mouth at the dentist. She sighed. "The Holiday Inn? Next to the airport?"

"Holiday Inn," her father agreed. "You can find there, the ambassadors."

"The Chinese ambassador to Ghana is there?"

"No, no, no." He shook his head and spoke rapidly to the rest of the group. All of them laughed, including the daughter. "Big men." He rubbed his fingers together, indicating money.

"The Holiday Inn. Okay. Thank you, Mr. Wang. Can you write down your mobile number, here, in case I need to reach you?"

"No text," said Wang. He stabbed the table with his finger. "You come here again."

The daughter reached over and wrote, under one set of Chinese characters, a mobile number. "Me," she whispered.

"Mr. Wang, can I at least pay you for the food?"

He looked at her blankly. Dani realized it was a stupid question. She dug a few hundred cedis from her bag and handed them to Wang with both hands, to show her respect.

DARKNESS HAD FALLEN BY the time she got back to her neighborhood. Dani was utterly exhausted. But the thought of going back to her lonely room, to her whiskey and biscuits, filled her with a yawning horror.

Instead, she went and sat at one of the student canteens on the edge of the University of Accra campus. It was a nameless establishment lined with long tables, open to the street on both sides. The square meal at Mr. Wang's hotel had reawakened her appetite. She ordered tea and toast and tried to read the BBC news crawl on the small TV they had mounted up in the corner.

The way she saw it, there were two options. She could go back to the Holiday Inn and wait for the elusive Chinese "ambassadors" to appear—with no guarantee that they ever would.

Or she could take a different tack. And for that, there was only one person who could get her what she needed. There was only one person who had access to the financial data.

She WhatsApped her ex-husband:

I need your help.

One of the students got up and changed the channel to a soccer game: Liverpool versus Chelsea. Scattered cheers went up from a few of the tables.

Her pocket buzzed. Ben had written back.

Why should I help you?

Dani laughed out loud. Why indeed, motherfucker.

For a moment she sat there, listening to the students watch the game. This was what globalization really meant. This was what it really looked like to connect people across the artificial boundaries of the state. The world did not belong to the people who thought it did—the cynics at Davos, the women in the lobbies of the Sofitel collection, the men in suits who read the *Financial Times* in business class lounges at Heathrow. There was something else underneath all that. Something bigger. Something real. They were not imaginary—these connections between young human beings for whom nation meant nothing. Who in older times would never have met, bonded, drank together, joked, fucked, in dive bars and student neighborhoods, bumming cigarettes and sharing drinks, united by the vernacular English they had learned from American movies and music—drawn to one another by shared good intentions, whose only source was the awareness of their mutual vulnerability.

Chelsea scored. Grumbling from the students.

Her pocket buzzed again.

But it was not Ben this time.

It was James.

Hello, Dani
Kofi and I are going for dinner tomorrow

And then, after a thirty-second pause:

Would you like to join?

NINE

Billy and Ford stared at each other.

"And?" Ford said.

Billy cleared his throat. "Bekwai's about an hour due south of Kumasi," he began. "Little town out in the bush."

He had gone north to see if the Double was telling the truth about this alleged landing station in Bekwai. He had traveled at night, half expecting it to be a trap. Maybe Ford was setting him up to be captured by the local police; maybe his bosses wanted to get the David Ibrahim murder off their plates. Kumasi was a major city, as big as Accra, but when you left the urban center the population dropped off a cliff. It was in the part of the country where the Christian south began to overlap with the Muslim north. If Billy had kept going north, he would have left the jungle behind and hit the desert, where coastal Ghana started to bleed into the Sahel: Burkina Faso, Mali, the vast Sahara beyond.

But instead he had proceeded south from Kumasi proper. When Billy had come to the coordinates the Double had given them, he'd driven his truck right into the bush so that it couldn't be seen from the road. Then he had walked. Two hours on foot. No moon. No Ghanaian officials waiting to arrest him. His headlamp lit the three feet in front of him and the GPS in his left hand glowed an alien green. Otherwise he was alone with the sound of his breath and the fall of his feet, whacking away obstacles with the machete in his right hand. Always aware of the Ruger on his hip. It was a last resort only. You never, ever fired your weapon in a country where you were undercover if you could help it. If you killed somebody and got arrested by the local police before they could get you out, you would be disavowed. You'd rot in some tropical jail while your fingernails got pulled off one by one.

"Rivera," Ford said sharply.

"Yes," said Billy. "It's there all right. About five klicks east of the coordinates he gave us. In a depression at the base of a hill. Chain-link fence with barbed wire surrounds the entire site. Building's around one hundred meters inside the fence. One gate, easy to bypass. Well, you have the pictures there. Nobody around that time of night. Ground covered with cigarette butts and ripped-up food packaging in Chinese characters."

"What else?"

"The construction is pretty far along. They've already poured the concrete foundations and you can see the entry points where armored cables enter the building. Earth torn up pretty good from the heavy equipment. Footprints and tire tracks everywhere. Exterior is freshly painted, with the words *Jushu Marine* stamped above some Chinese characters. Construction materials under the name of a company called Dongsha. That word was all over the place."

Ford grunted.

"Bottom line—it looks like your Double is telling the truth. And it looks like the Chinese are close to done with this thing. So if you need to get inside, the window's closing fast."

Ford sat back. “Okay,” he said. “I’ll write it up.”

Billy knew from his tone that he was being dismissed. But something held him back. The instant he and Ford parted ways, Billy would be alone again: surrounded by people who did not know who he was. Who he really was.

“Any blowback on Ibrahim?” he asked. “What did you pull off his phones?”

Ford regarded him silently. Billy waited for him to say that it was not his job to worry about that. “His phones prove that he was in the thick of it,” Ford said finally. “And now the Chinese are definitely spooked. They know that we know that they’re here. And the other thing. The way he was killed. Hacked almost to pieces.” Ford’s tone was bland. “What was that about?”

“He fought back pretty hard. It was him or me.”

Ford watched him for several long seconds more.

“Never know who’s going to turn out to be a fighter,” Billy continued. “I remember this buddy of mine in basic training, Raul. He was from Puerto Rico. Joined the Marines fresh out of high school in San Juan. So of course the first English word he ever learned was ‘fuck.’ ” Billy laughed. “One time, we were doing Indian sprints, God, it was so hot. And this corporal comes along in a jeep. Don’t know why but somehow picks Raul out of the lineup to ask him—”

Ford cut him off. “Stop talking. I don’t want to hear about your life. That’s not what I am.”

There. Billy felt it again. The feeling of falling, from the car with Ibrahim. A roar in his ears. It flickered through him for a moment and then was gone. He swallowed, his throat dry. “All right.”

What this idiot didn't know was that Billy was trying to tell him about the girl. If he could have just sat there and listened for five minutes, Billy would have told him everything.

GOD, DID ANYTHING MAKE you go from feeling powerful to feeling ridiculous faster than jacking off?

Billy was in his apartment, doubled over his dick. The American reporter's face was below him. He could see her so clearly, he could feel her nails digging into his back. And then it was over, and he was a loser grunting over a wad of tissues.

His only consolation was that the Chinese probably didn't have this apartment bugged. If they'd known who he was and what he'd done to Ibrahim, he would have been dead by now.

He'd known going on a date with her had been a terrible idea. And not reporting it was even worse. Unreported intimate contacts like the one he'd had with Dani Moreau were serious protocol violations, because honeypot schemes were incredibly common. An adversary nation would send a hot woman to bump into an officer, just to see if he bit. And "journalist" would be exactly the sort of cover story a girl like that would use. The legend was that back in the day, the officers working in the American embassy in Moscow got so used to the Russians sending them honeypots that the whole station would just sleep with the same five Russian agents and pass them the same bogus intel. But it was easy to lose your clearance this way. It often happened to men cheating on their wives.

As Billy cleaned himself off, the thought crossed his mind that maybe losing his clearance wouldn't be the worst thing in the world. It would mean he could go home.

—

It wasn't that the agency had tricked him into joining. But Billy could not quite place how, exactly, it had happened—how he had decided to go this route, instead of the many other lives available to him.

At the end of his third tour in Afghanistan, he had been nearly four years into his Army career. That left sixteen more to go until he was eligible for a pension. But when the time came to start thinking about reenlisting for a fourth tour he had hesitated. What good was a pension if he never lived to see it? Two of his buddies had died in the past six months. Death was not something far away. It ate with you, walked with you, squinted with you in the morning sunlight and lay down at night with you in your bed. Already he could feel that death itself had taken on a darkly seductive quality. Sixteen more years was a hell of a long time to live that way.

So Billy had started talking about what he would do when he got out. It wasn't some single dramatic moment; guys were always talking about what they'd do when they got out. He spoke with his commanding officer, who sent him to their unit's human resources liaison—people whose whole jobs were to help soldiers think through their career options. Billy's liaison was a kid named Raymond, who far outranked him but looked like his balls hadn't even dropped yet.

"What is it you want to do, Specialist Demirjian?" Captain Raymond had asked in their first session.

"What do I want to do?"

"In life. With your career."

"Well." Billy frowned. "I guess nobody's ever asked me that."

Captain Raymond had leaned forward like this was good news. "We can start by doing an exercise. I want you to close your eyes."

"Man—"

"Specialist, this is all part of the process. Close your eyes. I'm going to share a question with you, and I want you to answer immediately, without taking even one second to think it over. Just start talking and we'll see what comes out of your mouth. Ready? Here it is. Picture your life five years from today and tell me what you see. Go. *Go*!"

"I don't know," Billy had begun haltingly. "I'm settled down, I guess. A wife. A family. Every morning I get in my truck and go to work. Stop at Dunkin' Donuts, order my usual. The girl behind the counter knows what my usual is. And just, you know. I'm living." He'd opened his eyes. "How's that?"

Captain Raymond helped him write up a résumé and encouraged him to spend some time looking at USAJobs, the federal government's job application portal. The possibilities had made Billy dizzy, like looking too long at the night sky.

"I stare at these applications," he complained at their next meeting. "All the DoD jobs are some random shit on base in some Podunk town. They're literally like, 'Welder.' 'Meatcutter.' Swear I saw 'Gravedigger' on there one time. And then when I try to apply for a normal job, I can't check any of the qualifications boxes. Only one I can check is 'Do you claim five-point veteran's preference?' What the hell has the Army been training me for?"

Captain Raymond had looked at him blankly. Billy knew the answer: they'd been training him *to be in the Army*. That was the beginning and end of their concern.

He had tried talking it over with the guys in his unit. Some of them were going to school; the Army would pay, but then they would owe back more years of service. "They'll help you," one buddy told him, "but they're going to take their pound of flesh."

So the next time they met, when Captain Raymond asked him, "Have you ever thought about the agency?" Billy didn't need to think hard.

"I'm all ears."

Which was clearly the answer Captain Raymond had been expecting, because he told Billy to sit tight and then disappeared for about twenty minutes. When he returned it was with a short Asian man in civilian clothing. Billy went to shake his hand, but the man just nodded and sat down in Captain Raymond's seat. He didn't give his name. He waited to speak until the captain left the room.

"Specialist Demirjian." He waited expectantly.

"Yes sir."

"William J. Demirjian."

"Yes sir." After a moment Billy added, "Family's from Armenia, originally, sir. My parents fled the first war there in the nineties."

"You speak the language?"

"No sir." Billy stuck out his chest proudly. "My father insisted. We are Americans. We speak English."

"No Russian? Turkish?"

"No sir."

"Too bad." The man's voice was flat, his expression unreadable. There was nothing notable about him at all. It was a type Billy would come to know well. "I've spoken to your commanding officer," he said. "You'd be a natural candidate for paramilitary officer, and we could certainly use men like you, if you're interested. You are interested, correct?"

"Hell yes. Yes sir."

"Here's our offer. You're in at just under four years now at E-4, right? So that's sixteen until you retire. If you do the next twelve with us, we'll call it even at a major's pension."

It took Billy a second to digest. "Who will call it even?"

Finally the guy had smiled. "The United States," he said. "Your country."

AND NOW HERE HE was, just over a year later—awake in the middle of the night in Ghana, throwing away his tissues like some dumb horny teenager.

Regret was dangerous. But nights like these, he wondered if he should have just toughed out the next sixteen years in the Army. At least it would've been in a world he knew, in an institution that he'd grown up in.

Billy picked up his book and tried to read. But the words went in and out.

He had not been with a woman who hadn't expected to be paid in more than three years—not since his last time home, when he was still in the Army. He had gone back to Rochester and messaged a couple of the girls from high school on Facebook. Erin McConnell had agreed to go to Chili's with him. He'd had a couple of Long Island Iced Teas, she'd had a couple of those drinks that look like blue Powerade with a pineapple skewer on top. They went back to the basement apartment she was renting from her aunt. She had let him hit but he'd been too drunk to come, so they'd ended up just lying together for a while, both knowing that this wasn't anything. It wasn't anything at all.

Besides that, just whores. They hung around outside the base. Wear a condom, you'd survive.

But Dani was different—if that was her real name. Smart as hell, he could tell. Older than him. And somehow angry. She burned with an energy that he couldn't quite identify. He was willing to bet that, like him, she also knew what it felt like not to be sovereign in your own life. He wanted her, badly. And by the way she looked at him, he thought she wanted him too. Like actually wanted him, the way a normal girl would. If only the lights hadn't come on like that and startled him.

After a while Billy tossed his book aside and picked up his phone.

Carlos Rivera sent a message to Marc Rutland on WhatsApp.

Tell me more about this Dani.

A few minutes later his phone pinged.

Oh ho. Up late?

Billy had made a decision. He was going to go on another date with Danielle Moreau. And he was not going to tell Ford.

Was it a mistake? Probably. But the hours that he had spent with her were the most like himself he had felt in Ghana. His real self. That and the night he had spent in Bekwai, casing the landing station—hearing the sound of his breathing and the swish of his boots in the vegetation, marching alone through the dark.

TEN

When Dani had first arrived in London after Beirut, it had been a shock to discover what ordinary life felt like when stripped of the threat of death.

She had secured a flat in Islington, bought an Oyster card. She had settled into her job as a desk reporter at *The Guardian*. She had begun to make friends with her colleagues.

And at first it had been a letdown. Physical danger had been like a drug for her. But gradually, she had begun to unclench. This was what she had wanted, after all, after Laurie's death. This safety, this predictability. Laurie had gotten closer to the truth than anyone. But she was dead. And Dani had at last understood that the truth did not lie in death. That death was the one place from which she would never be able to discover it.

And then Ben had entered the picture. They drank together a lot; it was how they were easiest with each other. In wine bars in Shoreditch after work, and down the local pub in Islington on Sunday evenings in Britain's long summer light. The drinking gave a dangerous undercurrent to their domesticity. They pushed each other. Some mornings she had woken up naked in the living room, Ben snoring on top of her, chairs and sofas in disarray. Once she had found him passed out in the kitchen, slumped around the expensive cast-iron soup pot they never used, which brimmed with his vomit.

But after they had showered and changed and washed down paracetamol with sparkling water in green glass bottles, they were really nothing more than a nice, boring, upper-middle-class couple. Dani was a little astonished at how conventional she had allowed her life to become in such a short space of time. They spent their weekdays at the office and their weekends with a circle of friends who were multiracial, wealthy, educated, perfectly at ease with their positions in the world. They deployed empathy when they needed to—feeling sad for those less privileged, but never letting it overwhelm them. Ben would read the *FT* every morning, making notes with a pencil on the margins. She would reach over and tousle his hair.

"Piss off." He would swat her away, laughing.

"I love you." The words rolled off her tongue easily.

But this was what she had wanted. She had been chasing a death wish most of her life. Finally she could admit that to herself: she had wanted to die. And now that Laurie had gone and died for her, she didn't want to anymore.

And then she had found out she was pregnant. What a startling thing: to discover that her body could be remade so fundamentally. To witness what alien currents ran through its sinews. To find out that your body is not just yours, when you are a woman: that it is also the terrain for life itself. The male body, by contrast, is inert, impotent. It just sits there. Dani got a kick out of this, thinking about some of the men she had known. She looked down at her belly—at the gentle, muscular swelling—and imagined the life to come.

This world is yours.

All her checkups were good. Her doctor's office was in Marylebone. The nurse was Belgian. When she saw Dani's last name, they had begun speaking French with each other. The jelly on her belly was cold. Running the ultrasound wand, the Belgian nurse had smiled softly.

"Félicitations."

ON THE MORNING BEFORE her dinner with James and Kofi, Dani found herself at the library of the University of Accra, staring at a list of hundreds of companies. In the solemn quiet, students turned pages of textbooks, looking stressed. The room had the particular damp paper smell of official buildings in tropical climates.

Dani felt chilly, almost feverish. She hugged her arms around herself. At the table next to hers a boy whispering with a friend laughed too loudly, and the librarian hissed at them. Librarians were the same all over the world.

She had asked Ben for two datasets: (1) all the major Ghanaian oil companies and their investors, and (2) all Chinese companies of any size operating in Ghana, along with information on their ownership structure.

He was the only person she knew with ready access to Bloomberg terminals. And to his credit, he had given her all of it. But on her other request—details on Oscar Aidoo's investment interests—he had come up short.

"This Aidoo chap, afraid there's not a lot on him that's publicly available." Ben was chewing gum on the phone with her.

She could picture exactly his bland, handsome face. The same one that had drawn her in three years ago when she first saw it ordering a lager at The Clachan on Carnaby Street. The last time she had gazed upon that face, it was contorted with rage—its mouth shaping the words *cruel, vindictive, bitch.*

"Okay," Dani said. "Thanks anyway. This is good stuff."

"I suppose you're in trouble, are you?"

She hung up on him.

He had sent her a zip file with information on nearly five hundred Chinese companies with operations in Ghana. Methodically, one by one, she went through them, using Google to fill in the gaps.

Over the course of an afternoon, some themes began to emerge.

Since the early 2000s, trade between China and Ghana had shot up from almost nothing to billions of dollars every year. And it was a lopsided exchange. Ghana's exports to China were gold, cacao, crude oil; in return, China sent heavy machinery and telecommunications equipment, and Chinese consultants and trainers to teach people how to use them.

Again and again, one name kept reappearing: Jushu. Founded in the 1980s, by the 2010s Jushu was the leading telecom equipment manufacturer in China and one of the largest in the world. Jushu had opened schools across West Africa, training young Nigerians, Senegalese, and Ghanaians in telecom skills, just as mobile phone ownership on the continent was beginning to skyrocket.

And they weren't just focused on telecoms—they were expanding into the African financial system as well. Jushu consultants had fanned out across the continent, working with the local banks, including the Bank of Ghana, to build out online pay portals and mobile banking facilities. "China is completely cashless," said a Jushu representative quoted in the *Daily Graphic*, the most widely read newspaper in Ghana. "We are helping in Ghana to make the same."

All interesting. All important. But none of it gave her what she needed. None of it got her any closer to the missing $7 million.

She scrolled back through Ben's list. Page after page of companies whose purpose she couldn't identify, with bland, one-word names.

Finally she came to Dongsha Limited.

She clicked her way through the links. Some of the info she had already come across in her research, but a lot of it was new and proprietary. International shipping registries confirmed that Dongsha leased container ships that moved goods from Shenzhen through the Strait of Malacca to points west, primarily ports on the African continent. Customs duties paid in Djibouti, Mombasa, Durban, Lagos, Abidjan. Inventory: truck axles, mopeds, industrial ceramic fixtures, electrical switches.

She clicked on the *Ownership and Key Executives* page. It was blank, except for one name: LU ZHONG, CHAIRMAN. She recognized it from the Hong Kong securities filing that had first clued her into the missing $7 million. There was no picture, but below the name was a link to the company Weibo account.

This page is in CHINESE. Would you like to translate it?

Dongsha had 112,000 Weibo followers and was following four hundred accounts. She clicked on *Following*. Mostly other Chinese companies. A smeltery in Shenyang. A chemical processor in Chongqing. A few large global conglomerates: Maersk, Rio Tinto.

Her feet were freezing. Her head was pounding. She needed to drink water. She hugged herself and thought, unexpectedly, of Carlos Rivera's hands on her hips. So long since she'd been with a man. She hadn't realized how much she had missed it.

She went back into Ben's files and searched by Lu Zhong's name, in both English and Chinese characters.

She found that he was also the chairman of a company much further down the list called Red Wing Capital, which appeared to be a venture capital firm that had invested in dozens of African companies. She double-clicked on its investments one by one.

A palm oil exporter.

A scrap metal consortium.

Halfway down, she came to a company called Paragon. When she clicked on it, she froze.

James Aidoo was the CEO.

She had heard *Paragon* before—it was the name of the nightclub in Takoradi that they had driven past.

There was no description of what Paragon did, or any details about who worked there besides James. But there was a single entry under *Investment Activity*.

In August 2016, Red Wing Capital had invested in James's company.

Seven million dollars.

For a moment Dani sat back, unable to do anything but marvel. The sheer rush of it—of digging something out that others did not want to be found. Better than any drug.

Pulse quickening, she bent her head over the desk, writing up several new note cards and placing them beside her old ones.

- Dongsha executives had met with Kwesi Adjepong on July 24, 2016.
- The next day they had paid $231 million for the right to explore Parcel 42, which had turned out to be a worthless stretch of seabed.
- Official Ghanaian government receipts showed that Parcel 42 had cost $224 million—$7 million less than what Dongsha claimed to have paid for it.
- Kwesi Adjepong's boss was Oscar Aidoo.
- The chairman of Dongsha was a Chinese man named Lu Zhong.
- Lu Zhong also ran a VC firm called Red Wing.
- One month after the purchase of Parcel 42, Red Wing had invested $7 million in Paragon.
- Paragon's only employee appeared to be James Aidoo.

Dani could not square what she was reading here with the tubby, awkward kid who had made her laugh on the veranda—or who had looked so frightened and humiliated running down the hallway from his father. That James and the James whose name was undeniably on the screen in front of her did not seem like the same person.

But there was only one way to know for certain. She had to ask him straight out.

Tonight.

When she was six months, she turned thirty-two, and Ben gave her a birthday party at the Chiltern Firehouse. Summer in London, the city thick with cranes. The champagne was on ice.

Back home, as they lumbered up the steps to their flat, Dani with her strange new center of gravity, he with half a dozen Scotches, they began to argue about something one of Ben's friends had said. When Dani called Ben an idiot for the third time, he smacked her casually across the face with the back of his hand. His hand was heavy; a weapon. He hadn't exerted himself: he didn't need to.

That night she watched him while he slept. The baby rustled within her. Ben snored heavily, drool pooling on the pillow. The next morning, he didn't apologize. She was not sure he even remembered.

Two days later, she was sitting in her office, working late. She was writing a story about China's Belt and Road Initiative. A port in Sri Lanka had defaulted on a loan, and a Chinese shipping company was taking ownership of the facilities.

The frustrating thing about desk journalism was that everything was oblique. You kept looking for that one quote where someone came right out and said the thing you were looking for, but you almost never found it. You were like a lawyer; you needed explicit admissions. But people rarely wrote things down. And without proof, you couldn't write the story.

Sitting at her desk, reading about Xi Jinping, Dani felt a pressure moving around her rib cage, like an odd balloon lodged below her armpit. A strange pain. But she was always having strange pains these days. Her organs were squeezed in odd formations.

That night, she got up to pee around four in the morning. The light in their flat's bathroom was on a pull chain. When she pulled it, the toilet bowl was full of blood and mucus. That was when she noticed the pain. It was everywhere, all around her. So huge and sudden that she hadn't perceived it immediately, like a wave that was over her head before she knew what was happening.

In the ambulance, the paramedics were two men. English boys with round faces. Dani wished she had a woman with her. Someone who would hold her hand. Her mother. Her sisters. Anybody. "Please," she whispered, but nobody answered. She wished she had been born a hundred years ago, when they handled things differently. When the men were banished, and a mother in labor was secured behind a locked door with a room full of somber and efficient women. Women who would know, without needing to be told, that what she wanted was a cool washcloth on her forehead. Who would know that what she wanted was someone to hold her hand.

Anybody.

THE PLACE THAT JAMES and Kofi had invited her to was a restaurant called Sandbox Beach Club. Dani had looked it up in advance, but the pictures had not done it justice. She was taken aback as she was escorted in by the slinky-hipped hostess—passing a large pool surrounded by sleek loungers, and wealthy-looking young people lying out on top of them, Ghanaian and obruni.

The two men had taken a table at the back, sitting together, watching her approach. Just like last time, when she had met them on the veranda of the Aidoo home in Accra, Dani was struck by the physical contrast between them: James short and round-cheeked, Kofi a head taller, with his intense stare. Both of them somehow self-important. Like children playing at kingpins.

"Hello," she said uncertainly.

"Good evening." Kofi got to his feet and shook her hand. "You are welcome."

Dani acknowledged him briefly, but her eyes stayed on James, who remained sitting. The cut above his eye had not quite healed.

"I forgive you," he said, preempting her. "All is forgotten." He was smiling but his tone was slightly anxious. "Let's order some beer, huh?"

For a moment Dani wanted to say that she did not accept his forgiveness.

"Okay," she said.

The three of them scooted in the booth together awkwardly. James gestured at the bright blue pool, at one end of which huge block letters lit from below spelled SANDBOX. "A bit like Miami?"

Something about his half-bashful, half-boastful expression brought her right back to the car ride to Takoradi. Charming, a little cocky, a little insecure. Yes, she was going to ask him about the missing $7 million. But it was a different feeling than when she had sat across from Kwesi Adjepong, from Oscar Aidoo. She was not here to trap James. She was worried about him.

"Please do not take what I say as an insult, Dani," James continued, "but it was Kofi who really insisted that we invite you tonight."

"Is that so?"

"I think he is a bit starstruck by the famous American journalist."

"Ah!" Kofi said indignantly. "The man is cheeky, bloody cheeky."

"Since your name is Kofi," Dani said, trying to smooth over his discomfort, "that means you were born on a—"

"Friday," James answered for her. His eyes were suddenly bright, amused.

"Yes," said Kofi. "Friday's child."

"Party animal," James grinned.

"You guys used to go to Paragon, right?" She spoke to Kofi but she tried to watch James's face for a reaction. "That nightclub in Takoradi?"

"Yes," Kofi nodded gravely. "We would go with our friends there. Our younger brothers were always so jealous. And then we would eat at Bocadillos."

"Do you both have siblings?"

"For me, just the one brother," Kofi said. "For James, his younger brother and his older sister. But really, James and I are like siblings too."

"Come now, come now," James pushed his glasses up his nose again. "Enough Kofi, didn't we say that we must be serious with Miss Moreau, we must give her the true picture of what is happening in Ghana? Let us discuss debt-to-GDP ratios, enh? But first we will order some food, some French fries, some Smirnoff? And then you will learn the truth about what is happening in Ghana, Dani." He didn't quite wink at her, but she could tell the gentle mockery in his tone was meant for her alone, and that Kofi did not notice it.

As they waited for their food to arrive, and as she thought about when she should ask the question about Lu Zhong and his $7 million investment, Dani considered the two young men sitting across from her. The second generation, the sons of power and privilege: "princelings," they were called in China. Xi Jinping himself was one—his father had fought alongside Mao during the ChineseCivil War in the 1930s. They bore the burden of their parents' achievement. On the climb to power and success, there was much more room below them than above. Their privilege was a new, surprising thing. It had been dug out of their earth with bare hands just one generation earlier—the very hands that had swaddled them, fed them, smacked them. Oscar beating James, the individual pops echoing like gunshots: *one, two, three.* In those hands they must have been able to feel their parents' uncertainty, the tenuous hold on safety—always braced for the raised voices in the streets, the brick thrown through a window.

"Cheers, enh," Kofi said, clinking his Smirnoff against hers. "Cheers to good American friends."

"How about just good friends?" Dani said. "We can drop the American."

"But you are," said James softly. "You *are* American."

"A nation is just a story that people believe. I'm a New Yorker, a journalist, a woman—the United States is just what my passport says."

Neither Kofi nor James seemed to know how to respond to this. Suddenly loud music began to thump from speakers behind their heads: the DJ was beginning his set.

"I love America," Kofi said eventually, raising his voice. "You know, I studied there too, like James? At George Washington University, in DC. For me, the best thing Ghana could do would be to become like America. But here is the problem. *Debt.*" He said it like a curse word. "Debt, debt, debt. The presidents who promise that everything will be free."

"Here it is," James sighed.

"Ah, ah," Kofi shook his head, shaking off James's objection. "She must *know.* It is a great tragedy. Ghana has had so many blessings. Just five years ago, we had one of the highest GDPs per capita in Africa. We had tourism. Well," he nodded at Dani, "it seems the tourism has not changed. But everything else has become worse, much worse, much worse indeed."

Beneath the house music, distantly, she could hear the sounds of the waves crashing on the beach. It took some effort to resist the urge to correct him: she wasn't a tourist. "How so?"

"Suppose I told you that in the last election the president promised that he would make high school free and pay room and board for the students also? Suppose I told you that he said he would build a factory in each district of Ghana." Kofi waved his hand. "He knew that the country could not afford it. But he promised it anyway. And when he became president, suppose I told you that he had one thousand presidential staff? The most that a president of Ghana has ever had. Of course, we cannot complain too loud. My papa and James's papa are among them. But this is democracy, enh? There are many people who need to be included in the spoils, because they gave you something along the way."

James shook his head. "Such a cynic."

"But this is not sustainable for any country. It is *not*! Cost of living is up. The ingredients for soups and stews. A bag of peppers at the market costs over two hundred cedis! People are tired of the NPP's management. It is not so good news here for our heir apparent." He nodded at James. "So what will the government do, of course? Spend more money. Promise the people everything. It flows downhill, from America, excuse me, Miss Moreau, but it does. The Americans capture the politicians, because they promise them money. Once the politicians have this promise, they turn around and promise the people, you will have stadiums, you will have new roads, you will have hydropower. You will be able to do whatever you want."

"Enough," James repeated, sighing heavily. "I am tired of your preaching, brother. We are all tired of your preaching."

"Preaching?" Kofi was indignant.

"You talk of my father? You like to hear yourself talk—more than he does!"

The two men began arguing in Twi. Dani tried to follow at least the direction of what they were saying, but it quickly descended, or ascended, into pure masculine scorn. She didn't need to speak the language to recognize it. They were posturing.

"Gentlemen," she interrupted. "Please."

"Excuse me," said Kofi in English. "I must go to the toilet." He stomped away, clearly flustered. In his absence James turned to face her, looking amused.

This was her chance.

"What did he mean by 'heir apparent'?" she asked.

James shook his head dismissively. "Sour grapes. As they say in Texas."

Dani felt a sharp pain in her side. A cramp. Her body protesting its mistreatment once again. She shifted her weight, silencing the dissent.

"James," Dani said. "I have to tell you again that I'm sorry about the position I put you in. With your father, in Takoradi. That was not fair of me."

"It is forgotten, like I said."

She took a breath. "Well—now I have to ask you something else."

"Oh?"

"In my research, I've found that the chairman of Dongsha, a man named Lu Zhong, also runs a venture capital firm that invested in small businesses across Africa. A firm called Red Wing Capital. One month after Dongsha overpaid for the rights to the oil parcel by seven million dollars—the one I asked your father about—Red Wing made an investment. Also of seven million dollars." She swallowed. The cramp in her side was worsening. "And you know what company he invested in."

For a long moment James looked at her, unreadable.

"This is all credible information," she added.

"This is your strategy, I see." His tone was high-pitched. "You bide your time, you pretend to be friendly, but all along you have the knife behind your back. The question you are truly waiting to ask." But he did not seem angry. He did not even seem particularly surprised. He tossed his napkin onto the table and leaned forward, shoulders hunched. A posture of defeat.

Dani gasped softly as another wave rolled through her belly, like a hot wind. James did not notice. He was staring at the tablecloth.

"You cannot write this story, do you understand?" He spoke in a monotone. "Everything I am about to say is off the record. But here is what it is. My father has always loved China and disliked America. You know this, you heard it from his own mouth. Everybody who watches his videos knows this. Maybe it is old Third World solidarity, maybe it is resentment against Anglo-Saxon imperialism." He sighed. "Maybe it is just greed. And he has always had big ambitions for me. So, yes, he worked with this man, Lu Zhong. The seven million dollars went into an account controlled by me because," he hesitated but did not look up at her, "because I am to use it to finance my campaign for Parliament in the next elections. Seven million dollars will easily get me to victory, with a well-known last name. My father believes there is no limit to what I can achieve, with my brains, my American education, his fame, and China's money. Member of Parliament, he will say. Maybe even a Ghanaian president, one day." He laughed dully.

Dani was squeezing her eyes shut, trying to remember everything he said so she could write it down later.

"So that is what it is," James concluded. "That is what you have been chasing. That is the truth. But you can never write a word of it. Not unless you want me dead. Do you understand? *Dead*, Dani." Finally he did look up. He frowned. "Are you all right? You don't look so well."

"I'm fine."

But when Dani tried to stand, she fell over. For a moment she lay on the floor, feeling the bass of the DJ's beats pulsing in her cheek. In a disoriented haze she looked up at James, castigating herself. It was not the drinking this time, but still. Stupid, reckless *again*. Alone with a man she barely knew, in a country where she was a stranger.

James got his hand under her armpit. "Up, up," he said gently. "Let us bring you home. You must rest."

"I'm fine," she whispered. "I'm fine."

But she allowed herself to be led.

SHE LOST THE BABY. A stillbirth. Old words; an old story. *Birth*: the forward motion, the breaching, the unfolding. *Still*: the silence, the infinite patience, the lack of regard. The life to come, vanished. The paths that would never be walked.

Her son.

Her doctor assured her that this was not her fault, but Dani had blamed herself. She'd felt certain that her worldview had poisoned the child—that her pessimism was like a toxin leaking through the amniotic sac.

At first, she had wanted nothing more than to hold her nieces. Emma and Claire. She wanted Caitlyn to send them to her, she wanted to clasp their warm bodies in her arms, kiss the tops of their heads.

And then, suddenly, the thought had turned, and she wanted never to lay eyes on either of them ever again. She wanted to deny the cruelty of their perfection—to insult and denigrate it. She wanted to claw out her doctors' eyes. She wanted to go out into the street and hurt a stranger. The force of her grief astonished her.

And then there was the matter of Ben.

He appeared in her hospital room after her doctors had left. Blubbering, clutching her hand. "Unfair," he'd sobbed, "this is so unfair." He'd laid his head down on her thigh, his snot on the gray blanket. His anguish had been obvious, and it was genuine. This was definitely the worst thing that had ever happened to him.

He revolted her.

"Ben," she had said softly. "Do you remember slapping me? The other night. After my birthday, at Chiltern Firehouse." Her voice had been weak with exhaustion. A nurse had promised to bring her some ice chips. "You were drunk, and you hit me."

"No," he said. "No I didn't."

"You did." A faint smile rose to her cracked lips. "You hit me. And two days later, this happened."

"What are you saying, Dani?" He had held out his palm as if to stroke the back of her head.

"You are a weakling and a fool. The baby was half you. And that's why it died."

He had frozen, arm outstretched. For a moment he'd just looked at her. "I knew you were mad," he said slowly. "I always knew it."

The nurse had come back with her ice chips.

Two days later, she had filed for divorce. Five days later she had quit her job at *The Guardian*. She realized that this had been a mistake. All of it. Letting herself slow down.

Two weeks later, she had moved out of Ben's flat in Mayfair.

Four weeks later, she'd had her dinner with Marc Rutland, when he had first told her to look into Ghana and its oil.

Twelve weeks later she'd been on a flight to Accra. The minute she'd gotten off the plane, Dani had closed her eyes and known she was where she needed to be. West Africa had a smell. Peaty, smoky, sweet.

Alive.

ELEVEN

"New orders from up top," said Ford. "We need to infiltrate the Chinese network before they seal off the landing station. We need to get inside the air gap and get a vampire tap on it."

Billy had looked up what an air gap was. It meant that a given network was an internet unto itself, with no physical connection to the rest of the internet—no way for data to jump in or out. It was a physical separation, like a moat.

"You saw the pictures, you saw what I saw," Billy said. "It's too late to get inside that air gap, unless your Double can help."

"That's exactly what he's going to do. The Double is going to get you to the door. It'll be on you to place the taps. Point and shoot. He's the pointer."

"I see." For a second Billy pondered the floor. "How do you know he's not ripping us off? Taking our money and jerking us around? They do that in these parts, you know."

Ford was brusque. "He's been accurate so far. Ibrahim. The landing station. And we aren't paying him."

"Then what does he get out of this?"

"You heard it the other night." Like Billy, Ford also had the ability to stay very still when he needed to. "He wants his US passport. He wants citizenship."

Dangle the promise of the US in front of a man, he'll throw just about anybody under the bus for it. Billy had seen it happen in Afghanistan. Boys sold out their fathers, uncles gave up their nephews. They did it for bags of food, new winter coats, sometimes straight cash. They would walk away bewildered, holding crisp hundred-dollar bills.

"And is he going to get it?" he asked Ford. "His citizenship?"

"Hell no. You think I have that kind of authority?" Ford's laugh turned into a grimace. "He's just ignorant. Thinks we're all-powerful."

Billy felt an instinct, below the level of conscious thought. Something was off here. The Double was clearly an amateur, but he was arrogant too. And people like that were dangerous. Like Billy, the Double was at the very end of long chain—on the wild frontier where there was no one to save either of them from the responsibility of their own decisions.

"How do we know he's not running some other game?" Billy asked now. "Maybe he's not just a Double but a Triple." When Ford didn't respond he felt compelled to add, "I'm just saying. It's my ass. If he is."

He knew Ford wasn't going to like the question, but he was still surprised by the look he gave him. Open disdain. "My orders are my orders," Ford said. "I get them same as you. And this guy is the key to all of it. You know how much work it took to bring him over the line? He's going to lead us not just to their landing stations in Ghana but into the heart of their operations all over West Africa. It's my career too, and I'm the one running him, not you."

Billy couldn't stand these creeps. Talking about his career like they were sitting in some air-conditioned office stateside, instead of sweating in the dark in a country where everyone wanted them dead. Talking about running a human being the way you would run a car or a gun. Fake Ghanaian accent fooling nobody; Ford had Harvard written all over him. Probably never fired a weapon in anger.

"I'll let you know once I've briefed the Double on his role in all this. Meantime, you do what you need to do to get prepared. Because one way or another, by next week I want to be pulling every single gigabyte off those wires."

Billy stood up, dismissing himself. "Yes sir," he said, saluting.

THE FEELING OF FALLING was getting worse. Billy felt it at random moments—when he was getting out of the shower, when he was haggling for food in Makola Market, when he nodded at the neighbors at Carlos Rivera's apartment complex. He could feel himself starting to slip from his own reach, and he did not know how to make it stop.

And now these new orders. Get inside the air gap. Something had clearly changed in the United States' operational posture towards China in West Africa. Decisions had been made by people high above his pay grade, or Ford's for that matter—in rooms with soft lighting and soft voices, black shoes on red carpets and unopened bottles of water on mahogany tables. For years the US had been fine with Chinese companies growing and spreading their footprint across the world. They were cheap, and they were fast, and American investors were getting rich. But now the Chinese weren't the crappy alternative anymore. They were the *better* alternative. All the tech that everybody wanted—the 5G that let your iPhone download apps faster, the AI assistants that could talk back to you—would run faster, more reliably, and cheaper on Chinese hardware. Pretty soon, not just the developing world but the *entire* world would run on Chinese technology. Which the American military obviously hated—because in a shoot-out you can't give your enemy the ability to turn off your guns. And American investors weren't so happy about it anymore either—since they were getting squeezed out of the Chinese market themselves, stonewalled by Chinese Communist Party officials who wanted control over their companies.

The wind had changed direction, and Billy was blowing in it. He didn't understand how cell phones worked or what radio spectrum was. He didn't care about who won the contracts to deliver 5G to Europe. All he knew was what was happening on the ground in front of him. Which was looking more and more like a war.

He had been violating protocol: first Ibrahim, then Dani Moreau. Yet no one had called him on these failures. It dawned on Billy that he was at the limits of his government's ability to surveil. There was no one checking his work. No one watching him. The chain of authority that stretched all the way back to DC ended on a street in Accra, with him. It made him feel oddly exposed, like he was out on a ledge.

Nobody would stop him if he decided to step off.

TWELVE

So she had it. She had her truth.

The seven-million-dollar plan, for her seven-million-dollar man. It *was* a scandal. China was corrupting a current Ghanaian politician, socking away cash for him to launch his son's political career. If the scheme succeeded, both Oscar and James would be in China's pocket forever, no matter what their Ghanaian voters expected of them. She had the proof—the data Ben had sent her—and she had confirmation from James's own mouth, even if it was off the record. Beijing was corrupting African politics in the most venal possible way.

It was the kind of slam-dunk story that could make her career. But more than that, it was the kind of story she had become a journalist to write—the kind the world needed to know, that could expose something hidden and malevolent to the fresh air of public scrutiny. Ghana didn't deserve this.

She knew what Laurie would have done next. Use her leverage. Keep pushing. Find proof that did not require James's confirmation, that got around what he had told her off the record and arrived at the same facts by some other route. Contact her old editors at *The Guardian* and tell them she had hooked something big.

But that was the problem. Could she even write this story? James had been clear: if people knew the truth, he would be physically in danger. "*Dead,* Dani."

This was the same kid who had walked her up the stairs to her room after she had collapsed at Sandbox, his hand under her armpit, steadying her, gentle as a mother. A future president, if Oscar Aidoo and this Lu Zhong had their way. A serious man, a leader in waiting. A chubby twenty-six-year-old in glasses, face shining with sweat.

Her cramps had ceased for now. Dani was unsure what had caused them. It couldn't be related to the stillbirth; her British doctors had given her a D&C, and two cycles had passed without incident since then. Dimly she worried that something more serious was wrong—maybe an ulcer, exacerbated by the Mini-Mart whiskey. But as long as the pain wasn't literally killing her, she wasn't going to worry about it. She had bigger problems to consider.

Alma was right: the ethical demands of journalism never let you off the hook for an instant. James had not chosen his life; what was he supposed to do if Dani blew it up? Was it fair to subject him to even more suffering, even for the sake of the truth? The kid had no fallback plan, no escape hatch. Whereas Dani always had the option to retreat. The seven-million-dollar story would revive her career, *The Guardian* would hire her back, and James would be left behind.

What did it say about her that she could even consider it? Was she only claiming that she cared about the oppressed in order to extract something, just like every other imperialist? Even if it was a story, even if it was a great one?

Dani thought about her mother. About her nieces at her wedding. About Laurie Balfour. About her thirty-second-birthday party, about the faces of her husband's friends, that afternoon at the Chiltern Firehouse. You thought there was a life beyond politics—you thought there were afternoons you could spend with your feet up, closing your eyes with the sun on your face. You thought it was only fair that there should be patches of respite, of beauty, of breakfast spreads in fancy hotel rooms, of penthouse views. You thought you were doing nothing wrong by enjoying them.

But instead there was violence—always, everywhere. Violence did not have to mean guns and bombs and blood. The everyday economy of the modern world was built on it. An airplane is violent as it rips through the air at five hundred miles per hour, as you sit with the shade down reading your magazine. The trucks that deliver your groceries are violent; cold as a morgue, thousands of pounds of hoofs, loins, breasts, their weight bending the asphalt of the bridges they cross. The ships that deliver the chassis of those trucks from one continent to another are violent—hulls heavier than a skyscraper, dead fish and dirty water drifting in their wake.

Dani wanted to show this violence to all the people she had ever known—to say to them that you may live with ease but you can never quite get away from it, and deep down you know it, and *that* is the source of your relentless fear, a distant faint echo beneath the surface of your days. You sometimes heard them say, of generals or criminals or the victims of war, that "he lived a violent life." Meaning: he lived a life in which violence was present. But all lives are violent lives. Even the ones in which violence is never visible.

Especially those.

When Carlos Rivera's name appeared on her phone, Dani had to look at the message for a few seconds before remembering who he was.

Let's try that again?

In the rush of learning the truth about the seven-million-dollar plan, and in her anguish about her moral dilemma, she had almost completely forgotten about him.

But something had changed. She was different, and he was too. Still young, still intense—but he seemed more real. Like he had stopped pretending about something.

"Sorry about the other night," he said, sipping his beer.

"Don't mention it."

They were at a dimly lit watering hole—little more than a couple of plastic stools beneath a tarp where an old man sold Star Beer out of a cooler. Much better than To God Be the Glory, with its noisy foreigners and people they both knew. And they were skipping the small talk, the unsexy history of families and careers. Also better.

"How's the story going?" he said.

"It's eating me alive."

He nodded. Suddenly he slapped his own neck, killing a mosquito.

"You ever come across any American troops in Kabul?" she said. "When you were with WFP?"

"All the time. Why?"

She shook her head. "I've just been thinking about them. American troops. Chinese troops. All these goons, all these people who put all the rest of us in danger, because they're busy worrying about each other. Like some kind of weird insular club. But because of them, everybody else needs to be afraid. When without them maybe everybody else would get along with each other just fine."

After a few seconds of silence he shrugged. "I don't think most troops are afraid of the Chinese. It's the people who give them orders who are afraid."

"These goons are all the same," she muttered, looking down at the dirt at their feet. Then she felt Carlos's hand on the side of her neck, gentle but firm. He held it there for a second while she met his eyes.

"Mosquito," he said, pulling it away slowly. He showed her the smudge of her blood on his palm. "Don't think I was quick enough."

"Here." Dani pulled his hand back towards her and let it drop onto her shoulder. "Easier access."

For an instant Carlos appeared to hesitate. Something crossed his face that she couldn't identify. Silently she willed him on. He took her chin between his thumb and forefinger and turned her face towards him, deftly as you turn up the collar of your coat.

"Back to your place?" she muttered.

"Better not. Messy roommates."

Back in the guesthouse, Dani drew the curtains and stood for a moment in darkness at her window, feeling Carlos's presence behind her. The awkward desperation of the other night had vanished. It had been a bad joke, a clumsy dream. Everything was different. She knew what she wanted him to do, and wordlessly he obeyed.

He moved slowly. In silence he pressed his weight against her. Her breaths shortened. She stretched out her hands along the window, poured her weight into her wrists, like she might break the glass. Accra slept below them, silent in the heat.

In the half-light his naked shoulders were bony, almost brittle. You could see every sinew. She told him what to do with her hands, and he was unresisting.

The front of her right hip tightened: always the right hip. Her leg moved just a millimeter, but her whole body knew what it meant. Dani groaned in recognition, in farewell.

Yes, this was what it was like.

This was what she remembered.

Breathing quickened and shallowed. "Bismillah," she whispered. Multilingual dirty talk. She had learned it in Lebanon. The last syllable lengthened, fading like a sigh. She was alive. This was what it was like to be alive. She turned her face this way and that. She bit his chest. "Bismillah, bismillah." In the name of God, in the name of— "Fuck," she said, not whispered now but announced, declared: "Oh *fuck*."

She came and almost immediately erupted into sobs. For a long time they washed through her. She did not know how long. When finally a break appeared between the swells she looked up and saw Carlos sitting back on his heels, panting slightly, watching her. Her eyes met his and he looked away quickly, head bowed.

Another swell of sobbing began to rise within her and she shut her eyes tight, tight against the world, feeling the grief like steam rising off her body, hot, hot, everywhere was hot, her skin was red as a boiled animal's. Sometimes between a swell she would crack her eyelids open slightly as if coming up for air. But mostly she was helpless, bobbing like a piece of plastic in a storm, borne unstoppably by a power much greater than her own, which it was not even worth trying to fight.

She lay like that for minutes, hours. When it was over she felt far away from where she'd started.

Her tears had ended. The room was silent.

Dani suddenly sat up and looked around.

Carlos was gone.

THE NEXT DAY SHE went walking through the city in the heat of the morning. She wandered down alleys and into markets, aimless. A Muslim girl tried to sell her a headscarf and Dani remembered Priscilla and her dress. She needed to knock on her door and ask for it. When she got tired she sat in the shade of a ceiba tree and watched the schoolkids pushing each other while they waited for the bus home.

"Obruni!" A hawker with a bucket of water bags on his head had spotted her. "Bra, obruni." It was unusual to see a man selling water; they were almost always women. He beckoned her. "Bra, bra." Ghanaians had a funny gesture for *come here*, which to her American eyes looked more like *give me.* Palms down, fingers raking the air.

Dani bought two water bags, and drained the first one in a single gulp, the water tinged with a taste of lukewarm plastic. She ripped the corner off the second with her teeth and sucked on it, watching the kids.

The water seller had not moved on but was lingering nearby. She waited for him to say something.

"Oh please, obruni," the man said finally. "Can you give me your address? Your address?"

"You want my address?"

"Yes, your address? In Canada?" He made a gesture like writing with a pen.

Dani ripped a page from her notebook and propped it on her thigh to write her name. "I don't have a Canadian address," she said. "British or US only."

"Oh," he frowned. "Not Canadian?"

"Sorry. How about Britain?"

"Britain." He nodded, but he still looked unhappy. "Britain is good."

Dani had encountered this before in West Africa. People asked for Westerners' addresses, thinking they could help them secure visas—thinking that all you needed was proof you had a place to stay, and the white people would give you a passport, would let you into their country. She felt ashamed picturing the cruel, blank faces of the immigration officers at JFK. She thought of the confidence with which she traveled in the opposite direction.

"Here." She passed the sheet back to him. "Good luck."

"Oh please, oh thank you, thank you!" he said, folding it carefully and putting it in his pocket before striding away.

Skin in the game. That was what the world demanded of her. She had dug up the truth, she acquired real leverage through hard work—through being good at her job, damn it. And now she had a choice. And her choices had to matter—like this man's life mattered, like the seven-million-dollar plan mattered, like the contest between the US and China mattered. No frivolity, no warmth, no softness. Just the bare facts of the world.

She was hungry. Next to the tro-tro stand was a KFC, and she ducked into it. The place was brand new—freshly painted, bright, clean, and cold. Rihanna played on the speakers, and the fatty, peppery smell of the oil wafted through the room. She ordered chicken strips and cheesy biscuits, which came in a wax paper bucket. Ghana had suffered severe food shortages within living memory, and this was not a ritzy part of town. But the restaurant was packed with well-dressed Ghanaians, mostly young, laughing, flirting, looking at their phones. Dani let the endorphins from the sugar and salt wash through her. She was feeling strong. Confident. Unsure of what would happen next, but unafraid of whatever it might be.

But when Dani got home and pushed open the door to her room, James was standing there, a finger to his lips.

"Jesus—*fuck*." She stifled herself mid-scream.

"Dani." He crossed the room and made as if to give her a hug.

She pushed him away. Her scream had produced an odd gurgling sound that died away as James stood smiling at her, oblivious. "How did you get in here?"

"I picked the lock."

"You're telling me it was that easy to pick?"

"It was rather a good lock actually. But I am rather a good picker."

"Fuck you, James. You can't just—" Dani realized she was shaking. "This is not a game."

"I agree," he said. "It isn't a game at all."

"Did anyone see you come in?"

"No. And fortunately, I stick out less in this country than you do." He frowned. "I am sorry if I frightened you. But I could not very well loiter in the hallway."

"Why are you here?" she said. The jolt of seeing him in her room, unexpected, uninvited, had made her feel an emotion towards James she had never felt before: anger. So now that he knew her address, he had decided he could let himself in whenever he wanted? Was this how vulnerable she'd been this whole time? She hadn't even cleaned up since Carlos had been there.

"I came to impress upon you what we discussed the other night." He cleared his throat, seeming slightly embarrassed. "You were, uh—not well. So I want to be sure that you understood. You *cannot* write your story. You cannot tell anyone what I told you about Lu Zhong and the seven million dollars."

"I understood," Dani said briskly. His apology, so brusque and insincere before moving on to what he actually wanted to talk about, reminded her of nobody so much as Ben. "And I have been thinking about what you told me. And I have decided you're right—I can't write this story."

He exhaled with relief.

"But. *But.* There is a story here that I *am* going to write. That needs to be written. And I will need your help to do it."

"It's too dangerous, Dani. You saw my father, what he is like. The others are even worse." He was speaking quickly, panicked.

"James, James." Dani held up her hands. "If you tell me that writing about the seven million dollars will put you at risk, I won't do it. I can set that aside. But for the sake of the truth, not to mention my integrity, I *have* to write something about what China is doing here in Ghana. The world must know."

He opened his mouth as if to speak, then closed it. He pushed his glasses up the bridge of his nose: a nervous tick that she had always found endearing but that today made her angry. *Stand up straight,* she wanted to bark at him. *Look me in the eye.*

"And what story is that?" he asked quietly.

"You said it yourself in the car ride to Takoradi. Data—the richest trove of all. The resource that really matters, that China and the West are really competing over. It isn't the oil. It's the data. Telecoms, Wi-Fi, mobile payments, social media. All of it. If you can help me with *that* story—then yes, I will kill the seven-million-dollar man." She stared at him. Her heartbeat was slowing down, her breathing becoming more regular.

James did not answer at first. His eyes had drifted to the corner of her room, where her papers and notebooks were stacked in messy piles next to the half-full bottle of whiskey. "I have been wondering," he said eventually, "how it is that you found out the truth about Lu Zhong and Paragon and the seven million dollars."

Dani hesitated. But she saw no reason to lie. "I asked my ex-husband to send me the names of all the Chinese companies operating in Ghana," she said, "and their financial information. I have data on hundreds of businesses."

"How did he get this information? He works in government?"

"Banking. He pulled the information for me from the Bloomberg terminals at his office. Rather helpful of him, actually."

"If you can get that from your husband, what do you need from me?"

"Ex-husband. And what I need from you is to tell me where to look. I will keep your name out of it, but I need your insights, your leads. I need to know what you know about China in Africa."

"Like what?"

"Well, start with your job. Vodafone Ghana. Tell me what they do and how China is involved."

His face blanched. "*Dani.* I cannot."

"James." She tried to inject an air of finality into her voice. "Do you trust me or not? I told you I would keep your name out of it, and I will. That's more than you would get from any other reporter, believe me."

After several long moments he nodded. "May I sit?"

They sat together on the floor, James with his back to the bed frame, Dani cross-legged in front of him, trying her best to block her disheveled pile of clothes from view.

She picked up her notebook. "So. Tell me about Vodafone Ghana. Teach me about telecommunications. Mr. President."

He frowned at the floor. "You know, a few of the tech companies around Austin tried to recruit me. Dell, Microsoft. I had an electrical engineering degree, I could have written my own ticket." He puffed out his chest. "But my business was here in Ghana. And not just because my father demanded it. Telecom is big money in Africa. The local people, even if they cannot afford a computer, everyone has a phone. Every market woman, every toothless old man in the bush, every young man in university. They all use WhatsApp. And the money is often stored on the phones. Because they have nowhere safe to keep it. So it is the phone, and also the bank." Suddenly James stood up, seeming excited. "Do you know how the internet works, Dani?"

She looked at him blankly.

"I mean, how it works practically. Mechanically. Most people don't really understand it. People think the internet flies through the air. But it does not. It flies *underground.* On wires and cables that wrap around the world, under the ocean. That's how your data gets from here to there. In fiber-optic cables that sit on the bottom of the sea. Highways for data, going so fast, you cannot imagine. *Zzzzp*: you sent an email from London to New York. Almost as fast as the speed of light: that is the 'optic' part. So fast, it looks instantaneous to you. But the data has run along the Atlantic Ocean in that time. Flying beneath the fishes."

She wrote fast, flipping the pages of her notebook. "And who owns these cables? Governments?"

"Mostly they are privately owned. By the telecom companies, and also by the big internet companies. Facebook, Google, Amazon. And Jushu—you've heard of them, right? Jushu builds the cables through a subsidiary called Jushu Marine. Dongsha also happens to be an investor in that—but so are half the companies in China." The words were spilling out of him, he was rising to his theme like a professor in a lecture hall. "Here, give me something I can draw on."

Dani ripped out a page from her notebook. James began to draw shapes, irregular blobs, with thickets of thin lines curving along their edges and crossing the blank spaces between them. It was a crude world map.

"The most recent project from Jushu Marine is this one." He drew a single, straight line across the page. "Cameroon to Brazil. It is a direct connection across the southern Atlantic Ocean. It's a new approach, you see. Most of the cables go like this." He scrawled a half-dozen lines lengthwise, one on top of the other, hugging the curves of the shape of Africa. "You see? They stay near to the coastline. From Asia, they loop around India. When they meet the Horn of Africa half of them go up the Red Sea and straight into the Mediterranean. The rest go all the way down and around the Cape of Good Hope, on the way to Western Europe. They bundle together near London, and then shoot over the northern Atlantic"—he drew a series of thicker lines—"to the northeast US. This is the major route of the world's information. And here, in West Africa"—he drew a circle around a tangle in the crook of the Gulf of Guinea—"many of them crisscross each other. If anyone ever wanted to cut off the flow of information from Hong Kong to New York, this is one place where they could do it."

A droplet of sweat from his forehead fell onto the page.

"Why here?" said Dani. "Why West Africa?"

"There are several switches located in the region. A switch is like a train station. They control the route the data takes. They determine which one of the cables will carry the data on its way from Asia to Europe and then to the US. There are some agreements between the owners of the cables. And there are capacity requirements—you know, traffic gets backed up on the lines, just like real train tracks. The whole thing only works because of cooperation between the owners. Between the American technology companies and the Chinese ones. And, therefore, between the US government and Beijing."

"But why Ghana, I mean?"

"Because it is the most stable country in the region. The one with the most internet bandwidth—thanks to companies like Vodafone." He smiled, satisfied. "Ghana is a relatively connected country. That's why they all build their switches here. The internet is the future, Dani. My father is right about that at least. The internet is the best thing America has ever done for the world, and it is not even close. A community without borders, impossible to close off and police. Where nothing is truly disconnected. A pure meritocracy of talent and determination."

Abruptly as it started, his energy seemed to run out. James put his hand over the world map he had drawn. "Maybe I should shut my mouth right now." Suddenly he put his head in his hands. "Damn it. I cannot do anything right."

"James, come on." Dani set her notebook aside. "Let's have a drink, huh? You'll feel better."

"Dani, you drink too much. It's not good for you."

"I agree." She grabbed the bottle of whiskey.

He half laughed. "I'm serious. It can be unsafe. For a lady."

"Thanks for your concern."

James's whiskey pull almost came back out of him in an explosion of coughing.

"Better, no?"

"A little," he wheezed. He took one more small sip but then shook his head when she offered him more.

Dani rested her back against the bed. This small room had become her home these last five weeks in Ghana. This thin mattress, this patchy carpet. That pile of dirty clothes and papers scattered in the corner. Really, when you looked at her life objectively, she was only a notch above homeless. She thought of Carlos, sitting back on his heels, watching her shut her eyes and weep, her body raw. She understood abruptly that she would not see him again.

"The other night," she said. "Kofi mentioned your siblings. You've never told me about them."

"My brother is only a little boy. He is still in secondary school. My parents had him late in life, before—before Mommy got sick." James waved at the air as if swatting an invisible fly. "He is a good boy, but young. We don't have so much in common. And Jasmine, my older sister. She is the true star of the family. She went to Princeton and stayed in America after school. If she had been a man, my father would have put all his ambition onto her, not me. I disappoint him."

"Oh come on."

"You haven't met Jasmine."

"But *you're* the one who is going to be president. You're the one running Vodafone Ghana."

James's eyes were shining slightly from the booze. A novice drinker. He shook his head when Dani tried to pass the bottle back to him.

"Why did you divorce?" he asked quietly. "You and your husband."

"I had a child. But the child died. I mean," she cleared her throat. "I had a stillbirth."

"I thought . . . you didn't want children. Forgive me, but you did not seem like the type."

"No," she said. "I wasn't."

James was silent for a minute. "When I first went to Texas, to Austin," he said eventually, "I was so happy. My father was so proud of me. My mother. And I was proud too. Because America was *it*. There was nowhere else you could go, except maybe Oxford or Cambridge—but even in Ghana, we can see that Britain has lost its luster. And you know what? I liked Austin. But UT, the campus, the students there." His face and his voice darkened with anger. "Gradually, I came to despise that place. I wished I had never gone." He gestured for the whiskey. "Obama used to say, 'That's not who we are.' When he was trying to convince people of something. Not to blow up civilians, for example. What he wanted to say, but could not, is 'That is morally wrong.' But he never said that. And do you know why? Because America has no vocabulary for morality. Americans today are too comfortable. 'Someone else has made the rules already, so don't look at me.' Americans have never lived in the real world, the world of right and wrong, that the rest of us live in. It is all a game to you. A dream. Ghana?" He laughed bitterly. "You do not know such a place exists."

"Not all Americans are like that. Some of us do want to live in the world of right and wrong."

He wasn't listening. "When I would fly back to school, the first thing I would notice was how fat everybody was in the airport, and all the little kids playing video games on their phones. Is that what Ghana will become? Is that what we want? What can these people turn to when the violence comes, when they have to choose between right and wrong?"

She was trying to get him to listen to her. "I agree with you James. That's why I'm here in Ghana. Not back home looking at Instagram in some New York City coffee shop."

"I'm not saying that I love the Chinese." He was speaking to the air now, to some invisible audience. He was drunk. "The Chinese are not moral either. But at least they are up front about it. At least the Chinese are honest with themselves." He looked at her. "At least, when they kill you, they know they're doing it."

THIRTEEN

THE DATE IN THE corner of the Double's computer read November 20. The deadline that Ford had promised for his US passport was still weeks away. But tonight his American handler had called him to another meeting.

He was worried. This time, he walked the whole way: there was no chance he could tolerate sitting squeezed in a tro-tro.

Today's meeting place was an apartment complex in the neighborhood of Kaneshie, on a side street tucked behind Accra Academy, where many of the Double's rich friends had gone to secondary school—wearing their socks pulled up to their knees in the British style.

As instructed, the Double went up to the second floor and knocked on the third door on the left. After a moment it swung open onto a darkened room.

"Hey friend." Ford's voice came from the shadows.

"Good evening," said the Double cautiously.

"Just me today. Mr. Rivera is not around."

The Double stepped inside. It was an empty apartment: no chairs, no bed, no sign of life whatsoever except for a map of Ghana spread out on the floor. Something about the place was deflating. He clasped his hands in front of him and turned to face his American handler.

"You wished to see me?" He tried to keep his voice even.

"It's about Bekwai," Ford said. "There have been some developments."

The Double opened his hands. "Whatever you want to know. As we agreed."

Ford cleared his throat. He gestured at the paper map on the floor, and the two of them bent over. "The operation is scheduled for 2300 on November 23, just about seventy-two hours from now. Our friend Mr. Rivera will lead the mission. He will place the vampire taps themselves. Your role will be to get us inside the building without attracting suspicion."

It took the Double a moment to process what he had heard. "*Me*?"

"Yes. You are going too."

The Double physically started back from him. This could not be the plan; it made no sense. In his shock he forgot about the passport for a moment. "Surely there is no need for me to be there, in person? What do I have to offer?"

Ford looked at him blankly. "You're Ghanaian. You speak Twi. You know how these landing stations work and what to look for. Carlos doesn't have any of those attributes. Don't worry," Ford smiled. "You would be amazed where you can go in this life just by holding a clipboard. That's how the Israelis busted the Iranian nuclear reactors back in 2010. You know the story? Tehran thought they had their network air-gapped. But sooner or later even an air-gapped internet has to connect with the outside world. The Iranians needed to update the software that controlled the plumbing. The plumbing—kid you not. So these Israelis put the Stuxnet worm on the USB of one of the water maintenance guys who came in to do this. Simply walked right in with his clipboard. Just like you will. And Carlos is highly trained. Believe me, anyone who tries to mess with you will be in more danger than you are. You will be in and out of the landing station in less than ten minutes."

The Double was momentarily speechless. "If we get caught, it could start a war."

"The war has already started," said Ford impatiently. "That's why we need to hear what the Chinese are saying."

The Double tried to keep himself from panicking. He could not actually *go* to Bekwai with Carlos Rivera; it was out of the question. Not only was it not what Ford had agreed to, but it was unacceptably dangerous in itself. The Double could be recognized or caught on camera by the Chinese, who would realize that he was betraying them. He could be killed in the cross fire, if the mission went badly. Or he simply could be dispatched by Rivera. A bullet in the head by the side of the road, a shrug of the shoulders in the debrief to Ford.

In that moment the Double had a sudden insight, too late and too obvious: *Rivera* was the man who had killed David Ibrahim. He was Ford's assassin.

Cold dread settled like a weight in his stomach. Now that the Double considered it, the Americans' intentions were obvious. He hadn't managed to make himself indispensable to them at all. He had only delayed what they had been planning to do all along: extract what they needed and then remove him from the equation.

"Look," said Ford, as if reading his mind. He put a hand on the Double's shoulder. "If you're having second thoughts about any of this, you can stop. We can wrap this up, find you somewhere to lie low for a while. Maybe your company sends you on a long business trip—couple months in Mombasa, Addis Ababa. You keep your head down and come back like we never met."

"And my passport?"

Ford hung his head as though gravely troubled. "Yeahhh," he stretched out the word. "Unfortunately, I think if you bail now, it's not going to be enough for them to take that step for you. The powers that be."

"You said three weeks. You gave me your word."

"Three weeks *and* you get us inside the landing station."

"That's not fucking good enough!" the Double barked, trying to sound rough. But it was not convincing, and they both knew it. The swear word sounded false coming out of his mouth. His mother would have slapped him for it.

His words died out in the barren room. There was no hiding the truth: the Double had no leverage. Either he fled now, without the passport, and all his sacrifices were for nothing—or he went north with a man who would kill him the instant the utility of his knowledge was exceeded by the deadweight of his presence.

Looking sympathetic, Ford drummed his fingers on his belt. "If it were up to me, of course, you'd have the passport tonight. You've done so much for us already, really you have. You've sacrificed more than most Americans ever do for their country."

"Naturally," said the Double bitterly. "If it were up to you."

"You're *very close*. I promise you that. Very close to getting what you want. But we need results. I need to be able to go back to my people and tell them you're a good investment. Then it will be done. You'll get your passport." He laughed. "And you'll be able to tell me to fuck off just like any other American."

The silence stretched between them. The Double felt enervated, almost drugged. He knew this was the critical moment of his life—that he was supposed to be thinking hard, calculating, solving the engineering problem in front of him. But the circumstances overwhelmed him. He was sliding into fatalism.

"All right," the Double said. "I will go to Bekwai."

"Excellent." Ford looked at his watch. "The time is 2200 hours, Wednesday, November 20. Sometime soon, Carlos will meet you to go over the logistics of the plan. No need to look for a sign, he'll find you. Saturday, November 23, you will travel north—separately, as Carlos will explain. By Sunday morning, this will all be over. And then I promise you." He clapped the Double on the shoulder again. "Your US passport will be in your hands."

THE DOUBLE WALKED THE whole way home from Kaneshie. He felt sick, impotent, and angry—at himself most of all.

For trusting Ford's word—the man was a spy, he was paid to be dishonest! For letting himself believe that they would let him walk away from this with a passport in his hands. For the ignorance to think that he could ever satisfy America's relentless greed, its need to collect it all, control it all, know it all, and share none of it with anyone. Even the smartest ant could not trap a giant. That was precisely why he needed to become a citizen—so they could never dislodge him, even if they wanted to.

But it would never happen. He could hear them laughing at him—Ford and Rivera. Did they think he was a stupid animal, chasing shiny silver flashes of light, always just out of his reach? It was all so obvious at last. There was nothing to stop them from breaking their word again and again.

The Double lay down on his red satin bedsheet, miserable and afraid. He could not go to Bekwai: Rivera would kill him as soon as he had helped get the American inside the landing station. And he could not refuse to go to Bekwai: Ford would have the perfect excuse to back out of their agreement.

Problems pressed on him from all sides, and he was running out of time to solve them. Going to Bekwai was only one of them. The other problem was perhaps less immediately dangerous in the physical sense, but it threatened to unmask him totally—and thus in the end could prove just as fatal.

The Double's eyes drifted to the clock on the computer screen.

NOV 21 | 3:15 A.M.

He sat up abruptly. A solution had appeared that would solve his two problems at once. Like major and minor chords in a symphony, he could play them off each other. It was genius in its simplicity.

The Double was not going to go to Bekwai. He was not going to risk his life for a US passport that he must finally admit to himself he was unlikely to receive. Instead he was going to do what smart men did when circumstances changed on them: enable his enemies to destroy each other, and survive to fight another day.

And if people had to die so that Double could live—well, he had learned the hard way that in Ghana, personal feelings did not have the luxury of impeding political choices. Maybe for Americans they could. Maybe even for the Chinese. But not for a Ghanaian. To be included in the future, you had to pay your debts.

3:23 A.M.

The Double picked up his phone and scrolled to the number he was looking for.

But now his hands were shaking. What had he become, that he could even think this way? Could he really go through with it?

3:24.

"Eh te sen?" a voice answered.

"Wo ho te sen," the Double responded. "Listen, mate—keep this between us. I have a job for you."

FOURTEEN

Dani could not quite shake the memory of seeing James standing in her room. The sudden shock of it: unannounced, uninvited, in the place where she was meant to feel safe. A distaste for him lingered, a spark of real anger, smoldering like the last red ember beneath the ash.

If she nurtured that anger, leaned in its direction, she could feel herself starting to doubt her choices. Had she made the right decision by setting aside the story about the $7 million and James's political future? It was a hell of a get. Maybe it was too good to bury. Especially for someone who didn't respect her privacy.

But then she pushed the thought aside. She had given James her word. And for all his faults, James was a genuinely good person. It was evident in the way he had been kind to Yaaba even while fleeing the house in Takoradi after his father had beaten him; in the way he had gently escorted her home from Sandbox, when he had had no obligation to her. A kind and smart kid. Clearly tormented by the circumstances other people had placed him in. A little pompous perhaps—but she'd seen worse.

She went back to the library and spent several hours with Ben's data. She wrote up dozens of fresh note cards, moving them around on the desk. As she did so she felt the recognizable hum of well-being that came from living in a story, the moral clarity of being oriented towards a defined purpose.

Jushu Marine controlled only a small proportion of the four hundred active submarine cables and the nearly fourteen hundred landing stations that carried 95 percent of the world's internet traffic. But it was still one of the biggest submarine cable companies in the world. Although the US had banned Jushu technology, many of the cables it built touched US allies, including Britain, Canada, and France. Which meant US data was going to travel through Jushu-built cables whether Washington liked it or not.

The maps she found online bore these facts out. Mankind had added a new geologic feature to the surface of the world. Veins. They snaked between New York and London, made a web in the Caribbean, looped down around Brazil's bulge, bent around Argentina and Chile, and shot cleanly up along the Pacific coast to LA, San Francisco, Seattle, Vancouver. But the thickest bands of all connected these cities to Asia. The knots where they ran together made it obvious where the great cities lay: Tokyo, Seoul, Shanghai, Hong Kong. There was a sinister beauty in the striations hugging the coastlines. It was startling to see the echo of the blobs James had sketched in her room. He hadn't been making it up. It was all here.

Each cable was about as thick as a garden hose. When they hit the continental shelf, they moved up the hill, eventually puncturing the crust of the earth itself and carrying the fiber-optic lines the rest of the way underground—surfacing, finally, on dry land, in a building called a landing station, which was filled with terminal equipment, from which new, different sets of fiber-optic cables sprouted inland, carrying data to computer terminals, televisions, phones.

Dani felt exhilarated. She might have set aside the $7 million—but here was a truth just as compelling. This story was related to the oil and the missing $7 million, but it was bigger than that. Broader. She had never imagined that the miraculous speed of modern technology lived in *physical* things. She had thought, vaguely, of satellites. Of signals bouncing from tower to tower. She had pictured red squiggly lightning arcing through the sky and down to each person's phone and laptop. She had not realized that the limitations were physical. The hardiness of the cables was extraordinary, but they were not impenetrable. They could be cut by ships' anchors or landslides, plunging whole countries into darkness. Sharks ate them. Google had started wrapping their cables in Kevlar to prevent that.

And if the limitations were physical, then the competition really wasn't so different from any of the things men and countries and companies had ever fought over. Gold. Oil. Data. The need was the same as always: to control the ground. To physically be in a certain place, and to prevent your opponents from being there too. Even if that place was on the bottom of the sea. Even if that place snaked around the entire world.

Halfway through the afternoon, a new message dropped into her email. It was from Isabelle.

The engagement party—of course she'd completely forgotten. As they had known she would.

SUBJ: Flights booked!!

The party is in two weeks. At the 21 Club in Manhattan. Don't be mad at me . . . but I booked your flights! BA437 Accra—London—New York. (I'm sorry about London, but it was the only stopover they have, and you'll only be in Heathrow for an hour or so.)

I know you don't want to come. But it would mean the world to me.

Please come, Dani. I love you.

Dani closed her computer and looked around. She felt suddenly impatient, annoyed. She should keep working. But she could not stay sitting there any longer. The walls of the library stared back at her. She drummed her hands on her knees, deliberating.

SOMEHOW SHE WAS NOT surprised to see Kofi at To God Be the Glory. They had never properly said farewell when she had gotten sick the other night at Sandbox. And she had felt, whenever the two of them were together with James, that there was something more Kofi wanted to say to her—another presence that lingered unspoken on the edge of the conversation.

"Good evening," he said, taking the seat next to her at the bar and shaking her hand formally.

"Hey dude," she said. After a beat she touched his shoulder in an attempt at warmth, but her hesitation was obvious to both of them. "Can I buy you a drink?"

"No, indeed, no thank you." Kofi's imposing physical presence was diminished when sitting. Perched on the edge of the stool, his back slightly rounded, his large shoulders hunched. It made him seem disarmingly timid. "Are you feeling better? James told me that you were taken ill, at Sandbox."

"Much better, yeah, thanks."

"I see." He sat there silently for a minute. Dani felt entirely uninterested in drawing him out. She had enough on her mind with James and Lu Zhong and a full day's worth of research swimming through her head. She was enjoying her cold beer. A beer that she'd earned. If Kofi wanted to unburden himself, which he obviously did, she was not going to beg.

"I wish to say something." He drew himself up.

She sipped her beer. "All right."

"You should leave Ghana."

"Excuse me?"

"You should not be writing the story that you are writing. Chasing facts about scenarios you do not comprehend." He lowered his voice. "And you should be careful about James."

Dani leaned back on her barstool, checking to see if anyone could overhear them. "Are you giving me a warning?" she said. "Or giving me an order?"

"I do not understand."

She set down her bottle of Star Beer. "You approach me, unprompted, and you tell me to back off. I'm trying to decide how to interpret that. Maybe you are giving me friendly advice, because there is something I'm not aware of that could put me at risk. Or maybe you just have a belief about what a woman like me should and should not be allowed to do, and you want me to know what it is." She narrowed her eyes, challenging him. "Which one is it?"

He frowned. He seemed to be seriously considering the question. "Not everything is about you, madam," he said finally. "You are now involved in something that is dangerous, it is true. But that is not why I say that you should leave Ghana. I say that you should leave because you should never have come."

"I'm here to try to help Ghana."

"Ghana does not need help. We do not ask for your help, and we never did." Kofi's expression clouded. "You see? A continent of 1.4 billion people does not need help. A society that is as old as the human species does not need advice."

"I'm not here to advise."

"What do we look like to you? A starving child in a television advert?"

"Oh, come *on*."

Kofi's lip curled, a nastiness puncturing his polite veneer for the first time. "Friendship that is not freely given is not true friendship. It is just another kind of control." He was glaring at her. She recognized the look that Kwesi Adjepong had shot across the table at her, when she had interviewed him at the beach two weeks ago, when she had first stumbled on the missing $7 million. Kwesi Adjepong had hated her then too.

For the first time Dani considered the possibility that Kofi might become violent with her. She would not stand a chance if he did. They were surrounded by other people now, but what if he followed her home? What if James had told his friend where Dani lived?

She spoke slowly, picking her way around each word. "So why should I be careful about James?"

"His mother is very sick, you know. Blood cancer. They say she will not live out the year. She is a noble lady, a God-fearing lady. It is very unfortunate."

"And that's why I should be careful around him?"

Kofi pushed the stool back and stood up, unhunching his shoulders and unrounding his back, until he loomed over her in his full striking presence. "I have said what I have come to say," he intoned. "You should not have come to Ghana in the first place. You are here for the wrong reasons. You should go home."

"I don't have a home."

He held her gaze for a moment, an unreadable expression on his face. He and James were so unlike one another. The silent, imposing purist, and the boisterous, indecisive softie. Of the two of them she knew which one she trusted, which one she could place her faith upon. Maybe Kofi was simply jealous of him.

Still, as she watched him stride away through the laughing customers, she felt uneasy. Had Kofi been so disgusted with her all along? What else was she missing? What else was she not seeing?

LATER, SHE WOULD TELL herself she should have just been patient. Everything might have been different.

But she was a reporter, and the story was out there. Not in the library with its charts and maps, its shushing librarians. Not in her dingy guest room with its soiled sheets and its room-temperature whiskey. And not at the bar at To God Be the Glory, watching the acrobats come around for tips every night. The truth would not be given to her on a plate. She had to hunt it out and rip it up by the root.

And she couldn't get Kofi out of her mind. Not just what he had said, but the look of hatred on his face as he'd said it. She had told James that she would not write about the seven-million-dollar scheme. But that did not mean she had to take everything he said on faith. There was something more at play here—perhaps something that not even James could see. She could still feel the facts giving way beneath her hands. Something about Kofi's enigmatic warning. Something about James's face when he had broken into her room. He had followed her, after all. It was only fair.

That was why Dani found herself slouched in the back seat of a taxi, watching through the windshield as office workers emerged from the Vodafone Ghana building at the end of the workday.

"There," she said, when she saw James getting into his Highlander. "Follow that car."

The taxi driver seemed to enjoy the novelty of the task, speeding around other cars to stay close, once almost hitting the back bumper of the Highlander, causing Dani to slouch down low to avoid being seen.

Eventually James pulled over and parked off the main road leading to Madina Market. Fifty meters back, the cab pulled over, too, and Dani got out. But her driver demanded a better tip, and in the thirty seconds she spent arguing she lost the trail.

Cursing, she jogged across the road and into the market. Food stalls, catcalls, liquid splashed against her foot. Smoke gusts, dried fish, slabs of meat buzzing with flies. She walked down the aisles looking for him. James was big but not tall. His shape was less distinctive in a crowd. She wished the back of his head were more remarkable.

There. The dark-navy suit jacket stretched over his round shoulders. Dani watched as he disappeared through the door of a squat building daubed with a drawing of a computer and the words "Jericho Internet Café."

She paused at a stall of soccer jerseys and immediately attracted a team of attendants. What shirt, what shirt you like, obruni? She tried to talk to them with one half of her attention, while keeping the other half pinned to the entrance of Jericho Café. After five minutes, most of the shopkeepers melted away, bored, except for one—the stall's actual owner—who touched every article Dani did, looking at her questioningly.

She went up the steps into the internet café. The stairs squealed loudly under her feet. The air was quiet and stuffy, and when she stepped into the room itself, she was hit with the sickly smell of overheating plastic.

A row of five computers. Three of them in use. There was a door behind the counter that was shut, but no sign of James anywhere.

"Hello," Dani said to the man at the cash register.

"Good afternoon." He was wearing a Liverpool soccer jersey. He didn't look up from the book he was reading.

"I'd like to use a computer."

"Five hundred cedis ten minutes."

Not knowing what else to do, Dani took a seat at one of the machines, next to a teenage boy playing a computer game.

"That one is broken," said the man. "Use the other one."

Dani switched seats, irritated. Why hadn't he said so in the first place? She logged on, dialed up. She clicked *History*. It was blank. Of course it would be.

She did not know what she would say when James confronted her about what she was doing. She had never followed anyone like this before. All she could offer was that she was doing her job.

Dani stood up. "I'm sorry to bother you," she said to the man at the counter. "My name's Rebecca Smith."

Again he did not look up. "My name is Kwabena."

"Eh te sen?" Dani was trying to catch his eye, to pass him some smile of complicity, of alliance. "Listen, Kwabena, I am writing an article about Ghana for an American magazine, and I would like to ask you a question."

Two seconds: suspicious, then flattered. "An American magazine?" He closed the book: *The Hitchhiker's Guide to the Galaxy*.

"The gentleman who came in here a few minutes ago. Do you know him?"

Kwabena rubbed his chin and said nothing.

"This gentleman." Dani pulled out her phone and showed him James's profile picture on WhatsApp. "He is my associate."

Kwabena peered at her phone. "I never seen this man," he said with a shrug. He opened his book again. "Your time is nearly finished. You must pay more if you want to stay. Five hundred cedis."

Dani's eyes rested on the door behind him. For a moment she bent over her backpack, as if she was going to pull out more cash. She couldn't tell whether Kwabena's apparent disinterest was genuine or not—but before he could stop her Dani had darted around behind him and yanked the door open. In a single motion she stepped through it and pulled it shut behind her, muffling Kwabena's cry of indignation behind a sudden seal of silence.

The room was empty of furniture, except for a big desk with two computer monitors on it. James was sitting with his back to her, typing furiously. In the instant before he turned around Dani tried to read what was on his screen: lines of computer code, a language she didn't speak—endless scroll of weird diacritic symbols and cascading indentations.

His head whipped up. "What are you doing?" In three quick strides he crossed the room to her. He grabbed her wrist and yanked her towards him, so close she could smell his sweat. "You followed me?"

"I wanted to help."

"You should not be in this place." He was hissing in a low voice, ribboned with panic. "It is very dangerous here."

"I'm not frightened."

"Dangerous for *me*, idiot. Come," he said, pulling on her. They left by another door, an exit she hadn't noticed. What was this place? A nondescript internet café, with rooms upon rooms?

Now they were flying down concrete steps, her arm in James's hand, she was sure they were both going to fall and break their knees. Now they were outside. Random thoughts raced through her mind. *I don't know this part of Accra. I should have told someone where I was going.*

"Come on!" They were pushing through the crowds of Madina Market. James turned a small boy out of his way with his foot—gently, like he was making a soccer pass. A momentary corridor opened in the tangle of people, and Dani locked eyes with an albino woman with a basket on her head. Then they were off the main road, moving away from the shouted din and honking horns. They were jogging down another back road of red earth, quiet with the stunning heat of late afternoon. She was clutching her notebook, as if it were something that could help her. The yellow wall of a building said: *God Lives.* They were ducking through a narrow lane. Then suddenly, impossibly, they popped out and were standing right in front of James's Highlander.

"Get in," he grunted.

"Where are you taking me?"

"Somewhere safe."

"Safe from what?"

He drove fast. They roared through traffic, roundabouts. A motorcade of SUVs surged past in the other direction, some flag she didn't know flapping on their antennae. Official vehicles. She almost rolled down her window. Official vehicles were for people like her, to get her out of danger like this.

"Burkina Faso," James said, as if reading her mind. "In town for the ECOWAS Summit."

"What was that place, James?" Dani said. She was trying to steady herself, to regain the initiative. "What were those computers for?"

He shifted gears violently. "Not yet."

She concentrated on tracking the landmarks as they drove, the details of the streets flicking past her, the colors of the houses, the gas station signs. They left the highway and entered a quiet neighborhood she had never seen before.

Then, at last, they stopped.

They were parked in front of a nondescript home. It was cinder block, unpainted, on a street of buildings that were also cinder block and unpainted. But it was the only one with its blinds drawn. The Highlander pinged softly with the door-open signal.

"Quickly," James said. "Before you're seen. They don't get a lot of obruni around here."

"Where are we?"

He waited until they were inside to answer. "We are in Ashaiman in Tema," he said, deadbolting the door. "To be specific, we are on Kofi Portuphy street near the Pentecostal church."

Dani looked around. There was duct tape over the electrical outlets in the wall. A cardboard box on the floor was full of outdated 2016 phone books stamped VODAFONE GHANA. She sat down on one of them and started to scribble notes: the name of the street and the neighborhood where they were hiding. The color of James's suit. The name of the man at the counter in the Jericho Internet Café. Kwabena. Last name? She didn't know. Hadn't asked. Didn't matter. She'd go back tomorrow and find out.

Now that they were indoors, James moved more slowly. But she could still see the anger and the fear coursing through his whole body. His hands were shaking. He pulled a handkerchief from his back pocket and wiped the sweat from his face.

"And so?" he said. "You thought you could follow me."

Dani set her face. "I thought you might be in danger."

"Ah! Please do not insult me. You care only about one thing in Ghana, and that is your story."

"James," she said sternly. "Tell me what is going on."

Suddenly he was crying. It was a shock, to see the young man's face dissolve into a boy's grief. Without thinking she put her hand on his back.

"James, what is happening?"

He shook his head, shoulders softly shaking. "No."

"Let me help you," she said.

"You don't care about me."

"Of course I care. I have nothing else. No one else."

Hearing herself say it, she realized how true it was.

James looked up at her in cautious surprise. Dani squeezed his shoulder.

He wiped his eyes and swallowed. "Don't write this down."

"THE COMPUTERS THAT YOU saw," James began. "Are connected to my work with the man you know as Lu Zhong."

Her hands itched towards her notebook, but she kept them still.

"Do you remember what I told you the other night about the internet? About the fiber-optic cables and how they work? The Chinese are building a new landing station in Ghana. It will be the biggest one they have yet built in West Africa. It is in a village called Bekwai, near the city of Kumasi. They are partnering with Vodafone Ghana to build it." He swallowed. "And I am the engineer in charge of the project."

"Okay," said Dani slowly. "But what does it have to do with Lu Zhong?"

"Jushu Marine—it's a real company, but it's not. Dongsha Limited—it's a real company, but it's not. Do you understand? Lu Zhong, he is a real employee, but he is not." James paused. "He is more accurately called a spy. A Chinese intelligence officer."

Dani felt calm, focused, alert. "Okay," she said. "A Chinese spy."

"Yes."

"And this is the man your father introduced you to. To run the seven-million-dollar campaign and get you elected. A Chinese spy."

"You are thinking about this too much like an American. In China, the state and private enterprise are the same thing. It's like. . . ." He thrust his palms together, as if in prayer. "So the spies come embedded with companies doing business here. Lu Zhong is like that. There are Chinese spies all over Ghana, but they're not normal spies. They're employees of private companies."

In the road outside the window, a car or a truck sputtered by. It made them both jump. They turned, in tandem, and listened to its engine fade into the distance.

"So what is Lu Zhong's job in Ghana?" Dani said.

James sighed. "The Chinese are building their own landing station, like I said, in Bekwai. It is to be their most secure communications hub in Ghana, for all their diplomatic and military assets across West Africa to talk to one another. And why? Because they do not trust the Western telecom operators. They do not trust the Americans. They are afraid the US will tap the routers of the other operators. Probably they're right. The only real way to protect yourself from that happening is to physically secure the building where your server rack is located. That's why the landing stations are the real prize. The cables, the wires—they are the highway. But the landing stations tell you where the traffic is going."

"So is that what Jericho Café is? A landing station?"

"No, no." He laughed. "You can't hide a landing station in a place like that. They are massive buildings full of server racks. Noisy, because of the cooling systems that keep the servers from overheating. They're often built in cold climates for that reason. The staff sits there in winter coats. Jericho Café is just a safe place for me to work. Looks like nothing from the outside, but its internet connection is secure and powerful. Most importantly, it is not my home or my office."

"What was in the computer code that you were writing?"

"You wouldn't understand." He waved his hand. "Not without an engineering background. All you need to know is that I am helping Lu Zhong—by which I mean, I am helping China—ensure the Americans are not able to break into the new landing station that Jushu is building in Bekwai. I am helping him keep that network secure."

She stood up, paced to the window. Between the blinds she could see a strip of the yard: scrub grass, thatch yellow. She had a million more questions. She needed her notebook, cash in hand, a visa extension. She needed to call her old editor at *The Guardian.* She felt it again—the hunger to know. The familiar urge, like a drug addict's fix. Curiosity, curiosity, curiosity.

"I don't get it," Dani said. "Why are the Chinese so obsessed with keeping their network secure? Why are the Americans so obsessed with getting inside?"

"If the Americans control the world's internet with back doors—which they have done until the last decade or so, when Jushu came on the scene—they can deploy those back doors at any time. It would be like letting your enemies build your bridges and hide sticks of dynamite in them. Would you drive over them every day, hoping they're in a good mood about you?" He exhaled. "And, naturally, the Americans ask the same about the Chinese. You don't let your enemy build your pipes. You keep them out of yours with your left hand, and try to get inside theirs with your right."

"So you're helping the Chinese spy on the US."

"Yes."

"With Lu Zhong."

"Yes."

"It's not just that Lu Zhong is helping *you.* It's that you are helping him."

"Well. That is the problem."

"What is?"

James's voice had a flat, resigned quality. "Lu Zhong is not happy with me. He wants me to do something that I cannot do. That I refuse to do."

Dani waited for a moment. "What is it?" When James hesitated she threw up her hands. "Oh come on. It's a little late now to wonder if you can trust me."

He took a deep breath. "Lu believes there is an American in Ghana. An assassin. Who has been sent here to kill Africans who work with the Chinese."

"An *assassin*?"

"A few weeks ago a Nigerian man named David Ibrahim was murdered, hacked to death inside his car. He worked closely with Lu and with Dongsha. If he really was killed by the Americans, others like me could be at risk. And more importantly for Lu, their landing station could be compromised. So Lu wants me to find the American who killed David Ibrahim. Use my official position at Vodafone to hack into the Americans' systems and find the assassin, before he can threaten Lu's plans any further."

Dani sat still for a minute, absorbing all of this. It felt unnatural not to be taking notes. "Why can't you do it?"

He hung his head. "First of all, because there is no guarantee I would succeed. Why should I be able to find the assassin when China's own intelligence service cannot? Second, because it would violate every principle of professionalism. It would make me not an associate of Lu's but his slave." He laughed bitterly. "But above all, it is too dangerous. Far too dangerous. It is one thing to partner with a Chinese spy to advance my political career. It is another to fight against actual murderers."

"But you are the seven-million-dollar man. Surely Lu has too much invested in you to put you in physical danger."

"I am a Ghanaian," James said simply. "There are many others for Lu to choose from, if I fail to meet his needs. Indeed, he has threatened to withdraw his protection and assistance if I do not comply. Threatened to blow up the whole seven-million-dollar plan. Lu is pressing me, my father is pressing me, my God—you would not believe how my father rages and storms."

She could picture it. "I'm so sorry, James."

The silence between them stretched and grew. Dani realized with a start that it was getting dark in the room. It was already evening.

"Now I will take you back to your hotel," James said heavily. "We will say farewell. And you will be on the first flight back to London tomorrow. We won't speak again. And this is my gift to you, Dani. Your life."

Dani's heart thrummed like a car engine. But it was not out of fear. It was because a decision was rapidly appearing in front of her. She could not straddle this fence anymore. She could not both care about the world and leave it to its fate. James could not be both her source and her friend. She could not be neither Aztec nor Cortés. For better or worse, she needed to choose a side. To stake a claim.

"And if I say I'm not afraid?"

She had tripped from one life into another—without meaning to, without deciding to. She had reentered the world of violence that she thought she had left behind after Beirut. And she was in danger now. The proximity of death was electric. Almost erotic.

Dani had never trusted herself more. All her life she had been the beneficiary of privileges she had done nothing to deserve. There was only one way to repay that debt: to put her neck on the line. To come off the fence. To finally leave the sidelines. To be in danger, like everyone else was in danger, all the time. To stand with the Aztecs and tell Cortés to go fuck himself. Even if her whole life had taught her that Cortés always won.

When she looked up, James was staring at her.

Sometimes we hear ourselves speak as if listening to a stranger; sometimes we are double and triple within ourselves.

But this was not one of those times. Pay for the fucking cups.

"Take me to Lu Zhong," she said.

FIFTEEN

Ford was correct: the Double did not need to go looking for Carlos Rivera. He was sitting in the kitchen of the Double's apartment in the dark when the Double came back from work on Friday evening.

"Rivera," said the Double softly in greeting. Pleased at how unfrightened his own voice sounded, even though his hands shook a little. Ford was obviously the superior officer, but even he had seemed a little intimidated by the man standing behind him in the shadows.

But the Double knew something Rivera didn't—which was that he was going to send this man to his death. The asymmetry of information rebalanced the power.

"Evening." Rivera's tone was short, almost bored. "Ford told you to expect me."

"Yes."

The Double flicked on the light. Rivera stood up, not looking at him. And then he did something unexpected. He opened the Double's refrigerator and peered into it.

"I'm thirsty," he said. "Do you mind?"

The Double swallowed. "Help yourself."

Rivera pulled out two Coke bottles. Handed one to the Double, opened the second for himself. Audibly exhaled after his first sip. The Double had to credit him. He gave every appearance of bearing his existence lightly. As if they were friends meeting for dinner, not coconspirators in acts of war between superpowers.

"I love Coca-Cola," the Double said, playing along for the moment. "When I was a child, my favorite restaurant was a place called Bocadillos. They served Western food. We used to go there after school for a treat. Of course, you know, we say it with an *l* (el) sound, in Ghana. *Dill*-os. Not *dee*-yos, the correct Spanish pronunciation. I would go to Bocadillos after school and order a Coca-Cola and fantasize about America. We all did, every Ghanaian. I do not understand why your country has retreated. Turkey is coming to us. India is coming to us. China and Japan, Russia, Indonesia. But not the US. You are disappearing over the horizon."

Rivera grunted. "We're here," he said. "Ford and me."

"You are two men," said the Double. "China is bringing thousands."

"I wouldn't count us out. History shows that's not a smart bet." Rivera's wide eyes fixed hard upon the Double. Liquid and alive, tracking him like a python. Abruptly he got to his feet, and in spite of himself the Double flinched slightly. From his back pocket Rivera withdrew a paper map, which he unfolded on the table. "We will travel separately to Kumasi," he said, pointing. "Make up some reason you need to be there. I will meet you at 2300 hours tomorrow, Saturday night, in the parking lot of the Lancaster Hotel, which will be our home base. Until I approach you in that parking lot, *you do not know me.* When I pull up, you get in the car and shut the door. I'll drive. Once we get to Bekwai, we will enter the landing station by cutting the fence and slipping through the gap. Your role will be to show me what the server racks look like once we are inside, and if necessary to run interference with anyone we encounter."

"Run interference? What does that mean?"

"Make up an excuse for who we are and what we're doing. Speak Twi. Stall." Rivera held his gaze for a moment. His eyes became still. "I'll place the taps in the racks. We'll be in and out in under ten minutes."

The Double regarded the map on the table, his hands on his chin. It was a simple plan. It could even work. But the risk to himself was as obvious as it had been the other night in Kaneshie. As soon as they were finished, all the Double's leverage would disappear in an instant, and Rivera would be free to eliminate him. Did they think he was so stupid? So desperate?

"You can't really believe this is the right thing to do," he said now. "You're going to storm the landing station with nobody but an untrained civilian to help you? It puts me in unacceptable danger. It puts *you* in unacceptable danger."

For a moment Rivera's eyes went blank, like a shade had been pulled down over them.

"I don't make the rules," he said. His voice was gravelly, and he seemed to be pulling himself with some effort out of the momentary trance he had fallen into. "Neither do you. Neither does Ford. You think anyone in Washington or Beijing gives a shit about any of us? There are always more Fords and Carloses to be found." The Double was surprised at the bitterness in his voice. "We get our orders, we execute them. If we decide we don't feel like it, or we falter, then we cease being useful to them. And then—" Rivera made a gun with his fingers and pointed it at his own forehead.

The Double stared at him. He had never heard someone articulate his own dilemma so precisely before. For the briefest moment he sensed that in another life, he and Rivera could have been friends. Comrades, at the very least. They had more in common than either of them shared with the leaders of their own countries.

But not in this life. In this life, it was Friday evening, November 22, and the symphony was about to begin. The audience was seated. The lights were dimmed.

THE SOLUTION HE HAD hit upon was this. The Double was going to tip off the Chinese that the Americans were going to move on the landing station on the evening of November 23. He was going to make sure they knew when and where Carlos Rivera would be there. And he was going to have Carlos Rivera killed. One enemy would confront another; one problem would eliminate the other. And the Double would be left standing to fight another day, with Ford even more reliant on him than before. It was elegant; it was clean.

Except for one thing.

The success of the plan depended on speed: it was only now, with less than twenty-four hours to go, that the Double possessed the information on Carlos Rivera's whereabouts that he needed. The plan therefore contained a dilemma: how to get this information into his Chinese handler's hands immediately, in a manner sufficiently compelling for the Chinese to act on it, without them knowing who it had come from. An anonymous letter would take too long to reach its audience, and the Chinese would have no reason to trust its veracity. Anonymous phone calls could be traced, even from a burner phone. He couldn't write the information on a rock and chuck it through his handler's window.

What the Double needed was a cutout. A courier. Someone to whom he could give the information, who could then deliver it directly to his Chinese handler and get away without being detained.

And that was where all the Double's bravado turned to confusion.

Because he would need to eliminate this cutout after the job was done.

There was no other conclusion. If the Double allowed the cutout to live, the Chinese would eventually find the cutout and connect the information to himself, and they would know that the Double had been working for the Americans. While the cutout lived, the Double would be in just as much danger as he was now. Killing a human being was not something he had ever believed himself capable of. But there was no one who could do it for him—paying someone to kill the first cutout would simply create another, and so on: an exponential function.

He had bought a gun. Holding it in his hands in his room, he felt clammy, sick. He felt absurd. But the clock in the corner of his computer screen did not lie. His dilemma had not changed. Rivera would kill him if he went to Bekwai. He needed to get the Chinese moving against Rivera *now.* Getting them moving required a cutout. Using a cutout required eliminating the cutout. The conclusion was brutal, but the logic was undeniable. If the Double wanted to live, this was what he must do.

There was no other way out.

THE CUTOUT HE HAD chosen was a man he knew who was always looking for ways to make a little extra cash.

The Double had typed out a message, addressed to his Chinese handler by name, containing the details of Carlos Rivera's operation in Bekwai, including the hotel he would be staying in and the details of his movements, and sealed it in an unmarked manila envelope. He had promised the man 10,000 cedis for delivering this envelope to the home of the handler and getting away cleanly. Five thousand cedis in advance, the rest when the job was complete.

His Chinese handler would of course want to know how somebody knew the details of an American spy operation. But the Double's bet was that the handler would not know which of his many grains of sand to suspect, and that the time-sensitive nature of the information—the operation in Bekwai was scheduled to begin in less than twenty-four hours—would force the Chinese to scramble to intercept the threat and neutralize Carlos Rivera without asking too many questions about where the tip-off had come from. Those questions would come later—by which time the Double would have ensured that the path had gone cold.

The cutout appeared at exactly 9:30 P.M.

The Double handed him the envelope. "Remember," he said. "*Absolute* secrecy."

The man nodded gravely. He pocketed the envelope and the first 5,000 cedis and got on his moped. As soon as it turned the corner and vanished the Double got in his car. He drove quickly, knowing that the man would be whizzing down backstreets and blind alleys. They had arranged to meet for the second 5,000 cedis not at the Double's home but in a parking garage on the other side of town.

When he got to the garage the Double pulled over and cut the engine. He picked up the paper bag in the passenger seat and took out the gun. Its weight was unfamiliar in his hands.

He checked his watch. Fifteen minutes had elapsed. Sudden nausea overwhelmed him and he gagged, opening the car door to let in the night air.

Right on schedule, the single headlight of a moped appeared at the end of the road.

The Double steeled himself. He tried to take comfort in the fact that there was no going back. The symphony was in motion. The music was playing. He could not stop it from unfolding even if he wanted to.

The moped's engine sputtered as it slowed, looking for him.

"Eh!" he hissed into the shadows. "Is it you?"

"Eh yeh."

"Is it done?"

The cutout puffed his chest. "Yes man. Gave them the message. They asked who I was but I didn't say nothing. They started to try to grab me but I drove away." He snapped his fingers, smiling broadly. "Absolute secrecy man, yeah, yeah." He laughed.

"Oh!" The Double suddenly pointed at the featureless night sky behind him. "Look at that!"

The man turned around. The Double raised the gun.

But he could not do it.

"Oh?" The man turned back to face the Double, and in a startled moment threw his hands up in front of his face to protect himself. “Fuck wa bo dam!” he shouted, grabbing at the Double’s gun, pulling it towards himself, twisting the Double’s arm away. The Double was going to lose his grip, the cutout was going to take it from him, the cutout was going to kill—

A single shot spun the man away and crumpled him to the ground.

For a moment the Double stood there. He heard the cutout’s wet grunts: nonwords, gasps. He saw only his back.

Somewhere nearby, a dog began to bark.

Dark blood pooled onto the ground beneath the cutout’s torso, spreading quickly. To the Double’s horror, he was struggling to raise himself to his feet.

He was still alive.

The dog’s barking grew louder. Now a light came on in a building at the end of the road.

The Double took two steps forward and shot the man in the head.

SIXTEEN

Another sleepless night.

Billy had met with the Double and provided detailed instructions on the mission, just as Ford had ordered him to. Now he was back in his apartment, staring at the wall.

The clock was ticking down to game time, and he needed to rest. He tried to regulate his nervous system with the breathing exercises his shrink had taught him. The agency had a full staff of psychiatrists on the payroll, who were responsible for medically clearing them for service, and making them as normal as possible when they came back.

In for four. Hold for four. Out for eight.

In for four. Hold for four. Out for eight.

Nope.

Still here.

Turned out, it wasn't just the honeypot risk that made getting involved with women in the field a bad idea. It was the way they made you too stupid, too happy. Made you question and doubt yourself. Wormed into every other thought.

He remembered Dani Moreau's naked body beneath his. He remembered the smell of her neck where her hair met her skin. And the way she had cried—cried like he had never seen anyone cry before. They were tears that didn't involve him, or anything he knew about. They were a glimpse of something older and bigger and more powerful than even the United States, than even China.

But at other times, his thoughts curdled into anger. "These goons are all the same," she had said, tossing back her Star Beer. She had meant people like him, although she didn't know it. She meant the soldiers and NYPD cops who had protected her all her life. Who she could always walk up to and ask for help, and who always would help her, because that was their job. Men who didn't have the luxury of agonizing over their personal and political views before deciding what course of action to take. Men who saw a world filled with threats, so that people like her could see a world that was safe. If Dani had known who he really was she would have spit on him, not fucked him.

He turned on the light, picked up his book and tried to read. The novel was *Kim,* by Rudyard Kipling. On Billy's first tour in Kandahar his sergeant had constantly quoted Kipling's poem to them:

When you're wounded and left on Afghanistan's plains,
And the women come out to cut up what remains,
Jest roll to your rifle and blow out your brains
And go to your Gawd like a soldier.

Billy had loved the deadpan joke of it all. So when he had gone home on leave, he had ordered a used copy of Kipling's complete poems and taken it with him on his second and third tours. He knew he was supposed to think "The White Man's Burden" was terrible, but damn if its lines hadn't come back to him when they were clearing a village of Taliban sympathizers:

Take up the White Man's burden—
Send forth the best ye breed—
Go bind your sons to exile
To serve your captives' need;

He respected Kipling for just coming out and *saying it.* That was more than most Americans did. And the fact that Kipling's poems were about troops like him. Poor British bastards—fighting the exact same people in the exact same country, two centuries earlier. The world had changed completely in two hundred years: imagine trying to explain 9/11 to those boys. But it also hadn't changed at all.

"These goons are all the same," Dani had said. "Maybe everybody else would get along just fine." She had said it with confidence, it had rolled off her tongue easily. The rich kids she had gone to school with would surely have approved. But Billy felt certain that that was a more impoverished way to go through life than people like Kipling's soldiers did, people like his father, like his buddies in the Army, like him—people for whom it did matter, actually, where you came from. For the people with money and passports, the world was just a bunch of airports you glided through on your way to an Uber to take you to some fancy restaurant, where the menu and table settings and art on the wall will look the same as the ones in the city you've just left behind. For the rest of us out here in the sticks, a nation is our neighbors. Our parents. Our cousins. And guess what? Most of the time, those people happen to look like us.

Billy blinked. Falling, then steady. Like turbulence in a plane.

He tossed *Kim* aside. Not nearly as good as Kipling's poetry. The language was heavy and dry, a mouth stuffed with cotton. Whereas the poetry zipped and swerved—you could practically sing it.

Maybe that's what Billy was really meant to be: a poet.

He smiled softly. What a waste of the millions of dollars the United States had spent training him. He couldn't imagine what his father would say.

His mother might approve, though. All his life, Mariam had encouraged him to read more.

Dani reminded him a little of her, actually. Same sad dark eyes.

Billy sighed and, without warning, dropped off to sleep.

SEVENTEEN

Lu Zhong. In all those long hours of research she had never been able to find a picture of him.

The chairman of Dongsha, the general partner of Red Wing Capital, the chairman of Paragon. The man who Beijing trusted to move millions of dollars through the Ghanaian government, to sponsor politicians and run influence campaigns aimed at capturing the country's future leaders for China. The man who, if James was to be believed, oversaw a counterintelligence operation against the United States—keeping America out of China's telecom networks with one hand while inserting China into America's networks with the other.

In person he was disappointing. He lived in an unassuming house in a middle-class neighborhood in the center of Accra, much like the street where she had first met James and Kofi. A small, thin man, wearing thick, round glasses and a collared shirt that was slightly dirty, the neckline and shoulders ringed with the faint brown watermarks of yesterday's sweat.

A TV was going on in the background, playing CNN.

"Why are you here?" Lu said.

"Mr. Lu—" Dani began.

"Not you." He looked at James, ignoring Dani. "You brought an American journalist into my home. Today, of all days."

James licked his lips nervously. "Because I thought she might become an asset to us. And as you see, here she is."

Lu turned his head sharply to look at her, then swiveled back to James. "You blew your cover to an American journalist. And then you let her walk around freely, going where she wanted, meeting who she wanted, speaking on the phone to whoever she wanted. Placing calls to London. Receiving large files via email from London. And what could be in those files?" He swiveled his head back towards Dani and laughed, which became a smoker's cough.

"Mr. Lu," said Dani. "James is not to blame for my sneaking around. I followed him against his will."

"And you let her?"

"No sir," James said firmly. "When I caught her following me, I told her that I would shoot her dead. Indeed, even this very moment, if you order me to kill her I will do it. But when she volunteered her services, I thought that you would want to hear this offer."

James had warned her that he was going to have to be rough with her. He was inhabiting his role very convincingly, but his voice slid registers like it was slipping on ice: *hear this offer* came out very Ghanaian, *shoot her dead* very Texan. She had no way of receiving signals from him, nor he from her. They were in it now. They were comrades and there was no going back.

Dani tapped the pack of cigarettes on the table. "May I?" Without waiting for an answer, she withdrew one and held it out for Lu to light.

She was trying to test Lu Zhong early—just as she sensed that he was trying to test her. Because a part of Dani was convinced that they had more leverage than James thought. She didn't buy James's dejected contention that he was "just another Ghanaian" and that Lu viewed him as disposable. James had assets Lu could not overlook. He was a Ghanaian princeling, with a media-savvy father. He had technical expertise in the communications infrastructure that China was trying to protect. And he had Dani on his side—an American journalist with, yes, a little bit of profile herself. The truth was James was *not* just another Ghanaian, and Lu could not simply dispatch either of them like they were anonymous. She was determined not to start from a place of weakness or let Lu think that she was frightened of him. If the chairman of Dongsha was really capable of putting either James or her in danger, she was going to make him prove it.

Lu leaned over and took the cigarette from her mouth and threw it to the ground, calling out something in Twi. The man who had answered the door, a broad-shouldered bodyguard with a mean-looking face, came into the room and stood behind James.

"Leave us now, my James," Lu said.

Dani tried to sustain her confident tone. "James should be here," she began. "We have discussed—" But Lu stayed her with a single uplifted finger. The silence was filled only by the background noise of the television.

"Leave us, James," Lu repeated.

For another moment James stayed absolutely still; then he stood up and shuffled out of the room behind the bodyguard.

Once they were alone, Lu took off his glasses and carefully wiped them on his shirt. "Maybe you can be great for me, Danielle

Moreau, from Manhattan. Maybe you can become a problem for me. How do I know?"

"You don't," said Dani.

He laughed and nodded, taking Dani's hand in his. She flinched, she couldn't help it. "Very well. So here is an arrangement. If you leave this place and go to the Americans and tell them, go to the house of Lu Zhong and find him there, and stop him in the name of America—if you do this, my James and all his family will be killed. My people will chop them and throw them in the sea. And then we shall kill you as well, if you are still in Ghana. We could try to kill your family, but ah, they are in America . . ." he sighed. "So you must not betray me, Danielle Moreau. You hold many lives in your hands. Okay? So, now that we know the terms of the arrangement, tell me again, Danielle Moreau," he squeezed her hand a little tighter, "why are you here?"

"I'm here because James is in danger."

"From whom?"

Be honest, James had prepped her. *Once we get inside and I put you in front of him, there is no point trying to hide the truth from him.*

Dani narrowed her eyes. "From you."

"What did he tell you?"

"You want him to do something that he cannot do."

Lu raised his eyebrows in a small gesture of surprise that she read as faintly mocking. "What thing?"

"I suppose I should start at the beginning." Dani took a deep breath. "Several weeks ago I uncovered the fact that Dongsha had overpaid for the oil parcel known as Parcel 42 by seven million dollars. Do you remember Parcel 42, Mr. Lu? And then I combed through the public records to identify you, Mr. Lu, as the chairman not just of Dongsha but also of a company called Red Wing—which, shortly after this overpayment occurred, coincidentally invested seven million dollars into a company called Paragon. James's company. When I confronted James about it, he told me about the plan for him to stand for election and to spend the seven million on his campaign. But I still wasn't satisfied. I followed him to the internet café where he does work on your projects. I tailed him as thoroughly as any foreign spy would." She could not keep a note of pride from her voice. "James was shocked and angry to see me there. I pressed him about what he was really doing. And when I confronted James about it, he told me the truth."

"Which is?"

"That although you are helping advance his political career, he also works for you—I mean, for your government. But that now you have asked him to do something he feels is too dangerous. And he does not know where to turn."

"So I say again: what thing? What does James tell you that I want him to do?"

Dani set her face. "Use his position at Vodafone to hack into the Americans' electronic communications. So that you can find the American assassin who killed David Ibrahim."

Lu seemed to consider her for a long time. "For his big mouth, I should have him killed, yes?"

"James revealed nothing to me of his own volition. I found out about everything myself."

"Then I should have *you* killed."

"I think that would be a waste of a valuable asset to you."

"Is that what you are? An asset? Hmm." For a moment Lu stared at her, arms folded across his chest. Then with a grunt he stood, his knee joints cracking. He walked past her into the kitchen and started pinching tea leaves between his fingers and dropping them into a porcelain pot. Dani listened as intently as she could for any sounds from elsewhere in the house, but there was only the murmur of CNN.

"Seven million dollars to launch James Aidoo's career is a good investment for China," Lu said conversationally. "It is a win-win, you know. Harmonious win-win cooperation. For Dongsha, for China, for Oscar Aidoo, for James Aidoo. You understand, yes? We are all on the same team. A cost-effective way to bring friendly politicians into the future with us."

Dani felt her hand clutch at a nonexistent pen, like a phantom limb. She was shocked to hear him speaking about corruption so casually, so directly. But she was not sure how to read what he was saying. Was he speaking to Dani as an ally? Was it trust in his voice, or disdain? Were they complicit together, or was his thuggish bodyguard in the next room, James dead at his feet, waiting for a signal from his boss to come back and finish Dani off as well?

"Where is James?" she said. "Can he come back and join us?"

"Ah," said Lu dismissively.

The smell of the boiling leaves filled the kitchen. From time to time, Lu's mobile phone, which lay face up on the kitchen counter, buzzed with a new notification. He did not bother to hide it from her. Texts in Chinese characters, and sometimes English ones. Notifications from apps she did not recognize. Other than the TV, the house was bare. No family photos, no books.

Before her she saw two Lu Zhongs. She saw a VP at Dongsha, a mid-level executive at a foreign-registered shipping firm, far from home, fluent in the local language, working diligently on behalf of his firm and his country—a vital channel of the foreign direct investment that was growing Ghana's economy. And she saw a spy for Beijing, who casually directed clandestine political corruption operations, and who threatened to kill his Ghanaian sources without blinking.

"Yes," Lu said, as if a noiseless timer had gone off. He picked up the porcelain teapot and poured out two cups—one for him and one for Dani. He raised his own to his lips and sighed with satisfaction. "The problem is when our investment becomes difficult to manage. Then it is not so cost effective anymore. This is where James has become a disappointment to me. I ask him to do something, and he does not do it. Complaining, making trouble, bringing you here. Complications," he sighed. "Very disappointing." Lu laughed again, coughing. "This seems to me like an investment I should sell. Like an asset that is junk. You understand, yes?"

"Hurting James won't help you achieve any of your goals."

Lu blew on his tea, then sipped it. His eyes closed slowly. He seemed to be deep in thought.

Dani waited.

Eventually the man appeared to come to a decision. He cleared his throat and sat up a little straighter. "It is auspicious that you have come today. We think the Americans have developed a source in the upper levels of the Ghanaian government," he said softly, eyes still closed. "For the last few months, they have been a step in front of us. Starting with this David Ibrahim incident."

"You think the Americans did it?"

"Oh yes." Slowly he opened his eyes again. "The killing was clearly the work of a professional, made to look like a crime of passion. Very violent." Wreathed in cigarette smoke, he was like a philosopher. "Even James himself could be in danger. It seems they are picking off Africans who work with us. It is not at all *predictable.* David Ibrahim was important, but—why kill him? And so violently. It must be a message of some kind, but what kind?" Lu shook his head. He seemed to genuinely want her opinion, but Dani stayed still, not daring to interrupt. "The Americans are devious. Indeed, we strive diligently to learn from them. 韬光养晦. Do you know this idea? Deng Xiaoping said it. It means: *Hide your strength and bide your time.* So we learn from them. Americans are talented. It takes skill to look someone in the eye and lie to them, year after year. Not many people can do it."

"Why would the Americans choose to get more aggressive now?"

"We have recently constructed a new landing station, in a town called Bekwai, for the Jushu submarine internet cable that crosses into West Africa." Lu frowned. "All of which you know, it seems. What you do not know is how upset this is making the Americans. Because we will now control our own communications, with Jushu technology. We will not need to use theirs. And this, more than anything, is what frightens America. They will not be able to hear what we are saying. So we expect them to attempt to interfere with the construction in some way. Maybe they try to compromise the building. Gain access to it, so they can get inside our networks. They have tried this before, in other countries." He paused. "Or they could simply try to stop us by killing people. The landing station was what David Ibrahim was working on. And it is what my James is working on. *That* is why he must find the assassin. His own survival depends on it."

Your life; another person's life. They were right next to each other all along—without any guardrail to keep you from moving from one into the other. All you had to do was step sideways.

"I can do it," Dani said. "I'll be your spy, instead of James."

"You?"

"I will find the assassin for you."

Lu leaned back, frowning, his cigarette burned down almost to a nub against his lips. "Why?"

"Because James is my friend."

"Think carefully. For this, you would betray your country?"

"A nation is just a story that people believe. It's not China that I want to help, or the US or anybody else," she said simply. "It's James."

Lu coughed and stood up, wiping his hands on his shirtfront. He stood at the stove, refilling his teapot. His face twisted into a papery smile.

"Okay. It is an arrangement."

Dani blinked. Was that it? "So what are my orders? How do I stop the assassin?"

He laughed—a deep belly laugh. "No, you cannot stop them. More simple, more simple. For us, you are like a bright and shining fish. Where you swim, the sharks will show themselves."

"I don't understand."

Lu sat down beside her again and coughed, rocking from side to side on his hips. When he became still again he fixed her with a hard stare. "You must go north to Kumasi at once. The assassin is on his way there even now."

"Wait—" Dani cocked her head. "You *know* where the assassin is?"

"We think that we do. Yesterday evening, we were tipped off about his plans by a reliable source. Even as we sit here, my people are moving to intercept him. We are going to catch him."

Dani thought for a moment. "And what will I do in Kumasi?"

Suddenly he grabbed her forearm. She resisted the urge to pull away. "The problem with being obruni is that you cannot hide. No more than me. So when you arrive in Kumasi, you will continue to pretend to be a journalist. By the time you arrive, the assassin will be in our custody. You will ask questions about this American whom we have caught, to anyone who will listen. Your presence will complicate matters for the Americans. You have a great advantage. You are an American citizen. They cannot kill their own people, unless authorized by their president. Your family is wealthy, yes?" Dani realized that his grip was tightening. "They will not hurt you. You are the silver fish. Too pretty for the shark to eat. He only wants to watch you swim. And while the shark is busy watching, distracted by your beauty, we will catch him in our nets."

"You're hurting me." Dani tried to move her arm, but Lu squeezed tighter still.

"You will report to the Manhyia District Hospital in Kumasi no later than twenty-four hours from now—tomorrow morning, the twenty-fourth of November."

"A hospital? Why?"

"When you arrive you will be given specific instructions." He was crushing her hand with no obvious effort—some obscure science increasing the torsion, twisting her bones away from each other. "And if you fail to appear as scheduled, or if you run away, James Aidoo will be killed, Danielle Moreau. He will simply be killed."

Dani gasped from the pain. Just when she thought her wrist would break, Lu released her. He coughed into his fist. "What do you know about China?" he asked, as if nothing had happened. "Danielle Moreau from Manhattan?"

"Nothing," Dani admitted, trying to keep herself from rubbing her aching wrist. "I know nothing. I've never been there."

"You will go someday." Lu closed his eyes. "It is a magnificent country. Very big."

"That makes it magnificent?"

"Oh yes. It is much like the United States. China fills up the whole sky. Blocking out the sun with its size and its power. We have the coast with its cities. Inland, we have our mountains, our rivers, our farms. Mm, we have more in common, our two countries together, I think, than with our allies. And what allies are those? The United States has Britain, mm. China has Russia." He made a face. "We do not have an equal. Except each other." He closed his eyes. "I was born in Shenzhen. You know Shenzhen?"

"I know Dongsha is headquartered there."

Lu nodded. "When I was a boy, Shenzhen used to be a fishing village. The road from our house to the sea was a dirt track. My mother used to take me in the morning. We would walk down to where the fishermen brought the fish. When rains fell, you could not pass. Muddy." He wiped his hands on his thighs. "Nowadays, it is a global technology hub. So much money. So much construction. Xi Jinping says it is the Greater Bay Area—Shenzhen, Guangdong, Hong Kong, Macau. Filling the whole sky. Blocking out the sun. My mother is dead now." He exhaled. "I was sorry to hear about your son. In London."

"Excuse me?"

"Do not suppose there is anything we do not know about you. What was his name?"

Dani swallowed. "We did not name him."

"For myself, no children. No wife." Lu closed his eyes. "Sometimes I think it is very sad to be Lu Zhong. So far away from my country."

Dani hesitated for one last moment. "The US and China," she said. "It's like the world doesn't change at all."

"But it does change," said Lu softly. "Manhyia Hospital, tomorrow morning. Do not be late." He smiled. "Good luck, silver fish."

TEN MINUTES LATER, DANI was walking up the street, lost in thought in the quiet of the afternoon, when someone fell into step with her.

"You okay?" James said.

"Yes." There was so much to say she was having trouble forming the thoughts into sentences. "Are you?"

"I'm fine." His voice was ragged. He seemed weary, somehow defeated.

"That other guy didn't hurt you?"

"*Lower your voice.*" James gestured with his eyes. Following behind them, at the far end of the street, was Lu's thuggish bodyguard. "It will be safest for both of us, if we do not speak for a while," James said in a rushed whisper. "But first I must tell you some things—urgently. Will you meet me at Sandbox, in two hours? Safer in public. And the staff know me."

"Okay."

"Be very vigilant. Assume you are being watched, being followed, being listened to, at all times. Say nothing you would not want to be overheard." An SUV drove past them, axles bouncing along the ruts of the road, kicking up a cloud of dust that drifted past their faces. She coughed, turned her head away.

"Arrive at Sandbox at 5:00 P.M."

"I will."

"And Dani? Thank you."

"You don't—" She started to say that he didn't need to thank her. That she had nothing to live for, and he did.

But James was already disappearing into the crowd.

EIGHTEEN

BILLY SLEPT FOR A couple of hours and woke up midday Saturday feeling uneasy, his room filled with bright, flat sunlight.

He had prepared for the mission to Bekwai like any other. Study the map. Review the coordinates. Rehearse the plan: be quick, be clean, be gone.

But something wasn't right. Billy could feel it in his gut.

Exiting his apartment, he passed a Chinese face in the street. He kept walking, but he memorized the features. For a second he thought he saw Dani coming down the road towards him. But it wasn't her, it was a different white woman—Australian maybe, leading a group of evangelical Christians. Young, early twenties. Identical T-shirts and fat pale calves. They left a packet of booklets at a bus stop. He picked one up. "*What is happening to me?*" the cover said, above a picture of two scared and confused-looking Black teenagers. It was a book about puberty; it told them not to masturbate or they would go to hell.

Billy threw the whole stack in the trash.

His gear was packed and ready to go. The vampire taps themselves were small, little plastic things you wouldn't look twice at. Besides that, he had a transistor radio, to monitor the frequencies that the Double had told them the Chinese used. He had a bowie knife for his ankle, and one for his belt. And the Ruger. His last resort. If he needed to use it, that meant the mission had been a failure.

All of it had been dropped off by the only other agency employee he had met in Ghana besides Ford, a weapons supplier he knew as Gabriel. Billy wondered how many other people like him were scattered across West Africa, right at this very moment. Working for the American people like he was. They flew in on fake names, on foreign passports. British, Canadian, South African. Passports were nothing, the agency gave them out like candy. They traveled on commercial planes, in seat 10A, in seat 22F. They watched movies on the screen in the seatback in front of them like everyone else.

Billy's task tonight was about offense: getting US vampire taps inside the Chinese telecom networks, to ensure that no data transiting through Ghana could stay hidden from the eyes of American intelligence. No doubt there were others like him focused on defense: preventing the Chinese from getting their eyes inside American telecom networks. If any of them failed, China would gain a little more control of the fiber-optic cables that were the pipes that the modern world flowed through. Your mortgage payment, your love letters, your medical records. And if China controlled the pipes, they could shut them off.

On paper, the plan was solid. The Double had promised them that the landing station's security team liked to get drunk in Kumasi on Saturday nights; no one would be guarding the site.

But Billy could not shake his doubts. They had been building for a long time.

It was something about the way the Double looked at him. The fact that the Double looked at him at all. Dangle the promise of America in front of a man, he'll throw anyone under the bus.

How could you take somebody like that at their word?

Billy didn't know much about geopolitics or the World Trade Organization or the fluctuating commodities market. But he knew how to stay alive, and he knew how to kill. He found himself imagining how he would take the Double down. He wasn't a fighter, that much was obvious. He would tire easily. You get them moving and you go at the soft places: the armpits, the guts, the neck.

Now it was 1700. Bags were packed. Weapons loaded.

He picked up his final piece of gear. It was another passport, for a cover identity that the Double didn't know about. Israeli. "Uri Katsman." To the left of the name, Billy's own face scowled back at him.

The oppressive heat of the day had broken and storm clouds were beginning to pass before the sun; the sky threw a square of silvery light onto the wall of his apartment. For a moment Billy sat there and stared at it.

The adrenaline of the hunt always used to lift him up. When he was in high school, he could never sleep the night before football games.

But now he was feeling something unfamiliar. A kind of dread.

His instincts had never failed him yet. That was what had unnerved him so much about what had happened in the car with David Ibrahim almost a month ago. The moment came back to him now. The desperation in Ibrahim's hands reaching at Billy's face. The strength in them. Was Ibrahim thinking of his children then, or his wife, or his mistress inside the house he had just left? Or was it the terror of death alone that gave his hands such power?

Billy had never felt that up close. The limitless energy a human body will discharge to stop its own destruction. The strength of billions of years of biology. And the rage it had ignited in himself, white hot, like dropping the pin of a grenade.

Boom.

He missed Dani Moreau. He wanted to call her. He wanted to bury his head in her lap and confess everything to her. Tell her who he was, tell her who Ford was, tell her who the Double was. After all, *she* was who they were doing all this for. The American people.

But he knew he could not go to her. Not just because his own government would throw him in jail for the rest of his life for revealing its secrets. But because Dani had made it clear what she thought about men like him. What she thought about everyone who had worked day and night, her whole life, to keep her safe. Without her knowing—without her needing to know. Every soldier, every cop, and yes: every spy.

Did she think he was doing this for fun? Because he got his rocks off by killing? She had it backward. The point wasn't the killing. It was the constantly trying *to avoid* being killed. She had no idea what it was like to live that way. To live in a world where people are never *not* trying to kill you. It made you feel half dead already. Like it wasn't so far from here to there.

Still, there had been a kind of honesty in Dani's waves of tears, the last night they had spent together. Just like there had been honesty in David Ibrahim's desperation.

Billy wanted that too. To be honest with the world. He could never live like the Double. Dishonest with everyone, even himself.

Billy sat up, startled.

He looked at his watch.

1800. The square of metallic sunlight was gone. Darkness had fallen, and he was behind schedule; he would need to gun it to make Kumasi in time.

He looked around the apartment—Carlos Rivera's apartment. The thought flickered through him that he might never see it again.

He grabbed the vampire taps and his pack and his weapons. He grabbed Carlos Rivera's passport and Uri Katsman's passport. Loaded up. Pointed the truck north and began to drive.

NINETEEN

LISTEN, HERE'S HOW YOU do it. It's not as hard as it sounds. You continue to be yourself, just the way you always have been. But you are also conscious of some other fact, locked in a compartment of your mind, behind a door that you only open when required. Being a spy is not so different from journalism, actually. All that is new is the fact that if you slip up, somebody might put a bullet in your head.

And it was liberating! It was liberating to have chosen a side, to have come off the fence and out into the open where retreat was no longer an option. All of this was complicated, but the task in front of her remained simple. She would do whatever she could to make sure James was okay. She was not a journalist, not a wife, not a mother. She was not American, not Chinese, not Ghanaian. She was James's friend and that was enough.

Finally, some unease had been put to rest. You are white, your family has money, you glide through airports and immigration halls without fear, your blue and gold passport protecting you. You know the only way to make a difference, to stand in genuine solidarity with your fellow travelers on this earth, is to place yourself in the path of real consequences. Because only then do your choices really matter.

Not that it ends well. You've seen this in others—the lust for danger. Handsome videographers in Syria: one minute the aviator shades, the next kneeling in the sand, wincing at the blade. Or Laurie Balfour, for that matter.

But that is the point. Welcoming the threat of death is the point. It levels the playing field. That's why Alma Hortensia had faced down death squads in Guatemala. Why Marie Colvin and Martha Gellhorn had risked their lives. That was what James was doing every day, through no choice of his own.

She would not let any of them down.

To God Be the Glory was quiet for a Saturday afternoon. Storm clouds were blowing over the Atlantic, bands of rain: shadows falling on the oil rigs that sat just over the horizon, out of sight, bolted to the seafloor.

Dani ordered a Ghana Star from the kid on duty and took it to a corner, finding a seat with its back to the wall, and waited.

A few customers trickled in. She poured half her drink into a potted plant next to her. She wouldn't let a drop cross her lips. She needed to be sharp.

Eventually she saw someone she recognized—Marc, sidling in from the street, an arm curled possessively around a Black woman's waist.

"Oh ho," said Marc. "Alles klar? Have you been hiding?"

"Hi." She addressed herself to the woman he was with. "I'm Dani."

"Joan. Pleased to meet you."

Dani was playing for time, casting her eyes around the room. Where was he, damn it?

"I have heard you have been on a date with my friend, Mr. Rivera," said Marc. "How was it?"

"He was nice."

Marc wagged his finger. "Nett ist der kleine Bruder von Scheisse."

She rolled her eyes at Joan. "Of course."

"It means *Nice is the younger brother of shit.* When all one can say about a person is 'he's nice,' this means *he's shit.* Do you know that, Joan?" He answered for her: "Everyone knows that."

And there, finally, was Yaw, the owner behind the bar. Dani was up and across the room in an instant.

"Yaw!" she said. "Hi!"

Yaw paused, smiled, took her hand in his. The slow way he always did. "Akwaaba, Ms. Danielle. You are welcome."

"Can we speak for moment? I need to ask you something."

"Tell me what has happened," he said. His tone was worried but his gaze was kind. "Come, come. Sit." He motioned at a stack of beer crates. "How can I help you?"

She could sense Marc watching her from across the room.

"Yaw." She fingered the lip of her Ghana Star bottle. "You know I'm a journalist, right? That's why I'm here, in Ghana. But I don't speak Twi and I don't know my way around."

"Yes, yes." He chuckled. "I know this."

"I have to go up north to Kumasi early tomorrow morning, for a story." On an instinct she added, "I'm reporting on something in a town called Bekwai. Have you heard of it?"

"Ah!" Yaw said indignantly. "Ah! This is your question? I am from Kokofu. Right next door. Why do you want to go to Bekwai?"

"Have you heard of anyone else talking about Bekwai? Some customers, maybe? There are some people I'd like to interview."

Yaw frowned. "Do you know? The other night there were some people talking about Bekwai in the bar."

"Any Americans?"

"Americans? No, no. Ghanaians only."

"Do you know their names?"

"No, I am afraid not. If I see them once more, I will ask their names for you." Yaw slapped his knee. "But why do you need to talk to these strangers, ah? Would you like me to call my aunties in Kokofu? They can tell you everything about Bekwai."

"That's okay, Yaw. Thanks."

"It is good to know someone, to have a friend if you go to the country," he continued sternly. "You will need some help. People do not speak so much English up there, as here in Accra."

Dani hesitated. It couldn't hurt. "Can you give me your aunties' numbers?"

He sat down on the beer crates beside her and wrote out two names and phone numbers in careful cursive handwriting. Christina Owusu, Yvonne Owusu.

"What was that about?" said Marc when she returned to where he was sitting with his date. "Conspiring?"

"Something like that," Dani said, brushing him off automatically. Then she reconsidered. "I'm going north tomorrow, to a town called Bekwai. Ever heard of it?"

"Near Kumasi," Joan nodded. "But why are you going there?"

"For my story."

"For your story?" said Marc.

"Joan, does he repeat everything you say too?" Dani pushed herself to her feet. She sipped what remained of her Ghana Star. It was lukewarm after two hours in her hand. "But I've got to run, guys. Enjoy your evening. Joan, don't believe a word he says."

"Don't forget your umbrella!" Marc called after her. "Big storm tonight!"

SANDBOX ALSO WAS NEARLY empty, with the weather already turning. Dani stood across the street from the entrance for a while, hidden in the shadow of a doorway, watching to see if anyone had followed her. When she felt it was safe, she crossed to the host's stand and gave her name.

The hostess's eyes flicked over her, a short appraising glance.

"Come," she said.

They went through the kitchen and emerged onto a back porch that faced the darkened sea, where the wind was picking up but the rain had not yet begun. James was holding a Smirnoff Ice. Dani was brought back instantly to the interview with Kwesi Adjepong that had started this whole thing.

Barely four weeks ago. A lifetime.

Today, though, she saw that the umbrella above James was covered in branding for TelTel, a Chinese telecom company. One of Alma Hortensia's lectures came back to her: *What is it you're noticing? What is it you're discounting?*

James gave her a weak smile. He looked exhausted. He looked older. Dani tried to give him a hug but he held out his hand to stop her.

"Not here. And first. . . ." He held up his cell phone and mimed taking out the SIM card. "Make that a habit," James said. "Anytime you talk to someone. Lessens the chance you'll be overheard. Best would be to throw out your SIM card each time you use it. And your passwords too—email, everything. Do you use a password manager?"

"I just use the same one over and over, but I add an exclamation point."

"My God." James put his face in his hands, half laughing. "No, Dani, no no no."

She tried to resist the urge to take his hand in hers and tell him not to worry, that everything was going to be all right. "James," she said. "How can you work for that man?"

"Lu? Believe me—as bad as the Chinese are, the Americans are worse. They say Jushu puts in back doors, to listen. But the Americans have been doing this forever. They say China will build bases in Africa. But the Americans have been doing this forever. They are in Burkina Faso, Cameroon, Djibouti, Ethiopia, Gabon, and yes, right here in Ghana. But you never hear about it. The base in Accra is at the airport, in a back hangar. Looks like nothing from the outside. You would never notice it. And why isn't the Pentagon saying so? It's because they want to pretend they're not putting their footprint all over this continent. Like every European power ever did."

A breeze crossed the beach and blew some mist onto her bare arms. "I still can't believe," she said, "that I thought it was the oil."

James looked at her thoughtfully. "Your mistake was to think the discovery of the oil was a bad thing for this country in the first place. You think we want our power to cut out every time there is a drought in Akosombo? We want what everyone wants. We want to be rich. And we are, you know. Slowly. Ghana is getting richer all the time. Last year, the World Bank . . . ," he trailed off. "We are still in the dirt, but it's at our knees now. Not our necks."

"So then why spy for China at all?"

"But I am not a spy. I am a source."

"What's the difference?"

"Sources are only permitted to know certain things. Lu Zhong does not sit me down and say: here is the picture, here is how we Chinese do our work in Ghana. I'm quite sure even he does not know the whole picture. The ones who know are back in Beijing. America has spies, China has spies. In Ghana? No. In order to fuck with other countries, you have to be rich enough not to be worried about where your dinner is coming from."

Dani was silent for a moment. The wind spun the umbrella above their heads. Down by the waterline in the darkness, a lone figure was walking along the beach, bent in the wind, head down. She, or he, stooped and picked up an object from the sand: examined it for a second, then flung it away.

Dani changed the subject. "Does the name Zheng He mean anything to you? Admiral Zheng He?"

James tsked. "Come on, Dani—you should know this. It's in every Chinese schoolbook. The Seven Voyages of Admiral Zheng He, who sailed to India, Africa, Arabia. He died six hundred years ago."

"I heard about him from a Chinese man I met near the ports in Tema, a couple of weeks ago."

He nodded. "Of course, the Chinese think they are carrying on Zheng He's legacy, by being here. And they work, and they work, and they work. It is amazing, how determined they are. Africans could learn from them."

The wind was a constant mournful roar. "I don't buy it, James," she said, raising her voice. "You didn't just blow your own cover to me. You blew Lu's too. That's why he was so angry with you. I don't think you're really happy about what the Chinese are doing here. I don't think you're satisfied just being a source."

James leaned across the table. "Be careful, Dani. That's all I'm saying. These people will kill you if required. They'll torture both of us to death. And everyone who knows us will say: they got what they deserved."

She felt her hip bones pressing into the metal chair. "I'm not afraid to die."

"Good for you. I am."

"You're not the one whose assignment is to be bait for an American assassin."

For a while he said nothing. She thought she saw sympathy on his face. It was not a look he had ever given her before. "If you get into trouble up there," he said, "there is a property I keep in the hills above Lake Bosomtwe. Kind of a safe house, like the one in Ashaiman, where I took you after you found me at the Jericho Café. Amekom is the name of the town. Hardly a town. You walk northwest from the tro-tro stand, about twenty minutes straight into the bush. Lu doesn't know about it, my father doesn't know about it. Nobody does. If you ever need a safe place to hide, go there. Amekom. You'll remember it?"

Dani swallowed. "I will."

She looked out over the ocean, at the lines of white water appearing out of the inky expanse and falling onto the beach, like row upon row of infantry.

History is not a balanced ledger. Columns grow unevenly, and some debts are never repaid. Suffering and progress flow like separate rivers into a great ocean, where they mix and blend. But there are billabongs—sometimes the river changes course and leaves behind ponds of suffering that will never be flushed out. Never made right. Ever.

"I'm going to send some information to someone I trust," she said. "About where I am and what I'm doing. In case—" She cleared her throat. "In case I die."

She expected James to object, to tell her she couldn't risk it, to lecture her again about sources and spies. But he nodded, as though it was sensible.

"Send it through a cutout," he said.

"A cutout?"

"An extra waypoint. Where someone else picks it up and puts it in a new envelope. Then they send it onward, listing a fake address as the return. A cutout breaks the circuit. You want to make it harder to track the package's ultimate journey from A to B? Give it a bunch of pointless zigzags in between."

Dani leaned across the table and took James's hand. She felt him pull away, then relax under her touch. "And what about you James? Are you going to be okay?"

He looked at her, his eyes tired. "We should be going." He stood up, his chair scraping backwards from the table. "I will be fine, Dani." He wedged some cedis under his empty Smirnoff bottle. "Do not worry about me."

WHEN DANI RETURNED TO the guesthouse, a small plastic package had been left in front of her door.

For a moment she just looked at it. There were no markings, nothing with her name on it. But it could not have been meant for anyone else. Was it from James? She bent towards it, expecting it to blow up in her face.

But when she opened it, she saw a fold of fabric. Green chiffon, with yellow stripes.

The dress that Priscilla had made for her.

She took it inside. For a moment she held it against her body, admiring the way it caught the light. She took off her shirt and pants and stood in her dirty underwear in the middle of the room. Her hand paused on her lower belly. She had grown thin, since the baby. Her body felt efficient. Boiled down to its essence.

Dani slipped on the dress. It was beautiful. It fit her perfectly.

Her gaze fell on her bag in the corner of her room. A packet of Hobnobs had been commandeered by ants, glimmering in a silent swarm.

Dani took the bag back outside and emptied it over the railing. The rain was picking up, thunder rippling in from across the dark Atlantic. She beat it gently, watching the ants fall.

Before she went in she knocked on Priscilla's door, intending to thank her. But Priscilla didn't answer.

Standing in the empty hallway, feeling Accra's dense wet air on her bare arms, Dani thought again of Carlos Rivera. Already he felt like a memory from another life. But it was a Saturday night, and she wanted somebody to see her in this dress.

She called him. It rang and rang.

But Carlos Rivera didn't answer either.

TWENTY

It was just shy of 2300 and the rains had started in earnest by the time Billy pulled Carlos Rivera's truck into the parking lot behind the Lancaster Hotel in Kumasi. He went inside and spoke to the man at the front desk.

"Just the one night. Rivera, that's right."

His room contained a bed and small table. He shut and locked the window and pulled the curtain halfway across it. He turned off the ceiling fan so the curtains became still.

For a moment he listened. Silence. Just the mumble of the rain on the roof.

He turned on light next to the bed, then he exited the hotel room, locking the door behind him.

The plan called for him to go pick up the Double and then be on the road to Bekwai by 2330. Instead, Billy got back in his truck and drove five minutes away to a deserted side street. He turned off the car and cut the lights.

Now was the moment to decide. Follow his suspicions or follow his orders. Either his gut was right or it was wrong.

He holstered his weapon, grabbed a pair of binoculars, and got out of the car.

Across the street and down the block from the Lancaster Kumasi was another hotel, the Asantewaa Premier. Billy asked for a map of the rooms.

"That one," he said, pointing to the far northwest corner.

"Your passport, please, sir."

He handed over Uri Katsman. The rain was really falling now, a heavy tropical downpour. He kept the lights off in his new room so his eyes could see more sharply across the deserted Kumasi backstreets to room 212 at the southeast corner of the Lancaster Kumasi, where the curtain was half open, unmoving, illuminated by the bedside lamp that had been left on.

Carlos Rivera's room.

Motionless he sat and watched through the binoculars, his elbows balanced on his knees. He felt thoughts emptying out of him, like a draining tub. He was on the football field, in the moment before the snap. The world was silent and slow. The world was nothing more than what he could see in front of him. He felt coiled. Spring-loaded. The rains came down harder. They pounded the streets to mud, then soup. He would have been having a hell of a time if he'd been out in the bush, advancing towards the landing station, vampire taps in hand.

There.

The light in Carlos Rivera's room flickered. The curtains were moving. The shadow they made against the lamp rose and fell.

Two individuals, he thought.

One of them came to the window and threw it open. The face was in shadow against the body, backlit by the lamp. Billy toggled the focus on the binoculars. Yes, he recognized that face. He'd been briefed on that face. A known Chinese intelligence operative. The object in his hand looked like a gun. A shadow moved behind him: there was another person. But before Billy could see who it was, the man with the gun shut the window and pulled the curtains closed.

Billy could feel his breathing rising. Consciously he slowed it down.

He checked his watch. 2314.

The facts were these. Only two people had known that Carlos Rivera would be staying at the Lancaster Kumasi tonight between 2300 and 2330: Ford and the Double.

So his instincts had been right. The Double wanted Billy dead. He didn't want the United States to win. He wanted China to win.

He became aware that the rain had finally stopped.

For all the anger Billy had felt as his suspicions had built up, now that they were confirmed he didn't feel upset. If anything, he almost wanted to laugh. He knew what he had to do now. He knew who he needed to kill.

For another hour he waited, watching Carlos Rivera's room for any further activity. But there was nothing. The Chinese must have concluded Carlos Rivera was already out in the bush and gone looking for him there.

Billy exited the Asantewaa Premier Hotel. He got back in his truck and started to drive south.

TWENTY-ONE

One day, when the Double was sixteen—a few years after he had begun delivering monthly reports to his Chinese spymaster—he had gone with his best friend to look at a soccer stadium that a Chinese construction firm was building outside the city where they grew up. Warm air had whipped around their faces, bringing the threat of afternoon rain. The two of them stood on a hillside that rose above the stadium construction site—far enough away not to be noticed by the light-skinned figures working on the building, pushing wheelbarrows of cement. The men looked like obruni, but their skin was not as pale as the British and the Americans on television. From this distance, they appeared to be working in complete silence.

"Henanom ne wan?" his friend said.

Who is down there?

"Daakye," the Double had answered.

The future.

Everywhere the Double had looked, his country was being flooded—Chinese sneakers in the market, Chinese brands in the electronics shops, Chinese characters on the sides of the huge container ships in the harbor, Chinese construction workers assembling in camps beneath the steadily rising shadows of new stadiums, power plants, airports, hydroelectric dams. The Chinese were popping up in remote cacao farms, in mining towns, in villages in the bush where nobody spoke anything but Twi. With cash. With jobs. And with a seemingly boundless energy and appetite for everything Ghana had to offer.

But as he got older, the Double read in *Daily Guide Ghana* that Chinese workers were installing solar power panels in remote villages; that Chinese drilling crews were taking over the oil industry; that Jushu trainers were embedding in the offices of Ghanaian telecom companies and overbidding for contracts to install 4G and then 5G equipment. The Chinese wanted to suck Ghana dry of every resource it possessed, whether that was cacao from its trees, bauxite from its mines, or data from its citizens. And Ghanaians, his own people, were letting it happen—selling out his country from underneath his feet.

The Double and his best friend had terrific arguments about this. The Double could not understand his countrymen who were so eager to work with the Chinese. Could they not see that Beijing was dividing and conquering, like others had before them? By the mid-2020s, there would be more Africans than Chinese people—but China was dividing them with the same combinations of promises, cash, and threats that the Europeans had used generations earlier. The playbook was depressingly familiar, because it worked.

That was why, on the morning Ford had first approached him after church, the Double had been ready. He had been waiting for this moment for a long time, convinced that this fealty to China could not last. Not just because it was the death of his country—but because he could feel the arrangement sapping his own life force. While he reported to the Chinese intelligence officer, his livelihood, his position in society, his very existence did not belong to him. And no nation was worth the waste of an individual life.

SUNDAY MORNING, THE TWENTY-FOURTH of November. A fierce rainstorm overnight had given way to a still, cloudless dawn, the fading full moon suspended in a pink sunrise. The Double waited for the news that the Chinese had intercepted and killed Carlos Rivera. It had most certainly happened by now.

The problem was how to *get* the news. It was a strange epistemological state: to be aware that the most important question of his life—was Carlos Rivera dead or not?—had a straightforward answer, that the answer was known to others in close physical proximity, and that in fact you knew who those others were, and in theory you physically could go and ask them. But to be unable, in practice, to do any of those things. He could not ask his Chinese handler if Rivera was dead. He could not ask Ford. He was utterly alone with the responsibility of what he had done. Confirmation, if it ever came, would be indirect. Unsatisfying.

He supposed that he had to get used to living with the feeling. He wondered what it must be like, to be one of those people who were briefed on the whole picture. One of those principals in a softly lit, air-conditioned room, handed a manila folder with the truth laid out neatly in bullet points. The whole truth. Seeing the world from above like that was not the luxury afforded to Ghanaians. There were people who saw how things connected, and people who were the things to connect. He was the latter.

As the cutout had been.

He tried to tell himself that he had had no choice in the matter, that he had been forced into this position and that the moral stain of his action thus belonged not to him but to others. He had been required to kill the cutout because the man was the only person who could link him back to the message he had passed to the Chinese about Carlos Rivera's whereabouts. That was the fate of most cutouts; it would have been the Double's fate too. You were somebody's loose end, somebody's track they needed to cover. Sooner or later you were crossed off a list. Pluck the average American from his home in the suburbs and put him in the Double's position, and see if he or she would behave any differently.

But these attempts at reassurance didn't work. A man was dead at his hand. *Dead,* forever. Even if he got what he was trying so hard to achieve—even if he held the blue and gold passport in his hands—how would he ever forget the look of confusion and fear on the cutout's face when he had turned around and seen what the Double was pointing at him? Or the choking sounds as the cutout had lain on the ground, a bullet through his belly, trying to get up? Or the weight of the pistol in the Double's own sweaty palm as he had stepped forward and delivered the coup de grâce?

He pleaded with himself: *But that was the whole point!* These things did not happen in America. Being American was the only thing that could insulate you from the shocks to which the rest of the world was so rawly and repeatedly exposed. That was all he was trying to do: reach safety. And he daresaid he was doing better than an American would in his shoes. At every step his choices had been rational, defensible. When Ford had asked for David Ibrahim's name, it had been reasonable to provide it. When David

Ibrahim had been unexpectedly killed, and the furious Chinese had begun to search for a mole, it had been reasonable to tell the Americans about Bekwai, to accelerate the pace of events. When Ford had promised a passport in three weeks in return for what the Double knew about the landing station, it had been reasonable to agree. When Ford had told the Double he himself would be required to go to Bekwai with Carlos Rivera, it had been reasonable to refuse.

Each step of the journey so obvious, so sensible. Yet somehow, in total, they had deposited him here, in this calamity. He had killed a man. *He had killed a man.*

The Double waited, his hand on his phone, for someone to get in touch. Ford, his Chinese handler, anybody. It would all work out. He needed to believe that it would. Something would happen soon. Some new fact would be revealed, some new decision would be called for, and he would take the next rational step, and then the one after that. And he would survive.

He had to.

TWENTY-TWO

BY SUNDAY MORNING THE rain had stopped.

Dani had been unable to sleep, and it wasn't just the adrenaline of what she was about to do: travel to Kumasi on direct orders from a Chinese intelligence officer. *By the time you arrive, the assassin will be in our custody*, Lu Zhong had said. If he was correct, an international incident was underway five hours to the north, and Dani was about to walk into the middle of it—on China's side.

But that was not what was keeping her up. Something else was eating at her, something that she could not name. It flickered just on the edge of her awareness—evading her whenever she tried to pin it down. She kept replaying everything that had happened since she had first arrived in Ghana. Those early days chasing the oil, that long-ago dead end. She had been focused on the right activity—something precious being pulled from the West African ground—but the wrong substance.

How had she gone from there to here? Surely she had missed some turn, some trick along the way, for her role in the world to have altered so drastically.

She lay on top of the bed, staring at the ceiling, watching the fan swivel in uncertain circles.

When dawn broke, she called her ex-husband.

"Don't hang up. I don't have much time to explain, Ben."

A long sigh. "Dani. It's early."

"Yesterday I sent a package by post to the pub where we first met your parents. Remember the barman? Remember his name? He helped us jump-start your parents' car when the engine wouldn't turn over?"

"Dani, your mother's worried about you. I've had a call from her."

Beads of moisture had risen on her collarbone. The phone was sticky against her cheek.

"*Remember his name?* It was snowing. The car wouldn't start."

"Wasn't it Fra—"

"Don't say it. Not on the phone. Just go to the pub in a few days' time and look for a letter from me to you, care of him. Open it, read the instructions, and send it on to the next person listed there."

"Dani—"

She hung up, took out the SIM card, and broke it in half.

She had sent Ben everything. All her notes since she had stepped off the plane in Accra. Her notes on Kwesi Adjepong, on Oscar Aidoo, on Dongsha and Jushu. Names, dates, receipts. Her trip to Takoradi. Her conversations with Oscar and James Aidoo. Everything she could remember, she had written down and sent to him. The Jericho Café. Lu Zhong, and who he was, and what she had agreed to do for him. Her assignment to help the Chinese disrupt an American assassination plot. The address of James's safe house in the hills above Lake Bosomtwe. A complete package—with instructions for Ben to forward it on to her former colleagues at *The Guardian.*

Her journalistic instincts had not disappeared. Whatever happened to her next, whatever curtain she disappeared behind, she wanted to put the truth on paper in black and white, in her own words. Because she knew that, sooner or later, American investigators would comb through her past. Men in sunglasses, holding notepads, unsmiling, would talk to everyone she had ever known.

And she was going to miss Isabelle's engagement party. She hoped her sister would be angry with her, rather than sad or hurt. Anger was fine. She hoped her sister would hate her for what she did. Both her sisters. Her nieces too. That would make all this easier: if they hated her. To think otherwise was unbearable—to imagine their grief, to imagine Cait and Isabelle in shock and Emma and Claire confused, crying, asking what had happened to their Aunt Dani.

As for the others—Ben, her mother, her doctors, her former colleagues—she knew what they would say. That she had gone mad. She could almost hear them. Dani was always unstable; it was crazy, what she'd done. They would all agree. She was a Crazy Woman.

Well fuck that. And fuck them.

She had hung up Priscilla's dress in its full length from the curtain rod. When she looked at it indirectly it almost felt like there was somebody else in the room.

Your life; another person's life.

The assassin is in Kumasi, Lu Zhong had said. *Report to the Manhyia District Hospital.* If she failed to appear, James would be killed. Never again would he push his glasses nervously back up his nose, or shoot her one of those half-raised eyebrows.

Her time was nearly up. Sunlight was flooding her room. She had to go.

And yet.

And yet.

Dani's instincts tingled in her fingers like nerve endings. She was pressing against the facts and there was still some give beneath her hands. She pictured the striations of the fiber-optic cables hugging the coastlines of the world map. She pictured the thin wires half buried in sand, snaking their way through the salty darkness.

Dani got to her feet. She had made a decision. Before she went north, there was one final thing she needed to check.

VODAFONE GHANA'S HQ LOOMED over her head, a cuboid box of concrete and blue-tinted plate glass—like any midsized office building anywhere in the world. Dani walked right up to the front door.

"Good morning. I am here to see James Aidoo."

The security man regarded her balefully for several long seconds. Then he waved her toward the lifts. "Third floor."

This early in the morning on the weekend, the office was mostly empty, but there were still a few support staff around. She heard a ringing phone, smelled warm paper and glue. Gray carpets; undoubtedly, somewhere, a watercooler.

"Good morning, madam," said a woman on the third floor, sitting at what looked like a receptionist's desk. "May I assist you?"

"James Aidoo's office, please."

She frowned. "I am sorry, Mr. Aidoo is not in."

"Yes, I know."

For the first time, suspicion. "Ye-es," the woman said slowly. "He is not in the office." She picked up a pen. "What is your name please, madam?"

"My name is Danielle Moreau. I'm a personal friend of the family's. I'm here on behalf of Mr. Aidoo's father. Deputy Minister Aidoo."

Oh shit looks the same on your face, wherever you're from.

"I'm sorry." The receptionist stood up, flustered. "Deepest apologies, madam. As I say, Mr. Aidoo is not in the office, but he will be in tomorrow. May I take a message for you on his behalf?"

"Can you show me to his office? I've been sent to pick something up for him. A letter," she added, lamely. But dropping Oscar Aidoo's name had done the trick and the receptionist showed no hint of defiance now. Dani walked down the long hall, past a few people with their backs to her, with headsets clipped over their ears. The blue and white button-downs, the soft clicks of keyboards. Powering Ghana's telecom industry, ensuring that people all over the country could make calls, browse Wi-Fi, and plug into the engines of the global economy.

His office was the largest on the floor. A nameplate read *James A. Aidoo, Executive Vice President.*

The receptionist winced expectantly. "He is not in. As you see."

"I'll just be a moment." Without waiting for her to reply, Dani stepped in and shut the door behind her. She heard a yelp of muted protest from the woman. Then silence. No attempt was made to open the door. Still, she had to move fast.

James's desk was orderly, completely devoid of personal effects except for a mug labeled UT AUSTIN and a framed diploma on the opposite wall. Two computer monitors faced the window, which looked onto Bypass Road. Next to the keyboard was a black binder fat with papers divided into slivers by red plastic tabs. She flicked through it. Nothing helpful.

She opened the top drawer: staples, paper clips, AA batteries. Middle drawer: stacks of papers in manila envelopes. She wished she'd brought a bag big enough to take them with her. Bottom drawer: a locked safe. The door was sealed by an alphanumeric keypad.

Shit.

Hopelessly she pressed 1-2-3-4-5. The keypad turned red and beeped its disapproval.

Voices in the hallway.

When was James's birthday? She counted the years. It must be 1994—but she had no idea what day or month. She pressed 1-9-9-4 and the pad blinked red again.

Somebody knocked.

Dani put her hands on her hips. So this was as far as she got. At least she had tried.

The knocking grew louder. In desperation Dani looked around the room. Her eyes fell on the diploma on the opposite wall. Hit by a sudden idea, she bent down and typed in the numbers that corresponded to M-A-R-I-N-A. The name of the girl from Mexico City whom James had dated in college.

The safe popped open. Inside was a solitary envelope, bulging in the middle. Dani had just slipped it into her pocket when the door barged open and the receptionist appeared on the threshold, the building security man looming over her shoulder.

"Did you find the letter?" The receptionist was chipper but the guard eyed her coolly.

"Yes. I'm all set. Thanks for your help." She brushed past them, walked quickly towards the entrance. People were staring at her, leaning back from their computers.

"Madam," said the guard behind her.

She waved dismissively and called "Thank you!" over her shoulder.

In the elevator, she opened the envelope.

A cell phone, with two SIM cards in a Ziploc bag.

She turned on the cell phone and inserted the first SIM card. There was only one number in the contacts and only one text message.

It read: *Ford confirms Lancaster Hotel 2300.*

She stared at it for a moment. A quick Google on her personal cell told her that the Lancaster Hotel was in Kumasi.

Straightforward enough—not necessarily incriminating.

She plugged in the second SIM card. Again, only one text message, sent to a different number than the first:

Ezekiel, soula st

She stared at this for a moment. Was it a code? Was "Ezekiel Soula" someone's name?

Then she saw it.

Soula Street.

An address.

As Dani approached Ezekiel Garage on Soula Street, she suddenly noticed two things at once: that the neighborhood was crowded for a Sunday, and that the flow of people had a direction, a purpose. Everyone seemed to be walking one way.

She followed the crowd. Horns honked, kids flitted. Old people stood watching in silence. Something was definitely up. The flow carried her down the next side street, where a line of people had formed in front of an automobile repair shop. *Ezekiel Garage* read the sign.

Dani pushed her way through and stepped forward into the building. Four men were inside, talking to one another. Confusion filled their voices. On seeing Dani they paused—then resumed their debate.

Behind them a rusting hulk of a Peugeot sat on cinder blocks without its tires. Dani stepped around it.

There was a dead body on the ground. A man in a red shirt. Hand thrown in front of his face, as if to cover his eyes from the last thing he saw. The elbow was bent at a weird angle. He had been dead for some time. His limbs were stiff, and the blood beneath his head and neck had already dried. The left side of his face was missing below the cheekbone. A gunshot wound.

"Who are you?" one of the men suddenly demanded from behind her.

Dani looked closer. The shirt was a jersey. Liverpool.

She pulled out the phone she had taken from James's office, popped in the second SIM card—the one James had texted *Ezekiel, soula st.*

When she dialed the number, the dead man's pocket began to ring.

She became aware that she was running. Her shoes were sandals, not made for sprinting, the rubber was eating into her skin. Down earthen alleyways and down cracked asphalt streets. Useless, all useless. The sound of gunfire behind her and she ducked and screamed. But it was not gunfire. Just a motorbike backfiring. Animal terror. She knew this feeling—from the night she lost her son, from the day of the car bomb in Beirut. Panic. It almost had a smell—your breath became metallic. Movements quicker, vision blurry. Feral. Like prey.

The SIM card in her own phone was not safe to use. Nothing was safe. Everything was fucked, fucked, *fucked.*

Along the roadside there was a man who sat in a plastic chair under a TelTel umbrella. She paid him to use his phone.

James's mobile rang several times before somebody answered. "Hello?" But the voice was not James. "Wo ho te sen?" the person demanded.

Dani dropped the phone. Because a new piece of knowledge had swum to the surface of her mind. She felt it moving up inside her before she had consciously formed the words, the understanding traveling upward while her hand dropped to her waist, the equilibrium between the rising and falling holding her in place like gravity.

She took out the phone from James's office and plugged in the second SIM card, the one that had received the text that read *Ford confirms Lancaster Hotel 2300.* The message had been sent yesterday at 5:00 P.M., around the time James and Dani had been sitting at Sandbox as the rainstorm closed in.

The other number.

She had seen it somewhere before.

For a moment Dani felt pinned by the universe. Perfectly still. She took out her own phone. Scrolled through her messages until she found it.

Let's try that again?

Carlos Rivera was texting James.

The truth, like a roaring in her ears. A set of facts solid as a rock. No more give beneath her hands.

The Americans have developed a source in the upper levels of the Ghanaian government.

James had texted a location to the guy who worked the counter at Jericho Café.

The man had been shot to death at that location.

The assassin is on his way to Kumasi even now. We have been tipped off about him by a reliable source.

Carlos Rivera was texting James about a meeting at a Kumasi hotel.

James was the mole.

Carlos was the assassin.

And they had met in Kumasi last night—walking right into Lu Zhong's trap.

DANI TOOK A TAXI back to her dorm. Stomach jolting stop and starts—why *couldn't* these people drive more reasonably? She rolled down the window and sucked in the air, Accra's heavy-sweet smell.

She packed her bag in a mad rush. Looking down, she saw that her hands, unnoticed, had begun to shake. Her mind flung images at her in rapid succession. The man reading *The Hitchhiker's Guide to the Galaxy* behind the counter. The man dead on the dusty ground. James sitting on the floor of her room at the guesthouse, coughing after taking a shot of whiskey. Her nieces smiling and laughing at her wedding last summer.

She walked to the tro-tro stand, breathing shallow, thoughts racing. Dani had seen violence before. She'd seen dead people in Senegal, bagged in neat rows. She'd seen bits of limbs scattered across an intersection in Beirut. She had replayed the violence of Laurie's death over and over again in her imagination. And she had seen her own precious son pulled from her body—perfectly formed, unnaturally small, utterly lifeless. She had seen all this and survived. But this time felt different.

She pushed her way through the tro-tro line, people enjoying the fresh air that followed in the wake of the storm; the drivers' mates leaned out the passenger side windows and called out destinations into the shuffling Sunday morning crowd. Obuasi, Mampong, Tamale, Wa. Twice she heard Kumasi but was unable to muscle her way to the front.

After the second failed attempt she looked up.

Carlos Rivera was watching her from across the street.

Dani panicked. Swimming through people, her elbow connected with a forehead and somebody shouted. She pressed on, half blind with fear and rage.

But when she looked back again, Carlos had disappeared.

SHE TOOK A SEAT by the window. The tro-tro was pulling out of the city, bouncing over ruts in the red clay road. It was just after 9:00 A.M.

She was going to find James.

She was going to find Carlos.

She was going to—what?

Save them from Lu? Confront them? Kill them?

She would find out when she got there. No way to know. No way to prepare.

Nothing to do but press forward.

Dani breathed. Tried to breathe. She thought of her nieces. A wedding in the Cotswolds in the summertime. It was June, the leaves were flush. Her nieces in crepe de chine dresses, running through the long grass, laughing, smiling, innocent. . . .

No. No. Not so fast.

You are submerged deep down in the world's dark messes, its cruelties. And it is possible to resurface. You can survive. It can be done. But not too quickly. Otherwise you get the bends.

TWENTY-THREE

BILLY DITCHED THE TRUCK on the outskirts of Accra just before dawn on Sunday and threw his passport in a sewage ditch.

Carlos Rivera was dead. Billy wouldn't miss him.

According to protocol, his first move after discovering that his cover had been blown and that the Double was a traitor should have been to report to the embassy. Brief Ford, and the agency section chief. Let them figure it out. Let them tell him what to do.

But he was finished with Ford and everyone like him. The agency had trusted the Double, and the Double had set Billy up. Nobody cared. There were countless more Billys where he came from. Captain Raymond was probably talking to one right now, sitting in front of some poor bastard, cocking his head like an idea had just occurred to him. *Have you ever thought about the agency?*

Billy didn't need someone else to decide for him what had to be done. He knew.

He crouched for a while behind a car outside the house of the Chinese operative Lu Zhong. The sun was coming up. For once Accra's air felt fresh, a cool breeze after the overnight rains. The moon was still in the sky, hanging low, round as a coin in the clear pink light.

Billy knew that Lu Zhong was the man who ran the Double. Billy knew that, on paper, Lu Zhong was the chairman of the Dongsha shipping and construction company, but that in practice he served Beijing's security services. He was a businessman, but it didn't matter: if you were Chinese, you worked for the CCP. And Billy knew that Lu Zhong was an older man. Physically weak. Easily disarmed.

Fair game. A legitimate target. Just like Billy was, and just like the Double was.

And when he had finished with Lu Zhong, James Aidoo would be next.

It was 0545. The street was asleep. The house sat silent. Like other homes nearby, it was surrounded by a tall wall studded with glass shards. Several cameras faced the street from above the entrance, capturing every angle of approach. But no security personnel were visible. All of Lu Zhong's muscle was probably still crashing through the jungle outside Bekwai, where Billy was supposed to be. He had to move fast.

Billy took off his shirt and ripped it in half, wrapping both his hands as thickly as he could. The Ruger was holstered on his left hip, the bowie knife on his ankle. Crouching, he jogged along the street behind the few parked cars between him and the gate. When he got to the last car he vaulted up onto hood, roof, up over the wall, sharp stabbing pain in his right hand, and then he was on his feet on the other side.

Soft feet. Hardly breathing. He looked down. The glass had ripped the fat pad below the base of his thumb.

No time to feel it. Forward.

He was standing inside the kitchen now. There was definitely no security present. The only person inside this house was asleep.

He knew it without needing to think about it consciously. Sometimes it surprised him, the intelligence that lived in his body, the creativity. He just knew.

The old man was in his bed. One hand clutched a sheet pulled up under his chin. Mouth hanging slightly open, lips twitching when he inhaled. Billy stood in the doorway of his bedroom, watching. Everybody looks like a child when they're asleep. Everybody looks unafraid. Lu Zhong had no reason to suspect anyone would be coming for him. Completely unaware. But that was the one thing you could not be. That was what this life taught you. You could never feel safe, never be at peace, never be yourself. You either learned that lesson or you ended up killed. There was no third option.

No feeling of falling this time. Billy felt calm as he crossed the room to the sleeping man and pulled the blanket out of his knobby hands and slid the knife up under his rib cage and into his heart. Elderly flesh. So soft it was almost indecent. Like wet tissue paper. Lu Zhong's eyes popped open and he let out one long choking sigh. He did not even have time to be shocked. Billy sat on top of him until he stopped moving, then pulled out the dripping knife and plunged it in one more time, as a courtesy. Dribbles of muck all over the blanket. He wiped the blade across Lu's forehead, first one side, then the other.

Cold sweat on the back of his neck. He wheeled around.

Nobody there.

Billy looked down at his right hand. The cut from the glass was bleeding heavily. His DNA was all over the scene.

He clambered off the dead man and walked into the kitchen. A packet of cigarettes lay on the table. Billy took one and lit it.

He opened the refrigerator; he hadn't eaten in twenty-four hours. But it was empty.

In a drawer he found a roll of duct tape, which he wrapped around his hand a few times. The cigarette was delicious. It made his head swim.

Billy walked through the rest of the house. The sound of his boots too loud.

In a back room he found what he was looking for. A false door, flimsy. One good kick broke it down. Inside was a small, dark workspace. A table with a computer and stacks of colored folders on top, and a safe underneath. He flicked on the light. Spun the safe lock a few times. Pointless, he would never get it open. The folders were filled with papers in Chinese characters. Maps of Accra, Kumasi. Bigger maps that showed the whole of West Africa and the coastline of the Gulf of Guinea. Here and there a set of coordinates circled in red pen. He turned on the computer. A log-in screen, also in Chinese. No use: hacking was not his expertise. And besides, he was running out of time.

Billy went back to the kitchen and found a garbage bag for the paper intel. He wanted another cigarette and reached into Lu Zhong's pack for one.

Something small and hard was hidden at the bottom.

A thumb drive. Black plastic, the size of a fingernail.

He carried it into the back room and plugged it into the computer. "Password required," it said in English, with the icon of a fingerprint. For a second Billy looked at this.

He walked back into the bedroom. Climbing onto the bed he pulled back the index finger on the dead man's right hand and sliced it off below the knuckle with his knife. The rest of the hand flopped away, unresisting. Billy felt a strange pang of sympathy for it.

In the back room he touched the tip of Lu's disembodied finger to the password pad. The screen flickered, and then a new display appeared. A digitized library, with folder after folder of names of places and people.

He saw *Bekwai* and clicked on it. Heard a slight "Wow" escape his own mouth.

There were detailed coordinates and plans for the landing station. Dates of shipments of equipment from China. The names of Chinese officials. The names of Ghanaian officials.

He clicked on OSCAR AIDOO. Written in English he saw SEVEN (7) MILLION USD, above a list of names. At the top of that list were the words JAMES AIDOO AND ELECTION CAMPAIGN—MP FOR KUMASI REGION.

Billy backtracked and clicked on other folders at random. The thumb drive appeared to describe the totality of China's operation to control and expand its telecom networks in Ghana. And not just in Ghana: he saw the names of cities in Nigeria, Togo, Senegal. The names of politicians. The names of companies.

Then he stopped. Two other names he recognized.

DANIELLE MOREAU. And beneath that: CARLOS RIVERA.

He clicked on Dani's first. ASSET, the document said, in English. The rest of the document was in Chinese, but by picking out proper nouns he could follow the arc. DANIELLE MOREAU. Aged 32, born LENNOX HILL HOSPITAL, MANHATTAN, NEW YORK. Father: LUC MOREAU. Mother: CLARISSE MOREAU. Siblings: CAITLIN, 36, ISABELLE, 29. After UC BERKELEY, she spent time in WASHINGTON, DC. Then she was in SENEGAL. Then BEIRUT. Then LONDON.

Married BENJAMIN WHITCOMB. Then she arrived in ACCRA. She met CARLOS RIVERA. She met JAMES AIDOO. And then there was a final bullet point dated about two weeks ago. It was mostly in Chinese, but CARLOS RIVERA appeared again.

He clicked on CARLOS RIVERA. This time the header was dated two days previously, next to the name of the employer for his cover job in big bold letters: UNHCR.

But the Chinese knew exactly who CARLOS RIVERA really worked for. They had photos of him and Dani at *Stars of the Future*, at To God Be the Glory. China knew everything that had been discussed in front of the Double. They knew what he had done to DAVID IBRAHIM. There was a lot about David Ibrahim, in fact. The date and time of his death. The make of the car it had happened in. They did not yet seem to know Billy's real name—but they would get it sooner or later, especially now that they had his picture.

He checked his watch. 0700. The sun was up at Bekwai, and the Chinese would know that he wasn't there.

Time to go.

AS HE WAITED IN shadow in a doorway across the road from Dani Moreau's apartment, Billy considered the facts.

The first was that the Double had tipped off the Chinese about Carlos Rivera's mission to infiltrate the landing station at Bekwai. No doubt about it: James Aidoo had tried to have Billy killed.

The second was that the Chinese had been more invested in David Ibrahim than he had realized. Ever since Ibrahim had been killed in that car, the Chinese had been hunting the man who had done it.

The third was that Dani Moreau appeared to have been recruited as an asset by the Chinese intelligence services in Ghana, and that her assignment was somehow related to her relationship with Carlos Rivera.

A honeypot. The same old story.

He had been careless. He was lucky to be alive.

Beneath the duct tape bandage his right hand throbbed hotly. Breathing shallow. Although it was still early, the sun had begun to beat down on the street and his back was damp with sweat. It was the fourth quarter and he was driving down the field. No time-outs left. Not for your side or theirs.

With his left hand he patted the thumb drive in the pocket of his jeans. He had left the garbage bag full of papers behind: the drive was immeasurably more valuable, and easier to carry. As soon as he was done here, he would make contact with Ford and show him what he had found. The value of the intelligence trove was the only thing that could save his career after the trail of violations left behind him. Hell, maybe the only thing that could save his life.

His eyes swept back and forth across the facade of the guesthouse. Two stories, pale yellow stucco. Dani's room was the third from the right on the second floor, behind a thin iron balcony. On the street in front of him the traffic blurred past in both directions. Permanent fog of diesel smoke hovering at eye level. Tro-tros honking, motorbikes accelerating, chatter in Twi.

Killing an American citizen was the cardinal sin. But he could not let her live. Dani's life story was pathetic, laid out in the official bullet points of a Chinese intelligence brief. Lurching from one thing to the next, never finding what she was looking for. A journey of self-discovery. The problem for her was that *this* journey had led her to become an agent of a hostile power. Before, she had been his boss: the American people, possessed of immense power, radiating it like heat, even when they didn't know it—a flood, an earthquake, an act of God, villagers scattering before the sheer relentless weight of Whatever the American People Wanted. But now she was not his boss. She was his enemy. She had thrown in with a pretender. With Beijing. An action, a step, decisive: it could not be explained, could not be walked back, could not be forgiven.

Billy would help her understand that the world was not a journey of self-discovery. It was a fight to the death.

There she was. She was shutting the door of her room behind her. Hefting a full pack onto her back.

"Where are you going?" he murmured to himself.

Dani adjusted the red bandana that was tied around her neck, pulled the straps of her pack tight over shoulders, and walked quickly along the second-floor balcony and down the external staircase to street level. She was obviously in a hurry, unaware of being watched, unaware of any of her surroundings. Looking more like a backpacker than a spy.

Come on, Dani. You need to try harder than this.

She began to walk east. Quietly Billy slipped from the shadows and followed.

He kept his left hand hooked on his belt, easy access to the thumb drive and the Ruger. His wounded right hand was becoming numb. He tried to make a fist and the pain almost blinded him. Keeping her in sight, he reached across his body and slipped the knife from his right hip to his left. Even with his nondominant hand, he was confident he could do it in one strike if he moved on her quickly. Slip his bum arm between her pack and her back and pull her tightly to him. Knife to throat.

Up and back, hard as you can.

Across the street he saw Dani stop at a tro-tro stand. Billy stopped too, and stepped into the shade of a nearby TelTel mobile phone umbrella. A thought flickered through him, unbidden: *Get on it.* And when the tro-tro pulled away, and he saw that she was still standing there, waiting for the next one, he felt something like dread.

"You want minutes, obruni?" asked the Teltel man. He held up a brand-new Android. "Five minutes, one hundred cedis good price."

Billy stepped away, taking a few paces along the street parallel to Dani.

He swallowed a few deep mouthfuls of dirty air.

Now was the moment.

Be quick, be clean, be gone.

He looked left, looked right. A gap in traffic. He could be across the road in seconds. She would not have time to react. She would not know what to do even if she saw him coming. He would overpower her instantly. He had felt her in his arms. She was slight, she would break like a bone.

"Do it now," he said aloud. Willing himself. Where was the feeling of falling when he needed it? Dani was as bad as David Ibrahim. She was as bad as Lu Zhong. She needed to die. She was helping people who were trying to kill him. She would have killed him herself, if their roles were reversed. Billy's life meant nothing to her. It never had. Do it *now.*

But all he could see was what she had looked like sobbing. Eyes closed, head turned away from him. Defenseless.

Now the traffic was roaring back. Billy stood rooted to the spot, his left hand on his hip, his right hand hanging useless, throbbing with pain.

Dani's head turned in his direction and stopped. Her whole body tensed.

She had seen him.

But by the time the traffic cleared again he was gone.

TWENTY-FOUR

An hour outside Accra, the countryside began. The window framed snatches of Ghana like a camera lens. Trees bending low in the humidity. A spilled orange in red dirt on the side of the road. A man in the street drinking from a Guinness bottle, swaying his hips to the music from a transistor radio. Between the villages, thickset jungle ran past the window. At one point, Dani saw a large dirt field installed with solar panels, with signs in Chinese characters.

The other tro-tro passengers sat silently. No one paid her any attention at all.

Unexpectedly, she dozed.

A swerve smacked her head against the window and woke her. They were approaching Kumasi. The tro-tro stopped to let off two passengers and a crowd of hawkers surged towards the bus. Dani played middleman, passing cash through the window in one direction, balls of dough wrapped in wax paper in the other. She bought one for herself.

As she munched on the dough, watching blurs of people pass, Dani took stock of what she knew.

The time was now—she checked her phone—just after 1:00 p.m. on Sunday. Yesterday, at approximately 1:00 p.m., Lu Zhong had told her that an American assassin was on his way to Kumasi, that the Chinese had been tipped off and would detain him within the next twenty-four hours. Lu Zhong had ordered Dani to report to a local hospital, without telling her what she would find there. This morning, she had stolen a phone from James's office that contained two text messages. The first text, sent to an unknown number: *Ezekiel, soula st.* At the Ezekiel Garage on Soula Street, she had found someone shot dead: the man who worked the counter at the Jericho Café. Jericho was where James kept the computers he used for his work on behalf of Lu Zhong. The second text, received from Carlos Rivera's number: *Ford confirms Lancaster Hotel 2300.* The Lancaster Hotel was in Kumasi.

There were some logical leaps between these facts. But Dani knew the truth in her gut. James was the Ghanaian mole and Carlos Rivera was the assassin. There was no other reason that James and Carlos Rivera would be texting each other. There was no reason James would be texting a man shot dead. There was no reason James and Carlos would be meeting in Kumasi, together with whomever or whatever "Ford" was.

There was no explanation that bound all of them together. Except one.

Some doubt had gone quiet, a lonely thought that had been shouting dimly on the edge of her awareness for a long time now. That had brought her to the Vodafone HQ and led her to break into James's office. That had driven her to follow James to the Jericho Café in the first place. That had kept her digging through Ben's files, even after James had told her about the $7 million scheme, even after he had confessed that he was passing information to Chinese spies. Even as she had committed herself irrevocably to James's life, not just in her actions but in her heart, even as she had felt herself becoming more and more bonded to him, more and more protective of him, more and more identified with him, some stubborn part of her had remained aloof and unsatisfied. The barest thread of resistance. Just enough.

Her journalist's instinct. Alma would be proud.

But where did that leave her now? James was the only meaningful relationship left in her life. He was a friendly, goofy, pompous kid. There had to be some comprehensible explanation for his role in all this. Yes, she had a set of facts in her hands that implicated him in violence—but there was also plenty she didn't know. Was James complicit in the murder of the man in the garage? Was he in danger himself?

And Carlos? She had a sudden memory of the first night she had spent with him—how hard he'd gripped her arms when the lights came on suddenly. The bruises had lingered for days. She thought about his eyes watching her at To God Be the Glory, that deceptively small, thin build. God, she had *slept* with that guy. She thought of Lu Zhong's description of the murder of David Ibrahim. "Very violent." Had David Ibrahim begged Carlos Rivera for his life?

Would she have to beg for hers?

Because that was why she had go to Kumasi. To stop whatever was happening. To put herself in the path of whatever danger James was in. Dani had come to Ghana looking for a story—and what she had found was a person who needed her help. James was not blameless, clearly. But neither was she. Neither was anybody. He deserved someone in his corner. She was going to get James out of this mess—whatever this mess was. And if necessary, she was going to put herself in harm's way to do it.

"Kumasi, Kumasi," the driver's mate shouted from the front seat.

They had arrived.

THE BUS DROPPED HER off in front of a Standard Chartered bank across the street from a mosque. The minaret was painted mint green.

Dani picked her way down the street, boots crunching on the dirt road, which the recent rains had churned up into waves of mud that the searing sun had dried into spikes. She passed women in hijab and men balancing boxes of bread on their heads. A white backpacker with dreads caught her eye, then looked away.

It took her a second to register what she was hearing. The muezzin's call, echoing through the streets. Kumasi was a border city, in its own way. You could feel the proximity of another world.

Above a roundabout bustling with traffic three billboards loomed over the roadside. The first said *Welcome to Kumasi,* with a smiling picture of the local Member of Parliament, an NDC man: one of Oscar Aidoo's enemies. The second was an ad for Oxo laundry detergent. The third showed a young man with his arm around a woman in a bikini. It said: *Have fun, but think about AIDS.*

Dani remembered Laurie Balfour exhaling sheesha smoke on a beach in Dakar. She remembered Laurie resting her hand on Dani's sweaty forehead in the malaria ward, telling her: "In some ways you remind me of me." What would Laurie make of her current predicament—of the turn Dani's life had taken? Would she be proud of Dani for not being afraid to die? Or would she be screaming at the top of her lungs for Dani to stop, halt, turn around—that death was not the answer to anything, only the permanent absence of answers? Was she screaming in Dani's face even now? If Dani closed her eyes and listened hard enough, could she hear her over the sounds of traffic?

The Manhyia District Hospital was in a quiet neighborhood, across the street from the Manhyia Palace, the home of the Asantehene, the king of the Ashanti people. Dani walked past the entrance to the hospital twice without seeing any obvious indications of activity. A piece of paper was taped to the front door, but from a distance she couldn't read what it said. On her third pass down the street she muttered "Fuck it" and walked up to the entrance.

The sign read simply: HOSPITAL CLOSED.

Dani peered through the glass door into the darkened room beyond. She knocked on the glass, timidly at first, then more forcefully.

Nobody came.

Dani crossed the street and loitered in front of the entrance to the palace museum, blending in with the handful of obruni who stood in line, guidebooks in hand.

She waited. After thirty minutes, she had still seen no signs of life at the hospital. Unsure what else to do, she decided to buy a ticket to the palace to kill time.

For a while she wandered in a musty twilight of placards and dioramas, one hand hooked through the straps of her backpack. She saw a replica of the Golden Stool: the throne of the Asantehene, the sacred center of the Ashanti nation. In 1900, the British governor had traveled north from the coast and demanded to sit on it. The Ashanti Queen Mother, Yaa Asantewaa, called the people to arms. Dani proceeded along the displays, reading. She paused at the word Kokofu—where had she seen that before? Yaw's village. She still had the phone numbers of his aunties, Christina and Yvonne. Kokofu was the site of an Ashanti fort, where a British attack had been repelled, causing many casualties. In the end, the Ashanti had won the war. No white ass ever sat on the Golden Stool, and the British retreated back to the Gold Coast. Though not before leveling the fort and town of Kokofu on the way.

When she emerged back into daylight, another sound competed with the muezzin's call: church bells. Dani counted: 3:00 P.M.

Across the street, the hospital entrance was as dark and silent as ever. There was no indication of anything unusual having occurred there. Indeed, no indication that it was even a functioning hospital.

Dani frowned into the sun.

There was only one other location in Kumasi she could think to go.

AT THE LANCASTER HOTEL, Dani rang the little bell at the front desk and waited.

"Hello?" A young man poked his head around the corner.

"Do you have a guest here named James Aidoo?"

"Eh?"

"James Aidoo? Or Carlos Rivera? Are they staying here?"

The man frowned and came closer to her. "Rivera?"

"Yes. I'm supposed to meet him, to talk to him for an article for my magazine." Dani took out her phone and showed him a picture of James. "And I'm looking for this man as well. What room is he staying in?"

The clerk laughed for some reason. "Aw," he said, seeming suddenly shy. "Who are you?"

"I am a reporter, an American reporter. He has information for me."

The clerk looked around the deserted lobby. He scratched his chin. "Reporter?"

"Just tell me what room," Dani snapped.

He considered her for a moment. "Wait here, please. Wait here." Then he disappeared into the back.

Ten minutes passed. Twenty.

Dani rang the bell again. "Hello!" she shouted.

She sat on a bench by the door and waited. If she thought too far ahead, panic would set in. She could sense it, just beyond her awareness, like a wind at the door.

For a moment she held her head in her hands. When she raised her eyes, a Chinese man was standing in front of her. In confusion Dani tried to shake the man's hand, as if greeting a colleague.

The man grabbed Dani's wrist with one hand, her neck with the other, and threw her to the ground. Fluid and forceful. Later, she would remember thinking: *I have never been thrown before.*

BOTH HANDS WERE WRENCHED behind her back. Blackout goggles over her eyes, then a hood over the goggles: she felt its heavy wool weight on her exposed collarbones.

Her ankles were shackled together. They were dragging her somewhere. She heard a thump, a door slam. Sudden silence.

They drove her for what felt like an hour. The hood and the vibrations of the floor of the vehicle made her feel almost sleepy.

When the goggles were yanked off her head, she was in the middle of a large, empty room, with a concrete floor that sloped gently to a drain in the corner. In the center of the room was a chair with butcher paper pulled over it, like you see at a dentist's office. Restraints dangled from it. The metal bottoms brushed the floor.

Two youngish women with Asian faces were in the room with her. One of them stared at Dani with a fierce, undisguised hatred. As if Dani had killed her child. The other looked almost bored.

"Undress," said the bored one.

Dani stared at her. "Excuse me?"

The bored woman turned her head slightly and yelled something over her shoulder. The door opened, and the man who had yanked her out of the Lancaster Hotel's lobby entered. He strode across the room in two quick steps and grabbed Dani roughly, pulling on her shirt, her belt, her bra strap. She felt his breath on the back of her head, felt his fingers nearly encircle her arms.

"Wait, wait," she pleaded, "stop, *stop*—"

The woman said something in Mandarin, and the man released Dani. He stepped back against the wall and waited.

"Undress," the bored woman said again.

"Can he leave?"

The woman shook her head. "Undress," she said simply.

Dani began to tug her shirt over her head. She was shaking. After a few seconds the woman spoke again, and the man left, closing the door softly behind him.

Dani continued undressing until she was naked. She was photographed: front, side, back. She was weighed and measured. Then she was given a hospital gown to wear: thin, papery; somehow it made her feel colder. Her pulse, blood pressure, and temperature were taken. Blood was drawn. "Make a fist," said the bored woman, tying on the tourniquet above her elbow. She provided a urine sample. There was no curtain. No toilet but the drain in the floor. Seeking privacy, she backed into a corner of the room and squatted against the wall. The women watched her, expressionless. "Up," said the bored woman, gesturing toward the dentist chair. "Open your legs." The other woman, the angry one, put on a latex glove. Dani resisted. She couldn't help it. Her body twisted away from the contact. "You want the chains?"

Dani forced herself to relax. She tried to deepen her breath. She thought of the night of her son's birth. The cold, the pain. Still. Birth.

The angry woman said something in Mandarin to the other woman, who made a note on a clipboard.

Then the women left. No instructions were given. Dani had nowhere else to sit but on the horrible dentist's chair. She was freezing, and her stomach hurt. She picked up her underwear from the floor and put it on gingerly. After a few minutes she put the rest of her clothes back on too.

The door opened again, and three people filed in. The man who had yanked her out of the Lancaster lobby, and another, similarly mean-looking goon, each carrying a chair. Behind them, a new woman. Different from the others. She wore a Western-style pantsuit, and shoes with heels that clipped on the wet concrete. Her hair was a bob cut at a jagged angle, so that one end of it almost obscured her right eye. She carried a manila folder, and her hands were freshly manicured. Dani felt it: power, like a shift in temperature. This was the person in charge.

The two goons placed the chairs they were carrying in the middle of the room, facing each other, and then stepped back against the wall, motionless. They reminded Dani of Lu Zhong's bodyguard. Where did they manufacture these guys? Chinese, Americans, Ghanaian—the models were all the same. Identical musculature and jawlines rolling off a thug assembly line, stamped with a humorless expression and put in their boxes with packing peanuts.

The stylish woman sat down and gave a delicate little cough. "Please sit," she said. Her English was perfect, barely an accent.

Dani stayed standing. Her whole lower body felt frozen from when the other woman—nurse? guard? jailer?—had stuck her fingers inside her.

"Who are you?" she said.

"My name is Florence Xiao. Please." She indicated the other chair with an open palm. "Sit."

"You want to what? Have a nice chat? After your people physically abused me, violated me?"

"I simply thought you might want to sit," Florence said pleasantly. "We will be here for some time."

"Where are we? By what authority are you detaining me here?"

Florence ignored Dani's questions. She flicked open the slim folder she was holding and took out a picture.

"Do you know this man?"

Dani looked down. It was Carlos Rivera.

"Yes."

"Did you know he was a CIA officer?"

"Where is Lu Zhong?" Dani said. "I am here on his orders."

"Lu Zhong is dead." Florence took out another picture, and then another. "These were taken at approximately six A.M. this morning."

Dani bent over them. They appeared to be stills from a security camera. The images were in black and white but the resolution was clear. The first one showed Carlos Rivera inside the home of Lu Zhong—sitting at the very same table where Dani had been sitting yesterday, receiving her orders to proceed north to follow the American assassin in Kumasi.

The second picture showed Carlos getting to his feet, holding a knife in his hand.

The third picture showed Carlos walking through the kitchen with a cigarette in his mouth.

At the next picture Dani gasped, she could not help herself. It was not a still from a security camera but instead had been taken directly over a gory heap in a tangle of bedsheets, somebody's hand in a latex glove holding up the chin of a face that it took her a second to recognize as Lu Zhong's.

"Oh my God," she heard herself murmur.

Wordlessly Florence handed her still more pictures from her folder. Carlos and Dani with Marc at the Holiday Inn pool bar, a time-stamped image from a security camera. A long-lens photo of Carlos and Dani at To God Be the Glory, leaning into each other. Another of Carlos and Dani kissing over a beer. Florence moved her finger across the picture. "And this man?"

Dani swallowed. "That's Yaw."

"Nana Yaw Owusu. Ghanaian."

"Yaw knows nothing about any of this. He is innocent."

"And yet he runs a bar where American intelligence officers feel safe meeting their sources."

"I'm not a source."

"No? Then what is your relationship, Danielle Moreau, with the intelligence officer known as Carlos Rivera?"

The tone was suddenly sharp. This was an interrogation.

"We had a personal relationship," Dani said in a shaky voice.

"An intimate relationship?"

"Yes."

"Did you know he was in the CIA? Did you pass him information?"

"No. Never." When Florence cocked a perfectly sculpted eyebrow, Dani continued, "You must know that I entered Ghana as a journalist. I collect sources and acquaintances who might help my reporting. I met Carlos at Yaw's bar. All of it stemmed from my work as a journalist."

"And now Lu Zhong is dead," Florence said. "Throat cut in his own home. Killed very brutally, very." She made a face, as if she had seen or smelled something unpleasant. "Just as David Ibrahim was. Our only conclusion," Florence continued, "is that we have been betrayed. The question is: by whom?"

And now Dani was realizing something else. Lu Zhong *passed* orders. He didn't give them. He was a cutout. *You want to make it hard to track the journey from A to B? Give it a lot of pointless zigzags in between.* Because it was obvious that Florence was the one giving orders here.

Florence flipped to a new page in her folder and began to read. "Danielle Moreau," she said. "Age: 32. Born Lenox Hill Hospital in Manhattan, New York. Parents Clarisse and Luc Moreau. Previously married to Benjamin Whitcomb, a British national."

As Dani listened to this woman narrate the facts of her life—they seemed pretty thin, laid out like this—she tried to calculate whether the Chinese knew that James was the mole they had been hunting. Why had nobody been at the Manhyia Hospital, where Lu had told her to go? How had they known to look for her at the Lancaster Hotel, when the only two people who should have been there were James and Carlos Rivera? If the Chinese had figured it out on their own, then they knew that James had betrayed them, and he was in grave danger—maybe even already dead. But Florence had not mentioned James once. She seemed entirely focused on Dani.

Florence paused and clicked open a pen. She showed Dani a photograph. "Who is this woman?"

"Priscilla. She's Nigerian. Stayed in the next room over from mine in Accra."

"And her? And him?" It was amazing what details the power of a state could uncover when it turned its greedy eyes upon someone. She had pictures of everyone. She had video of her and Marc and Carlos Rivera at the taping of *Stars of the Future.* She had the name of the librarian at the University of Accra who had helped her print out Ben's diagrams on Jushu.

But still the state wanted to know more. Florence asked question after question. Provide the names of everyone who knew you were in Ghana. Provide their addresses. Provide the location of the first time you met Marc Rutland. Where in London. Who were you with.

Dani felt she was learning, even through her exhaustion and terror. Espionage, like journalism, was simple. Relationships. That's it. Figuring out who knows whom, who owes favors, who is owed them. You map the truth, as best you can, from incomplete information: you move pictures across boards, drawing lines between them. But in espionage, unlike journalism, you must also understand that on other boards, in other rooms, your pictures are being moved around too.

"You haven't asked me about James Aidoo," Dani said finally.

Florence nodded as if she had been waiting for this. She slipped shut her manila folder and stood. "Come with me."

OUTSIDE THE CONCRETE ROOM, Dani saw that the place they were in was little more than a large garage with dirt floors. In a back corner, fake plastic walls had been erected, creating a miniature room within a room. A small hinge door was visible in one of the walls, a guard stationed on a chair in front of it, arms folded across his chest. He moved aside when Florence and Dani approached. The hinge door swung open.

And there was James.

She felt again, unprompted and uncontrollable, the same maternal feeling that had bloomed inside her back at the truck stop on the return trip from Takoradi, the day she had watched James being beaten by his father. Dani wished that she and James were alone. She wished they could just talk.

He was clearly agitated, his hands twisting each other in his lap. But he appeared unharmed.

"There you are," he said—speaking not to Dani but to Florence. He got to his feet. "I demand to be released at once."

"We are holding you here for your protection, as I have told you, Mr. Aidoo," Florence said. "The American intelligence officer known as Carlos Rivera has killed Lu Zhong, and we suspect he was the same individual who killed David Ibrahim. He may be coming for others next."

"My safety is my own concern. You cannot detain me in this, this"—James stumbled for the words, gesturing around at the walls of the plastic cell—"this *place.* And stick some impudent men at the door who threaten and glower. Is this how a great nation behaves?" He was breathless with indignation. Trying his hardest to be imposing, but still coming up short. Like a child inhabiting a role that he was not yet ready for. "You invest seven million dollars in me. You ask me to hack into the Americans' systems to help you find the assassin. At every turn I meet your demands. More than once, Lu Zhong has told me I am the most valuable asset that China has in this country. And now you treat me this way? You, you," he stuttered again, "imprison me?"

"It is for all those reasons that we do keep you in custody," Florence said patiently. "For your protection. It is temporary."

"It is intolerable! I demand that you release me at once." He was breathing heavily, striding back and forth in short bursts. But Dani had to credit him. If he was afraid, if he thought he was in any danger of being found out as the mole for the Americans, he was hiding it well. All she saw was anger. She thought of something Lu Zhong had said, the smoke from his cigarette filling his little kitchen. *It takes skill to look someone in the eye and lie to them. Not many people can do it.*

"I will not permit this to continue."

"You do not have a choice."

"My father will not allow it."

"Your father does not have a choice either."

"I promise you, whoever you are, you are making the mistake of your career. I do not even know you, and you come to Ghana and presume to give me orders."

"Of course, I apologize," Florence dipped her chin, a precise and insincere bow. "But just as you do not know me, Mr. Aidoo, I do not know you."

"Lu Zhong knows me," he said, lowering his voice "He has known me since I was a boy."

"Lu Zhong is dead." Florence made a small chopping gesture at the air with her open palm, a movement that managed to be both gentle and brutal. James stepped backwards. Finally he turned his eyes onto Dani, like he was noticing her for the first time.

"*She* is the one at fault," he growled. "Her and her CIA boyfriend. She is the one who should be in custody."

"I am in custody," Dani retorted.

"If she is so much at fault," Florence said, "then perhaps you should have killed her when you had the chance."

James looked up eagerly. "Let me kill her now."

A long silence that Florence did not break. Dani looked down at her hands in her lap, at her thin, dirty fingers. There were no windows in the room, but her eyes had adjusted to the darkness somewhat.

She remembered the way James had first greeted her with a "howdy" on the Aidoos' veranda in Accra. She remembered the way that he had stopped to comfort Yaaba, as they had fled the house in Takoradi under a hail of Oscar Aidoo's abuse. The softness with which he had hoisted her to her feet when she had collapsed at Sandbox, gently depositing her at her own front door. Yes, all along she had suspected he was not telling the full truth. Her journalist's instinct had been right about that. But could *everything* have been a lie? And if some or even most of what James had told her had been true, didn't that excuse the rest?

"Ms. Moreau?" Florence said finally, her voice rising—as if an idea had just occurred to her. Dani recognized the interviewer's tell, an eagerness, a slight leaning forward. "I wondered if you could answer a question for me."

"Of course."

"Why were you at the Lancaster Hotel today?"

She watched James's head tilt as if he had heard something faint: the whisper of his own death brushing past his ears. She tried to calculate it all in an instant, the moral equations, the fair thing to do, the right answer. But there was no right answer. Her mind was unchanged and her task was the same.

She had to get James out of here.

"Because Carlos told me he would be there," she said easily. "He wanted me to come meet him at the Lancaster Hotel. So we could have sex."

If James felt relief, he did not show it. "You see?" he shouted at once, voice choked with disgust. "This is why Lu is dead and we are all at risk. This ignorant American troublemaking bitch. And instead of killing her, you put me in prison? Is that how you repay me for fifteen years of loyal service?"

"Oh grow up, James," Dani said, sensing her moment. "You're sorry you met me? *I'm* sorry I met *you.* But we all made our choices and you need to stop whining about yours. Like that Bible verse you told me on the drive to Takoradi, in your flashy Ford truck. Ezekiel 22, verse 30, right? *I put away childish things*?"

There. A slight widening of the eyes. That was all it took but it told her what she needed to know. James understood her.

"Corinthians," he muttered.

Florence cut in. "You confirm that you were at the Lancaster Hotel at the behest of Carlos Rivera?"

"Yes," said Dani. "I was waiting for him when your people showed up."

Florence opened her folder and made a small note.

"You should let James go," Dani continued. "It's my fault we are in this situation. It's my fault that Lu Zhong is dead. James shouldn't be detained because of something I've done."

"James is here for his protection," Florence said again. "As you are."

"If you hurt him in any way, then you can forget about me being of any use to you. You want an American to die in a Chinese prison? I'll smash my head into the wall."

Florence smiled sympathetically. "You have had a long day, I think. You must be tired." She closed the folder, and at the same moment, as if by some wordless signal, the door to the cell opened, and the two women who had examined her stepped inside once more.

Dani glanced at James but he was resolutely not meeting her eyes.

"We will continue our discussion tomorrow," Florence said, as the bored woman's hands closed around Dani's arm. "I wish you a pleasant rest."

THE DOOR OF HER cell was plastic, just like James's had been. Dani felt as though it was the middle of the night, but she had no way of being certain. The light in the prison outside her door's one tiny window was the same relentless industrial halogen it had been all day, all night, whatever time it was—however long had elapsed since she had been snatched from the Lancaster Hotel and brought to this place.

She tried to push the door open, without much conviction. It was locked from the outside. Immovable. Things take up space in the world. They're solid, you can't pass through them. Neither can you pass through people. They're solids too. They collide, damage, scuff one another. Displace and suffocate one another.

When had she last slept?

Twenty-four hours ago it had been Saturday night. She had been in Accra, in her dorm room at the guesthouse, listening to the pounding rain. Lu Zhong had given her an urgent assignment to head north, because the Chinese were about to capture the American assassin. She had lain on the same scratchy blankets that she had pulled around herself every night in the last two months, and she had listened to the rain.

And now she was a Chinese prisoner.

It could not be.

But it was.

Doubt ate at her. What did she know about any of these people? What did she know about Ghana and China, Jushu and fiber-optic cables, CIA spies and Chinese intelligence? Maybe they were all lying to her. Maybe this was a ploy, a scheme, a dream.

You can see how quickly it happens. Insanity is not something far away. You are deprived of sleep, you are moved from place to place, hands on your body. You are taken to a room you don't know, and you are locked inside, with nothing to distract you from your sprinting mind. You are fed information that may or may not be true. You are made to fear for your life. And then you are made to wait. She thought about the men in Guantanamo Bay. The men who were still there today. This peculiar privilege of her American family, or of Ben's friends at Chiltern Firehouse, to shake their heads and say, "Yeah, man, we are the *worst,*" as if being rueful would let them off the hook—when what they meant by "the worst" was that we hung people by their wrists from walls until their shoulders strained at their sockets and their toes dragged on the floor. When what they meant was that we poured water down their throats until their brains thought they were dying.

TWENTY-FIVE

HERE IS A THUMB drive. Here is your duty.

The mission is clear: stop China. Offense: get inside their systems. Defense: keep them out of ours. Until when? Until forever. Until the Chinese go away or learn to toe the line.

The mission is straightforward, and somebody just handed you the other team's playbook. The names of the politicians to watch, the locations of the present and future landing stations. You have done well, soldier. You hold your country's victory in your hands—or at least a powerful tool to stave off defeat a little longer.

Billy spun the thumb drive like a top. The little piece of black plastic swiveled for a moment then fell. He righted it with his good left hand. Flicked it again. Watched it wobble.

He was waiting for Ford. He'd left a signal for him with the bread vendor at his old drop spot, where he used to buy his Nescafé every morning, before everything had gone to hell. He was prepared for Ford to come bursting through the door with a dozen armed Marines from the embassy and place him under arrest. Billy had gone rogue after all. He had killed without authority.

But Billy was hoping that Ford would come alone. His case officer had no way of knowing the state of Billy's mind. No real indication he was anything less than fully loyal, fully committed to the mission. If Ford was alone, then Billy would have more flexibility to do what he needed to do. Once he decided whatever that was.

He picked up the thumb drive and spun it again.

When he had signed on with the agency, he had thought he'd be getting closer to the center of American power. But early in his training he had realized how wrong this was. His superiors had hammered it into them: We do not make decisions, the elected officials do. Which is to say, the American people do. They give us our orders and we carry them out. None of his bosses had authority, not at the agency nor in the military. Ford sure didn't. Billy felt as sorry for him as anybody. They were all tools. And when a tool stopped being useful, you junked it and got yourself a new one.

"William Jefferson Demirjian" was known to no one in Ghana. Not even Ford. Hiding your true name was good opsec—operational security. But it also meant that he was lost to the world. Compare that to all the names he had scrolled past on the thumb drive on Lu Zhong's computer. African politicians. Tech CEOs. People who really *existed.* Who could not just be killed and erased. People whose lives would have to be answered for. But nobody knew where Billy Demirjian was. Not his dad, not his mom, not his sister. None of the kids he had grown up with in Rochester. Not Erin McConnell, who had let him take her to Chili's.

He dropped his bad right hand heavily onto the table and touched it with his left index finger. Trying to feel his own skin the way a stranger would. Was Billy Demirjian here, right now?

Did he even exist anymore? When Ford opened the door and saw him sitting there, who did he see?

"Rivera."

Billy slowly turned around. Ford was just inside the door, back to the wall. Alone, it looked like. But there was no way to know who was outside.

"Sir," he replied.

"Tell me what happened."

Billy started with the truth. "Aidoo betrayed us. I went to Kumasi. But something didn't feel right. I could tell I was being surveilled."

"What gave you that idea?"

"Just a feeling. You know how sometimes the back of your neck gets cold? And I was right. A team of Chinese agents broke into my room. Right away I knew the plan had to be aborted. Hustled back to Accra and went straight to the source, to Lu Zhong. Because the Double told us he was running things. I know I should have sent up a smoke signal. But there was no way to know if Aidoo had compromised you too. I'll admit it: I wasn't thinking completely straight. And then Lu attacked me with a knife." He held up his bandaged hand. "No choice. I had to ice him."

Ford considered him for a long moment, leaning back against the wall by the door. Billy sat listening. If there were other men outside, they were not making a sound.

"You need to report to the embassy immediately." Ford's voice was soft, authoritative. He did not sound worried. "Whatever you did at Lu's house, the Chinese are up in arms about it. We've been monitoring their chatter. First it exploded. Then it went dark. At least four suspected Chinese intelligence assets from across West Africa have transited through Ghanaian immigration in the last twenty-four hours. The cavalry is here. If you were trying to start a war, you got your wish."

"Thought we were already in one."

"Aidoo disappeared somewhere outside Kumasi. Together with an American journalist named Danielle Moreau. Who I understand you have gotten friendly with."

"Moreau is working for the Chinese too."

"Yes. Aidoo told me."

"And you didn't share it with me?"

"Didn't think I had a reason to." Ford shifted his weight from side to side. "It's not my business where you dip your stick, Rivera. But it is my business when it interferes with a play I'm running. Anyway, it doesn't matter now. We can't find either her or Aidoo. Possible they're already dead."

Billy sat back. "You lost them."

"No, *you* lost them." Ford took a quick step forward and stuck a finger in Billy's face. "So these are your orders. You are to come with me to the embassy, now, and you will be put on a plane back to the States. That's the best I can do for you, and I suggest you don't make this difficult. Because believe me, there are people in the embassy who want to turn you over to the Chinese and let them rip you limb from limb."

Billy felt sorry for Ford, yes he did. It couldn't be easy being a case officer. Your results were never good enough, and you were responsible for the behavior of people you could never really control. It must have been a life of constant tension. A life where every victory was only a temporary respite.

"No one's going to want to turn me over to the Chinese," Billy said quietly, "when you see what I took from Lu's house."

"And what is that?"

"A thumb drive." But Billy was surprised to hear that his own voice sounded not triumphant but vacant. Listless. He was running out of steam. Not just for this conversation. For all of it, and all of them. "It has everything. The locations of their current landing stations, and future ones. The politicians they've bribed in Ghana, Nigeria, everywhere. How much they've paid. The shell companies they use. All of it."

"Give it to me."

Billy didn't answer.

Ford took out a gun and pointed it at him. "Give it to me, Rivera." He reached forward and his hands grazed Billy's arm, and—

—and suddenly Billy had Ford's windpipe in the crook of his right elbow and was pulling backward, a shot had gone off and hit the wall, its echo was ringing in all directions, if there were other men outside he was finished but nobody came, Ford was alone, and his neck was at the mercy of Billy's right arm, Billy looped his good left hand on top and shoved it into his right armpit so that the weight of Ford's own head would seal both of Billy's arms in place. He looked away. Could feel Ford's rib cage fighting to breathe. The diameter of its expansion getting smaller and smaller. The interval between its attempts getting shorter and shorter. Ford's hands swiped uselessly at anything, at the floor, at Billy's legs, trying to gain purchase on his arms to pry them apart. But it would never happen. The science of the grip was immutable. "You taught me," Billy grunted. "You taught me this." Ford's eyes were wide with shock, pleading. Then the moment passed, and they slid out of focus.

Billy let him drop to the floor. He emptied Ford's pockets. Two passports, two cell phones. He threw the passports aside and shoved the phones in his pocket with the thumb drive.

Before he shut the door behind him he started to clean the fingerprints off the handle. But then he realized there was no point. There was nothing to hide anymore.

TWENTY-SIX

James Aidoo was neither so heedless nor so optimistic as to have believed that the appearance of Danielle Moreau in his life would have made things simpler. But he could never have anticipated how intertwined their fates would become.

And how quickly! As he lay on a cheap bunk in his cell, separated from the rest of the safe house by a plastic partition, he remembered the day, barely four weeks ago, when she had first appeared on his veranda and sat with him and Kofi, asking her questions about the Jubilee Oil Field.

And now here he was: an American double agent held prisoner by the Chinese, somewhere in the jungle outside Kumasi—his survival utterly in this stranger's hands.

Twenty-four hours ago it had been Saturday night in Accra. James lay on his red satin bedsheets, unable to sleep. He had been up for hours, reading and rereading the article that had appeared on *Ghana Today*'s website.

"MURDER IN DANSOMAN!" screamed the headline. A thirty-one-year-old man from Dansoman, Kwabena Oppong, had been shot by an unknown assailant and discovered by a mechanic at

Ezekiel Garage. Robbery was suspected. The victim's father was the cousin of a prominent MP. The family declined to be quoted. Their pastor was instead.

"Kwabena was a smart man, a God-fearing man," said Reverend Arthur Adu. "For money? May these devils who have done this be struck down by God. For the wages of sin is death."

As James had stared at the article, he considered how little he had actually known about Kwabena's life. The man was—had been—a relative of his best friend, Kofi. A second or a third cousin from one of the poorer branches of the family. That was how James had met him in the first place. He had been looking for someone to mind the till at Jericho Café, and Kofi had said, "My cousin Kwabena needs a job."

James had known that Kwabena loved science fiction; he was always reading some American or British book about robots or aliens or zombies. He had known that Kwabena was always doing odd jobs for extra cash. But other than that, the man had been anonymous to him. James did not know if he had a girlfriend, he did not know where he went to school, he did not know what he liked to eat or what football club he supported.

And now he was dead.

Restless, James had walked out onto the veranda of his family's home. As Saturday night's rainstorm had faded into Sunday morning's pink sunrise, he had sat down in the chairs where he had first talked with Dani and Kofi a month ago, and waited for confirmation that Carlos Rivera was dead.

In that hour, the city was asleep. So when the car had accelerated down the road in his direction, James had known it was coming for him.

Two men. Chinese faces he didn't recognize. One of them had a gun on his hip.

"Come with us," the armed man had said.

James had risen from his chair as if in a trance. "What is happening?" he had said.

Gently but insistently they had kidnapped him, keeping him moving with fingers pressed into the joint where his spine met his skull. He had not been sure if he was under arrest: had his betrayal been discovered? There had been violence coiled behind the two men's movements—in the gun on the waistband and the casual but precise aggression in their hands. But there has been also, perhaps, a certain deference.

They had pushed him into the back seat. He had tried reaching for the door handle but it was locked. Watching the front yard of the Aidoo family home falling away through the window as the car accelerated into the morning, James had never thought he would be so sorry to see it go.

"What is happening?" he had said from the back seat. "I demand to speak to Lu Zhong."

The men had said nothing in reply.

"I demand to speak to my father, Oscar Aidoo."

Silence.

He had tried to absorb what he could from the scenes out the window. The car had left Accra behind, driving through the sprawling settlements on its outskirts, places with no character, with nothing to distinguish them but the presence of hundreds of thousands of people. He had thought they were heading north, but he couldn't be sure.

He had almost begun to feel safe—surely if they were going to hurt him they would have already done it—when he had felt the car pulling off the road and into a darkened space, some kind of garage. Then floodlights were pointed into his face. His eyes had stung at the suddenness of them, and he had braced for a beating, or worse. Was this the end?

But to James's amazement, the questions they had shouted at him were all about Carlos Rivera and Danielle Moreau. This American woman. Where she had come from. What James knew about her. What she had to do with Lu Zhong, who was apparently dead.

Gradually the picture became clear. They were looking for Carlos Rivera. They thought that Dani was the one who could lead them to him. And they were interested in James because they thought he could bring them Dani.

James could not tell them, of course, that *he* knew who Carlos Rivera was. That *he* was the one who had tipped them off. All he could do was repeat over and over that this was not fair, that he demanded to speak to his father.

And then, without explanation, the questions had ceased. He was moved to his current location, a kind of dormitory in the back of the garage, lit by a single fluorescent bulb. "I am hungry," he had said, before the door had slammed shut.

It looked like a cell in an American prison. There was a small bed, and a steel toilet in the corner. The false walls and lack of sunlight and uncirculated air made him feel as though he were underground. For hours he sat there, shivering despite the heat. At any moment, he had expected the door to swing open and a bullet to be put into his head.

But then the door had opened again, and Danielle Moreau had been standing there.

The stranger who held his life in her hands.

Because it was clear to James—after Dani and Florence had left him alone again in his cell—that somehow Dani had found out about his communications with Ford and Kwabena. She had been snatched up by the Chinese at the Lancaster Hotel—exactly where he and Carlos Rivera were supposed to have met. She had misquoted the Bible verse as Ezekiel 22:30—referencing both of the last two text messages that had been on his burner phone SIM cards. She must somehow have broken into his office and accessed them. She had even referenced his *Ford* truck—when everybody knew that Highlanders were Toyota.

There was no way these facts were a coincidence. Dani had figured him out from top to bottom. And she wanted him to know that she knew.

Evidently she had decided not to give up his secret for now, but he could not rely on her goodwill forever. There was nothing to stop her from changing her mind. And he suspected the Chinese agent who called herself Florence did not believe her story about being at the hotel to meet Carlos Rivera for sex.

Which itself raised other questions: how had Carlos Rivera survived? Had he somehow figured out James's plan and escaped? Or had he escaped without learning that James had double-crossed him? Where was Ford? Why was Lu Zhong now dead?

Events had spilled their banks, and he was being carried along at their mercy. If James thought too intently about what might happen to him next, about the paths that had brought him to this juncture, about the choices and mistakes he had made, he would be lost. Panicking would only put him in more danger.

The better approach was to consciously, artificially calm himself down.

Now he drew a circle in the dirt at his feet. Breathe. Be still.

Events had their own momentum. Their own energy.

Trying to fight it was impossible.

At some point, he supposed he slept—because the next thing he was aware of was the hinge door in the false plastic wall opening again, and one of his guards entering with a bowl of soup.

"Thank you," said James. "May I speak to Florence?"

The man shut the door wordlessly.

James gulped the soup, its heat filling his belly. But somehow the rush of nutrients made his exhaustion far worse, as if throwing it into relief. For a long time, all he could do was sit on the bed, leaning his head against the wall, eyes shut.

If he had not been so scared and exhausted, he could have cried. Or perhaps laughed. What a story. Forced into circumstances he would never have chosen for himself, by people whose aims were inherently selfish, by beasts like his father. He had tried to find his way out of the labyrinth with all the integrity and self-reliance of which he was capable. And now he was a murderer. A traitor to his country, to his friends, to Kofi, a traitor to his father, and worse, to his mother—his eyes stung, and now he actually was crying. How could he have done this? He was a *murderer,* and whatever happened next, he would remain one for the rest of his life, no matter—

His thoughts were interrupted by the sound of one of his guards hawking mucus into the dirt floor outside his door.

He twirled the empty soup bowl in his hand. The Chinese had been treating him better since Dani's visit, which had evidently eased some of their suspicions. But he was still a prisoner. What was it Mao had said? "Revolution is not a dinner party." How could anyone fault him for the actions he had been forced to take? He was an ant in the dust. Trying to survive, trying to leap to safety amid the chaos of the world's two giants fighting each other. You couldn't blame an ant for seeking higher ground. You couldn't blame the desperate for their desperation.

Indeed, revolution was not a dinner party; it was a logistical nightmare. A math problem. A computer code that needed to be debugged.

Yes. That was what he faced. An engineering challenge.

And he was a good engineer.

So what does one do with code? Start with the parameters, the facts that could not be changed. One: Dani now knew everything about his Double arrangement with the Americans. Two: she had decided not to tell the Chinese, at least for now. Three: Lu Zhong was dead. Four: Carlos Rivera, apparently, was not. Five: the Chinese were obsessed with one thing and one thing only: finding and neutralizing Rivera. Six: in the meantime, they had decided to park James here, apparently unsure of what to do with him.

Now, how to rearrange these parameters? How to make them talk to and interact with one another, so that the result was something useful?

At the moment he saw only bad options. He could try to escape and seek shelter with the Americans. But if Carlos Rivera had figured out that James had double-crossed him, and if he had told Ford, then of course the Americans would no longer protect him. What use was an asset you couldn't trust?

Could he go to the Chinese? Confess all, beg forgiveness? He had valuable information about the Americans' plans in Ghana, about their interests in vampire taps and telecom networks, about David Ibrahim's death.

But the Chinese would never forgive his betrayal either. They would kill him as soon as they realized what he had done—no matter who his father was.

His stomach tightened, and he tasted the soup at the back of his throat.

Softly now, softly. Panicking meant certain death. Follow the logic instead, one turn at a time. Logic was safe. It was regular and predictable. It made of the universe something obedient.

Start again.

Whatever had happened with Rivera, it did not necessarily follow that *Ford* knew of James's double-cross. Ford's role in all of this was a mystery, a black box.

And in that box, possibilities resided.

Because what was indisputably true was that Ford was the only person who could help him. The only one who knew all that James had done for the United States.

And what was also indisputably true was that if he could get to his safe house on Lake Bosomtwe, he could make contact with Ford.

And he was confident that if he could escape this prison, he would make it to his safe house. This was his land. These were his people. He spoke Twi. He blended in. He could dress in rags if he needed to, travel through back roads and small villages and slums: any Chinese pursuers would see another poor Ghanaian and would look right past him.

Of course, he was not the only one who knew about the safe house on Lake Bosomtwe; he had told Dani about it as well, in an inconvenient fit of conscience.

But that was a problem for later. For now his only chance of success was to proceed stepwise, methodically.

And so the first task, the first command in his computer code, was very simple:

Get out of here.

"I need," he started to say—but it came out a whisper. Then in one great breath he shouted, "*I demand to speak with Florence!*"

No answer from beyond the false plastic walls. He heaved another breath and shouted again, "*You are illegally detaining a Ghanaian citizen! I demand to be—*" but before he could say "released" the words died in his throat.

It didn't matter, of course, that he was a Ghanaian citizen. That was the whole point. That reality was what had gotten him here. Dani was protected, whatever mistakes she had made. She was American. No matter what she did, she would always have value as a bargaining chip between governments. But he had never gotten his blue and gold passport. He was still just a Ghanaian.

James banged his fist against the hinge door. "Hello!" he demanded. "Hello?"

Silence. The impassive disinterest of a world too crowded to take note of the most important events in its people's lives.

James shut his eyes.

He must have fallen asleep again, because sometime later—it might have been ten hours or ten minutes—he was awakened by a splash of cold water in his face. Florence was standing over him, flanked by two of her goons.

"Stand up," she said. "You are coming with me."

TWENTY-SEVEN

DANI OPENED HER EYES and bolted wildly awake—scratching at the air like a cornered animal, remembering all at once who and where and what she was.

A prisoner of the Chinese. A traitor against the United States.

The door of her cell was opening, the plastic making a soft scraping sound against the dirt floor. The women who worked for Florence were back. Her tormentors. Bored and Angry.

"Up," said Bored—the one who spoke English.

Dani went willingly this time; what choice did she have? They brought her back to the room where they had first examined her, with the dentist's chair and the drain in the corner of the floor. They made her sit. They shoved her back against the chair and dumped cold water over her head, wetting her dirty T-shirt and the sports bra she had been wearing when she had left Accra. They rubbed dye into her hair, its chemical smell harsh but familiar and therefore oddly comforting.

Dani kept trying to hug herself to fight the cold; they kept pulling her arms away. The angry woman yanked her head this way and that, rubbing in the coloring. Then they cut it close to the scalp. The dry click of scissors. Another familiar sound, from a different life.

They took her pictures again: making her stand in front of the blank white wall. Front, back, side. Then they did something new. They held out her forearm, turned towards the ceiling. A tool like a miniature drill-bit was pressed against the bony flesh of her wrist. She felt an instant of blinding pain, and the tool was removed, leaving behind a small, circular red pockmark.

As before, Florence had waited until the unpleasant work was finished before making her appearance.

She sat across from Dani now, her folder in her lap. Dani wanted to tell her the interview would have been more effective if she had brought a partner. Alma had once taught her that trick: you can interview in pairs. You fire questions rapidly at the subject one after the other. They can't keep up.

"Something has changed," Florence said.

"Yes?" Dani's fear had entirely evaporated. She was angry. "Are you going to tell me what it is?"

Florence cleared her throat, a small sound: *hmm.* "After killing our Lu Zhong, we had assumed that Carlos Rivera was heading to the landing station in Bekwai. We believed that was the Americans' target. So we posted our people there, but we have seen no movement. Now we know why." *Hmm.* "He took something from the home of Lu Zhong, something very important to us. And now we need to find it. But we have lost the trail. He is not to be found anywhere."

"What did he take?"

"A thumb drive."

Dani crossed her arms coolly. "So you fucked up," she said. "You wasted your time kidnapping and abusing me, and keeping James under suspicion. When all along you should have been out there trying to track down the man who is the real danger to you."

"The man we are chasing is a professional. Highly trained. I accompanied my men to the Lancaster Kumasi hotel to apprehend him. As soon as I entered his hotel room I knew at once that he had figured out what was occurring and had fled. And I knew that we would have to become creative to find him. Of course"—Florence lowered her eyes—"What I failed to anticipate was that he would proceed immediately to killing our Lu Zhong. I predicted he would try to get farther away from us, not come closer. The conclusion? He is not behaving according to rational calculations. And you are correct: failing to recognize this was my error. You will help me fix it."

Dani uncrossed her arms. "How?"

Florence took something small and green out of her folder and handed it to her. A South African passport. The cover was slightly mussed, the pages stamped occasionally. A very convincing imitation. Still warm, as though fresh from the printer.

She flipped it open. Christ, was that what she looked like now? In pictures Dani had always compared unfavorably to her sisters. She had a slightly wide face, a bigger nose than theirs. Now she just looked gaunt. Beside the picture were a name, date of birth, nationality. Lindsey van Broek. Thirty-three years old.

She had a sudden memory of trying on the dress that Priscilla had made for her, back in her room in Accra. Of admiring the way it fell on her hips.

"The silver fish," she said now.

Florence looked at her quizzically.

"You want to use me as bait. Just like Lu Zhong did."

Florence inclined her head slightly. "In a sense, that is the heart of the matter."

"So, what? I go back to Accra and I text Carlos *Wanna fuck?* And then I ask him where he hid the thumb drive? How stupid do you think he is?"

"Success is not guaranteed. But we do not have any other way to try to tempt him out in the open."

"If you want me as bait, why the new haircut? Why the fake passport?"

"This was the agreement I reached with my superiors," Florence said. "They are skeptical that the experiment will work, but I convinced them to try. We need you, the real you, out in the open, because you are the only person in Ghana to whom Rivera has any kind of intimate connection. The only person he might tell where the thumb drive is. But of course, the risk of leaving you in the open is that you will be tempted to run away. To make this more difficult, we take away your US passport and make you a different person."

"You think Carlos will recognize me?"

"We both know that he will."

After a moment Dani said, "How do you know he's not already back on a plane to the US with your thumb drive?"

Hmm. "Of course it is possible. But something about the way he has behaved thus far makes us doubt it. All the way back to David Ibrahim. Our people who examined Ibrahim's corpse reached the conclusion that this was a man losing his grasp on rationality. The behavior that we captured on security cameras in the home of Lu Zhong confirms this. I have watched it myself, many times now. Rivera is not *well.*" Florence raised her eyebrows slightly, as if to include Dani in that assessment. "So while you are correct that we may be too late, it is also possible that we are not. And we have an asset that we can use to try to cause him to reveal himself. So we must try."

"Bait," Dani said angrily. "That's the best use you can think of for me? For an American citizen who has volunteered to spy for the Chinese? Not once have any of you thought to use me for what I really am."

"Which is?"

"A soldier."

Florence laughed. Her teeth were immaculate. Everything about her was. Her skin, her hair, her nail polish. Sitting across from her, in her prisoner's clothes and her violated body and her new shorn haircut, Dani felt dirty and stupid. In a burst of frustration she said, "I demand to contact the American embassy!"

Florence sat quietly, letting it pass.

"I can hurt people if you want me to," Dani continued, more calmly. "I can put my body in danger. Look where we are—haven't I proven yet that I am not afraid?"

Dani was expecting Florence Xiao to tell her to shut up, to close her petulant mouth, to be grateful that she was still alive at all.

"Patience," Florence said. "You are still new at this."

"And how do you know I won't make a break for it? Why shouldn't I run to the Americans or call my family to let them know where I am? You think a haircut and a fake name means you've erased Dani Moreau?"

But even as she said it, Dani doubted herself. Hadn't she been living her life in exactly this way—cutting the threads that bound her to others, one by one by one? Who was left to vouch for the real her?

"If you try to flee during those twenty-four hours, you will be killed. If you try to contact anybody besides Carlos Rivera during those twenty-four hours, you will be killed. If Carlos Rivera has not surfaced within twenty-four hours after you contact him, we will have to assume he will not surface again, that he has left the country, and that all our information has been exposed."

"And then I will be killed?"

"That has not been decided."

"I would like to negotiate for James's freedom. If I agree to be bait for you, you must let him go."

Florence looked disappointed. "Worry about yourself, Danielle Moreau. That is my advice to you."

"But what will happen to him?"

"James Aidoo has been released." Her face was still, watching Dani carefully for any reaction.

Dani fought just as hard to stay unreadable. "Prove it," she said.

"Prove that we do not have him?" Florence smiled. "We do not. His father secured his release. And I assure you, James Aidoo did not try to negotiate for *your* freedom."

Dani held her gaze for another moment. "Good," she said.

"Besides"—Florence handed her a bundle of papers bound with a rubber band—"if you reappeared again, I think your family would be very surprised."

Folded inside were printouts of news clippings:

JOURNALIST FEARED DEAD IN RURAL GHANA.

EX-GUARDIAN REPORTER MISSING IN AFRICA.

She had even made *The Washington Post.* There were quotes from Ben. He had been worried about her for some time. It seemed she was not well.

Dani looked up. "So who am I now? Dani Moreau, or Lindsey van Broek?"

"For the purposes of attempting to make contact with Carlos Rivera, you will be Danielle Moreau for one more day. We will even let you have your old phone back. But in general," Florence nodded, "you are whoever we say you are, at any given moment."

Dani looked down at the fake passport. Lindsey and Dani stared back at each other, each knowing the other's worst secrets.

Your life; another person's life.

SHE WAS DROPPED OFF in an apartment block in a run-down looking neighborhood in Kumasi with a key to Unit 20. They gave back her phone and 500 cedis. "You will not have time to need more," Florence had said.

The building smelled of palm oil. The apartment was small, not much bigger than the prison cell. But there was a tiny kitchen and a tiny bathroom. There were noises somewhere above her head, a radio or a TV in a neighbor's apartment.

The red divot on her inner wrist ached. Beneath the skin she could feel something hard and round, like a plastic BB gun pellet.

Before she left, Angry and Bored had stood over Dani while she did as Florence instructed. She had texted Carlos Rivera from Dani Moreau's phone. Fresh life beneath their last exchange, from the night when she had wept in front of him.

Hey, she wrote.

I'm in Kumasi.

Thinking about you.

They had given her a detailed script to use if he responded, to slowly reveal her location and tempt him to reveal his. Then they had retreated to whatever vantage point they had chosen from which to monitor her. Far enough away not to rouse Carlos's suspicions.

The thought kept coming back to her: she could run. There must be some Americans around here somewhere. She could find a fancy hotel, go into the lobby and cause a scene.

But what if she tried it and failed? They had threatened to kill her. What if they turned Angry loose on her and allowed her to hurt Dani for real—the way she clearly wanted to?

She thought about James back in the prison cell: "*Let me kill her now!*" So eager; he had meant it. But Dani could not fault him his fear, his panic, his need to flee. He had more to live for than she did.

And now James had been released—China evidently unaware of his betrayal of them. If he was smart, he was long gone.

But if James no longer needed her help, what was she doing here? She was actively serving a foreign power hostile to the United States and helping them catch an American agent.

People went to jail for the rest of their lives for something like this. People were killed for it.

She longed to write down everything she had seen and heard and learned in the last two days. What she needed was time, and money, and safety, and something to eat. What she needed was more information. Travel records, phone records, bank records, access to CCTV tapes. Subpoena power would be nice too. What she needed was the power of a state. With the power of a state, she could figure it all out, trace the paths that had brought her from A to B to C.

But then, even states got it wrong. They got it wrong all the time. States weren't anything, really. They were just people. And the needs and desires of Ghanaian people or Chinese people were no less legitimate than those of American people. No less jealously guarded or deeply mourned. "A nation is just a story that people believe." She had meant it flippantly when she had said it to James and Kofi, wedged in the booth at Sandbox, the DJ's house music echoing over the distant waves. But it was true.

In the flat's tiny bathroom there was a bucket shower, which she filled up with cold water from the spigot. Dani took off her clothes and stood naked on the dirty tiles. She touched her hip bones. She had lost a lot of weight since London. Since the baby. She ran her hands along her thighs and felt herself, tenderly as possible, where the Chinese woman had jammed her fingers inside. *Cunt*, she thought savagely. She resolved that if she ever saw Angry again, she would kill her.

Dani's hand came to rest atop the small red bump where they had implanted something in her arm. A burst of Twi in the hallway made her jump. But it was only neighbors: a child's voice, and an old woman's, just beyond the thin walls.

THE TUMULT OF KUMASI was almost physically painful after the hushed stale air of the prison. She walked hesitantly at first, like a child learning how to do it. She tried looking around for anyone who might be tailing her. But it was no use; she was not trained in this. Dani kept expecting someone to stop her, for Florence's troops to emerge from some unseen shadow. She rehearsed excuses for when Bored and Angry dragged her away—her body flinched at the thought. She was doing what they had asked of her; she was not fleeing, not making a dash for freedom. She wasn't even drawing attention to herself: there were white tourists everywhere.

She entered a market. Byways of stalls, stacked with goods shipped in from everywhere on earth. The same crap you could buy in Accra and Takoradi. Packs of white undershirts. Mops, drill bits, fake Adidas sneakers, coils of HDMI wire. Finally she found a row of shops with the kinds of goods she was looking for. Cheap liquor in multicolored bottles, with elaborate stoppers in the shape of the African continent and the colors of the Ghanaian flag. On a table farther back in the stall, a row of knives in cheap leather sheaths, with AFRICA painted on their sides.

"You like knife, obruni? Six hundred cedis."

"One hundred. With that." She pointed at the liquor.

The seller scoffed at her. She scoffed back at him. "Fine," she said. "Let me borrow your SIM card and we'll call it even at four hundred." It was almost all the money Florence had given her. But she would not need it for anything else.

He leaned slightly backward, considering her. "Borrow phone?"

"Yes. I need to call someone. Quickly. Only two minutes."

"Okay, it is fine, obruni, it is fine. Four hundred."

While the man bagged the tourist tchotchkes Dani stepped still farther into the stall, trying to shield herself from whoever might be watching her. She called the number that Yaw had written down for her on top of a beer crate at To God Be the Glory, a few days and a lifetime ago.

She told herself that she was not putting these women in danger. But she knew that wasn't true.

On her walk back to the apartment block, she made a show of swigging from the ridiculous liquor bottle. If the Chinese were watching, they made no move to stop her. Dani was certain her plan would not work. How could somebody like her fool the Chinese state security apparatus? But she was not going back to that horrible prison with its dentist's chair. If she was destined to die, she was going to get it over with.

BACK IN THE DIRTY bathroom, she took a final gulp of the liquor and poured the rest of it over her wrist. In the close air a thin line of sweat clung to her skull, where Lindsey van Broek's haircut exposed several inches of new skin.

Her veins stood out against her thin bones. She slapped herself a few times, like a junkie in the park.

The knife was dull, which she had feared. A bead of blood appeared, then a flood. She bit down on the fake leather sheath, her tongue slipping over the painted AFRICA. Its chemical taste ran into her throat. Pools of saliva drooled to the floor with her spots of blood. Which kept coming. She reached blindly. Could feel the metal of whatever it was. But could not gain enough traction to pluck it out. Her eyes trying to close against the pain. She fought them open. Would not let them shut. Fell to her knees on the concrete. Dug the knife in deeper. Too deep. Heard herself sigh. *Ahhh.* Was this her death? Her chin was black where the melting AFRICA paint ran down it. She reached in with her fingers once again.

It was out.

She had it.

Panting, she lay on her side in her mess and held the tracker in her good right palm. A tiny piece of metal, roughly the shape of a washer on a screw. She marveled at her unruined right wrist, at its pink skin pulsing. With her teeth she tore a strip loose from her shirt and tied it tightly around her wounded left arm. In an instant the blood had soaked straight through. She stumbled to her feet and back into the apartment.

A pillowcase. That would do.

Shreds and shreds. With her mouth and her good hand she managed to wind them around the wound once, twice, three times. Pulled as tight as she could. The pain was excruciating, the fingers stiff and numb. Had she cut a tendon? The blood pulsed through, slowly turning the bandage a dark red.

It would stop or it wouldn't. She had to keep going.

Down the hallway and out the door, the tracker in her pocket. The sky had turned hazy and the sun was setting: a feeble, flat light. Her breaths were coming short and sharp. But Dani was still on her feet.

In the tro-tro to the Standard Chartered bank she sat next to a middle-aged man in a collared shirt and glasses, who stared straight ahead, stiff with the effort of trying not to touch or be touched by this filthy white woman with the bleeding arm. At his feet was an old-fashioned briefcase. At the next stop, as the tro-tro slowed and pulled over and the driver's mate called out their destination, the man cleared his throat and stood up. Dani grabbed his briefcase and got to her feet, moving aside to let him pass.

"Here you are," she said politely, handing him back his own briefcase. The man frowned and took it, stepping around her without a word.

The bus continued on. Dani let herself exhale just a little.

—
IT WAS AFTER 7:00 P.M. when Christina and Yvonne showed up, pulling to a stop in front of the bank in a battered Mercedes sedan. She had been expecting old ladies, but both of Yaw's aunties appeared to be in their thirties. They spilled out of the car, pinching her skin, voices piling on top of each other. "Akwaaba, akwaaba, akwaaba. You are welcome!" They touched her hair, speaking rapid Twi, rubbing the exposed skin on her arms. "Welcome to Kumasi! How did you travel? You are well? Ah, your arm, your arm, you are hurt!"

"Let's get in the car—quickly please. I will explain."

"Do you hear the Twi?"

"No. I'm sorry. Quickly, *please*."

If the Chinese had eyes on her, none of this mattered. But if they did not, and were relying on the tracker to keep her in sight, then they were following that man from the tro-tro home from work. And that meant Dani had a narrow window to get out of the city before Florence realized she had been tricked.

"Where are you from?" Yvonne demanded.

"As soon as you start driving, I'll tell you."

Yvonne clucked impatiently and they pulled out into traffic. Dani braced for the raised voices, the gunfire, the sirens. But all she heard was the honking of horns, the steady hum of the evening commute.

"You know Houston?" Christina was friendlier. She was the one Dani had spoken to on the market seller's phone. "We have cousins in Houston."

"You must add us on Facebook!" said Yvonne.

"Thank you for finding me," Dani said after a minute. Her voice was hoarse, her chest unclenched only slightly. She sensed that if she let herself go, let herself feel any real relief, she would be lost completely. "I'm very grateful."

"What happened to your arm?" Yvonne said. "Somebody hurt you?"

"Yes. Yes. But it's okay."

From the passenger seat Christina pulled Dani's hand towards her, turning it over to examine the dirty bandages. Dani yelped, dizzy with pain.

"We must change it," Christina said somberly. "It will become infected."

"We will change it in Kokofu," Yvonne pronounced.

"Kokofu?" Dani said. "I need to get to Amekom—to Lake Bosomtwe."

"Kokofu first." Yvonne's tone was final.

"You must rest there," Christina said. "You will be better."

"Listen, I cannot tell you why, but you need to keep me away from your friends and families. Please just bring me to Lake Bosomtwe."

"Bah," Yvonne said to Christina. "She says bring me to the lake? It is ten kilometers from side to side. Where? Eh? Where?"

"To a house," Dani wheezed. "In the town of Amekom."

"A house?"

"Yes. I don't know the street address. But it will be hidden, probably in the bush. You wouldn't find it on any map."

Christina and Yvonne looked at each other doubtfully.

"Kokofu first," Yvonne repeated.

They swerved around potholes and darting chickens in the long light of the setting sun. The two women chatted away in Twi to each other, while Dani, behind them, sat with her hands in her lap, weak with pain, with thirst, her left hand curled into a horrible claw in her lap. She was thinking about the generosity of strangers. She had told Yaw only that she needed to go to Bekwai to work on her story, to interview someone. She hadn't said who or why. Yet without suspicion he had arranged for her a place to stay, contacts. His own family.

And now she was putting all of their lives at risk. She was no better than James or Florence or any of the rest of them, playing human beings like chess pieces.

Arriving in Kokofu, they passed a little marketplace being packed up for the day. Yvonne parked the Mercedes outside a bigger building than the rest. Dani opened the door with her good hand and stumbled to her feet. After spending all her time in Ghanaian cities, this place felt utterly foreign. A handful of streetlights were strung along the main road, but otherwise the town was already dark. She had lived in this country for nearly two months, all of it amidst the loud voices and car horns and reliable cell phone service of cities. If someone had asked her "What's Ghana like?" she would have thought she knew the answer.

Yaw's aunties had brought her to the home of the town's big man; really it was a complex, several structures wrapped around a large central courtyard. Christina led her into a small room at the back of the main house, where she made Dani sit on a wooden stool and unwrapped her dirty bandages.

Dani forced herself to look. A huge jagged gash, frozen in a mess of congealed black blood. What might have been a tendon or a long flap of skin curled backwards up the wrist, bent like a rip in a pair of tights.

"Oh," she said.

Christina's tone was motherly, murmuring. "We must get you to the doctor."

"No time. I need to get to Amekom."

The woman shook her head. "Not this evening."

"Then just bandage it back up as best you can. Please. And tomorrow morning I'll be gone."

Christina muttered something in Twi, shaking her head at this rude obruni. But she took Dani's hand in her lap and sat down beside her.

"Thank you," Dani said.

But when Christina picked up a mug of steaming hot water and poured it over the wound, Dani passed out.

WHEN SHE CAME TO, she was wearing a clean shirt, and her wrist was bound tightly in fresh white bandages. Her whole body was sending one message, sounding one single alarm: she had nearly died. Everything hurt. Everything felt broken.

Christina and Yvonne were awake, murmuring in the corner. Dani gestured, clutching her stomach. The women gave her a flashlight and pointed. There was an outbuilding behind the home; the toilet was a normal-looking toilet, but it sat above a deep pit dug in the earth. Flies buzzed around Dani's head and buttocks. She heard not the splash of water, but a smaller, more distant sound.

Gingerly she walked back through the courtyard. Hurricane lamps hung from the rafters, too bright to look at directly. She could not find her way back to the room where she had been.

Christina and Yvonne had disappeared and Dani was lost, alone, disoriented.

Suddenly a young girl flitted across the courtyard in front of her.

"Bra, girl," Dani called. "Bra." The girl halted and cocked her head at this strange apparition. She said something in Twi.

"Water," Dani croaked. "Do you have water?"

The girl shrieked and ran away into the house.

Dani followed. Dark rooms. Low ceilings. She heard the girl's footsteps and listened for their echo, like a bat. Then she was in a smaller side courtyard, full of six or seven women and girls. The low light of a cook fire flickered in a corner. In the middle they were pounding the fufu for dinner. It was a two-woman job. The pestle was as tall as the girl who was holding it. She raised it above her head and brought it down on the mortar, where a second girl crouched, flipping the dough between strikes: fingers deft, flicking cavalierly, millimeters from the hammer blow.

Dani looked down; the girl she had followed was tugging on her sleeve, holding something in her hand.

"Yes?" Dani said.

It was an egg. Still warm and wet from the hen.

TWENTY-EIGHT

THE MIDDLE OF THE night. Accra was asleep, and Billy was in Dani's room at the guesthouse. If Ford had been telling the truth, she had gone over to the Chinese and would not be back.

He sat on her bed and spread out his worldly effects on the floor in front of him. It didn't look like much. Three cell phones: the two that he'd taken from Ford, plus his own. Uri Katsman's passport. Two bowie knives, one crusted at the base with Lu Zhong's blood. How long ago was that—forty-eight hours? When had he stood across the street from Dani and watched her waiting for the tro-tro? And how had he gotten from there to his meeting with Ford, and what had he been doing in the hours since he had choked Ford to death? Whole chunks of his life dropped clean out of existence like they had never happened.

He placed the final two artifacts on the floor: the thumb drive he had stolen from Lu Zhong, and the Ruger. The thumb drive was far too small to be so powerful. It looked like any old piece of trash you might never notice on the side of the road. And that's what it would have been, if not for the data inside it. The data that made it hum. That made it almost glow.

His gaze lingered on the Ruger for a moment. Never fire your weapon unless it's a last resort. And he still hadn't.

He stood up. His mind raced momentarily down a forking path. How far could he get on Uri Katsman's passport? Transiting through immigration and airports would be risky. In the past, when he had done it, the way was smoothed for him by his support staff back in the States, clicking away on their keyboards. But his minders would not smooth his way this time. They would bar the gates.

God he was tired. He tried to imagine the arc of the story that had carried his mom and dad from the foothills of Armenia to Rochester, New York, and that had led him from Afghanistan to Accra. From beginning to end the whole thing had taken less than forty years—and even then it was impossible to follow the lines that redirected a life from one fate to another. He couldn't find his way back if he tried. The world was too big and there were too many people in it.

His mother had always told him that Armenia was the most beautiful country on Earth. That in winter the snowpack rose like bread until it swallowed the lowest boughs of the mountain pines. That in autumn you could feed a whole family with the persimmons you scooped from the ground with your bare hands.

Billy had never been.

The illusion of a purpose was leaking out of him like air. He had tried to be as American as he could. He had done what his country had asked of him. But it had only ever been a borrowed jersey.

He was not like the others—the Americans whose Americanness could not be rubbed away by circumstances, whose nationality flowed unmistakably in their blood. Dani was one. She was American no matter what she believed or did. He hoped she would never forget it. The Chinese certainly wouldn't.

An unfamiliar feeling gnawed at him. Grief, he supposed. He looked around Dani's room. People usually took a drink before they did this, right?

But she seemed to have thrown out her stash of whiskey.

He sat back down on the bed, feeling it sag beneath his weight. People usually shut their eyes when they did this. Right?

But that was not for him. He would go eyes open. *Roll to your rifle and blow out your brains.* The quicker the better. A flash of noise, heat, and then the relief. Finally the relief. He sighed out loud, imagining it.

Okay, Billy. It's time.

He clicked off the safety of the Ruger.

Then a faint buzzing sound started up on the floor.

One of Ford's phones had started to ring.

TWENTY-NINE

THE CARS STOPPED TEN meters apart from each other on a deserted stretch of road, the asphalt darkening in a light rain that had just begun to fall. James had no idea what was happening or where they were going. There were no road signs, no landmarks. Only jungle.

Florence sat in the seat beside him, impassive.

The truth was that James was too exhausted to fight whatever they were going to do to him. He felt utterly spent. He was past trying to stop it.

The rain began to fall harder, flicked aside by the rapid motion of the windshield wipers. After several long moments he raised his head uncertainly and peered at the car facing theirs, ten meters away. It was a black SUV.

The passenger door opened. Oscar Aidoo got out and stood beneath an umbrella, glaring in their direction.

Florence turned to James. "Our apologies for the misunderstanding, Mr. Aidoo." One of her goons came around to his side and opened his door. She indicated the empty space with a flat hand, palm up. "You are free to leave."

James did not hesitate. He stumbled out to the roadway. Shuffled his feet forward. Into whatever future awaited him.

Nobody moved to help him. His father watched him approach impassively. The rain splashed against his bent neck. After ten meters he had reached the far shore. He heard his father's voice. "Hurry now, boy." Oscar was pointing at the back seat. Looking not at him but forward into empty space. Face set in a scowl, haughty and proud. James grabbed the door handle and pulled himself up into the back seat of the SUV, sighing with the effort. His father said nothing more to him. He spoke only to the driver, a single word: "Go."

THE RUMBLE OF THE car over dirt roads, pitted highways. The workaday beeping of tro-tros slowing to the shoulder, mopeds honking as they passed. His father's snarling face, twisted around from the front seat, taking in his son with pure contempt. Yelling in English, in Twi. *Stupid boy. Ruin everything. Your mother. Such a beating I will give you. Kill you myself.*

James hardly took it in. Beneath the confusion, something was becoming clear. Something so unlikely that he could not keep a weak smile from his face.

They didn't know he had betrayed them.

He was smarter than these people. He had known all along that he was, but it was still a shock to have the undeniable confirmation. His father. Florence. Lu Zhong. They didn't know the truth. They did not even suspect it.

Why are you smiling boy? Gyae serew! Gyimifow! Stop laughing, idiot!

But he couldn't, James couldn't stop smiling. They didn't know he had betrayed them. He was still breathing.

He still had cards to play.

EVENTUALLY IT BECAME CLEAR that they were bringing him to Takoradi, to his family's stronghold. His father had ceased yelling at him and now appeared to be asleep.

James was thinking about the day all this had begun—the day Lu Zhong had come into his life. He had been told to wait in the back room of the house in Takoradi, the place where he was usually sent when he was being punished. He had fidgeted nervously with a loose thread on his Michael Essien Chelsea shirt, wondering what he could have done to deserve this detention. And then a middle-aged Chinese man had entered the room. James had never met a Chinese person before. "Be a good boy now," Oscar Aidoo had said. "I am counting on you." Then he had shut the door quietly, leaving James and Lu Zhong alone. And James had realized, young as he was, that his life was already too big for him, that the decision that he would spy for China had already been made.

The world comes and finds us, not the other way around. The great decoupling between the US and China. The reversal of forty years of globalization and economic integration in favor of hard borders, high tariffs, arms races. The fight over the internet itself. The battle for the pipes that carried the data that was the oil of the future, and that powered the technologies that would determine whether your life was worth living: your bank accounts, your medical records. The sudden reversal of globalization, the flow of information itself slowing, contracting, thickening. What chance did any individual have in the face of such titanic forces? James Aidoo was just one small chapter in the story of a century that would swallow them all without regard and without slowing down.

It was only once he became the Double that James had truly understood for the first time what it meant to be a man. To take ownership of your destiny, to make decisions rather than receive them. Even his father had noticed. "Your confidence is growing, boy," he had said approvingly, two years ago, back when James had first begun meeting with Ford. "Finally you may be ready to rule." James had had to bite back his laughter. His confidence was growing—because he was betraying his father! He had discovered steel in his spine that he had never expected. At every turn he found he was stronger than he thought. How often Oscar had intoned that Corinthians verse to him, the one Dani had misquoted: "*When I was a child, I spake as a child, I understood as a child, I thought as a child; but when I became a man, I put away childish things.*"

And what more steel could he have shown than what he had done to Kwabena? Backed into a corner, he had not hidden and cried. He had fought. He had killed. It was only his bad luck that had spoiled the symphony. The world was a dangerous game with cruel rules. Kwabena had lost.

But here his bravado faltered.

A human being. His best friend's cousin. Dark blood spreading beneath his twisted body on the floor of the garage. The sounds that he had made as he had struggled to get to his feet. The feeling of the gun in James's hand as he had stepped forward. The back of Kwabena's head exploding in the moonlight.

Without warning James vomited into his own lap. For a moment the total surrender of the body overwhelmed individual sensations, his torso contracting again and again, long after he had evacuated the thin soup the Chinese had fed him.

In the front seat his father awoke and started screaming again—but the judging voice James heard was Kofi's.

All this for an American passport?

He tried imagining what his friend would say, to know that he had become James's conscience personified. But Kofi would never be his friend again after what he had done. Nobody would.

"Pull over please," he murmured. "Pull over."

Oscar's driver guided the car to a shoulder off the highway.

"Out, out, out, out!" Oscar was yelling. "Clean yourself up, boy."

James stood for a while behind the car, wiping his mouth with a tissue the driver had handed to him. He grimaced at the acrid taste of the vomit.

But the act had cleared his head. He knew what he needed to do. His father's influence had freed him from Chinese custody. But Florence was bound to discover his work for the Americans soon enough. Even Oscar Aidoo would not keep him safe then.

Follow the logic. One turn at a time.

He walked around to the driver's side window. "Where are we?" he said in Twi.

Before the driver could answer Oscar began snarling again, pounding the center console with his fist. For what felt like the first time James saw his father's rage for what it was. The raving of an old fool. Fundamentally impotent.

James turned around and considered the view. They had been driving for thirty minutes. Starting point somewhere outside Kumasi. Destination presumably Takoradi. That meant Lake Bosomtwe was still in reach, if he could get to a main road and catch a tro-tro heading the right way.

He could be in his safe house before nightfall. Call Ford on the emergency number. And make a plan to evacuate the country.

"Get back in the car, boy!" his father shouted.

James took one last look at him.

Then he ran.

THE FIRST TRO-TRO TOOK him back into Kumasi. He stayed out of sight as much as possible—easy to do in a city that was packed to the gills with human beings, and where he looked and sounded like everybody else.

From Kumasi he caught another tro-tro out to Amekom. He slumped low in his seat, pretending to be asleep. His mind kept returning to Dani. Did the Chinese still have her in custody, or had they let her go? Was she still keeping James's secret, or had she told them everything?

Now the last tro-tro was pulling away from the tiny bus stop at Amekom, and he was finally alone. Night was falling. The air was vegetal and sweet from the surrounding forest and the nearby lake. It felt very far away from the noise and turmoil of the cities, where even now Chinese intelligence was probably swarming to find him.

James bought a plate of goat curry from the old man who staffed the bus stop and wolfed it down standing up. He was still in significant danger—closer to death than he had ever been in his life—but he was feeling unaccountably giddy. Engineering problems. That was all they were—Ford, Dani, Lu Zhong, his father. Even poor Kwabena.

He had been alone all his life.

He had been alone when Lu Zhong had come into that back room at the house in Takoradi.

He had been alone when his father had sent him to school in Austin.

He had been alone when Ford had approached him that morning after church.

And he had survived thus far—alone.

He did not intend to stop now.

The day's earlier scattered rain clouds had passed, and a last sliver of sunlight glowed like a grapefruit beneath the spreading darkness. Human beings were not meant to live in confined spaces. That was what they did not understand, Florence, his father: true freedom, even for a moment, was worth paying any price.

He asked the old man where he lived. Just up the road. Did he know someone who had a car? No. Pity. James would walk. Safer anyway.

One last thing: could he borrow the man's phone?

The voice that answered the emergency number was familiar, but it was not the one he was expecting.

"We've been waiting for you to call."

James hesitated. "Where is Ford?"

"We're coordinating right now," Carlos Rivera answered.

"Can you put him on? This is his emergency line."

"No shit." Rivera cleared his throat. "We're packing it up and burning it down. Ford wants to collect you and then the three of us are gone."

"Where is he?"

"He's on the phone with our superiors as we speak. Tell me where we can meet safely. So we can evacuate stateside."

James hesitated for a moment. But he had no choice.

"My safe house. It is in Amekom, above Lake Bosomtwe. A few kicks northwest of the tro-tro station. Get to the station and walk that direction about thirty minutes. And you will find it."

Carlos exhaled. James thought he sounded almost disappointed.

"I'm on my way."

THIRTY

In the morning, Christina announced that she had a friend in Amekom. “He says that he knows the building you are looking for. He will take you to the place.”

Dani tucked her passport inside her bra—Lindsey van Broek’s passport—and they walked down the road into town for breakfast. Her mangled left hand drifted uselessly at her side, fingers immobile. It felt permanently damaged.

Already, the sun had crested the low hillside behind the town: a white, muscular light, with nothing taller than a tree to impede it until sundown. The heat was astonishing, an underwater quiet. She felt weak; she needed water.

They bought rolls of bread spread with queasy-looking butter from a woman sitting under an umbrella near the big man’s house, and washed it down with Nescafé. Dani paid with the last of the cedis that the Chinese had given her. “My treat,” she said, “for your hospitality.”

Christina and Yvonne shrugged.

Dani kept waiting for something. Carlos Rivera to step around from behind a tree? A battalion of Chinese troops to burst through the doors and start murdering everyone? The sounds of a helicopter overhead?

She did not know what would happen next. She could not think beyond getting herself to Amekom. If you get into trouble, James had said, go to my safe house. Well, this was trouble. She felt sure that Florence must be closing in on her, that getting rid of the tracker had only caused a temporary delay. A cheap trick by a non-spy could not fool the power of a state for long.

Or maybe it could. Perhaps Florence had no idea where she had gone or what to do with her. Perhaps this whole thing had been a massive fuckup from start to finish, and everyone involved in Ghana or China had already gone to ground or been terminated by the masters in Beijing. Fuckups did happen. States were just people.

CHRISTINA'S FRIEND MET THEM by the side of the road in the late afternoon. He was an older man, wearing a dirty gray T-shirt that said PHILADELPHIA FLYERS. In one hand he held a flashlight, in the other a machete.

"Hello," Dani greeted him. "Wo ho te sen?"

He said nothing—he would say nothing, the whole afternoon.

"I will meet you here in the evening, right here, in this place," Yvonne said. "Do not go in the lake. You will be sick." Then she drove away.

The guide beckoned her to follow, and together they began to walk along the shore of Lake Bosomtwe.

Jesus, her arm hurt. Filtered through the lens of the pain, beneath the hazy sunlight, the afternoon felt like a hallucination. She saw Ghanaians bathing in the shallows. A man rubbed his bald head with a bar of soap. Nearby, on the shore, two boys were viciously fighting: wrestling, tumbling, punching each other in the dirt. Dani and the guide walked past them and continued up across a gentle slope of scrub grass, leaving the lake behind. To take her mind off the pain she focused on the rhythm of her feet. She stopped to take a sip of water, but the man didn't pause, didn't even look back.

She had looked at a map before they had left. Amekom was not terribly far from Bekwai, from the Jushu landing station that was at the heart of all of this. Dani felt dazed anew by the thought that the internet was really a physical *thing.* That the data that ran along thousands of miles of pitch-black ocean floor emerged up in the African soil, ran below her feet, and came crashing into the terminal equipment somewhere in this bush—before being rerouted and sent on its way to Lisbon, London, New York, Washington; or coming the other direction, to Johannesburg, Nairobi, Lahore, Mumbai. What had James said? An inexhaustible resource of incalculable value.

Like the data on the thumb drive that Carlos had stolen. It suddenly seemed clear how desperate Florence's plan was. To use Dani as bait? If the thumb drive was as valuable as they made it seem, Carlos had certainly disappeared with it already. Whoever he was.

Her guide kept going. There was intermittent jungle. They crossed a hillside planted with cabbage plants where three men were spraying pesticide. The men looked up and stared silently. Her guide didn't acknowledge them.

The ground leveled out slightly. They passed by a cacao farm. Rows of trees waited with their husky, yellow-green fruit.

Beyond the farm, the bush proper began. The jungle blocked the sun but trapped the heat. Her brain had melted to slurry in her skull. She drank. Half the water was already gone. She moved slowly, her head down.

The man had stopped. She walked smack into him.

A house.

It was a shock to see it, sitting there in the middle of the bush. It was a small concrete structure, surrounded by a tall fence. No signs of life inside, but it looked solid, well-built. It looked like the most expensive piece of real estate for miles around.

She hooked the fingers of her good hand through the chain link fence. "Thank you," she murmured. "Thank you for bringing me here." But when she turned around her guide was gone.

Dani blinked in confusion. She felt a burning prickle in her lower back. It was almost gentle, like hot wax.

Then everything went dark.

When she came to, night had fallen. Her right wrist was bound to a metal bedpost with a plastic zip tie. James was sitting beside her, cuffed to the pole like she was.

And Carlos Rivera was standing over them.

JAMES SPOKE FIRST.

"Where is Ford?"

Carlos seemed distracted, jittery. He kept moving around the room, hands at his sides. His eyes met Dani's then darted away as if startled.

"Ford? He had some trouble back in Accra."

Dani smelled something fresh and earthy: the lake? But she couldn't say what elevation they were at, or how far she had traveled, or how many hours had elapsed. Was she inside the same building she had just been looking at? Had that even been James's safe house at all? And where had her guide disappeared to?

No light, no sounds penetrated the room. Only a vague ringing in her ears. *Heeeeeeen.*

"Why are you here?" Dani said slowly. Her tongue felt thick in her mouth.

Carlos flashed a weak grin. "Could ask you the same thing."

"I mean—the thumb drive. You know they're looking for you."

Carlos held up a small black stick. "This thing?" He tossed it onto the floor at his feet. "They can have it."

"Let me free," James pleaded. "What is this? You're here now. We have to go." He tried to stand, but only got halfway before the arm that was handcuffed to the bed yanked him back down.

"You impress me, Dani," Carlos said, ignoring James. He sat back on his haunches, his eyes passing over her body. His arms were wiry and strong, and Dani thought again about the way he had hurt her when the lights had come on, the first night they had spent together. "Digging out that tracker? You've come a lot farther than I ever would have guessed for a civilian."

The pain in her left wrist made her want to scream. "Don't call me Dani. I don't know you."

Anger flared in his face, then faded. "Prisoner Moreau then."

"Rivera," James said hurriedly. "We don't have time for this. We need to get out of the country immediately."

Dani and Carlos both turned to look at him. For the first time Dani registered how unwell James looked. His eyes were pallid, and he had lost weight. Across his jaw were the patchy beginnings of a beard.

Carlos's face went cold with hatred. "Do you think I'm fucking stupid?" He nudged the thumb drive with his foot. "You think the fact that the Chinese gave you seven million dollars and you gave us the location of their landing station makes you untouchable? Ford was never going to give you a passport. That's not how it works. And then you tried to have me bumped? I could bring your head to Washington or Beijing, and they'd both have a reason to thank me. But you're not even worth that. You're worth nothing to anyone."

"You don't need James," Dani said, speaking quickly, alarmed by the uncontrolled edge in Carlos's voice. "Just take me. Rendition me. Whatever it is you people do."

A knife appeared in Rivera's hand. Dani flinched. But all he did was reach over and cut the plastic zip tie binding her hands. Then he did the same for James.

"Tell her," he said. He set the knife on the floor between the two of them. Dani's eyes had adjusted to the low light of the room, and the serrated edge glinted in the gloom. Rivera unholstered a 9mm from his waistline. He pointed it at James. "Tell her," he said again. "I want her to hear it from you."

In the fraction of a second that James looked at the knife on the floor, she lunged for it. James's fingernails scratched the top of her hand as he grabbed for the knife a moment too late.

Dani was on her feet, backing away from them both. "Don't!" she said, as James advanced on her. "I'll put this through your fucking heart."

"Dani," said James. "Stay very calm."

To her right, Carlos Rivera was watching them, the 9mm balanced on his knee.

Dani's palm was sweating and the knife felt heavy in her hand. James was looking at her, his expression a mixture of fear and contempt. She took a breath, trying to steady herself.

"James doesn't have to tell me," she said slowly. "I already know."

"What do you know?" said Carlos.

"I know that he's working with the Americans." She looked at James. "You planned to meet Carlos at the Lancaster Hotel in Kumasi. Someone—one of you—killed a man named Kwabena." She jerked her chin at Carlos, not taking her eyes off James. "Was it him?"

"You know nothing," James growled. "You came to Ghana for an adventure. You came to Ghana because you were bored."

"Enough," said Carlos. He cocked his weapon. In the close confines of the room, the click of it echoed like a shot.

"Rivera," Dani said. "You don't have to do this."

His expression sagged slightly. "My name is Billy."

Dani was not afraid to die. What could she do? There was a moment when it had all tipped from her hands, but she couldn't have said when, exactly, it happened. And somehow she didn't mind not knowing. She felt almost relieved. She was no longer responsible for making rational decisions.

"Billy," she said slowly. "Nice name. Why don't you give me the thumb drive? I'll take it back to the Chinese. And you and James can disappear wherever it is you want to go."

"The Chinese?" He narrowed his eyes. "Why would I do that? Why would you?"

"It doesn't matter why. Just take your life back and leave me with this. I'm offering it to you. The door is wide open."

For a moment Rivera, Billy—whoever he was—appeared to consider it. Then he lowered the barrel of the gun to the back of James's head.

"No!" Dani screamed, lunging forward.

The shot hit the wall behind them, sending a spray of plaster dust across the floor. James fell limply to his side, clutching his skull. Dani was on Rivera in an instant.

He moved.

She moved.

Dani aimed for the armpit. In and up. In and up inandup inandup inandup inandup.

"Wait," he murmured, his face in her collarbone. "Wait."

She drew back her hand, leaving the knife embedded in his stomach.

No blood emerged at first. The black bulk of Rivera's torso filled the doorway. His face wobbled, distressed. Dani saw that he had dropped the gun, and she bent down to reach for it.

Turning her back was a mistake.

Suddenly her arms were pinned behind her. Blinding pain shot up her damaged wrist. A foot kicked inside her ankle and her feet were no longer her own, a knee was behind her knee and she was being marched, her body moved by this other body, almost gently. Like a father teaching his daughter to dance. Then her face was on the floor and Rivera's knee was in her back, mashing her head into the ground. She gasped and gurgled. His full weight was pressing on her shoulder blades, and she heard him grunting with exertion. Her nose broke—she felt warm blood falling down her cheeks. She was going to die. She was going to be killed by an agent of the government of the United States of America. Her country.

What does a state do?

That is an easy question to answer.

What is a state for?

That is harder.

And if you think the answers are the same, you've misunderstood the questions.

Dani saw the gun on the floor several feet in front of her and reached out towards it with her busted left hand. Rivera kicked her fingers away and stamped on them. Across the room, James rolled over onto his back, whimpering. The bullet had grazed his skull and taken off part of his ear. Blood ran dark and slick down the side of his face. But he was alive. He was looking up at Dani. For a moment they stared at each other.

"Fucking cunt," Rivera grunted. His anger was incredible. It was like heat coming off him. And now his hands were around her throat.

She would not be able to dislodge them.

Dani closed her eyes. She had not found the truth after all. She had tried and failed. Maybe this was how Laurie had felt in her last moments. She thought of her niece at her wedding, Emma emerging momentarily into the light—laughing, her thin blonde hair pulled back in a pink barrette. Dani closed her eyes and felt the winch of this furious man's hands tightening like a bolt around her throat. Dying was easy. This was not really pain at all.

"Billy!" James yelled.

In the instant that Carlos Rivera hesitated, his attention pulled away, Dani shimmied out from under him, scuttling across the floor towards his gun. He lunged out and grabbed her ankle. Dani kicked him away. Her fingers found the handle of the 9mm. But Carlos Rivera had the knife in his hand. He raised it—a pained, slightly quizzical smile on his lips—and plunged it into her heart.

Four a.m. in Ghana. The world at its quietest. In Accra the market stallkeepers are pulling the tarps off their stands. The fishmongers are packing tilapia and mackerel and river crab in salt. In Kokofu, in the cook yard, the youngest cousin is turning over the ashes with a stick to salvage the embers, rubbing sleep from her eyes. In London the rubbish lorries are beeping as the binmen hop off, wiping their hands on reflective orange vests. The chambermaids at Claridge's are clearing the room service trays from the halls. In Beijing it is lunchtime. The smog lowers the horizon, and the noodle shops are full. In Singapore glass towers crowd the narrow streets. HSBC. Société Générale. Bank of China. Wafts of cologne follow men in dark suits, and you hear the brisk clicking of high heels on concrete. In New York it is midnight. Brightly lit: but the ads play mutely above dim streets. At JFK, the long hauls descend: Emirates, Lufthansa, Delta, Cathay. Engines scream above the darkened marshes.

A standard passport consists of thirty-two pages and is a quarter of an inch thick.

The point of a knife, driven by a strong arm at high speed, can exert a force of hundreds of pounds per square inch.

But sometimes the angle of attack makes all the difference. And sometimes a quarter of an inch is all you need.

The knife punctured Dani's shirt and sports bra and lodged at the thirtieth page of Lindsey van Broek's South African passport. Carlos Rivera looked from Dani's face to her chest, where the wound was supposed to be. By the time he realized what had happened and saw what her fingers had closed around in the meantime, it was too late for him.

Dani shot him in the head once. The thing practically jumped out of her hand, slamming her right elbow back against the floor. It was shockingly loud. Her ears rang. But otherwise easy as could be. A grown man's skull is eggshell delicate, it turns out. There is nothing to hold it together. It comes apart like wet paper.

Easy.

It was easy, this. Why did these men congratulate themselves for being able to do it? There was nothing to it. You almost did it by accident. Like dropping a book. Like not looking where you were going. No special effort. No special skill. Your finger made a tiny movement against a metal surface and—

The second shot was unnecessary. He was already dead. But Dani took satisfaction at feeling the weight of him slump sideways. Like a bag full of meat.

Silence.

It was over.

THIRTY-ONE

WHERE IS A BORDER?

Is it on the land? In the air?

How wide is a border? The length of a step? An inch?

Smaller?

Even a perfectly cut paper edge is jagged and uneven at the microscopic level.

So then: when have you crossed over?

JAMES HAD RAISED HIMSELF to a sitting position. One eye was swollen shut. The other stared at her, his nostrils flaring as he breathed.

"Are you going to kill me now?" he said.

Dani felt all the sensations return to her body at once. A shooting pain in her torso that said she had broken some of her ribs. Her bloody crushed nose. Her rapidly swelling throat, where she could still feel the imprint of Carlos Rivera's thumbs against her trachea. The deep ache in her ruined left wrist where she had dug out the tracker that the Chinese had implanted.

"We're in your safe house," she said.

"Yes." James's voice was very soft. His right arm dangled awkwardly. It looked like it had left its socket.

She rolled to her side, grunting. Keeping the weapon trained on James, she scooted along the floor, kicking Carlos Rivera's body aside. She peered out the bullet holes that her gunshots had left in the plaster. Dark jungle steamed in the predawn.

"Can you walk?"

"What are you going to do?" He was still staring at the gun in her hand.

"Can you walk?" she repeated.

"If you turn me over to the Chinese, you know what will happen? They will kill me." He was speaking quickly, breathlessly. "You know that, right? They will—"

"I haven't decided what to do yet." Dani winced, feeling the pressure of her own cracked ribs as she spoke. She glanced through the bullet holes again. A thin gray line was beginning to appear in the darkness above the trees. Dawn would not be their friend. Florence's people had certainly fanned out across the country, looking for them.

Bending low, she picked up the thumb drive. With her bad hand she just managed to wedge it into the pocket of her jeans.

"We can't go anywhere until we fix that shoulder," she said. "Come here."

He held out his dangling arm towards her. Dani transitioned the gun to her damaged hand for a moment, and with the other she yanked on James's arm as hard as she could—until they both heard the pop of the bone moving back into its socket. A small cry of relief escaped James's lips.

"Now open the door," she commanded. "Stay in front of me. Go slow."

James pushed aside the heavy deadbolt that lay across the front door, and they slipped down the steps into scrub grass. Through the trees to their right Dani could make out a larger, darker mass, which must have been the lake.

"If you're going to turn me over to the Chinese," James said—and she could hear the tears in his voice—"I would prefer if you just killed me now and made it quick."

Dani looked at the back of his head. Her breath had steadied. Her whole body screamed for mercy. But her mind felt fearless and clear. The morning was breaking. The sky was turning white.

"Move," she said.

THEY CLAMBERED THROUGH THE thick vegetation that covered the hillside. Dani gripped the gun tightly, vigilant to every creak in the undergrowth. But they were in a part of the world unbothered by human beings—no cars crossed the road, no crowds filled the street, no helicopters swept the sky. She heard only the sounds of their footfalls on the wet earth and her own labored breathing.

From time to time she patted her back pocket with her busted hand, making sure the thumb drive was still there. "It doesn't make sense," she said eventually. Her voice was low and ragged. "Why did he follow us here? If this thumb drive was as valuable as Florence said, why didn't he turn it over to his bosses? And how did he find us?"

In front of her, James did not speak. How many days had passed since she had sat with him at Sandbox and he had given her advice about sources and spies? Time had collapsed, but it had also ballooned: whole lifetimes had elapsed since she had been stripped and violated by Florence's goons; since she had walked through Asantehene's museum and read about the British burning Kokofu to the ground; since she had boarded the tro-tro bound north from Accra to Kumasi; since she had tried on the dress Priscilla had sewn in her room at the guesthouse.

"I called him," James said. "That is, I called Ford. My contact. We had a special phone number, in case of emergencies."

"Who is Ford?"

"An American agent. He worked with your lover. Rivera."

"He wasn't my—"

"They were colleagues," he talked over her. "But I preferred Ford because he was intelligent, like me. Rivera was just the muscle. Ford is the one who can vouch for me—for the work I did for your country." James's voice grew strained. "But when I called for help, he sent Rivera in his place. And now who knows where he is? Who is to say what he relayed to their superiors about what I did on their orders? I risked my life for America. I betrayed my father, my family, and my country in return for US citizenship." He spat into the bushes. "And it's all for nothing."

"And then he tried to kill you," she prodded. "Why?"

"Rivera was a madman," said James. "You know what he did to David Ibrahim? Even Ford was scared of him."

There was something that was bothering Dani more than the rest of it. But she was not sure which was more racist of her: to believe James was capable of evil, or to believe that he wasn't.

"And Kwabena? The one who worked the counter at Jericho Café—who I found dead at Ezekiel Garage. Who was he to you?"

James looked around at the thick bush enclosing them. "He is—he was Kofi's cousin."

"You killed him?"

"He was my cutout. I had no choice."

Dani stopped walking. "James."

"Blame yourself!" He turned to face her, his face twisted. "If it weren't for you, he would still be reading his space novels and eating fufu with his friends in the evenings. But what's another dead African to you, eh? Instead of oil or gold or data, you needed a story. And guess what, Dani—you found one."

"Don't lay this at my feet. It was not my intention for anyone to get hurt."

"Fuck your intentions." James sounded very American when he said it. "You're here for your selfish purposes, no less than anyone else." He put a hand to the still-bleeding wound on his neck.

For a moment they just looked at each other.

"Keep moving." Dani pushed him forward with her foot. "We don't stop until I say."

They walked on through the dense brush. The sun had risen, it was peeking through the canopy above them. The heat was building. Dani kept having to duck as the branches James pushed aside whipped back at her in his wake. She never let the gun move off him.

"Why didn't you just tell me that you were working with the Americans?" she said, stepping over a fallen tree. "Why tell me that you worked for the Chinese? I'm an American, after all. I might have helped you."

"When we went to Tadi, and my dad hit me—I wasn't expecting it, but let's say I wasn't surprised. That was when I first got an inkling that maybe you could be useful to me. I knew that if you felt sorry for me, it would blind you. But you kept following me.

You never took what I said for an answer. Following me to Jericho Café. Digging into Dongsha and Paragon and confronting me with your evidence. So smug and pleased with yourself." She could hear the anger and the hurt in his voice. "There was no way I could tell you I was working for the Americans. Far too dangerous. But I wanted to keep you close, in case I needed your help. So I told you about Lu Zhong. I knew you wouldn't be able to resist the story."

"Hell of a gamble."

"Of course, I couldn't predict where it would lead. But my ultimate goal was to get out of working for Lu anyway. If you blew up Lu's operation, my time as a Chinese source would be over, and the Americans would be obligated to honor their promises to me."

"But why, James?"

He stopped walking again. "Why what?"

This time Dani stopped too. "Why do any of it?"

After a moment he said, "Bocadillos."

"Bocadillos?"

"It is a café in Takoradi that serves Western food. Kofi was obsessed with it. Eggs, bangers and mash, that kind of thing. Going there after school—life was good. In Ghana we say it like that, with an *l* (el) sound. *Dill*-os. And then when I got to Texas everything was *dee*-yos, like Spanish. My daddy used to hate it when we went to Bocadillos. Said we were an indulgent, Western-loving generation. Fufu and fomfom aren't good enough for us?" James grunted. "Now nobody goes to Bocadillos anymore. They go to KFC."

"Fuck you." She put the gun to his head. "Give me a real answer."

"That is my answer. And if you were born into my shoes, into my country, into my family and my life—it would be your answer too." James closed his eyes. His right eye was completely swollen over by now, and his arm still hung at an odd angle, like it had been stuck on incorrectly. The sight of it made Dani feel again the aches in her own body, the parts that were broken and not where they were supposed to be. She licked her lips and tasted the blood from her broken nose that had pooled and dried along them.

"You know something," she said. "All along, deep down I was suspicious of you. Something wasn't right. There was always some give under my hands. I didn't know what it was, but my gut told me you were hiding something."

"I congratulate your gut."

"And all I ever tried to do was help."

"Very well." He made the sign of the cross in the air above her head. "You are redeemed of the sins of all white people. Abracadabra. The mass has ended. Go in peace."

"So you were more of a spy than you ever admitted. You played the Chinese off the Americans. You played Carlos Rivera off me. You played your father for a fool. Always, it was you in control." Dani gestured with the gun. "And now look at you."

James's expression deflated. He said nothing in response to this.

They kept walking. Soon the slope beneath their feet changed its pitch, and they began heading downhill. Through the undergrowth, they could hear a road at the bottom of the mountain, and the sound of the occasional passing car.

At last, they emerged into open space. In front of them was a small cluster of buildings, less than a town.

"Move slow," Dani said. "If you run I'll have no choice but to shoot."

He laughed harshly. "Run where?"

They found a position behind a tree off the road and waited. Eventually they heard a car coming.

"Now," Dani ordered.

Together they ran out into the street, blocking the car's path. The startled driver was an older man who looked at them with wide eyes: this Black man and this short-haired white woman, emerging from the jungle covered in blood. Dani came around to the passenger side door and trained the gun on the driver.

"We're going to Accra," Dani said. "We need your car. Get out."

The old man made a gesture of contempt. "This car is my livelihood."

She hesitated for a split second. "You drive us then. The American embassy, downtown Accra. You don't pull over, you don't stop, you do exactly as I say, or we leave you by the side of the road."

He considered her. "I will be late for work."

She waved the gun at him. "Then you better drive fast."

THE CAR TOOK THEM over bridges and around the sides of mountains where waterfalls cut through the acres of trees. Then it took them down a long, flat highway—empty green bushland to the horizon, occasional clusters of activity by the side of the road, food stands, petrol stations, a man sitting beneath a TelTel umbrella, a stray dog asleep in the shade beside him. After a couple hours, as they got closer to the coast, the traffic began to thicken. The rivers slowed and widened. Smog settled over the road like a helmet.

Dani felt herself fraying at the edges. Her throat ached. Her mangled left wrist had gone numb. Breathing hurt. She could not keep going for much longer. She was weak with hunger and her whole body weighed her down.

But it was more than just her physical disintegration. The accumulated revelations were beginning to catch up to her. She had tried to take real action in the world. She had tried to help. But Ghana didn't want her help and China didn't need it. All along, James Aidoo had been using her. She had got it wrong. She thought that if she wasn't a mother, or a wife, or even still a journalist, then at the very least she could help James.

But he was a grown man, and he hadn't asked her to.

And in her desire to prove her own importance, she had got innocent people hurt. Didn't that make her the worst kind of American? The worst kind of carpetbagger? As if the world and its complexity existed only to fuel her own sense of purpose?

"We're close," said James behind her.

Dani tensed, startled. For a moment, she had completely forgotten where they were and what they were doing. She gripped her weapon tighter, looking over at James. "I've been thinking," she said. "You *do* have something of value to offer the Americans. Carlos killed this man David Ibrahim, and he killed Lu Zhong, and you are the only one who knows the truth about why. Use that."

He frowned, suspicious. "What do you mean?"

"Americans don't like a failure. And something tells me that is what happened here. Does this look like a well-run US operation to you?" She cleared her throat. "*Use it.* Hold out, and don't tell them anything until they agree to give you asylum. You're the son of a Ghanaian politician with a lot of profile. You know about Florence. You know about Carlos. You know about me. Use all of it."

His eyes widened slightly—lit, for the first time all day, with something Dani recognized as hope.

"Why don't you come with me?" he said. "We'll tell them together."

For an instant she was tempted. A future opened before her like a gap in a crowd. There would be some punishment, some penance, but then the apparatus of American power would move on, and she would be left alone. She would settle down. A desk job, a house of her own, clean sheets on her bed.

She shook her head. "I've committed treason. I killed an American spy."

"But Dani." James looked confused. "What will you *do*?"

"I'll be fine." She raised her voice so the driver could hear. "Pull over across the street from the embassy. Slow down, but don't come to a full stop. If I tell you to hit the gas, you do it. Okay?"

The old man nodded, his eyes focused on the road. Only the subtle lift of his bushy eyebrows showed anything like surprise at the turn his morning commute had taken.

"Get ready," she said to James. "Once you're out of the car, we're gone."

"What if the Chinese shoot me before I make it inside?"

"That won't happen." Dani's energy was back. She was pissed off, and she was absolutely unafraid. James. Carlos Rivera. Lu Zhong. Her doctors in London. All these men, who spoke with such confidence.

"It is there," said the driver, pointing up the road. "The American embassy."

"Well," James said. He attempted a smile. "Despite it all, I am sorry, Dani. For everything."

The driver slowed down to a crawl. Behind them, somebody honked.

"Go!" she commanded.

They watched him run, a small figure, slipping quickly among the morning crowd. Dani winced, bracing for the report of a bullet, the swarm of plainclothes policemen, the rush of sirens that would end it all. But nothing came. James was stopped at the embassy door. She saw him conferring with the Marine guarding the entrance. His body language was very calm. Then something he said made the Marine snap to attention. James was pulled inside the entrance.

And he was gone.

HER BREATHING WAS GETTING shallower. Her throat was so swollen it had almost closed entirely.

She would never get the whole truth. She should never have expected to. You get one box of documents—if you're lucky. Just a sliver. When you're finished, you add your sliver to the pile, and hope that someone who comes after you can make better sense of the mess.

After a while, the old man turned to her. Ignoring the gun in her hand, he said, "You are American?"

"South African."

"Ah," he said, frowning. "The Empire."

It took her a second to realize he meant the British one.

"You must leave now," he said politely. "Please."

Dani raised her drooping head. "One more favor before you go."

—~—

THE STREET IN FRONT of the guesthouse where she had spent most of her two months in Ghana was crowded with schoolkids on their way to class. As Dani moved through the crowd, people were giving her odd looks. This filthy foreign woman in tattered clothes. A bread seller shooed her away.

Finally she sat down on the curb, too exhausted to go any farther. And now she saw that there were obruni here too, scattered amid the crowd. Asian obruni. They were broad-shouldered, and they were looking only at her.

"You have thrown caution to the wind, I see."

It was Florence.

Dani sighed, and opened her hands to show she was unarmed. She had ditched the gun in a rubbish bin two blocks away, after the old man who had driven them all the way from Lake Bosomtwe dropped her off and wished her good luck. She had apologized for making him late for work.

"Do not worry," said Florence now. "If we were really angry, we would already have grabbed you and we would be beating you, in private."

"What are you waiting for?"

Florence lowered herself to the ground and sat beside her. "Where is James Aidoo?"

"I dropped him at the American embassy. I'm guessing he's out of your reach by now."

"And Carlos Rivera?"

"Dead. I killed him."

"And the body?"

"In a safe house somewhere above Lake Bosomtwe. I can take you there if you'd like."

Florence picked up Dani's bandaged left wrist in hers, examining the absurd bloody stump with precise turns of her soft manicured fingers. "You will recall," she said, "I told you to worry about yourself. And no one else."

Dani thought suddenly of the letter she had sent to Ben, the day before she boarded the tro-tro to Kumasi. The written record of what she had uncovered about American and Chinese spying in Ghana—mailed to her deadbeat ex-husband, care of Frank the barman at the Hurtwood Inn Pub in Peaslake. Her cutout.

Had Ben gone and collected it? And what would he do if he had? Most likely he hadn't even bothered to lift his drunk ass off his sofa in Shoreditch. Most likely he had hung up the phone from their last phone call and rolled over to whatever new woman was filling Dani's place that night.

But what if he had gone to Peaslake? What if he hadn't been able to get her phone call out of his head? What if he was sharing what she had sent him with her old employers at *The Guardian*? What if, even now, her colleagues were working on verifying the claims she had made?

"And my thumb drive?" Florence said.

Dani looked at her for a moment. Then she reached into her back pocket. "Here."

Florence could not keep an instant of naked shock off her face. In one smooth motion she snatched the piece of black plastic from Dani's hands and slipped it into the pocket of her coat. "I am impressed," she said after a minute. "Very impressed." Her face resumed its position, watchful, expressionless.

"Where are you from?" Dani said suddenly. "In China?"

"I am from Shenzhen. Over the border from Hong Kong."

"Lu Zhong was from Shenzhen."

"Thirty million people live in Shenzhen," Florence said briskly. "It is growing very quickly. China would like to replace Hong Kong with Shenzhen. Because Hong Kong is too—" She shook her head. "Hong Kong does not fit so nicely with the rest of the nation."

"Nations aren't anything," Dani whispered. A small smile cracked her dried lips. "A nation is a story that people believe."

"Don't talk like that when you get to the mainland. Not if you want to work for us."

"Work for you? I don't understand."

"What else would you do? You have just killed an agent of the US government. There is nowhere and nothing else for you."

Both women looked at the ground, as if embarrassed by her frankness. Dani noticed, in the flood of chattering schoolkids, the well-built men beginning to move towards them.

"How will I learn?" Dani wiped her nose on her arm. "How will I learn to do what you all need me to do?"

The men were almost upon them. Florence's eyes were kind and soft. Like a teacher's. Like a mother's.

"You will learn by going slowly," she said. "Cross the river by feeling the stones."

"What if I can't do it?"

"You already have, on your own." Florence patted the thumb drive in her pocket. "And now you will have training. You will not be alone. I promise."

Florence's face opened into a wide smile as one of her men put his hand on Dani's shoulder.

THIRTY-TWO

ONE MONTH LATER

OVERNIGHT THEY HAD DOCKED in Luanda, the capital of Angola. After three weeks aboard the *Dapeng Star*, Dani was used to the constant tilting motion beneath her feet. But it was an undeniable relief when the massive machine came finally to rest.

During the ship's twenty-four hours in port she had stayed in her cabin, as she was required to do. But now that they had cast off again, she was allowed to come outside. She stood at the railing, watching the Angolan deckhands far below. They moved languidly, holding heavy ropes, unlooping them from the massive cleats that had held the ship steady overnight and tossing them to their Chinese counterparts on board.

For a long moment the untied boat remained stationary, held in place by its enormous weight. She looked out over the Luandan skyline, obscured by haze. The waves in the harbor were the color of milky tea. Bits of stuff bobbed in them: sticks, Styrofoam, plastic bottles.

"We are going to send you to Hong Kong for your training," Florence had told her. "There are no direct flights to China from Ghana. It is too risky to send you through a European airport, because the Americans might intercept you. We thought about flying you through Johannesburg, but the South Africans aren't such dependable friends either. Therefore, a ship."

A liquefied natural gas freighter, to be specific. The *Dapeng Star* was owned by COSCO Shipping Energy—the world's largest oil tanker company. Headquartered in Shanghai.

Dani gripped the railing. Her wounded arm had improved significantly under the care of the Chinese embassy doctors. A jagged scar stood raised like a sandbar in a slowly healing bruise. In the other arm, her right arm, a new tracker pulsed gently.

If they were worried that she would flee, they did not need to be. She had no home to flee to. No loyalty. Not to a nation, not to the craft of journalism, not to James, not to her family. She was utterly alone.

Utterly free.

The image of her nieces came to her, as it still did sometimes. Emma and Claire. The warmth that had risen in her heart the first time she had held them. She followed them through a field, heard their laughter in the tall grass. She caught up with them and scooped them into her arms.

And then she very deliberately put them down. Emma and Claire were already older than the last time she had held them. Already different people. Their memory of their aunt would fade. They were in their lives, and she was in hers. She could not depend on anybody, and nobody needed to depend on her.

Dani felt her pulse beating wetly in every joint of her body. With each minute that passed, the scale of her treason grew. It wasn't that she thought China would be any better an overlord than the United States. Power was permanently afraid, no matter where it resided. Power was hunched over a soft white underbelly. In her small way, she was both an agent of that power and a threat to it. And the truth was that she had never felt more alive.

From time to time she wondered about James. She had heard nothing about his fate—and she knew she never would. She hoped that he had managed to talk his way into asylum, into safety. She hoped he was in the States even now. Maybe sitting outside a tent in Zion National Park, watching something small and furry dive into a pile of dead leaves.

But it was equally possible he was dead.

Now the railing pushed itself upwards gently but insistently into her palms—the wave of energy generated more than a hundred feet below by the thirty-thousand-horsepower engines rippling back up through her body and out the top of her head. The ship began its turn out to sea, where it would steam along to the next port of call—roughly tracking the paths of the fiber-optic wires that ran through darkened trenches far below the surface.

She was unsure what Florence planned to do with her once she got to Hong Kong. Dani had given up trying to control the flow of her life. Unanticipated, mandatory: events overrun us. Her choices were not her own. And so what? What is history but one room after another full of ashen-faced men turning to each other saying how did it come to this?

And they were always men.

ACKNOWLEDGMENTS

Thank you to:

Graciela Watrous Martin; Stephanie Gangi; Kirby Kim, Lansing Clark, and the whole team at Janklow & Nesbit; Luisa Cruz Smith, Otto Penzler, Julia O'Connell, Charles Perry, and the whole team at The Mysterious Press; Ali Lefkowitz; Gretchen Koss; I.S. Berry; Paul Vidich; the Admirals: Cecile Berberat, Simona Blat, Josh Boardman, Ryan Boyle, Sidik Fofana, Sean Gill, Zack Graham, Dolan Morgan, J.T. Price, Anna Schwartzman, and Ashley Taylor; Thatcher Foster; Amber Dermont; Marianne Gunn O'Connor; Richard Socarides; Elizabeth Martin and Kelly Martin; Kelsey Martin and Jared Tishelman; Griffyn Martin and Shannon Fernandez-Ledon; Kevin Sullivan and Genevieve Sullivan; Stuart Martin; Steve Mortenson; Mary Ellen Olson; Cathy Mortenson; Philip Mortenson; Julius Goldman and Rachel Hunter-Goldman; the entire Goldman-von Unruh family; Bess Weatherman, Kate Weatherman, and Jeb Brown; Julian Watrous; Louise Eastman and Peter Watrous.